DAGGERS AND MEN'S SMILES

DAGGERS AND MEN'S SMILES

A Moretti and Falla Mystery

Jill Downie

DUNDURN
TORONTO

Editor: Cheryl Hawley
Design: Courtney Horner
Printer: Webcom

Library and Archives Canada Cataloguing in Publication

Downie, Jill
        Daggers and men's smiles [electronic resource] : a Moretti and Falla mystery / Jill Downie.

(Castle Street mystery)
Type of computer file: Electronic monograph in PDF format.
Issued also in print format.
ISBN 978-1-55488-869-6

        I. Title. II. Series: Castle Street mystery

PS8557.O848D34 2011a   C813'.54   C2010-905994-8

1   2   3   4   5   15   14   13   12   11

We acknowledge the support of the **Canada Council for the Arts** and the **Ontario Arts Council** for our publishing program. We also acknowledge the financial support of the **Government of Canada** through the **Canada Book Fund** and **Livres Canada Books**, and the **Government of Ontario** through the **Ontario Book Publishing Tax Credit** and the **Ontario Media Development Corporation**.

Care has been taken to trace the ownership of copyright material used in this book. The author and the publisher welcome any information enabling them to rectify any references or credits in subsequent editions.

                                        J. Kirk Howard, President

Printed and bound in Canada.
www.dundurn.com

Dundurn	Gazelle Book Services Limited	Dundurn
3 Church Street, Suite 500	White Cross Mills	2250 Military Road
Toronto, Ontario, Canada	High Town, Lancaster, England	Tonawanda, NY
M5E 1M2	LA1 4XS	U.S.A. 14150

To Ros and Frank

acknowledgements

My thanks go to the Guernsey Police, for invaluable help with the structure of the force and the unique administration of laws on the island. Thank you also to Elaine Berry, a former colleague of my mother's at the Ladies' College, who gave me books about the island occupation from her personal collection, and shared an afternoon of memories, tea, and roses, and to painter Brian Pinero Terris for his stories of buccaneers and privateers past and present. My heartfelt gratitude goes to my friend from Ladies' College school days, Ros Hammarskjold, and her husband, Frank, for their warm hospitality. Grateful thanks, as always, to my agents, Frances and Bill Hanna, and to my husband, Ian, for his constant support and encouragement.

... my dagger muzzled,
Lest it should bite its master, and so prove,
As ornaments oft do, too dangerous.

— William Shakespeare, *The Winter's Tale*

PART ONE
Cast and Crew

chapter one

*U*n *rocher perdu dans la mer.* A rock lost in the sea.

Viewed from above, the island of Guernsey reminded Moretti of Victor Hugo's description of the place when he was exiled there. Once upon a time, on a fine day, you were blinded by the glare of the sun shining off the greenhouses that covered the island, but many of those were now gone. Once, it was horticulture and tourists that brought in the money. Now, it was money that brought in the money, huge sums of it, most of it perfectly legitimate. Over fifty billion pounds of it. Drawn by low taxes — and no taxes on foreign-source income held by non-residents — the money continued to pour in.

The ATR turboprop was bringing them in across the harbour. First, Castle Cornet at the end of its long pier, looking from above like the eighteenth-century print he had on his sitting-room wall. He could see the projecting stones at the top of the Gunners' Tower, like the points of a giant granite starfish, the pale green and dusky rose of the castle gardens that cascaded down the cliff face. From the air the tidal swimming pools at La Valette looked like line drawings on a map. Hidden in the thickly wooded slopes beyond, just before the sweep of Val des Terres, the main road leading to the south, was a huge subterranean U-boat refuelling bunker, now refurbished as La Valette Underground Museum.

Not visible from above. Even from the ground, its entrance was well concealed. Beneath the rock of the island existed another world of passages, tunnels, command centres, a hideous granite honeycomb built by human misery. When he was a child, before the reconstruction of Fortress Guernsey for the tourist, no one talked much about that hidden world. They were anxious to move on, to forget starvation, deprivation, fear. Collaboration. Betrayal.

Love affairs.

"They came to Mr. Boutillier, asked him to dig seventeen graves — an explosion, they said. I was terrified. Numb. I only cried when I saw you the next day, alive."

His mother, talking to his father, late at night, the two of them reliving the agony. His father had been there, underground, digging, dragging trucks of rock in a harness, like a beast, with the Russians, the Poles, the Ukrainians, the Czechs, the French. All of them at the mercy of Hitler's Organisation Todt. Hidden from view, once. Now, reconstructed, open to the public. The giant blood-red oil tanks for diesel, the glass display cases of knives, stilettos, the steel-lined rubber truncheon, the whip with its leather strips.

From the air the Fort George enclave for the wealthy seemed no more remote than it did from the ground. There were two entrances to it: one through Fermain Road off Val des Terres, the other through the gate, all that was left of the old fort. He could see the mansions overlooking Soldiers' Bay from the Clarence Battery, glimpse the far reaches of forbidden ground from the cliff path that ran past them. Once, on a cliff walk, Moretti had heard loud cackling from one of the properties, saw a flock of geese running toward him beyond a fence, protecting their Capitol. "No, no," someone was saying.

No, no indeed. No parking on the roads, no vans allowed on driveways, no children playing on the pavements, not a sign of life. Inescapable, really, in a world of haves and have-nots. The rich needed to be as protective of their homes as they were secretive in their businesses, closed away in the Crédit Suisse buildings on the Esplanade or behind the elegant facades around the Plaiderie, near the law courts and the lawyers' offices, with the CCTV cameras trained on every entrance.

The one-storey airport building came into view, beyond it a couple of smaller buildings, one of them the club for the owners of the private planes that were now as common as gulls on the island. The ATR landed with a gentle bump, taxied to a halt near a couple of Trilanders, the three-engine airplanes used by international banks and financial companies, their logos writ large on their sides. The one closest to him read, "Royal Bank of Canada." Up on the open viewing area he caught a glimpse of his new colleague, leaning over the parapet. His feeling of depression deepened.

DC Liz Falla.

What had he done to deserve this? Fate in the guise of Chief Officer Hanley had given him this inexperienced girl-woman as his brand new partner. Even from here he could see the brisk, relentlessly youthful spring in her walk. Twenty-sevenish going on seventeen.

God almighty. He reran the phone conversation he had with her when he was in Italy, attending his godmother's funeral. The timing couldn't have been worse, leaving an inexperienced officer behind.

"Anything come up?" he had asked.

"Well, there's something, Guv. At the moment it doesn't seem like much. There's been trouble at that film they're shooting at Ste. Madeleine Manor. You know the one?"

"Of course."

Who didn't? Guernsey was agog from the moment it was announced that an international film company would be on the island to shoot the film version of the hit novel, *Rastrellamento*, by British bad boy author, Gilbert Ensor. They were the biggest movie-world presence on the island since Guernsey had stood in for Nova Scotia for the filming of *Adèle H.*, starring Isabelle Adjani as poet Victor Hugo's tragic daughter, and they had arrived about two weeks earlier, taking up the space and the facilities and the support staff usually reserved for tourists. On an island that measured about twenty-four square miles, with under sixty thousand inhabitants, they were markedly noticeable and far more exotic than the tourist trade. No buckets and spades and shandies for this lot; the hotels and watering holes had optimistically stockpiled magnums of champagne and crates of caviar. Some of the top hotels held on to their chefs, whose stay on the island was usually a summer's lease.

"What sort of trouble?"

"Well, it's all a bit freaky, really. Like they are. Involves a bunch of costumes. And daggers."

"*Daggers?*"

"Right. Daggers. Or *a* dagger, actually. Chief Officer Hanley's dead keen to get you back because you speak Italian."

"Italian? Oh, right. The director is, isn't he?"

"And some of the others. I'll tell him you'll be back tomorrow, shall I?"

* * *

"I see," said Detective Constable Liz Falla, wondering if she did. She looked again.

A group of dressmaker's dummies stood facing her against one wall, and in front of them lay six costumes on a foldaway table: three women's suits tailored in a style she'd seen in black and white films, a flowered dress, a man's suit, and a Second World War German uniform. They, and the dummies, were ripped and slashed to shreds.

It was stuffy and airless in the lodge, which was always called "the lodge," but which was in fact the ancient seat of the manorial court of the Manoir Ste. Madeleine, on the channel island of Guernsey. Its original function was long gone, and the building was now serving as storage for the international film crew shooting on the island. The freshly whitewashed walls of the long room were hung with costumes on hangers. Racks of costumes crowded the aisles between a series of tables on which lay a variety of headgear, from hats to helmets.

"I see," she said again. "When did this happen?"

Lack of oxygen — perhaps that was why I feel particularly dozy, thought DC Falla, looking at the very large, very blond, very angry Englishwoman at her side.

"Some time during the night. I don't know, but they were all right when I left yesterday evening. Whoever it was came in through the window." The costume designer indicated a broken pane beyond the lineup of dummies.

There was something undeniably gruesome about the ripped costumes, spread out in a row, the gashes in the fabric like open wounds. *Like headless corpses,* thought Liz Falla. But still — this woman had been as hysterical on the phone as if actual murder had been committed, and in her new role as Chief Officer Hanley's blue-eyed girl, she had been sent to investigate.

Eagle-eyed, to be accurate. That's what the *Guernsey Press* called her, for spotting the old spare tire with a stain near the rim in the boot of a brand new car that had rolled off the Condor ferry from Poole. Inside lay four one-kilogram packages of cannabis, wrapped in yellow foam, street value around thirty-six thousand pounds. A drop in the ocean, but it meant another mule — it was her third trip — put out of business. High-fives all round, and a foolish young girl sentenced in the Royal Court to a four-year jail term.

But this? It looked more like a destructive prank than the dangerous act of a crazy madman, which was how the costume lady, Betty Chesler, had described it on the phone, and why someone from plainclothes had been sent out. Liz Falla wished that her new boss, Detective Inspector Moretti, were with her.

Which was not how she was feeling when she got up that morning. Be careful what you wish for, the Chinese said — didn't they? — and she'd got it. Out of uniform, assigned to one of the premier investigating officers on the island, but not the one she'd have chosen. He had a reputation for being a maverick, since he played with that jazz group, but also a loner, and certainly not a laugh a minute. No merry chatter in the squad car to while away the hours, not with this one. Unmarried, not too long in the tooth, reasonably good-looking, if you liked your men darkish, thinnish, and sort of brooding. Which she didn't — she personally preferred the lively ones. Anyway, she wasn't in the least interested in finding a life mate. She was relieved when he told her he had to take a few days compassionate leave and now here she was, on her own.

"You look very young for this."

"Sorry?"

"Didn't they think this important enough for a senior officer, then?"

The costume lady's voice rose sharply and cracked in indignation at the end of her query.

Film people, stage people, thought DC Falla. All the same, just like her uncle Vern who hung out with the Island Players and tended to weep at the drop of a hat at family celebrations. The artistic temperament, he called it. Histrionics, her father called it.

"Do you know how the damage was caused?"

"Yes I do, because the bastard left *it* behind."

Betty Chesler pointed to something that gleamed on the table between a small black beret and a broad-brimmed straw hat.

"Like something out of an Errol Flynn movie. He came through the window, that — *butcher* — holding a dagger. And did this. With a *dagger*, for God's sake, which he had the bloody cheek to leave behind."

With dramatic theatricality the sun suddenly disappeared beyond the thick glass panes of the windows of the lodge and, just as swiftly, the room darkened. Liz Falla felt the skin on her arms prickle. No lack of oxygen now, but a heightened awareness of something hanging in the air. It's chilly in here, she told herself, nothing to do with those ancestors of yours, those poor benighted women who took the long, winding walk down from the prison of Beauregard Tower to the gibbet built above the brushwood, at the foot of Fountain Street.

By the pricking of my thumbs, something evil this way comes. The "gift," her grandmother called it.

"Now, young lady," said Betty Chesler, her hands planted aggressively on her voluminous hips, "what are you going to do?"

"You're a bastard, Gil."

"I know. It's one of my strong points. It's why you fell in love with me."

"Too true," said Sydney Tremaine wearily. She got up from the rumpled sheets on the floor, pulling her peignoir around her. Her husband lay spreadeagled on the carpet, naked and unashamed, the bird's head motifs of the Turkoman rug around him pecking at his privates. Or so, vindictively, she fantasized. *A man in his condition* should *be ashamed*, she thought. He should be the one covering himself, pulling the bedclothes over his ever-increasing belly. But he knew only too well the power he had over her.

Not love, not even sex anymore. Money. Moolah. The comfortable cushion of life in couture clothes and five-star hotel suites, even if it was a luxury hotel on some Godforsaken minuscule island that she had never heard of before the film shoot. That was why, instead of turning away from him with a yawn, she joined him on the floor, straddling him with her strong dancer's legs. His renewed desire for her was a sign that the only hold she had over Gilbert Ensor was restored to her.

"Christ, I don't believe it. The sun's out. Get me a Scotch, baby, will you?" He grinned as she cringed at his pathetic attempt at her American accent. "I'm going out on the patio."

"I don't know why you keep trying to sit out there. It'll still be soaking from that shower. This isn't the Riviera, you know."

"Don't I friggin' know. But I've got to keep close to these shysters, or they'll have my masterpiece in fucking tatters."

"Why do you bother?" Sydney called after his departing figure, legs wobbling slightly from his recent exploits. "They're paying you a fortune. And shouldn't you put something on?"

"Oh, right."

Gilbert Ensor picked up a pair of corduroy trousers from a chair and, hopping from foot to foot, hauled them over his legs, zipping them up around his protruding stomach where they hung comfortably and baggily. He opened the door onto the small private patio that adjoined the suite and stepped outside.

Beyond the high stone wall was a stretch of grass, and beyond that was the steep cliff that lay between St Martin's Point, the southernmost tip of the island, and St. Peter Port, the capital of Guernsey. A wrought-iron gate set in the wall led to one of the cliff paths that encircled the island — not that Gilbert had ever pulled back the bolt. Exercise was anathema to him.

"All that walking and running and huffing and puffing uses up creative energy. Any I have left over I save for sex."

Sydney knew that was true. She also knew that his precious spare energy was not always saved for her. She sighed and poured him out a triple Scotch. With any luck he'd then fall asleep and stay out of trouble. Not sexual trouble. She was used to that. The trouble she dreaded was the constant fighting with any member of the film company who came close enough. She poured herself a Perrier and picked up both glasses.

"*Sydney*!"

His scream was high-pitched, shrill. *Oh dear God*, she thought. Not his bee allergy again, not a mad dash to the hospital — in which of all those expensive matching suitcases was the Epipen? She put down the glasses and ran on to the patio, the stones unpleasantly moist beneath her bare feet.

"Have you been stung?"

"That's one way of putting it."

Gilbert Ensor's quivering forefinger was pointing at something that lay on the ground, gleaming in the slanting rays of the afternoon sun.

"It's a dagger." Sydney picked it up, turning it over in her hands.

"No kidding, genius. It came hurtling through the gate, just as I was about to sit down. Landed at my feet."

"Through the gate? You sure it wasn't just lying there?"

"Perfectly."

Sydney ran over to the gate. The design of leaves and ferns was certainly far enough apart to allow a narrow knife through, but hitting the target — any target — would have been well-nigh impossible. She struggled with the bolt, and pushed it back.

"Where are you going, for God's sake?"

"To take a look. You stay there."

The rough path on the grassy expanse beyond the patio was deserted. Sydney ran to the edge, and saw that beneath what appeared to be the lip of the cliff was another path. Above her head a couple of black-back gulls whirled and screamed in avian mockery of Gilbert's shriek. In the distance, somewhere, she could hear the noise of some kind of engine, or motor. Sydney stood on the edge of the slope and peered in the direction of the sound.

The path below her was thickly hedged, the undergrowth and trees beyond it hiding the edge of the cliff and the sea below, but it ran reasonably straight at this point. Out of the corner of her eye she was aware of movement, and turned swiftly to her right. A woman was running with athletic strides along the rough track and, even at this distance, Sydney Tremaine, the ex-ballerina, could see that this was no casual jogger.

"Hey!"

Either the woman didn't hear, or she chose not to hear. Sydney caught a glimpse of long blond hair flying, the faint gleam of the reflective tape on the heels of her running shoes before she turned the corner of the cliff and was out of sight.

Back on the patio, Gilbert seemed to have recovered. He had fetched the glass of Scotch and was already halfway through it.

"Well? Could you see anyone?"

"A jogger, a woman jogger. That was all."

She picked up the dagger again from the small table by Gilbert's chair. It was about twelve inches long, its steel blade bolted into a mother-of-pearl handle. She touched one edge of the two-sided blade and winced. "Sharp. And pretty, but I think that's imitation mother-of-pearl. Looks like a modern copy of a medieval one."

"How would you know? Oh, right, that godawful Borgia movie you were in."

Sydney grimaced. But he was right. A disaster, with herself as Lucrezia Borgia, and the casting directors had stopped calling. The arrival of Gilbert Ensor in her life had been a godsend. As her mother always used to say: you pay for your pleasures. Oh God, did you ever. Two of his nastiest insults were to call her a Moira Shearer wannabe and "Lucrezia to the ends of your blood-red nails, darling — typecast to a T." Both hurt, because both contained a grain of truth, and she knew it.

"I think we should call the police, Gil."

"For chrissake — it's just some idiot on this speck in the Atlantic who thinks he's still in the Dark Ages."

"Perhaps. But I think we should. After all, there was that creepy business with the costumes."

"Jesus. I'd forgotten. That was daggers, wasn't it? Right. Phone the police. But first, honeybunch, pour me another drink."

chapter two

"Good afternoon, sir. I hope everything went as well as could be expected. In the circumstances, I mean. I'm sorry about your loss."

Her voice took Moretti by surprise. He had forgotten how deep it was for a young woman, with a distinctly bossy timbre.

"Good afternoon, DC Falla. Yes, everything went fine. I really didn't know my Italian godmother very well. We weren't close."

"No."

Why did she say it like that? he wondered.

"What's going on at the Manoir Ste. Madeleine? Someone been hurt?"

"Well, it's weird." Liz Falla turned on him the large, keen-as-mustard, eager-beaver eyes that swallowed up her small face. "More like vandalism, really."

The police car, an 1800 cc BMW, swung smoothly around a corner, and Moretti acknowledged that DC Falla was a damn sight better driver than his last partner.

Which was good, because he only liked driving behind the wheel of his own Triumph TR 6.

"I don't get it. Why are plainclothes being called in at this stage?"

"That's what I wondered, but I think it's because of the Vannonis."

Moretti's eyebrows went up. "Are the family still around? I thought they'd just rented out the place to the film company."

No wonder Chief Officer Hanley wants me back, thought Moretti. When this branch of the Vannoni family arrived in Guernsey some time after the war, they had made it their business to become socially involved with the top figures in the island power structure — notably the handful of politicians who ran the island, the lieutenant-governor, and the bailiff. The former was now purely a symbolic position, but still influential, the latter was head of the judicial, legislative, and executive arms of government, appointed by the sovereign. The Vannonis spent most of the year on the island, but there was still a branch of the family in Italy somewhere, where they ran their traditional businesses: olive oil and wine.

"No. They're still on site and the son is an assistant director. I think he's the reason they're here in Guernsey in the first place. Or so I'm told. I don't really understand the set-up, and I'd have to look at my notes to see who else is doing what."

"Do you know anything about the film company?"

"A little. It's an American outfit, but it's not that straightforward. The company itself is called Epicure Films, and the producer is the bloke that matters. He's an American called Monty Lord. The director is an Italian called Mario Bianchi."

"Right, I remember. I read an article about him not so long ago. Wunderkind, who's going to resurrect the Italian film industry single-handedly. Any other major players I should know about? It's an adaptation of a novel by Gilbert Ensor, isn't it?"

"You've heard of him? What a piece of — sorry, Guv. Anyway, you'll see for yourself."

DC Falla braked with a crispness not entirely called for by the terrain.

"He's hot at the moment — writes about crimes of all kinds. Crimes of greed, crimes of passion, crimes of betrayal. Remind me, which one of his books are they filming?"

"*Rastrellamento*. I haven't read it myself. I'm not big on war stories." DC Falla replied, a note of disapproval in her voice.

"Right. I've read it. Set in Tuscany at the very end of the Second World War — escaped British POWs, fascists, communists, partisans. What are they doing over here, I wonder. Money, I suppose."

"I don't know about that. But one of the crew told me they wanted to use the remaining structures from the occupation: bunkers, gun emplacements, observation towers. That's one of the attractions of the Vannonis' place — that big command bunker in the grounds."

"Right. One of the principal regimental command bunkers. Isn't it linked to the house by a tunnel?"

"I wouldn't know about that. My uncle who belongs to the Occupation Society says they wanted to use the underground military hospital, but you know what that's like, Guv. Still looks like it must have done when those poor men were slaving down there."

Yes, he knew what it was like. Clammy and dark, a curved roof hacked out of the rock overhead, with moisture dripping from the fissures, running down the gutters in the passages, an abomination of desolation.

DC Falla shuddered. "Gives me the creeps, it does. Besides, all that mould and mildew gets my eyes itching. What's the title mean — *Rastrellamento*? Is it a place?"

"No. Ensor uses it symbolically as well as literally. The raking or searching of an area for escaped prisoners, the examination of the past for ancient evils, the exploration of one's mind and thoughts for hidden motivations."

"Not my idea of a good night out. But since he writes about violence, maybe there's a link there. To what happened, I mean. He certainly made me feel violent."

Something in DC Falla's tone suggested a personal revulsion rather than a professional observation of character.

"Violence? I thought you said vandalism."

"Well, I'm not sure you can commit an act of violence on a bunch of dummies — dressmaker's dummies, that's to say. Three nights ago someone got into the area at the manor where they're being stored and slashed at a collection of dummies set up with costumes of various characters in the film."

"They're calling us in for an attack on a lineup of dresses?" Moretti's cloud of depression settled more firmly over him. "Someone's playing games. They'll just have to tighten their security. We don't have the manpower to guard Epicure Films' wardrobe for them."

"That's what I said to Chief Officer Hanley, and the director himself had decided to keep the whole business quiet. But the costume lady was dead set against it from the beginning — there's a fair bit of damage and she's out for blood. Then this Gilbert Ensor turns up with his wife and the costume lady confides in her. Seems that the evening before — which was the evening after the incident with the dummies — someone threw a dagger onto the patio of the Ensors' hotel suite. It didn't hit anyone. Ensor was out on the patio when it happened, and when you meet him you'll see why someone might take a potshot at him — but I went out to take a look at it."

"A dagger? Not just a knife?"

"No. Fancy-looking thing, but sharp enough to do real damage. Mrs. Ensor says it looked medieval to her." DC Falla turned toward Moretti. The bronze tinge in her dark hair as it caught the light reminded him of the black cat who had been the family pet, Merlo. He hadn't thought about him in years. "Mrs. Ensor's like a film star herself, Guv. American. Funny, I had the feeling I'd seen her somewhere."

"You may well have done. If I remember rightly, Ensor married Sydney Tremaine." His partner shrugged her shoulders. "Principal dancer with, I think, the American Ballet Theatre. I saw her once, guesting at Covent Garden. You probably saw her in a film. She had a brief screen career and then retired. To marry Gilbert Ensor."

"Good *luck*," said Liz Falla, fervently. "I remember now. It was a film about a Russian dancer — Anna something or other. I didn't like it that much."

"Anna Pavlova. I didn't like it much myself. But you're right, she's a looker."

"I told the Ensors we'd drop by this evening. He wasn't thrilled at the idea. I get the feeling he just likes being a pain in the backside — as if it's good for his image, or something. My uncle Vern would say it's the artistic temperament, so you'll likely understand him better, you being a piano player."

"We'll see."

In what spare time he had, Ed Moretti played jazz piano with a local group, the Fénions, in a nightclub called the Grand Saracen. Named for a legendary Guernsey pirate, it operated out of the cellar of one of the eighteenth-century houses that faced the old harbour — a vault that had been used to store the wine, spirits, and tea that flooded in and out of the island from all over the world. Not everyone approved of a senior member of the small plainclothes island police force moonlighting in what used to be a smuggler's den.

"We might as well go there right now. Where are they staying?"

"The Héritage, Guv. St. Martin's."

"Did you meet the American producer?"

"No. He's been away on business in Rome, apparently. Something to do with renting equipment, someone called the location manager told me. He's Italian, by the way. Albarosa. Toni Albarosa."

"I'm sorry I had to take time off just as you were — assigned, DC Falla, and I didn't get everything done, anyway. I need more than a day to deal with Italian red tape and bureaucracy, and God knows when I'll be able to get back."

"Is there any way I could help, Guv?"

"I don't think so, DC Falla, but thanks for offering." Moretti restrained a smile.

"It's just that," — DC Falla's small, strong hands whipped the wheel in evasive action around a couple of late-summer hikers meandering near the middle of the road — "remember that inspector from the Florence carabinieri who came over here for the symposium about money laundering?"

"Nice bloke, I remember. What was his name?"

"Benedetti. Giorgio Benedetti. We — that is, Guv, we had a bit of a fling, as you might say, before he left. He calls me from time to time."

"Good Lord, DC Falla —" Moretti turned sideways in his seat and looked at his companion. Her profile showed no signs of emotion whatsoever, let alone embarrassment, "— should you be telling me this?"

"I don't see why not. I was off-duty at the time — well, not when we met, but I went on holiday and he — stayed on for a week. I could ask him to cut some of that red tape for you."

"Would he do that?"

"For me, yes. Mind you, I'd just as soon this didn't

get around Hospital Lane."

"Understood. I'll bear that in mind."

They had come to a halt outside the Héritage Hotel, one of the island's top luxury establishments. Behind its elegant Regency facade it offered ensuite facilities with all of its twelve individually decorated bedrooms, and the Ensors were occupying two suites on the ground floor, joined by a connecting door. One of the chief attractions for Gilbert Ensor was its dining room's international reputation.

"Greetings, Ed."

They were met at the door by the owner and manager of the Héritage, Don Bertrand, who was an old school friend of Moretti's. Both of them had attended Elizabeth College, the Guernsey private school for boys, and Moretti's father had worked for Don Bertrand's father, when he turned his family home into a hotel after the war. When Moretti senior returned to the island he had first worked in the greenhouses, and then he had moved into the dining room of the Héritage. It was with regret that Bertrand senior had seen Moretti senior leave, to run his own restaurant in St. Peter Port.

"Hi, Don. You can guess why we're here."

"Of course. Hello, Constable Falla. Did you have so much fun last time you couldn't keep away?" Don Bertrand's bright blue eyes twinkled in his deeply bronzed face — the tan of a sailor, rather than of a sun worshipper.

"Something like that, sir."

"Hope you can get some sense out of him. He's three sheets to the wind as usual. Terrific for the bar receipts as long as he doesn't disturb the other guests."

"Does that happen?" asked Moretti. "Could this incident be the action of an irritated guest?"

"Could be — who knows. Mind you, things are quieting down now, and I've been able to keep the suite next to his vacant for the last week." Don Bertrand was leading them along the corridor that led from the main foyer to the part of the hotel that overlooked the cliff and the sea.

"You checked, didn't you, DC Falla, as to whether anyone had heard or seen anything?" Moretti asked.

"Well —" Liz Falla looked sheepish. "I talked to the staff, Guv, but I didn't see any point in upsetting other guests, when no one had actually been hurt."

"For which I was bloody grateful," was Bertrand's reply. "As you know, Ed, we are a Five Crown hotel, which means we have a porter at the desk at all times, all night. However, we cannot patrol the land beyond the hotel, and I have suggested to Mr. Ensor that he keeps off the patio. It was not — well-received. Here we are."

They were outside a door with a peephole and a plaque on it that read GARDEN SUITE. At the end of the corridor was another, similar door.

"Is that the empty suite?" Moretti asked.

"No, that's the door to the suite which the Ensors have also taken — or, rather, the film company have. All arrangements were made by them. We have one of the actors here as well, and two members of the film company — a man and a woman — but they are upstairs. The actor is a German. Nice guy, the German. Well, all of them are."

Moretti remembered that Don Bertrand senior had been imprisoned somewhere in France or Germany for most of the war.

"I'll leave you to it. Good luck! See he doesn't break up the furniture."

Bertrand departed down the hall. On the other side of the heavy door, voices were raised. Liz Falla looked at her boss and rolled her eyes. Moretti knocked. Then knocked again, loudly.

The door was opened by a tousle-haired man of about forty in striped pajamas, holding a heavy cut-crystal glass containing a clear gold liquid. He was teetering on his bare feet. Clutching the doorpost he called out in an appalling fake American accent, "Honey, it's the hired help!"

Over his shoulder, Moretti saw Sydney Tremaine, a cloud of red hair loose about her shoulders, her slender figure wrapped in a brilliantly coloured silk kimono.

"Forgive my husband's bad manners, officers — as you can see, he's very drunk. Thank you for coming. DC Falla, we met the other night, didn't we?"

"'Course we did!" slurred her husband. "It's the cute little gamine from the cop shop — hello again, darling."

Beside him, Moretti felt his partner stiffen.

"I'm Detective Inspector Moretti, Mrs. Ensor."

"Come in."

Sydney Tremaine's voice was pretty, with a musical resonance and depth, unlike that of many dancers. Apart from her looks, Moretti could understand why she had been plucked from the world of ballet to be in film.

"Perhaps we could go through and take a look first of all at the patio."

"Of course."

Ahead of them staggered the rotund figure of Gilbert Ensor, glass in hand, his corpulence comically exaggerated by the thick stripes of his attire.

They emerged on to a flagged area, softly lit, the actual lighting concealed among the various plants that grew in raised beds and containers. The sound of Mozart's clarinet concerto sang sweetly from a speaker concealed somewhere in the vicinity of a potted palm tree.

"Show me where the dagger landed," said Moretti to Sydney Tremaine. There seemed little point in sending too many questions in the direction of the tottering Gilbert Ensor.

"Here. I was inside, and I heard Gil scream —"

"I was fucking startled," Ensor interrupted her. "I yelled. Anyone would've."

"Here, Inspector." Sydney Tremaine knelt down, indicating a spot close to a chaise longue. "Your partner took the dagger. Have you seen it?"

"Not yet." Moretti turned to Gilbert Ensor, who sank, groaning with the effort, on to the chaise lounge. "How did you first realize it was there? Did you see it thrown? Or was it the noise as it landed?"

"The noise, I think. Clatter-clatter." Ensor waved his hand as though it weighed about ten pounds.

"So you don't know for sure if it came through the gate."

"Mus' have done. There wasn't any assassin hidin' behind the friggin' ferns."

Moretti went over to the gate and looked out. Whoever threw the dagger must have been, even briefly, in full view.

"It wasn't dark, was it? Did you see anything, anybody?"

"I wasn't looking, mate. I bloody ducked." Ensor drank the last of the liquid in the glass he held in an unsteady hand.

"I did," said his wife. "But it was after the knife landed and after Gil — called out. I opened the gate and took a look outside."

"Did you see anyone?"

"Only a woman jogger on the lower cliff path."

"Show me."

Sydney Tremaine walked ahead of him and opened the gate. Moretti noticed the lock was both efficient and sturdy.

"Over there. I called out after her, but she was too far away. There's always a wind out here." She shivered in the light wrap she was wearing, pulling it closer around her.

"Let's go back. We'll get a description from you later, and we'll have to have a written statement." She walked back ahead of him and Moretti saw that her slender build gave her the illusion of being shorter than she was. For a dancer, she was fairly tall.

"Can you think of anyone who might want to harm you?" he asked the figure slumped amid the cushions of the chaise.

"Look, mate, there's lots of people out there who find talent and genius a threat, and don't I know it. That's besides all the loonies and the crazies. Anyway, this island's covered with pagan remains, isn't it? For all I know, it's some Guernseyman following some ancient ritual. For all I know, youse guys throw daggers at the drop of a neolithic hat." Gilbert Ensor fumbled for a packet of cigarettes in the breast pocket of his pajamas. He managed to extract one, and bent forward precariously to light it from an ornate lighter on a small wrought-iron table near the chaise, cursing as the breeze extinguished the flame.

"Not normally," said Moretti, stifling both his growing irritation, and the urge to comment on the crude anachronism, which was deliberate, he knew. This man was too intelligent to have made the comment for any other reason than to annoy. "Here —" He pulled out the lighter he still carried, although he was supposed to have given up smoking, cupped the flame, and held it close to the writer's wavering cigarette. Best to ingratiate himself, perhaps, if that were at all possible.

"Ah, a fellow sinner." Gilbert Ensor squinted up at Moretti through a cloud of smoke and intoned, "'There's daggers in men's smiles' — I tend to believe that, Inspector. Don't you?"

"No more than I believe in air-drawn daggers, sir," Moretti replied.

"Ah, so besides looking like Dirk Bogarde you've got a brain. The ladies must love you." Gilbett Ensor leered at his wife. "Eh, Syd, me darlin'?"

Sydney Tremaine was quite calm. Moretti thought, *She's used to this.*

"I'm sorry," she said. "Perhaps it would be better if —"

"— We left, yes. There's nothing more to be done now. The dagger is being checked for fingerprints, and we'll have a word with the hotel staff and the occupants of any of the rooms that face this direction. Maybe someone saw something, but it seems unlikely. Sir, perhaps it would be best if you went inside?"

"I'll go inside when I want to go inside, Mr. Plod, and right now I don't want to go inside." It was said with an oily, drunken calm, and more clearly articulated than anything Ensor had said during the policemen's visit. Moretti wondered if the drunk act was precisely that — a performance.

So much for ingratiating oneself, thought Moretti. Without responding, he turned and left the patio, followed by Sydney Tremaine and Liz Falla, leaving Gilbert Ensor puffing at his cigarette.

"I apologize for my husband's rudeness, Inspector. It's — nothing personal. It's the way he is," said Sydney Tremaine when they reached the door of the suite.

"Sorry to hear that, Mrs. Ensor." Sydney Tremaine's green eyes widened, but she made no response. "About this business with the dummies and the costumes — can you think of anything that has happened on the set, during the making of the film, anything at all, that could help us establish a link between that incident and this — or anything at all for that matter?"

Sydney Tremaine threw back her head and laughed. It was a hearty laugh that made the red curls bounce about her lightly freckled shoulders.

"Any number of things happen on a film set, Inspector, that make any number of people want to throttle someone or other — or throw daggers at them. But no, nothing specific, nothing that seems to connect with the attack on Gil — if that's what it was."

"A coincidence then — is that what you're saying?"

"No." The laughter was gone now. "I think not. I don't really believe in that kind of coincidence. I wish I did." A shadow crossed her face, and Moretti had the feeling she had been about to say something else, but had changed her mind.

"Has anything like this happened before? Your husband has a volatile approach to life."

"How kind of you to put it like that! Fights and fisticuffs, yes. But no, nothing to do with daggers. Not even knives."

"Well, if you think of anything, let us know immediately."

Outside in the car, Moretti and Liz Falla sat for a moment without speaking.

"Talk about Beauty and the Beast, eh, Guv? Felt me up when I came before — very slick. I'm sure his wife didn't see a thing. What a bastard!"

"A talented, successful, and therefore indulged bastard," said Moretti, deciding not to comment on Ensor's liberty-taking with his colleague. She seemed more than capable of looking after herself, and he hoped this wasn't yet another hazard of having a female as his partner. "If it weren't for the incident at the Manor I'd say it was some idiot teenager messing about out on the cliff path. We could be dealing with a personal problem, whatever his wife says. I had a feeling she nearly told us something else, but changed her mind for some reason."

"Could be any number of things with that creep."

"Too true. Let's go back to the station, Constable. I should put in an appearance to reassure Chief Officer Hanley."

* * *

The green Triumph negotiated its way out of the police station, bypassing the winding streets of the town, making for St. Julian's Avenue. Climbing the road past the eighteenth-century elegance of Regency architect John Wilson's St. James Church — now used as a concert and assembly hall — and the same architect's less felicitous drab Gothic pile, his own alma mater, Elizabeth College, Ed Moretti drove the familiar route, deep in thought.

His education had been like the curate's egg — good in parts, and one of the good parts had been an extraordinary English teacher, the other a history teacher with a fondness for Aristotelian logic. A quotation from the Nichomachean ethics had been a favourite of the history teacher, and it had stayed with the pupil: *Every art and every investigation, and likewise every practical pursuit and undertaking, seems to aim at some good: hence it has been well said that the Good is that at which all things aim.*

Between the three of them — the English teacher, the history teacher, and the philosopher — he had become a policeman. Not what his parents had in mind for him when he won the scholarship, but still. And, in becoming a policeman, he found himself dealing with members of the human species whose behaviour threw Aristotle's logic on the topic of Good out the window.

Shifting gears, Moretti headed up the Grange past Doyle Road, named for an earlier lieutenant-governor. Up here, he was in the Regency and early Victorian suburbs into which St. Peter Port had expanded from its narrow sea-edged site, with spacious homes built from the profits of smuggling and privateering, surrounded by gardens verdant and beflowered with subtropical plants and trees like camellia and palm that flourished in the island's temperate climate.

Just after passing the Guernsey Academy for Girls,
the distaff equivalent of Elizabeth College, the Triumph
swung left into a narrow lane between two sizeable
houses, finally coming to a halt outside a high stone wall.
Moretti slowly negotiated his way between the stone
pillars of what had once been a gateway and was now
merely a gap in the wall.

Facing him was the cottage left to him by his father
— a two-storey dwelling built of rough-hewn granite
that had once been the stable and coachman's quarters
for the grand home through whose gateway he had just
passed. A solid wooden doorway of faded grey, set in the
traditional curved stone archway of the Guernsey cottage,
a window on each side and three above, were all of them
framed by a deep-pink climbing rose, long ago left to
its own devices. On each side of the property, fuchsia,
honeysuckle, and ivy covered the old walls with a tapestry
of crimson, cream, and dark green that, in the island's
mild climate, lasted most of the year round. What had
been the stables to one side of the structure served as his
garage. But the manor house was long gone, and all that
remained of the fine estate was Ed Moretti's inheritance.

He loved the place. One of the disadvantages of
leaving the island, as he had done earlier in his career, was
that the property laws were so strict that inheritance was
not always enough to hold on to such a possession. But
Moretti had been lucky, because he had returned to the
island to work and thus qualified for the house when his
father died. It was the source of much ill feeling among
expatriate islanders that the rich might buy their way in
to avoid supertax, but a poor native might sometimes
not be able to return to his, or her, roots.

He had made few changes to the decor and
furnishings of the house, and it had taken a while to get
over the feeling of waking in the morning and expecting
to find his parents downstairs. The most significant

addition was the sound system he had installed, to carry the music that was so important to his sense of well-being — a vintage quad system that drove a set of ESL speakers. The large speaker panel gave an incredibly smooth, sweet sound that had not, in Moretti's opinion, been bettered in over forty years.

He had not had to add a piano. His own love of music came from his mother, and one of his earliest memories was of listening to her playing "Roses of Picardy," singing the words in her soft, crooning voice. A very early memory. She had been gone a long time.

"Going back to the womb, you are." That was one of Valerie's cuts, just before he walked out the door. "Grow up, Ed, and face the music," she admonished him in one of their final fights. An unfortunate image in the circumstances, since she was of the opinion that it was the musician who was "a bloody Peter Pan," and the policeman who was the grown-up. Not so simple. Having watched his father dwindle and diminish after his mother's death, he wondered if he'd ever risk an emotional involvement that brought so much pain.

You're terrified of commitment, shit-scared of it, aren't you?

The first thing he did when he went into the cottage was put a disk on the record player. Oscar Peterson.

How did the man do it? The marvellous internal rhythm that could sing without benefit of percussion or bass, creating melody and miracles of harmony, fireworks and lyricism and tenderness. Like the perfect love affair. Only, unlike love affairs, the mood created was constant, the same perfection when played for the umpteenth time. Now, that was commitment. And it was a commitment devoutly to be wished, of which he was not afraid.

Oh lady, be good to me.

The music continued to play in his head, long after he had gone to bed. Finally, sleep came.

* * *

It was barely light when Moretti was awakened by the persistent ringing of his bedside phone. It was the desk-sergeant from Hospital Lane.

"Sorry to wake you at this hour sir —"

"What hour is it?" Moretti surfaced groggily through the layers of sleep.

"Six-thirty. But it's the film people out at Ste. Madeleine Manor and you're down on my sheet as the one to call. There's been some sort of accident. Nasty business."

"Was it a human target this time?"

"Oh yes." Moretti could hear the surprise in the officer's voice. "It's the location manager. Albarosa. Italian." And, feeling it necessary to make the message even clearer to Moretti's sleep-addled brain, he added, "He's dead, Guv."

III

September 16th

The limousine wound its way through the quiet early morning lanes southwest of the capital, St. Peter Port, making its way to the parish of St. Andrew's. Even before Guernsey was divided into parishes, the island was separated into fiefs, holdovers from the ancient feudal system, in which tenants owed allegiance to the local seigneur. Many of the old customs were long gone, as were the ancient fiefdoms, of which the Manoir Ste. Madeleine had been one.

On an island the size of Guernsey the past and present were often juxtaposed with almost jolting speed. The driver made his way past one of the smaller former fiefdoms, the Manor of Ste. Hélène, now in private hands like the Manoir Ste. Madeleine, and on past St. Andrew's Church, carefully restored to its twelfth-century self. Hardly past the squat spire and castellations of the old church, then they were crossing the Candie Road, close to the site of the vast German underground hospital.

"The underground hospital's over in that direction," said the driver, Tom Dorey, a local assigned to transport the Ensors. Before Sydney could make any response, Gilbert surfaced from a fitful doze for his usual grumble.

"Getting up at this hour is insanity. If they weren't paying me big bucks I wouldn't be doing this, and the way I feel I will never repeat the experience."

"The way you feel now has nothing to do with the hour. It's the booze, honey."

"Bullshit. My body and my inspiration purr along beatifically when they're well-oiled with Guinness and Glenfiddich. They grind to a sickening halt when confronted with the fucking light of dawn."

Impassively, Tom Dorey negotiated the sharp bend that preceded the gates of the manor. He had by now got used to his passenger's tongue, and could restrain the audible intake of breath that had been his original reaction.

"You don't have to do this too often, do you?" observed Sydney. "You only have to be in early today because Monty Lord asked for a script meeting."

"Jesus *wept* — or he would have done if he was the writer on this movie. It's not as if I were responsible for most of the script — Monty put his Hollywood hotshots onto that — but now he's farting about with the bloody plot line."

"Well, they do that, movie people, don't they? What is he changing?"

"Don't know the details yet, but it seems he wants to add another strand to the story, which'll completely alter the balance of the plot — and Bianchi's going along with it. He's building up one of the minor characters — the countess."

"Is the actress who's playing the countess his mistress?"

"Now *that* I could understand. But no. Word is he's got the hots for the Marchesa Vannoni herself. Shoots high, our Monty."

"My, my," marvelled Sydney. "She must be all of — what, fifty, fifty-five?"

"She's in good nick — built like a brick olive press. Still, she's not your typical Hollywood producer bait, I grant you. Ah, at bloody last."

They had arrived at the main entrance to the manor, which stood open. On each of the lofty stone pillars that supported the gate stood the heraldic beast that had once been part of the crest of the old island family who had lived in the house — a greyhound-like creature with impossibly long legs. To the right, a short distance away from the gate, was what looked like the gatekeeper's lodge — a two-storey building of unusual construction, with a pointed roof and an upper storey jutting out over the lower. The car continued up the drive toward the manor, which hove into view, giving the first-time visitor a shock — of pleasure, amusement, or aesthetic anguish, depending on the arrival's sensibilities.

The original structure of the Manoir Ste. Madeleine dated from the seventeenth century, to which had been added an elegant Georgian extension. The crowning eccentricity was the new entrance hall, built around the middle of the eighteenth century by a seigneur who had obviously paid a visit to the châteaux of the Loire valley and come back enamoured of towers and turrets. On each side of the central doorway the turrets hung out over the main walls like stone torpedoes, with a slender tower just visible behind the pointed roof. It was surrounded by well-maintained parkland, presently covered with the trailers of the film people, with a coach house close to the main building.

"Thank God we're here. I've got to take a leak."

They had come to a halt in the courtyard behind the manor alongside a vintage Mercedes, a Bugatti, and a handful of army vehicles of various kinds dating from the 1940s.

"Where *is* everyone?" wondered Sydney, as she got out of the car. "It's like the *Marie Celeste*."

The usually busy courtyard was deserted. There was a complete absence of drivers, film people of every stripe, even the security guards who generally milled and shouted around the area, which was not being used for the film.

"Shut up, woman," enjoined her superstitious husband, hustling for one of the portable toilets set up in a discreet corner of the yard. "They're probably all on the other side of the building. You go on — I'm making a pit stop."

Sydney made her way around the side of the manor house. To one side of her she could just see the grass-covered hump near the ornamental lake that concealed the entrance to the command bunker. One of the senior German officers had lived in the manor during the occupation, and it was on his orders that work had started on what was intended to be an elaborate complex of underground rooms and tunnels. The only sound was the squawking of the ducks that lived on the lake and the crowing of a rooster somewhere. There was still no sign of life, and the sensation of separation from reality she had experienced since their arrival hit her so powerfully that she felt vertiginous.

Gil had roared with laughter when he first saw the Manoir Ste. Madeleine.

"Dear God, it's pure kitsch — if kitsch can be pure. Any moment now and Sneezy, Grumpy, and Doc will come waddling round that corner, singing their corny little hearts out."

It was not how she saw it. Pure Castle of Otranto more like. More Transylvania than Ruritania. Any moment now and Nosferatu might come, swooping round the corner.

Perhaps it was the subject matter of Gil's novel that made Sydney so aware of the island's traumatic past — the bunker looming in the midst of the manor's verdant parkland and, scattered throughout the island, the remaining traces of anti-tank walls, gun emplacements, artillery direction-finding towers, restored for the amusement and amazement of tourists.

And perhaps it was even earlier presences. For Sydney, the island was indeed full of strange noises: the ancient witches' colony at L'Erée, the fairies emerging from caverns like Creux ès Faies to dance at Le Mont Saint or le Catioroc on the western coastline. At first she had been intrigued by the stories told by the tour guide who had taken members of the film company round the island, but all they did after a few days was feed her depression — which, she knew, had nothing to do with Guernsey, past or present. She felt a shiver of apprehension.

"I shall turn around this corner," she thought, "and everything will change. The world I knew will be gone forever."

She came around the corner into a blaze of light, so strong after the half-light of dawn that she was dazzled for a moment. As her vision cleared, she saw that the broad terrace that ran the length of the manor was floodlit by one of the arc lamps used on the movie, perched high on one of the huge Sky King cranes brought in from Rome. In the half-shadows around the periphery were gathered all the people she had expected to see in the courtyard: electricians, extras, grips. But there was hardly a sound.

"They must be shooting," she thought.

Sydney looked around for the director, Mario Bianchi, and caught a glimpse of his dark ponytail and tall, slender figure under the lights, huddled with another tall man she didn't immediately recognize. The man turned, and she saw it was the detective inspector with the interesting face who had come to the hotel the night before.

Of course, the business with the costumes. Betty Chesler, the costume designer, must have insisted. As Sydney approached the outskirts of the crowd, one of the men turned and saw her.

"Sydney! Where's Gil?"

It was Betty's assistant, Eddie Christy, minus his usual cheeky chappy expression. He looked haggard and nervous.

"Using the facilities. What scene are they shooting?"

"Oh my God, love — you don't know?"

"Know what? Gil's here for the meeting about the rewrite, if that's what you mean."

"Some rewrite, darling."

Over his shoulder, Sydney caught sight of a figure on the ground, slumped in an unnatural position against the parapet of the terrace. A man wearing what looked like a white lab coat was taking photographs of him — stills presumably, for he certainly wasn't carrying a movie camera.

"Who —?"

As she started her question, the crowd suddenly parted, and Sydney saw the impressive figure of the Marchesa Donatella Vannoni, clutching the arm of Monty Lord's assistant producer, Piero Bonini. As she came closer, Sydney saw that the figure on the ground had the dark, curly hair and smooth bronze skin of the marchesa's son-in-law, the location manager, Toni Albarosa. She also saw the handle of the dagger through his chest glistening under the arc light.

Vertigo hit her. She swayed, and Eddie Christy grabbed her and called out, "Someone, anyone, get a chair!"

A chair was provided and the crowd parted again.

"Ms. Tremaine — where's your husband? Is he with you?"

Above her she saw the detective inspector's face, his grey eyes urgent.

"He should be — oh God, you don't think —?"

Was the policeman suggesting whoever this maniac was might still be around, and that Gil might be in danger? As Sydney turned around in her chair to see Piero Bonini and the marchesa walking toward the manor together, from the darkness beyond the floodlit terrace came the unmistakable roar of her husband throwing a tantrum.

Anxiety changed to relief. Gil had come around the corner and seen Monty Lord.

"That's him," she said. "Don't worry — that's not fear or pain. That's the cry of the wounded artist, Detective Inspector. Hell hath no fury like a writer scorned."

Sydney could hear what he was screaming at the producer, who stopped, staggering momentarily under the weight of his noble burden.

"You turd! Couldn't you wait until I got here to make changes? Or is this your idea of a joke, scaring the fucking daylights out of me with fucking daggers — get Toni off the set and send that rubber fake back to props before I — I —"

Gilbert Ensor was halted in mid-sentence by the sudden arrival of the distraught marchesa against his ample belly, temporarily winding him. She was screaming in Italian, so he had no idea what he had said or done to upset her. Her long red nails scored his face before Piero Bonini managed to restrain her. Through the searing pain he grasped one word, said over and over again.

"*Morto — morto — morto!*"

Dead?

Ahead of him he saw his wife in a chair, the detective inspector alongside her. Beyond them, two ambulance attendants were covering Toni Albarosa's body. His jaw dropped. Violent death had rendered Gilbert Ensor speechless.

There followed one of those uncanny moments of silence that sometimes comes on the heels of uproar. Then into the silence came the rumble of a powerful engine. From the half-light around the villa thundered a gleaming Ducati motorcycle, its streamlined scarlet and black body brilliant in the arc light. Sydney Tremaine saw long blond hair flying beneath a winged helmet, powerful leather-clad legs stretched against the sides of the monster as, with a dramatic flick of the wrists, the rider brought her mount to a shrieking halt and pulled off her helmet.

Ed Moretti, looking down at the face of Sydney Tremaine, was intrigued by what he saw.

"You know her?"

"No."

Sydney got up from the chair and went toward her shell-shocked husband. The Valkyrie ran over to the marchesa, putting her arms around her. Together, they went into the manor, with Piero Bonini behind them.

Other members of the island police force had arrived to help with the dozens of statements that would have to be taken from everybody in the cast and crew. The Ensors and the Vannoni family were waiting in the manor to be interviewed by Moretti and Liz Falla. Finally, some semblance of order had been restored.

Moretti waited until the body was loaded into an ambulance and then turned to the Vannonis' doctor, a local St. Andrew's man called Le Pelley.

"So — what can you tell me?"

"Only what I told you before." Le Pelley, clearly somewhat shaken himself, removed his glasses and put them in his coat pocket. "He was killed, almost instantly. Whether by luck or good management, the point of the blade got him right through the heart."

"Time of death?"

"We'll know more after the autopsy — but, what time is it now? Nine-thirty? I'd say about five hours ago."

"Five hours!" Moretti was taken by surprise. "I thought you'd say midnight — something like that."

"Definitely not midnight — he'd not been dead long when he was found around five o'clock."

"Who found him?"

"One of the security guards, apparently. A couple stay around all night to keep an eye on the equipment."

"Then he probably only just missed being another murder victim."

Moretti said goodbye to Le Pelley and joined Liz Falla, who was waiting for him with a very worried-looking director, Mario Bianchi, and the reason for his expression soon became clear.

"I've already lost about two hours shooting time today, and the Constable tells me I can't touch what has now become the crime scene for at least another hour. If then."

Mario Bianchi was almost cadaverously thin. Heavy lines ran down each side of his mouth, which was largely concealed by an unfashionably heavy moustache, and Moretti wondered whether the ponytail and the facial hair were to compensate for the receding hairline above deep-set, anxious eyes. His nails were bitten to the quick, and his hands fiddled constantly with the collar of his open-necked shirt, or stroked his forehead. His command of English seemed good, and Moretti decided not to switch into Italian, if possible. Otherwise, he would have to translate for his partner, which would slow things down considerably, or exclude her completely from the interrogation.

"We'll do what we can, Mr. Bianchi. Certainly we're grateful for the light we were able to use. Could you not work on something else while we're out here?"

"Work on something else," Bianchi repeated. "You don't understand, Inspector. We set up the day's work in advance — the actors and technicians are called for certain times, and the lighting levels have to be decided upon with the cinematographer and the cameramen, depending on the needs of the scene and the weather conditions, and so on. These lights and cranes were in place for the scene we planned to shoot first — and which required the early light of day. That's gone now. We've lost it."

"What scene were you going to shoot out here?"

"Well, that's the strange thing — as I was just telling the officer. It involved the violent death of a man suspected of betraying one of the principal characters in the film. And the murder weapon is a knife. It gives me the — creeps, you call it? Poor Toni!"

"Tell me something about Toni Albarosa — he was the marchesa's son-in-law, I gather."

"Yes, married to the eldest daughter, Anna. They live in Italy, not here. It isn't the first marriage between Albarosas and Vannonis — at one point, the family coat of arms was actually combined, so he told me. He was a very nice lad — very hard-working."

"Experienced? As a location manager, I mean."

"No, but he had what we needed, Inspector — contacts. Not all of the movie is being shot here, on your island, and Toni could open doors for me. He was the first member of the family I met, when he was on holiday in Venice, and it was he who suggested his mother-in-law's property on Guernsey, when he heard the theme of *Rastrellamento*. He was a charming man — I'm sure you're going to ask me if I can think of anyone who might want to do this, and I can't. He didn't have an enemy in the world."

"Then he was indeed a rare human being, sir. Few of us can say that."

"True. But compared with other members of his family —"

Mario Bianchi broke off in mid-sentence, one hand pulling frenetically at his ponytail.

"So there were difficulties with some of the Albarosa and Vannoni clan?"

Bianchi laughed in what he clearly hoped was a light-hearted manner. "Families, Inspector, families! Nothing in particular, but you'll see what I mean when you interview them."

"Which I should go and do now. Thank you, Signor Bianchi. We'll try to get out of your way as quickly as possible. Oh —" Mario Bianchi had started to walk away toward his waiting crew, when Moretti called him back, "— the woman who arrived on the Ducati. Is that Anna, his wife?"

Bianchi turned. He was laughing again, but this time he seemed genuinely amused. "No, Inspector. That was Giulia Vannoni, the marchesa's niece. She just arrived, and is visiting the marchesa at the moment. Wife —" The director pointed to the Ducati, which still stood on the terrace, gleaming in the light. Painted on one flank was a pink lily, its petals tipped with gold.

"I'm sorry — I don't —"

"That, Inspector, is the symbol of gay and lesbian Florence. That's what that is."

Moretti and Liz Falla watched the departing figure of Mario Bianchi.

"Before we go in to talk to them, DC Falla, is there anything you can tell me about the Vannonis?"

"Of course, you weren't on the island when they arrived, were you, Guv? Well, not much, except they don't mix — except with the high and mighty. A bloke I used to go out with says they've got a little message up on the front door that reads, 'Only personal friends of the marchesa may use this door. All other visitors must go to the back entrance.'"

DC Falla's love life was proving quite useful.

"Charming."

In spite of being a small island — or perhaps because of it — there were some clear-cut divisions in Guernsey society. There were the hundreds of families who had lived on the island since the beginning of its recorded history and beyond, with the old island names — Bisson, Falla, Gallienne, Roussel, Le Poidevin, and many more. There were the great families — Brock, De Saumarez, Carey — the island aristocracy, some of whom had fallen on hard times, like their British counterparts. There was a transient population, who came from Europe to work in the hotels and restaurants, or to teach in one of the island schools — some of these came and went in a summer; some stayed for years. Then there were the wealthy escapees, who came to avoid the high taxes of the mainland, and who bought their way into the higher priced properties on the island — what were called "open market properties."

Not that British escapees were any longer the dominant section of that community, since Prime Minister Tony Blair had altered the tax base in Britain. Now, the wealthy were more likely to be the managers and CEOs of the myriad banks and financial institutions that operated on the island. Many lived in the comparatively new development around Fort George; some purchased Guernsey's equivalent of a stately home — the Manoir Ste. Madeleine, for instance. All around the island, the old farmhouses and cottages were being tastefully renovated, painted in pastel shades of dove grey, apricot, ivory, and restored to greater than former glory.

But Moretti had rarely heard of such overt class distinction.

"So, let's beard the lioness in her den and start off with the family. Then we'll talk to Monty Lord and the Ensors again. Insiders and outsiders — only, which is which? Somewhere between the two groups we'll start to get some sense of this." Moretti recalled the expression on Sydney Tremaine's face.

"Mrs. Ensor seemed startled by Giulia Vannoni's appearance."

"So was I, Guv. It was quite an entrance. Those bikes cost a fortune, don't they? Mrs. Ensor's unlikely to be a — well, one of them —"

"— a lesbian," supplied Moretti. Interesting that Liz Falla had problems with saying the word, but it could be she was concerned about his own delicate feelings.

"Right. Is she? Mind you, that creep she's married to could put any woman off men, in my opinion."

"Quite," said Moretti, his thoughts elsewhere.

What point was the murderer making by using daggers? What was he — or she — saying? Was this all about love? It was much more likely to be about hate.

But nobody hated Toni Albarosa apparently. Still, it was amazing how often that was said about murder victims. In the Manoir Ste. Madeleine they might take the first steps toward the truth.

"Oh, by the way, Guv — I spoke to Giorgio Benedetti last night. He says if there's anything he can do —"

"Thank you, DC Falla."

DC Falla gave him a look he was beginning to recognize now, but for the life of him he couldn't make out what it signified. His mother would have called it "an old-fashioned look," but that seemed particularly inappropriate for this young woman.

If the outside of the manor house was Walt Disney or Bram Stoker, depending on your aesthetic point of view, the inside was as close to Renaissance palazzo as the designer could get, given the architectural constraints. Moretti and his colleague walked under a succession of high, embossed ceilings, past long stretches of walls hung with what looked like family portraits, heraldic devices, the heads of animals slaughtered long ago and in other countries. Overflowing baskets and jugs of flowers filled the empty summer grates of stone fireplaces built into the thick walls.

"Impressive," said Moretti, stopping briefly to admire a luscious still life of flowers and fruit. "I wonder how much of this was changed by the film company — or does it always look like a Medici palazzo?"

"All I know is that one of the staff who's my father's cousin said working here was like being in Tuscany, where she'd done a wine tour one year."

Ahead of them now was the principal reception room. And in the centre of the stateroom, amid golden brocade-covered walls, were gathered the marchesa, the woman Mario Bianchi had identified as Giulia Vannoni, and another man whom Moretti didn't recognize. He was young, in his early twenties, handsome, but with a softness in his features that suggested a character flaw rather than gentleness or any more positive quality. The incongruous presence of two movie cameras against the golden walls added to the impression that the group was waiting for someone to shout "action!"

The three sat side by side on a gilded sofa, unsmiling, staring unblinkingly at the two policeman. Giulia Vannoni stood by the fireplace, drinking from a bottle of mineral water. She had unzipped her tight-fitting red leather jacket, displaying a minute black lycra bandeau and a tanned length of torso. Her black leather pants looked as if they had been spray-painted onto her spectacular haunches. *The quintessential mesomorph*, thought Moretti. He introduced himself and DC Falla.

"I'm sorry we kept you waiting. If I could first make sure we have your names correctly. You are —?" Moretti directed his first question to the young man.

"Gianfranco Vannoni." He spread his hands and gave a shrug. "I do not speak much English."

"My son." It was the marchesa who spoke. "He lives in Italy, looking after our business affairs. But for the moment he is helping Mario on *Rastrellamento* — as assistant director. I can speak or translate for him, if necessary."

"No need, marchesa. I speak Italian, if necessary," said Moretti. He watched with interest as three sets of eyebrows went up.

"Moretti — you are Italian?" asked Monty Lord.

"My father was." Moretti went swiftly through the formalities and then said, "This is a trying time for you. I am very sorry about the tragic death of Mr. Albarosa."

"Murder." It was the marchesa who spoke. "Murder, Detective Inspector Moretti. A sick mind playing games, perhaps. But murder. My poor daughter has been informed. She is on her way here, to say goodbye to her dear husband, the father of her children."

The Marchesa Donatella Vannoni was, in her own way, as impressive physically as her niece. Full-lipped and full-hipped, with a mane of dark hair streaked with grey, she was an Anna Magnani of a woman, with an aura of raw sensuality about her. But somehow she conveyed an air of austere grandeur, a cold remoteness, a structure built to keep people out. There was a marked divergence between her physical opulence and her conservative style of dressing: her lush curves were controlled beneath a dark grey carapace of a dress, and a bruisingly thick gold necklace lay over the generous shelf of her bosom like a chain-link barrier against infiltrators.

Yet, in a moment of uncontrollable anger, those long carmine nails had raked Gilbert Ensor's face.

"Indeed. We will have to have written statements from everyone, but I'd like to ask you now where you all were around four o'clock this morning — and I realize that, for most of you, the answer will be, in bed. But I'd like to know who sleeps on the premises and who does not."

"I, of course, sleep here." It was the marchesa.

"Does your room face the terrace?"

"Yes. I imagine your next question will be, did I hear anything, or see anything. I did not. I sleep soundly and well."

"Signor Vannoni?"

Gianfranco Vannoni replied in Italian. "I was here last night. Does that make me a suspect?" *A man used to charming his way through life*, thought Moretti. *He cannot resist the dangerous question, asked with humour.* A charming *moue* of the lips and a gentle twist of his hands, their tan setting off the gleaming gold bracelet he wore.

"It could," said Moretti. "Tell me more."

"I went to bed early — I had to be on set by eight o'clock, and we had a meeting at nine scheduled for myself, Mario, Monty, and Gilbert Ensor. Mario was expecting fireworks."

"From —?"

At this moment a door on the far side of the room opened, and a middle-aged man wearing a black turtleneck sweater and black pants burst into the room. He rushed across to the marchesa, who stood up, fell into his arms, and started to cry.

"It's okay, *cara*, I'm here, I'm here," he said in Italian to her. They made a somewhat incongruous couple, because the marchesa was taller than her comforter and had to crouch to be consoled. He looked up and saw Moretti.

"Monty Lord," he said. "Forgive me, but I just got back from Italy. I met Piero in the corridor, and he told me about Toni. This is terrible, terrible." He sat down, taking the marchesa with him in his arms.

"You are the producer of *Rastrellamento*?" Moretti asked.

"That is correct."

Monty Lord was a small man in his fifties, whose shaven head seemed almost too big for his body. The darkness of his clothing brought into prominence a pair of piercing pale eyes set in a tanned face, and Moretti felt as if it were himself and his sergeant who were under examination from the shrewd, searching look to which they were both subjected.

"Mr. Vannoni was just telling me that he, you, and Mario Bianchi had a meeting scheduled for nine o'clock."

"Right. I was joining them as soon as I got in from the airport."

"He was saying that you were expecting fireworks and I asked from whom?"

"Gilbert," Monty Lord replied. "I gather from Piero you already had a preview."

Before Moretti could respond, Monty Lord went on. "Time is money, Detective Inspector. And the marchesa has had a terrible shock. Can any of this wait?"

"The sooner we get some sort of picture of the victim from those who knew him best — and an idea of the whereabouts of everyone on the set, the sooner we can establish motive, opportunity — and the guilty party."

"But surely," said the marchesa, "this is just a random act by some madman? You know, of course, about what happened to the costumes."

She was interrupted by her niece who turned away from the fireplace to face Ed Moretti and Liz Falla, giving them the benefit of an alluring smile from her beautiful, heavily lipsticked mouth. "— and the attack on Gilbert Ensor. And you didn't ask me where *I* slept, Inspector. But it wasn't here."

The intervention of Giulia Vannoni seemed to anger Monty Lord. He turned his pale gaze in her direction and exclaimed, "Oh for Christ's sake, if we all keep interrupting we'll never get out of here."

This room reeks of animosity and anxiety, Moretti thought. *But I'm not sure who mistrusts whom — or do they all dislike each other?* He saw a look of distaste on the face of Gianfranco Vannoni as the American put a hand on his mother's arm. Her niece, on the other hand, looked mildly amused. "Detective Constable Falla will take statements from each of you, separately. Is there a room close by she can use?"

"She can use my study," said the marchesa. She added, "The Ensors are in my private sitting room — you will, of course, be talking to them?"

"Of course," said Moretti. "I expected to find them in here with you."

Monty Lord snorted. "Donatella did not want to be in the same room as Mr. Ensor after the tasteless accusation he made out there. And the less I have to do with Gil the better — we have to meet from time to time, but I'm happier if I'm not breathing the same air as that literary lout."

"Were your disagreements limited to the script, Mr. Lord?"

"We didn't socialize, if that's what you mean. Gilbert's problem is that he thinks because he wrote a bestselling novel, and because we bought the movie rights, he can now tell us what to do. He can't."

"But as long as you didn't have to breathe the same air as Mr. Ensor, you were prepared to let him live?"

"Christ, yes! I was in Rome until yesterday at Cinecittà — all kinds of people would be able to confirm that. And I flew back by private plane to be here for our meeting."

"Thank you, sir. Just give DC Falla the details and any names." Moretti turned his attention again to Gianfranco Vannoni, speaking to him as before in Italian.

"I understand, sir, that it was on your initiative that Epicure Films came to Guernsey."

The marchesa's son looked startled. "No. Not that I remember. Why?"

"I just wondered — why you were all here."

"Detective Inspector," it was Monty Lord who intervened, "perhaps I could fill you in?"

"Thank you, sir. If I could speak to you later today." Moretti turned to his partner. "I'll leave you to it."

"Signor Moretti," the marchesa stood up, "my Anna will arrive soon, and we would like to take Toni back home."

"And home is —?"

"Fiesole — you know it?"

"It's quite close to Florence, isn't it?"

"*Si.*" The marchesa nodded, and reached out for Monty Lord's hand.

"I regret, Marchesa, that I cannot at this stage give you any definite day or time when we would be able to release the body. There will, of course, have to be a post-mortem, which will be performed at Princess Elizabeth Hospital."

"*Dio mio!*"

Whatever else the marchesa might have said was lost in the shoulder of the American producer's jacket, and Moretti took advantage of her dramatic collapse to make his escape.

As he left the room he could hear the sound of someone whistling. It was Giulia Vannoni. As she passed him she called out, "Don't worry, Inspector. I have permission to leave, and I have promised to be back."

She resumed her whistling as she passed him, running lightly and easily, her straight blond hair flopping heavily on her leather-clad shoulders. A long gone and, he had thought, long-forgotten love drifted back into his consciousness on the wings of her perfume. The name of both the woman and her perfume escaped him. The perfume's name had something to do with chaos, or uproar. Something like that. The tune was more instantly recognizable: "La Donna è Mobile."

Perhaps there is supposed to be a message in it for me, he thought. Although Valerie would say that in his case it was the man who was fickle. One minute committed, the next running in the opposite direction. Actually, he'd been committed — if not married — for years, but that was how she saw it.

The Ensors were waiting for him in the marchesa's sitting room, which was also on the ground floor, near the front entrance. It was a small room compared to the others, simply furnished with English chintzes and numerous family photographs in silver frames. Sydney Tremaine sat on one of the deep window seats cut into the thick walls of the manor, and her husband lay slumped on one of the beflowered sofas. He seemed to be asleep.

"He didn't know, you know," was the first thing she said to Moretti. She looked pale and fragile in a white shirt of thin Indian cotton and khaki pants. "He's had so much trouble over script changes, and he thought it was someone's idea of a joke."

At the sound of his wife's voice, Gilbert Ensor opened his eyes and sat up. The marks left by the marchesa's talons ran down his cheeks in parallel tracks of congealed blood.

"The bitch. See what she did? I could bring charges —"

"Probably not advisable in the circumstances." Moretti's crisp tones cut into the self-pitying whine. "But that must be your decision, naturally. Right now I would like to talk to you, Mr. Ensor, about your book and the film script for *Rastrellamento*."

"How long have you got? Where would you like me to start?" The whine had changed to a petulant snappishness.

"Tell me, first of all, about your initial agreement with Epicure Films — what were the original changes that were agreed upon? What are the main differences between your novel and the script?"

"You know my work?"

"I read *Rastrellamento* some time ago. Refresh my memory."

"You think all this has something to do with Gil's book?" asked Sydney. She was looking puzzled.

"I don't know. Perhaps we can rule it out. Go on, sir."

"Well, there are two central plot lines: one is about a British prisoner hiding out in Tuscany just after the surrender of Mussolini, and the other concerns the struggle between the various factions in Italy at the time — the fascists, the partisans, the communists, and the efforts of the local population to deal with all these warring parties, including the presence of German troops. But if you know my work, you'll know that I am interested in more than plot lines — I am interested in exploring the interactions of human beings, their philosophical stances and their justifications for their actions, conscious and unconscious. Much of this does not translate well to the screen, and I understand that. So much of that part of the book had to go."

"What, do you think, attracted Monty Lord and Epicure Films to *Rastrellamento*?"

"Apart from my international celebrity?" Gilbert Ensor asked the question without the slightest trace of irony or self-deprecation. "Intrigue and exotic setting and historic period — and lashings of sex and violence."

"I still don't really understand why you're so interested in all this." Sydney Tremaine unfolded her long legs and perched on the edge of the window seat. "Don't you want to know where we were and all that sort of thing?"

"Another officer will take a written statement from you both, but I am trying to establish some of the circumstances around the crime — the project you were all working on, what tensions may have arisen. Do daggers play a major role in the film, for instance?"

"Not a major role, but certainly knives were used by the resistance movement — as a silent way of killing, you understand."

"And is there any reason in the script for you to be in Guernsey?"

"None at all. Now, that had a great deal to do with the bloke who's just got a dagger in the chest. There's a thought."

"Yes." Moretti watched the shadow crossing the flawless skin over Sydney Tremaine's cheekbones. "I gather, Mr. Ensor, that you approved the initial cuts and alterations to your book, but that there have been changes since then that have given you problems. Why? Surely this is fairly normal in the film world?"

"The changes to the basic plot line are quite unnecessary. This isn't Gilbert Ensor's *Rastrellamento* any more — it's more like Dante's bloody *Inferno*."

"In what way do you mean that?"

"The whole project's become hell on fucking wheels is how I mean that — I was not speaking intellectually. Each day I spend in contact with the movie world I can feel my brain cells dying, my mental capacity shrinking like a weenie in cold water."

Moretti ignored the outburst. "Your book and the movie have political content. If I remember rightly, you are harsh in your judgments of both the peasant population — the *contadini* — and the local aristocracy, when writing about their politics and their loyalties. Is it possible you have opened old wounds?"

"See, I wondered that." Suddenly, Gilbert Ensor was quite serious. He leaned forward and offered Moretti a cigarette from a battered packet he pulled from his crumpled linen jacket.

"Thank you." In the interests of establishing rapport — a peace offering, Moretti told his conscience, as he accepted.

"At first, when someone hurled that thing at me on the terrace, I thought it was some madman who had it in for celebrities. Then I calmed down and thought maybe it was an accident — some moronic kid playing about. Then, when I heard about the damage to the costumes, I thought it was a malicious attempt to scare us off the project."

"But it's a possibility, isn't it?"

"But why Toni? If you wanted to make a point, you'd try for me again, or go for Monty, or maybe one of the actors taking political roles, wouldn't you? Toni was Mr. Sunshine — a kind of male Pollyanna. Most of the locations had already been scouted, you know, and Monty used him to appease the marchesa. He did damn all and nobody cared, because he was so bloody cheerful and good-tempered. Got up *my* nose, but I like my humans to be bastards or bitches — that's why I married Syd, isn't it, honeybunch?"

Sydney Tremaine slipped down off the windowsill. "I'll be right outside if you need me, Inspector," she said.

"I probably won't need to keep you today. Just be available to give a written statement some time." As she walked from the room, Moretti had the feeling she was removing herself before she lost control.

"I thought it was Mario Bianchi who hired Toni Albarosa, for his local contacts — at least, that's what he told me."

Gilbert Ensor gave a contemptuous laugh. "He would, poor sod. Trying to hang on to the illusion he has *some* sort of creative control over Rastrellotitanic, as I like to call it."

"You think the project's doomed?"

"Oh, it'll get made. But it won't be the movie we started with, and I am seriously thinking of removing my name from the project."

"Have you said that to anyone?"

"Most likely. When I'm in a blind rage or in my cups — which is most of the time lately — I say all kinds of things I don't remember."

"I see. Thank you, Mr. Ensor. The office will be in touch with you some time tomorrow."

Gilbert Ensor got up from the sofa and crossed to the door. For all his marital raging and sniping, he was a lost soul without his wife to guide him through the maze and morass of everyday life — such as where to find the limousine that would take him home.

"Syd?" His plaintive call reverberated through the echoing expanses of the manor house.

But Sydney Tremaine wasn't there.

chapter four

"Not one of them, Guv, can think of any reason why anyone would want to kill the marchesa's son-in-law."

Moretti and Liz Falla were exchanging information as they made their way across the park and up the flight of stone steps to the upper floor of the lodge where the first attack with a dagger had taken place. Liz Falla had acquired a complete list of everyone employed on *Rastrellamento* from the associate producer, Piero Bonini, and was compiling a record of who lived where. *Not just eagle-eyed*, thought Moretti, *but organized*. It wasn't her fault Hanley had said "eagle-eyed" until everyone was fed up to the back teeth with hearing it.

Most of the cast and crew lived in hotels and guest houses in St. Martin's and St. Peter Port, with the level of luxury matching their level of importance. There were a few exceptions. All the Vannonis and Toni Albarosa were at the manor, and three of the cast were staying there also. These were the two female leads: newcomer Vittoria Salviati, who played the young love interest,

Maddelena, and an established star, Adriana Ferrini, whose role as the Contessa Alessandra di Cavalli was creating the latest problems on the movie. One of the leading men, Clifford Wesley, an up-and-coming British actor, recruited from the classical stage, who was starring as the escaped British prisoner, Tom Byers, was also at the manor. The internationally known German film actor, Gunter Sachs, who was playing the commandant of the prison camp in the imaginary Tuscan village of Santa Marina, had stayed briefly, but had now transferred to the Héritage Hotel, where Betty Chesler and Eddie Christie were also billeted.

"Did Piero Bonini have any interesting comments to make about his cast?"

"Mostly he went on about Gilbert Ensor, who seems to be at the top of everyone's hit list. Hit-and-miss list, I suppose I should say. Do you think someone thought Toni Albarosa was Ensor in the dark?"

"Could be, but unlikely. What would Gilbert Ensor be doing skulking about outside the manor in the small hours?"

"Well, that was one of the things Bonini went on about — about Ensor, I mean. Seems there'd been a spot of bother in Italy somewhere. He wouldn't go any further, but he did say Ensor was lucky his wife was the forgiving kind, and if he'd heard that Ensor was the one with a dagger in the chest he wouldn't have been surprised."

"Interesting. So what was Toni Albarosa doing in the wee small hours? Did Bonini shed any light on that?"

"I was just coming to that. When I was leaving his office — he's got a trailer on the far side of the manor, quite close to the bunker — I could hear him through the open window. He was shouting at the interpreter they've got here — it must have been her, because she was the only other person there — and it was all in Italian, but I can understand quite a bit now, of course, and what

I managed to pick up was her name, Bella, and then another two names — Vittoria, and Toni."

"Ah," said Moretti.

"That's what I thought, Guv." DC Falla turned and grinned at Moretti.

Betty Chesler was waiting for them at the top of the steps, only too eager to speak her mind.

"I see you've brought your superior officer with you this time," she said to the young policewoman. She turned and glared at Moretti. "I'm so glad someone is now taking this seriously, and what a wicked shame it took poor Toni's death to do it! I can't tell you how upset I was with the cavalier attitude of just about everyone about the damage — mark my words, I said to Piero, this is like an *omen*. It's a warning, and there's more to come. But until Gilbert Ensor's wife said about the attack on her husband, no one cared a tinker's cuss about my costumes — here, let me show you the damage." She led the way inside.

The damaged costumes were still where Liz Falla had seen them, lined up on the foldaway table: the three women's tailored suits, one dress, a man's suit, and a German uniform.

"To which characters in the film do these belong?" Moretti asked, bending over them and examining the gashes in the German uniform. The dagger must have been sharp to have torn the tough fabric as it had.

"The dress and two of the suits belong to the countess, the other woman's suit is for a fairly minor character, the housekeeper, the man's suit belongs to the village priest, and the German uniform is for Gunter's character. Those are the dummies I was using over there."

Liz Falla went over and poked her fingers through the holes. "Through the heart," she said, "— or where it would be."

"That's exactly what I said to Piero," said Betty Chesler. "Through the heart, I said."

"I presume there'd been a break-in?"

"In a manner of speaking, though it wasn't that difficult. I wish now I'd opted for a trailer, but this was so roomy and I like the higher ceiling. Besides, I wasn't that worried with security guards patrolling the grounds. Whoever it was came in through the window." Betty Chesler indicated the broken pane. "And now that we've lost the location manager" — this was said with heavy sarcasm — "the police have dusted for fingerprints. The young lady took the dagger away."

"He — whoever — left the weapon."

"Yes. Very fancy, like something out of an Errol Flynn movie, as I said to the police officer here, but I imagine you're too young, aren't you, to know who I mean." Betty Chesler shuddered. "I just screamed when I got in here and saw what had happened. It looked like a massacre."

"Was it generally known that these particular costumes would be on the dummies that night?"

"Well, anyone coming in and out of here over the past three or four days would have known, because that's how long they've been up. Mr. Lord and Mr. Bianchi wanted some changes to the countess's outfits — they're building up her role, so I hear — and Mr. Sachs had put on quite a bit of weight since his original fittings, so we had to alter them."

"And the housekeeper and the priest?"

"Casting changes. For the housekeeper they'd gone from a jolly roly-poly English actress to a gaunt Italian lady, more of a Mrs. Danvers type — you know, like in Daphne Du Maurier's *Rebecca*? And they'd gone the other way for the priest — from cadaverous to cuddly, don't ask me why."

"I see. Thank you, Ms. Chesler. You've been very helpful. If you think of anything else, this is where you can reach me." Moretti handed her his card. Then, on the spur of the moment, he asked, "Do you have any theories yourself? You talked about an omen. A warning."

Liz Falla was standing by the table where the attacker had left the dagger. As he said this, Moretti saw her look across sharply at him, then away. She said nothing, so he continued. "About what? Or whom?"

Betty Chesler looked at Moretti. "I don't know for sure," she said slowly. "I work on a lot of historical films, and sometimes I get a strange feeling, standing in a room like this, surrounded by the past. It could be just that — but whatever this is about goes a long way back. That's my opinion."

"A long way back — in time, you mean?"

"Right. This isn't about what Gilbert Ensor did or said to insult Monty Lord, or what the marchesa did or said to upset — well, just about everybody, that one. I mean, I can understand why knives — guns aren't so easy to come by, unless you're in America — but why bother with decorative daggers? If you can find that one out, Detective Inspector, you've probably got the answer."

"So these are not like any knives or daggers used in the film?"

Betty Chesler shook her blond beehive vigorously. "I don't do weapons, but I know that much. There's guns of all sorts, and a few knives — World War Two army issue type things, I suppose. Plus the odd bomb or grenade. But no fancy handles."

As they went back down the steps, Liz Falla asked, "Was she helpful, or were you just saying that, Guv?"

"A bit of both. I'd like to know why such a major change in a minor character — it could mean absolutely nothing, but it could also be part of that feeling she has that all this has something to do with the past."

"Which past, that's what I thought when she said that."

"Exactly. But daggers, not just knives, have been used three times and that has to be significant. Murderers have quirks, but I can't believe this guy has managed to get hold of a handful of fancy daggers cheap, and is using them for reasons of economy."

Liz Falla reached into the pocket of her jacket and pulled out several sheets of paper. "I got what they call a shooting schedule from Mr. Bonini, as well as the list of cast and crew members. They usually make out a schedule for the whole project and it is updated each day. It gives names, times, and location. Who are we interested in next?"

"Vittoria Salviati, DC Falla — if your Italian steered you right."

They were in luck. The young actress was scheduled for a shoot that afternoon. By now it was late morning and, according to the schedule, she would be in makeup. Moretti went back up the steps and asked Betty Chesler where they would find her.

As they made their way back up the drive, Moretti asked, "Has anyone mentioned anything that might be of interest from any of the statements taken so far?"

"Nothing, Guv. I did ask about the security guard's statement, and apparently he saw and heard nothing unusual, until he came across the body — except that one of those big lights were on. There's nerve for you, illuminating the scene of the crime!"

"Unless," said Moretti, "it was Toni Albarosa who switched it on, because he saw something unusual — something he was not supposed to see. I think we're about to find out *why* he was on the terrace at night, taking a murderer by surprise. But I don't think he was the original target."

Vittoria Salviati was as pretty as a picture, chocolate-box beautiful. As she turned around in the chair before the brightly lit mirrors, Moretti could not restrain a sharp intake of breath. She looked no more than eighteen years old and, even allowing for the miracle of movie makeup, her pouting red lips, cloud of tousled dark hair, and huge dark eyes against her porcelain skin did indeed take the breath away. But the white around those huge dark eyes was bloodshot, and their expression was anguished. Moretti introduced himself and Liz Falla, and established that she was reasonably comfortable speaking English.

"Do I have to speak to you now? I have a difficult scene to do — could it wait until tomorrow?"

"We would like just a brief word now with you, Miss Salviati. It would be better, coming from you, rather than from anyone else — wouldn't it?" said Moretti, gently.

The young actress turned and nodded at the makeup artist, a middle-aged man with purple hair and a nose ring. As he left the trailer, he turned and rolled his eyes knowingly at the two policemen. As soon as he had left, Vittoria Salviati burst into tears.

"You know, don't you? Who told you?"

"Guessed would be a better word, Miss Salviati. Toni Albarosa was either coming to see you, or leaving."

"Leaving — oh my poor, darling Toni! It was always such a chance we took, with the marchesa so close, but we could not keep away from each other — you know how it is."

Moretti was aware of a quizzical glance in his direction from his partner.

"Did you meet on *Rastrellamento*, or had you known each other before?"

"We met on the first day and it was what the French call '*coup de foudre*,' Inspector."

"Forgive me, Miss Salviati," said Moretti, "but — you are a very beautiful woman. You must have had men making passes at you, falling in love with you, at every step. What was different about Toni Albarosa, that you would risk an affair with a man married to the daughter of the marchesa, who was on the premises, and who clearly has a position of importance on this project?"

Vittoria Salviati swung around from the mirror on her swivel chair, giving both officers a glimpse of slim brown legs beneath her cotton wrap as she did so.

"That's just it — he *didn't* make a pass at me. He just looked at me so sweetly with his big eyes, and told me — oh, the most beautiful things you can imagine! For a whole *week* before he slept with me! Oh, I'm sure this is all my fault. I'm sure this has something to with that bitch of a wife of his, or that bitch of a mother-in-law of his, or both of them!"

"I don't think you need blame yourself for his death in that way, Miss Salviati. I think that Mr. Albarosa was just in the wrong place at the wrong time. Did he ever say anything to you about anything he might have seen or heard during those nightly visits? Outside in the grounds, I mean?"

"No. Mostly we didn't talk once he got to my room."

Moretti could think of no adequate response to this.

"Does everyone have to know?" Vittoria Salviati leaned forward anxiously in her chair, affording Moretti a generous glimpse of her much-photographed and beautiful bosom.

"Not immediately, but when we find who is responsible, the reason for Mr. Albarosa's presence on the terrace at that hour may come out in court."

There was a knock on the door and the makeup artist put his head into the room. "Miss Salviati's due on the set in half an hour and — oh my God!"

With a wail and a shriek he ran across and held the actress's face between his hands.

"Vittoria sweetie, what have they *done* to you, what have they *said* to you!" He turned and looked accusingly at Moretti and Liz Falla, the brutal sulliers of his handiwork. "Look at this mess — she's got mascara and lipstick on her *chin*, for God's sakes. I'm going to have to start all over again."

At the foot of the trailer steps Liz Falla stopped and looked at Moretti.

"That Albarosa had a great act going, eh, Guv? Believe you me, that one works much better than that sleaze Ensor's slimy gropings."

"I believe you," said Moretti. "I want to talk to Monty Lord next, but first we'll head back into St. Peter Port, and I'll drop you off at the station. If Chief Officer Hanley asks where I am, you can tell him I'm making further enquiries."

"Right, Guv."

"Okay, DC Falla, give me your first impressions," Moretti said, as the police car pulled in to the side of a narrow lane to allow one of the town buses through. Through the open window Liz Falla called out cheerily to the driver as he passed.

"Well, first of all, I agree with the costume lady — find out why daggers and we're on our way. But I'm not sure I agree about the past. The French say '*coup de foudre*,' like Vittoria Salviati said, but they also say '*cherchez la femme*,' don't they? I think it's all about sex myself."

"You may be right." Moretti smiled. His partner's straightforward and unvarnished approach was a salutary reminder of his own tendency to intellectualize and embroider. "And Ms. Chesler may be over-exaggerating the importance of the daggers. When the purple-haired gentleman took a fit at some smudged makeup I reminded myself that we're dealing with people who act and think theatrically. The use of decorated daggers could be merely picturesque, for effect. And nothing more."

"The artistic temperament. Or histrionics, like my uncle Vern. So we go back to motive and opportunity?"

"For the time being. But we'll certainly take a look at the daggers back at the crime lab. If possible, I'd like us to interview Monty Lord and the other actors whose costumes were damaged when we get back to the manor in the afternoon. By the way, I thought you were about to say something when I asked Betty Chesler about her use of the word 'omen.' Were you?"

"No, Guv." There was a pause, and then Liz Falla said, "I just thought she was being fanciful."

"Okay. I'll pick you up from Hospital Lane when I've seen to some personal business."

"Right you are, Guv." Liz Falla cast a quick glance at Moretti. "That actress, then — do you think those were real tears?"

Moretti smiled and shrugged his shoulders "I do, but I don't think that was just grief we saw. She's genuinely scared that the marchesa will find out, and we'll have to talk to the widow before we can decide if Toni Albarosa was as sweet and genuine as everyone says. But my feeling is that your instincts are right. I'll see you in about an hour."

The restaurant Moretti's father had once owned was above the cellar that housed the jazz group, the Fénions. It was called Emidio's — Moretti senior's first name. It was now run by Rick Le Marchant, the younger brother of Emidio Moretti's former business partner — a solution that had kept the peace in the extended family, if not the immediate family. As was not uncommon on the island, it so happened that this branch of the Le Marchant family was distantly related to Moretti's mother, Vera Domaille.

Whenever Moretti walked in through the front door with its red awning, he was stepping into the past — which was why he so rarely ate at Emidio's, although it boasted some of the best and most authentic Italian cooking on the island. The restaurant smelled particularly enticing today. From the direction of the kitchen wafted the yeasty, fruity fragrance of freshly bakèd *panettone*, and through the side of the glass-covered counter shimmered the dark chocolate gleam of *dolce torinese*, the chilled chocolate loaf his mother had loved so much.

But while he ate his veal scallopine *al Marsala* or *scampi alla griglia*, Moretti preferred his digestive system not to be awash with memories of his mother laughing at his father over the low counter that divided the kitchen from the restaurant. That bright memory was gone too soon with her early death, and from then on it was the shadow of Emidio Moretti that wandered between the red tablecloths and took the orders of local and tourist until he sold the business.

Coup de foudre. Like a thunderbolt, his father once told him. *Como un fulmine, Eduardo.* Not just from the pain in the empty stomach, the ache in the bones from the physical labour, and the ribs cracked from the butt of the guard's gun. Like a thunderbolt when I saw her face — her great blue eyes and the pity in them. I smiled, and the next day there she was again — only this time she darted out and put a piece of bread in my hand. The day after that it was a piece of cheese — sometimes it was bacon or sausage, if they had any, and they had so little — we were all starving. We were lucky — we were never caught, but she took a terrible risk. *Como un fulmine, Eduardo.*

"Ed! What brings you here? Thought you stuck to the lower level of this establishment."

Rick Le Marchant was a small man — small in height but of expansive circumference, with a voice and a laugh as rich and mellifluous as his *stracotto* or *zabaione*. He was about fifteen years older than Moretti, so had never been a close, personal friend, but he had been at every family get together and had been around as far back as Moretti could remember. He had originally been the business manager of Emidio's, moving into the more creative, culinary role when his older brother retired. He had not substantially altered the decor of the restaurant, but a greater profusion of plants and vines now climbed in and around the stuccoed walls, thanks to his wife's green thumb.

When Emidio Moretti came back to the island and courted Vera Domaille, it had been the Le Marchants who had found him his first job with Don Bertrand at the Héritage Hotel, and for the penniless Italian immigrant, they became his island family. Moretti knew his father was not the voluble, emotional Italian of popular perception, who wore his heart on his sleeve and poured out his innermost thoughts to anyone who cared to listen, but if anyone knew anything about Emidio Moretti and his family back in Italy, it would be a Le Marchant.

"Hi there, Rick. I'll have some of your great bruschetta and, if I may, a little of your time."

"Done. Annette can take care of three tables." Rick Le Marchant called out to the pretty dark-haired waitress behind the counter, "Two orders of bruschetta and two espressos, Annette."

The coffee arrived, Annette returned to the kitchen for the bruschetta, and Rick Le Marchant looked speculatively at Moretti.

"Is this business? Any problems downstairs I should know about?"

"God, no. At least, not as far as I know, and I'm sure Deb would tell you."

Deborah Duchemin was the manager and hostess of the Grand Saracen, where Moretti played jazz piano, and in which he had a part interest. From time to time, the club ran into trouble with members of its clientele who thought it would be a fruitful drug-selling venue, and had to be dissuaded, arrested, or thrown out.

"Yup. She's a tough biddy, that Debby. Now," — Annette deposited the bruschetta on the table and departed — "what's up?"

"My godmother just died in Italy. I didn't know her that well, but she's left me with a request in her will that's a puzzle. I only remember meeting her on two occasions, although I think my father took me back to see his family quite soon after I was born. And yet she's kept quiet all these years, not spoken to anyone who might have helped her, and waited until after she herself had shuffled off this mortal coil to ask for my help."

"What does she want you to do?"

"Now *that's* real bruschetta," said Moretti, finishing a luscious mouthful. "Hold on —" he reached into his pocket and took out a piece of paper, "she wants me to find someone called Sophia Maria Catellani."

"Sophia Maria Catellani." Rick's cherubic face was uncustomarily solemn.

"Does that mean anything to you?"

"Catellani means nothing to me but — I don't know. What I mean is, Sophia Maria seems to ring some sort of bell, and yet — hold on. I'm going to make a phone call." Rick looked across the table at Moretti. "I would have to share this with my mother. She's in a nursing home on Mount Durand now, but her brain still functions fine. It's her body that has let her down. That okay?"

"Fine by me."

Moretti watched as Rick went through to his private office. He was aching for a cigarette. Instead he ordered another espresso, and exchanged a few words with Annette, who was dying of curiosity about the film people up at the manor. She was less curious about the murder than she was about whether Moretti had actually seen any of the stars, and disappointed that he had only spoken to Vittoria Salviati.

"What's she like?"

"Beautiful."

"I know, but what's she like? Was she nice?"

"Yes, she was nice."

Rick returned, and Annette scurried off to the kitchen with her scrap of insider information. Vittoria Salviati was nice.

"Did I say my mother's brain was functioning fine? Understatement of the year. Firing on all cylinders, enough to continue to be a thorn in my side. I've got something."

"She knows something?"

"Well, depends on whether you think it's something. It may be coincidence."

"Not sure I believe in coincidence, not in my business. Go on."

"She says — after much hemming and hawing about what a negligent son I am, and how good a son-in-law Emidio was to his poor aged mother-in-law — that she seems to remember that if you had been a girl your name was going to be Sophia. Or Sophie. She's not sure which, but of that much she is sure. Sophia or Sophie."

"Well, well," said Moretti.

As Liz Falla turned the police BMW into the courtyard of the Manoir Ste. Madeleine and found a parking space between an immaculate period Mercedes and a battered contemporary Honda, an agitated figure rushed out from among a gaggle of helmeted *fascisti* making their way across the courtyard. It was Gilbert Ensor. He was shouting as he approached.

"Thank Christ you're back — where the hell have you been?"

"Having lunch, Mr. Ensor. How can we help you?"

"My wife has disappeared, and the security guards say it isn't their business." He was sweating profusely, his unseasonable linen jacket clinging to him.

"Disappeared? She has probably gone back to the hotel."

"Don't you think I'd have the sense to check that? She's not there. We've had an attempt on my life and a murder — my God, you're cool in the circumstances! If anything's happened to her, I shall personally see you're both hung out to dry."

Since "keeping cool in the circumstances" appeared to be annoying the hell out of a sweating Gilbert Ensor, Moretti stifled the desire to retaliate in kind.

"Have you checked with the limousine drivers? She couldn't have walked, and it's unlikely she'd have taken the bus."

"I got Bella to do that for me. She says no one has left in a limousine this morning — the only ones that returned to town were empty."

Into Moretti's mind drifted a vision of a *donna mobile* running lightly down the corridor in the manor, a humiliated young woman going out into the same corridor, the sound of someone passing, humming as she went by the door of the marchesa's sitting room. He decided to jump to conclusions.

"I think," he said, "she's in good hands. Safer than here, I should think. I suggest you take a limo back to the hotel and wait for her."

As a bewildered Gilbert Ensor turned to leave, Moretti allowed himself to add, "And stay off the patio, won't you, sir?"

When he was out of earshot, Liz Falla looked at her senior officer. "*Do* you know where she is, Guv?"

"Not really. I'm going to look for Monty Lord. I want you to check whether anyone saw the Ducati leave — and whether it left with a passenger."

"Brilliant!" said DC Falla. "Oh I hope so, Guv."

Moretti was spared a hunt for the film producer by his appearance in the courtyard. He was coming from the direction of the stars' trailers and he looked grim. As soon as he saw Moretti he said, "You questioned Vittoria, I hear."

"Of course." Moretti said no more.

"It's all right, Detective Inspector. I knew about the little affair, but I made sure nothing was said to the marchesa. This was the last thing she needed — and not the first time such a thing had happened."

"So Mr. Albarosa was a philanderer?"

"Yes, and a successful one. Donatella would never have told Anna, but I wanted to spare her the pain."

"Maybe that's why he was killed. From what I hear, Mr. Ensor is also a successful philanderer."

"Detective Inspector Moretti — if someone is going around killing off philanderers on this film set, I'll be lucky if I'm left with half my cast and crew."

Moretti looked around the courtyard, which was now filling up with dozens of laughing, chattering extras dressed as peasants, *contadini*.

"Is there somewhere we could talk, sir? If we could get it over with today, then hopefully I won't have to take too much of your time again."

"My office," said Monty Lord.

Monty Lord's trailer office was close to the command bunker entrance by the ornamental lake. They left the path that followed the side of the manor, and walked around the grassy hillock that had grown over the concrete curve of the man-made construction beneath. A couple of mallards hastened their steps ahead of them and made for the shore of the lake, which was partly obscured at this point by a giant chestnut and some large elderberry bushes. As they walked past, Moretti could see a heavy iron grille set in a concrete wall which was almost concealed by two massive beech trees. The approach to the bunker was brick-lined, but the sides were now overgrown with ferns, brambles, ivy, and moss, giving the installation an almost bucolic appearance.

"I understand you'll be using the command bunker during the filming of *Rastrellamento*, sir." Moretti bent down and peered through the foliage.

"Yes, we intend to," replied Monty Lord. "I've got the key on me, as it happens. Would you care to take a look?"

"Certainly I would. I've seen others, but this being on private property —"

"Sure."

As Monty Lord led the way down the slope to the entrance, Moretti saw that the iron grille did not extend to the ground, but ran across the top of a heavy metal door. The producer pulled a keychain from his pocket, bent down, and turned the lock.

The door swung open easily, revealing a long tunnel with openings on each side, stretching away into the darkness. The chill of the place was immediate, the exposed skin of Moretti's hands and face instantly damp with moisture.

"Do you have any lighting installed?" Moretti could hear his voice echoing ahead of him into the gloom.

"No. We'll use our own lights for that, on cables, but we always keep something here by the door."

Monty Lord bent down and picked up a powerful workman's lamp and switched it on. The intense beam of light illuminated the curved ceiling above, which had a large badly rusted pipe running the length of it. Somewhere in the darkness a creature squeaked and scuttled.

"Mice?"

"Bats, I think. I've seen them in here before. There's a humongous ventilation shaft farther into the chamber, and an escape shaft also. It goes deeper the farther we go away from the entrance here. We can go on in, but there's not really much to see." Monty Lord swung the light around, lighting up the entrances along the passage. Moretti felt a drop of moisture on his head. His heart thumped unpleasantly in his chest as he thought about his father.

"Even with a ventilation shaft, you'll need to pump in air, won't you, if you work at any distance from the door?"

"Yes. We have that set up. Fortunately, even on your small island, Detective Inspector, you now have air-conditioning experts, and we've been able to arrange that locally."

Moretti looked around at the encircling walls, the brickwork falling away in places from the granite, the broken rusting brackets holding the overhead pipe.

"One thing I don't understand, sir — this place is a mess. How are you going to film as if it were a fully operating command post?"

"Aha!"

Monty Lord patted Moretti's arm and shone the flashlight on the entrance closest to them on the right of the passage.

"Look in there, Detective Inspector."

The stones beneath his feet were slimy with some growth or other, and Moretti slipped as he walked forward.

"Careful — there now. Great, huh?"

"A surprise, yes."

The chamber had been set up as some sort of observation post or lookout. Moretti saw whitewashed walls, a grey painted cement floor, tables, chairs, wall maps. Bulky wireless equipment and headsets took up most of the central table, and a couple of uniform jackets hung on pegs on the walls. Some black-and-white photographs and a pin-up on the walls above a bunk bed were already showing signs of moisture damage.

"The set designer'll bring down most of the decorative vintage shit when we need it, but the damp down here is a killer. And of course we'll use the passages as they are. We need them for one or two scenes, also the escape shaft. Seen enough?"

"Yes. Terrible place."

The sun outside felt delicious to Moretti. He ran his hand over his face, and his skin felt clammy, as if he had sweated and cooled.

"You suffer from claustrophobia, Detective Inspector?" Monty Lord locked the gate and put his key chain back in his pocket.

"No. But my father helped build places like these, sir."

"So that's how an Italian ended up on Guernsey. The end of the war that would be, I guess. Was he a partisan?"

"Yes. He was betrayed by local police when the Germans arrived in his village."

"Yet he came back here?"

"To marry my mother."

"The power of love, Detective Inspector."

Monty Lord looked at Moretti, who had the impression that the film producer's thoughts at that moment were many miles away.

Monty Lord's trailer was the workplace of a fastidious and meticulous man. There were three or four filing cabinets with detailed labelling, a metal safe, charts and plans of various kinds on the walls. The huge aluminum desktop was uncluttered, with neat piles of papers — and no ashtrays. Moretti presumed the microwave and fridge were standard fixtures but, apart from a stereo unit, there were no personal belongings, no pictures or paintings, no rugs or family photographs. The trailer was a place of business — a place for everything and everything in its place.

When they came into the trailer, a woman was standing by one of the filing cabinets, putting away some papers. She turned to face them, smiling at Monty Lord. She looked to be somewhere in her forties, and she was tiny, with the narrowest rib cage Moretti had ever seen.

She was wearing a black business suit that emphasized her extreme slenderness, and a pair of heavy-framed glasses almost too large for her narrow face.

"This is Bella, my personal assistant, who is also acting as interpreter for the movie. Thanks, Bella, but I'll have to ask you to leave us for a while."

Bella Alfieri closed the drawer of the filing cabinet and smiled again at the producer. "Of course, Monty. I'll be in the other trailer when you want me."

She crossed to the door, and Moretti heard her heels clacking down the steps outside.

Monty Lord indicated a chair on the other side of the desk, and sat down himself.

"You speak Italian very well, sir," said Moretti, taking his seat. "How did you learn the language?"

Monty Lord tipped back his chair and laughed. "Because I've made what seems like hundreds of movies in Italy — probably dozens, anyway. I've spent much of the past ten or fifteen years there, making my living. Spaghetti westerns, that's what I made, by the reelful. I'll never sneer at them, because they gave me the money and the connections to make movies like this one — and they made me a great deal of money. Most of them feature someone who has since become a major Hollywood star, and at one time I owned a piece of him. Now he and I make the movies we always wanted to make."

The name Monty Lord dropped was major enough to raise Moretti's eyebrows and make him whistle in surprise.

"That, presumably, is why *Rastrellamento* appealed to you. But, with your connections, why take the trouble to bring cast and crew over here — let alone all that heavy equipment you need?"

"Costs, Detective Inspector. We could have rented a fabulous Medici palazzo near Florence, but at a price that would make your blood run cold. So when my major investor suggested using the family's Guernsey property at a rock-bottom price, I jumped at it. The other determining factor was the availability of authentic war sites, without having to build them. The room in the bunker is just one of our planned locations. We are going to use some of the coastal fortifications as well."

"So you haven't financed the whole enterprise yourself?"

"No. I have my major investor in Italy, and I have also set up another branch of my company — Epicure Films Italia. This is quite normal for movie work."

"I see. Who is your major investor?"

"The marchesa's husband and his company — *Vannoni Vigneti e Boschetti.*"

"I somehow thought the marchesa was a widow." Moretti was taken by surprise.

Opposite him, Monty Lord rubbed a hand vigorously over his shining, shaved dome. "For all intents and purposes, she is."

"The marchese is absorbed in the work of the company, you mean?"

"They live apart, Detective Inspector. He rarely if ever comes here. He has an apartment in Florence and runs the business from there."

"Does anyone in the family have contact with him?"

"I think Anna sees the most of her father. As a matter of fact, I met Paolo Vannoni before I met Donatella, at some government shindig or other. It was he who suggested using the Guernsey property."

"How did the marchesa feel about that, I wonder?"

"Like shit at first. Then we met and — got along."

Apart from a slight pause it was said simply, without any discernible subtext. For Moretti, who always listened for subtexts and hidden messages, it was a curiously empty remark, devoid of emotion. Either Monty Lord was brilliant at concealing emotions, or there was indeed nothing to conceal.

"It's a while since I read *Rastrellamento*, but I remember the action being quite scattered. Apart from the war sites, this film seems to be centred on the manor. Am I right?"

"Yes. The scenes in the book are far more diverse. We wanted to create a much more enclosed and claustrophobic feeling in the movie, so we focused in on the aristocratic Cavalli family in the novel, and spun the rest of the action around them."

"You say 'we.' I presume you mean yourself and Mario Bianchi? Is it usual for a producer like yourself to have that kind of input?"

"It varies. Some are just the money men, and some like to have creative control. Like me."

"Doesn't this make for problems — with your director, I mean?"

"Not in this case. Mario is brilliant, but he's also very unsure of himself in some ways. Often I simply reinforce what he has already decided — take the blame, you might say, and tell Gilbert. To the producer falls a number of unpleasant tasks, and that for sure is one of them." Monty Lord gave a grim laugh.

"Why the casting changes? Is this normal?"

"Perfectly, particularly if there are changes to the script. Obviously, we pay the original actor, if he or she has a signed contract. You may have noticed we haven't changed any of our leads — it would cost us a fortune."

"You say you were in Rome — we will, of course, be confirming that. Where were you when Mr. Albarosa was killed?"

"Still in Italy, I think, or up in the air. Depends exactly when he was killed, but I got back to Guernsey very early this morning, as soon as your airport opened up. I am a qualified pilot and was on my own, but you could check that with the airport."

"How long were you off the island? Were you here when the incident occurred with Mr. Ensor?"

"Unfortunately, yes, given our working relationship. I was only in Italy for just over twenty-four hours — possibly thirty-six."

"And where, precisely, were you?"

"Here." Monty Lord jabbed his finger downwards toward his chair. "Bella could confirm that. She was here with me taking notes that evening. I worked on my own for a while, and then called her back in to complete a couple of letters."

Moretti put his notepad away. He often wondered what useful purpose it served. "Thank you, sir. We'll check that with Ms. —?"

"Alfieri. Bella Alfieri. Highly competent and completely reliable."

"Good." Moretti stood up. "I was hoping to speak to some of your lead actors, but I see from the schedule they're filming right now. It will have to wait until tomorrow — oh, did you know that Mr. Ensor says his wife is missing?"

"No, I didn't." Monty Lord seemed genuinely surprised.

"Does she have a function of any kind?"

"Apart from being Gilbert's minder, you mean? Not officially. They've had some godawful fights since we started shooting, but there's no doubt he behaves better when she's around — or else she takes the crap he usually hands out to others. She is — was — a gifted woman. Gave it all up for that shit — what we do for love, as the song says, eh, Inspector?"

"Yes."

It was time to move on and end the interview. Moretti was beginning to worry about his assumption that Sydney Tremaine was safe, and anxious to get back to town. As he opened the door of the trailer, he asked Monty Lord, "What do you know about Giulia Vannoni? I don't see her on the list we were given."

"No — I only wish she were part of Epicure Italia. That's one hell of a dame, brainy as well as beautiful. She's head honcho of the olive oil side of the business and she's turned it into an international success. A lot of the family's income comes courtesy of that lady's smarts."

"Interesting. Thank you for your time, Mr. Lord."

"You're welcome."

"Oh, by the way, the story is that there's a tunnel leading from the house to the bunker. *Is* there one?"

Monty Lord shook his head. "There may have been once, but not anymore. If we'd gone farther into the bunker, you'd have seen that there are all kinds of other passages branching off the main tunnel, but they're all filled with debris, and some have caved in. I'm sure if one was still open into the manor, the marchesa would know about it."

The producer came to the door of the trailer and closed it as Moretti went down the steps.

Liz Falla was waiting for him back in the courtyard. She seemed excited.

"Good guess, Guv," were her first words when Moretti joined her. "Giulia Vannoni left on that motorbike with Mrs. Ensor riding pillion. There were quite a few eyewitnesses. Tongues are wagging."

"Why didn't anyone tell Ensor?"

"A conspiracy of silence, Guv. Most people hate his guts, and got a kick out of seeing him sweat. Besides, as one of the cameramen said to me, 'Let him get a taste of his own medicine.'"

"Meaning?"

"Meaning that Ensor plays the field — boys *and* girls, if you get me."

"What a charmer."

"I got the address of Giulia Vannoni from the art director, who's a friend of hers. Seems she has a place here she uses from time to time — somewhere out near

Icart Point. She's close to her aunt, so he says."

"Interesting. Let's get back into town. I'll have to report to Chief Officer Hanley before too long."

As they returned along the winding lanes that led to St. Peter Port, Moretti found himself thinking about love. About the marchese and the marchesa, still married, who lived coldly apart. About the tears of a young girl for whom kind words were as precious as the passion she felt for her risky choice of lover. About a redhead and a blonde on a scarlet and black Ducati, with the salt wind of the island blowing through their hair.

Fracas.

That was it. The name of the perfume. Uproar. Chaos.

He still couldn't remember the name of the girl. But he knew it hadn't been Valerie.

chapter five

Her heart was beating hard enough to burst the thin cotton of her shirt — as hard as the blows she would have liked to have given him, to wipe the taunting smile off her husband's face. When Sydney Tremaine found herself in the corridor outside the marchesa's sitting room, she was shaking with suppressed rage, the humiliation of being insulted in front of the civilized and quiet-spoken detective inspector. If they had been on their own, she would have picked up the nearest blunt object — anything that would have served as a missile — and thrown it at Gil.

What should she do now? Wait meekly around until the interview was over, babysit Gil for the remainder of the day, as she usually did, and then return to their hotel suite to scream and shout and rant at each other? Or to drink too much, have sex if Gil was not too drunk, and go to bed?

The prospect was appalling. Sydney leaned against the wall and closed her eyes.

When she opened them again, she saw a figure at the end of the corridor. It was the woman who had arrived on the motorbike, the woman she had seen running along the cliff path — and whom she had told the detective inspector she didn't know.

"Wait!" Sydney started to run toward her.

The woman stood and waited, her hands on her hips. As Sydney got closer, she saw she was smiling.

"You are Sydney Tremaine, the ballerina."

"Ex-ballerina. You are the jogger I saw on the cliff path near the Héritage Hotel."

One finely pencilled eyebrow was raised. "I don't jog. I run. Yes. Giulia Vannoni."

"You didn't hear me call out?"

"I hear nothing with my iPod. Not the birds, not the sea, nothing."

She extended her hand and Sydney took it.

"Someone threw a dagger at my husband at about the same time."

"So they tell me. And missed. If it had been me, *cara*, you would be wearing black right now."

Sydney saw that Giulia Vannoni had green eyes but, unlike her own, they were long and slightly slanted, and they were looking challengingly at her.

"Why were you standing outside my aunt's study?" she asked. "Are you looking for her?"

"No. The detective inspector is questioning my husband. I — left. I didn't tell him that I saw you. I'm not sure why."

"Ah? Perhaps you hope I will hit my target next time?"

The pent-up anger of the past few minutes — of the past few days, weeks, months — burst from Sydney Tremaine in a flood of tears. "Christ! No. Yes. I don't know!"

"Hey!"

Giulia Vannoni did not put her arms about her, pat her on the shoulder, talk in soothing tones. She took Sydney by the elbow and steered her toward the foyer that led out on to the terrace. "I've got to move my bike. Come on."

The Ducati stood where Giulia had left it, with a small group of admirers around it — English and American crew members, and some Italian *macchinisti*, brought in to handle the equipment rented from Rome.

"Hey boys — don't touch!"

"The bike you mean, Signorina?"

Puzzled, Sydney watched Giulia Vannoni explode. Most Italian women she knew enjoyed such remarks, or dismissed them with a shrug or a humorous comment. But this Amazon turned on the man with a burst of such rapid Italian that Sydney missed most of the meaning, although the language was pungent enough to make the joker flinch. The crowd quietly withdrew.

"My new baby. Superbike eleven ninety-eight, special edition. Beautiful lines, great control." Giulia was smiling again.

"I like the logo."

"Pretty, isn't it? It is the emblem of many of my friends in Florence." Giulia's smile grew wider. "Like a ride?"

Sydney indicated the intricately painted gold and black helmet with its dark visor hanging on the curved handlebar. "I don't have one of those," she said.

"We'll find one. Come."

Sydney found herself following Giulia and the Ducati around the side of the manor, along the path that had led to what she now thought of as her point of no return. One thing was certain: wherever the path and Giulia Vannoni were now taking her could be no more disturbing than the scene of violent death on the terrace. The shock of seeing Toni Albarosa with a dagger in his chest — a dagger that looked distressingly like the one that had landed on the hotel patio at Gil's feet — seemed to have deprived her of rational thought, and she was content to have this complete stranger decide what she should do next.

In an area to one side of the main courtyard, which was principally used for vehicles in the movie, were parked the hired limousines and the various cars, bikes, and motorbikes that belonged to the crew. Giulia propped up the Ducati and made for a line of motorbikes, sorting through any helmets that had been left as if she were in a store.

"No, *troppo grande* — mmm, no, *brutto* — *si*!" Triumphantly she held up a neat metallic black helmet with bronze highlights. "*Bello, perfetto* — from Roberto Stavrini, like mine. It will go with your hair."

"But I can't —"

But she could. The helmet was placed on her head, the strap fastened beneath her chin.

"Eh — Cosimo!"

Giulia called out to a tall bearded man crossing the courtyard, and Sydney recognized the art director, Cosimo Del Grano, who was on his way to the building where the costumes were stored. "Lend us your jacket."

"Darling, but why?" he protested, as Giulia started to remove his heavy denim jacket, kissing him profusely as she did so.

"Because, because, *caro* — I'll get it back to you."

As the two talked and laughed, Sydney began to put together the pieces of the past few minutes: the jibe by the crew member and Giulia's reaction, the way Cosimo spoke to this woman, even the emblem on the Ducati. Could it be —?

The jacket was huge on her. Sydney rolled up the sleeves and hauled it across her body. She could feel her heartbeat quieting, the delicious irony of the situation easing her sense of desolation. It looked as if the whirligig of time was bringing in a revenge far sweeter than she herself could possibly have dreamed up, in her wildest and cruellest imaginings.

"Come on, Sydney," said Giulia Vannoni. "Let's go."

* * *

And go they did. Heart in mouth at first, Sydney felt every muscle in her body stiffen as they roared away, the wind blowing through her completely inadequate sandals, the Ducati accelerating rapidly as Giulia put it through its paces, winding along the lanes to the south of the Manoir Ste. Madeleine, smooth as the feel of Giulia's soft leather jacket beneath her hands. Gradually, Sydney found her own movements blending with Giulia's, much as she had learned to move with another dancer in a pas de deux, relying on the strength and expertise of her partner.

They seemed to be heading for the southern coastline of the island. In spite of their introductory tour, Sydney was vague about the geography of Guernsey, but she knew that this coastline — unlike the flatter, gentler western coastline where much of the filming would take place and where many of the wartime installations were to be found — was craggy and spectacular. Wild and beautiful, its cliffs and coves were breathtaking enough to have attracted the painter Renoir on a visit to the island. They turned yet another corner in a small, winding lane and Sydney saw a sliver of milky blue horizon beyond a cleft in the pine-covered slopes. Sydney felt herself slip toward Giulia as the Ducati descended a steep slope between the trees.

"See?" Giulia called over her shoulder, her words blown back by the wind. "*Mio castello*."

Giulia's castle, set high above the sea, was one of the eighteenth-century Martello towers, built to protect the island against Napoleonic invasion. This one seemed to have been modified, because on top of the familiar circular construction with its tiny slit windows, was what appeared to be another storey, with wider windows, still elongated in shape. There was a stone wall encrusted with plants around the perimeter of a grassy enclosure, with a solid-looking gate set in it. Giulia brought the Ducati to a halt by the gate, and got off the bike.

"Here, let me give you a hand. I'll unlock this and we'll walk from here."

"*Your* castle? I wouldn't have thought they allowed anyone to buy one of these," said Sydney, removing her purloined helmet. She was grateful for the heavy jacket. They were high up, close to the edge of the cliff, and the wind was strong.

"Yes, it's mine. There are only one or two of these on private land — there's one out at L'Ancresse in the north of the island, I'm told — and I was lucky enough to be staying with my aunt when this one came on the market."

"The marchesa is your aunt?"

"She is."

Giulia pulled the Ducati through the gate, which she relocked. "Robbery is not such a problem here — it's the sightseers and nosey small *ragazzi* I want to keep away from the place," she said.

For a moment, Sydney hesitated. Ahead of her, the Martello tower loomed, grey, cold and forbidding, like something out of a tale by Grimm. No attempt at decoration had been made to the exterior, and the area around it was unkempt, rough beneath her feet with exposed rock and long grasses. Above her head a flock of gulls wheeled with their hideous shriek. Ahead of her she saw that Giulia had unlocked the door of the tower and was pushing the Ducati inside.

Well, she thought. *You've done dumber things in your life, woman.* And walked toward Giulia Vannoni.

"Welcome," said Giulia, "to my *castello isola*."

As Sydney stepped across the threshold, Giulia flicked a light switch by the door.

Sydney gasped.

Where the outside had been bleak and forbidding, the interior was warm, glowing with colour, ablaze with oranges, ruby reds, carmines, emerald and aqua, the glowing blue of stained-glass windows or Victorian enamels. Giulia was laughing as she flicked down the Ducati's stand, leaving it on a terrazzoed area by the door.

"That look of surprise on your face — you expected gloomy grey and black bleakness — no?"

"Yes. This is like — a secret garden."

"That is nice. I am away so much I do not want those beyond the walls to guess at what lies inside. The lady at L'Ancresse has a picture window where there once was a gun, but no landscaping, no tearing out of these narrow slits for me. I make my own light. Always have done, *cara*. I like to feel — protected."

Giulia's secret garden was contained in one circular room, with an iron circular staircase curling up close to one of the walls, its railings in *ferro battuto*, the spectacular wrought iron of Tuscany. The harsh stone of the round walls was largely hidden and softened by bronze silk curtains that had been used as an undulating backdrop, like an extra frame, for the paintings — most of them abstract, but again using the deep, glowing palette of their setting. Opposite the door through which they had entered, against a black wall — the one sombre note in the room — stood a bronze sculpture of a woman, arms raised as if she were about to dive on to the pale cinnamon terrazzo around the white translucent cube on which she stood, frozen in time.

I make my own light, Giulia had said, and it was the lighting that created the magic of her secret garden. Sconces in burnished metal mounted on the walls and standing on slender poles gave the feeling of candlelight to the space, while above their heads glittered a spectacular eighteenth-century Venetian chandelier.

"Where do you get the power from?" Sydney asked. "That's a practical question, not a philosophical one."

Giulia laughed. "I have a generator. The Germans used this place during the war. The bigger problem was water, but there once was a house on the site, and there is a good well. Another practical question — are you hungry?"

"Starving. My last meal was at about five o'clock this morning."

"Me too. Let us pour ourselves some wine and get something to eat. My kitchen, such as it is, is over here, by the lovely lady."

To the right of the sculpture was a small space semi-concealed by a screen made of the same material as the translucent cube. Sydney stepped on to the carpet that covered most of the floor.

Beneath her feet rode a knight — from the red cross on his shield, it appeared to be St. George — a deep blue surcoat over his silver armour. To one side of him stood a slender maiden, hands clasped in prayer over her deep pink dress. At her feet roared an emerald dragon in his death throes, his elegant ivory throat pierced by a sword — or a stiletto, or a dagger, since only the elaborately decorated hilt protruded.

"This is —" What was there to say? Coincidence? An omen? Sydney was at a loss for words.

"*Spettacolare,* no? I had it specially woven for me. I so love the legend — the king's daughter sacrificed to the dragon that threatened the kingdom, and the knight who saves her."

"Do you believe in knights on white horses, Giulia?" *Leave the other alone*, she thought. *For now*.

"That save us from others, or ourselves, you mean? No. But, see, his horse is chestnut. I asked for that. And above his head an angel — them, I believe in. Sometimes. Come, I'm too hungry for all this. We'll talk while I cook."

The small area behind the screen contained four burners set in an olive green ceramic counter, some wall storage, a small fridge, and two bar stools. Giulia patted one as she passed.

"Sit down. We'll start with some Brunello di Montalcino."

The wine went straight to her head, courtesy of her empty stomach. It felt good. "How often are you here?" Sydney asked.

"It depends. As you probably know, my family are in *vino e olio*. The *olio* is my baby. By the way, don't feel too sorry for Anna, Toni's wife."

Giulia made no attempt to explain her remark, and Sydney did not ask. Married to a man like Gilbert Ensor, she needed no further elaboration.

The wine was outstanding, filling Sydney's head with a humming sensation and the ability to ask the questions she most wanted to ask.

"Giulia, tell me about the symbol on your bike."

"It is the symbol in Florence for the gay and lesbian community. Does that bother you?"

"No."

Any worries Sydney might have had nothing to do with the sexual preference of her companion; in the world of dance she had worked closely with people whose tastes and orientation were frequently far from what some sections of society considered the norm.

"Besides," said Giulia, "I am celibate for a little while."

"Why?"

"Because it makes life simpler."

There was no disputing that statement, and Sydney had other, pressing questions she wanted to ask.

"Is it a coincidence that you were running past the Héritage Hotel just as a dagger was thrown onto our patio and that, woven into the rug on the floor of your *castello*, is the representation of violent death by a dagger, or a sword, with a decorated hilt?"

"Coincidence, perhaps — I think your husband is a bit of a dragon himself, no? Planned, perhaps. A warning, maybe." Giulia was taking eggs out of the fridge as she spoke and, although Sydney could not see her face, her voice was calm and unconcerned. "I often run on the cliffs in that area, and many people know that. Your hotel is only about two or three miles from here to the east of us, around the point, and there are cliff paths all the way. I am — easily noticeable."

"That's true. So if it wasn't you, Giulia, then who?"

With her back to Sydney, Giulia shrugged her powerful shoulders. "Someone is saying something — what they are saying I don't know. But take care, Sydney, because whoever they are, they are killing anyone who stands in their way — or gets in their way."

"Gets in the way of what?'

"Who knows? That, as you Americans say, is the sixty-four-thousand-dollar question."

Even the sweet numbness brought on by the wine had not removed the image of Toni Albarosa, the haft of the dagger protruding from his chest. Sydney shuddered. "Let's change the subject. What are you cooking? It smells delicious."

"Frittata, this one with some *carciofi* — artichoke hearts. Something simple. It is how I live here." Giulia's smile was back, her mood sunny again.

"You are from Florence?"

"Yes. You know the city?"

"Not very well. I find it — well, gloomy, almost scary, in some way."

"I can understand. A city of men, *Firenze bizarra* — Michelangelo, Leonardo, Brunelleschi — men who had little time for women. It's a city that turns its back on the stranger like you who passes in the street. Like *mio castello*, it hides pretty loggias, hidden courtyards, secret gardens behind ugly grey walls."

It was in Giulia Vannoni's grey Martello tower, on an island off the coast of France, sitting at a marble-topped table eating frittata and drinking Aperol, the honey-coloured aperitif of Florence, that Sydney Tremaine began to believe once more in happiness — as bizarre and unlikely a time and place as any, in which to believe in such a thing again.

"Come on now, Sydney!" Giulia sprang to her feet. "We go out on the town."

"Is that possible?"

"Of course! You don't know this place any better than you know Florence, do you?"

"But I think I should be getting back to the hotel."

"The night has hardly begun, *cara*. Why not — how do you say it? — get hung for a sheep as lamb, no?"

"Oh, why not!"

Light-headed with wine and good companionship. Sydney threw caution out the Martello tower window. *Go on*, she thought, *let Gil feel what I myself have felt, so many times*.

"I am hardly dressed to go out on the town."

"Here, anything goes. But I'll lend you something that is more fun. You won't be able to use my pants with that ballerina hip span of yours, but — let's see."

Giulia started up the circular staircase with her easy, powerful stride, and Sydney followed her. The staircase opened directly into a bedroom, as different as it could be from the lower level. The wider windows let in more natural light from outside, but that was not the only difference. The decor here was spare to the point of sterility, with a simply designed bed in a beechwood frame, a pristine white bedcover, a matching bedside table, chair, and dresser with the same clean lines. There were curved, sliding doors set into the wall, and a walled-off section of another wall presumably concealed a bathroom of some sort.

"This floor," said Giulia, "was added by the Nazis when they occupied the island — I think there is one other tower like this. I had the floor strengthened, and the walls covered with the wood panels you see, more for warmth than for any other reason."

"It's so different from downstairs." said Sydney.

"I sleep better in monastic surroundings," Giulia replied, without a glimmer of humour in her voice or on her face. "In that city of mine you do not understand, it took until the fourteenth century for women to be allowed to read — unless they were nuns." Before Sydney could think of an appropriate response, Giulia went over to the sliding doors and pulled them open.

The contrast with the spare, colourless room was startling. Scarlets, silver, golds, echoes of the riches below dazzled Sydney's eyes, cooled by the monochromes around her.

"I love clothes," said Giulia. "I love Versace, Gucci. Sexy, dangerous. My leather jacket is Gucci and so are these. I'll wear them tonight." She pulled out a pair of jeans that glittered with dozens of tiny beaded squares, with fringes of silk scattered over the blue denim. "Long ago, there was a wise woman whose home was in the portico of Santissima Annunziata — a street woman, who sewed pretty patches on her clothes. I think of her surviving *con eleganza* when I wear these."

"So Italian," said Sydney, "and yet, didn't an American once design for Gucci?"

"*E vero*. Such a small world — that can make things so dangerous."

Giulia Vannoni retreated for a moment into a mood that appeared to have come out of nowhere. Her warning came back to Sydney. *Someone is saying something — what they are saying, I don't know.*

She knows, she thought. *Or she knows far more than she is telling me.*

"Try this." Giulia held out a slippery satin shirt in a luminous apple green. "This is Gucci also. It feels wonderful on the skin and is perfect with your colouring."

She pointed to the cubicle. "You can use my little bathroom, if you wish. And here —" From the dresser she pulled a pair of black spandex tights. "These'll fit. Roll up the legs and your mules will go perfectly."

The cubicle contained an updated version of a hip bath, a toilet, a small mirror, and a tiny hand basin. As she started to change into her new clothes, Sydney heard Giulia going down the iron staircase. By the time she came back into the bedroom, Giulia was waiting for her, wearing a blue and grey striped bustier with the bespangled jeans.

"*Meravigliosa!*"

"*Grazie* — you, too."

As they returned to the floor below, Sydney's attention was caught by a heraldic device she had not noticed before, hanging high up on the wall near the stairs in an area shielded from the brilliant light of the chandelier. It was a shield, divided into quarters, each with its own device. In the bottom right-hand quarter was a hand, the wrist encased in chain mail, holding a dagger — a dagger with an elaborately decorated hasp. Sydney stopped in her tracks.

"Giulia —"

Giulia Vannoni looked back up from below. Her glance followed Sydney's eyes.

"You have a dagger very like the one that killed Toni on your family coat of arms — I presume that's what this is."

"Yes. The shield is on every bottle of olive oil we sell."

"So, Giulia —" Sydney sat down on one of the iron steps. "— what's going on? Is this some extremist group? Is it the Mafia? Is this an attack on your family and, if so, how does my husband fit into this?"

Giulia held out her hand. "Come," she said. "I have something to give you."

She pulled Sydney to her feet, then went over to a small desk near the kitchen area, took a key from the small purse she wore slung around her body, unlocked one of the drawers, and took out another key.

"Here," she said, holding it out toward Sydney. This unlocks the door to my *castello* — and the gate. You don't have a purse, but put it on that chain you have around your neck, and wear it under your shirt. If you ever need to, come here."

"But why? Why are you doing this?"

"Because I don't know the answer to your questions." Briskly, Giulia unfastened the chain around Sydney's neck. "Yes, it goes over the clasp. Good."

"You said, come here. But where is here?"

"You take a taxi, and you ask to be driven to the tower on Icart Point. This tower is the farthest to the east, one of the few where the cliffs start to climb — he'll know. And one other thing I will show you."

Giulia took Sydney by the hand and led her toward the statue of the girl. She reached behind it and the black wall opened.

"Not magic," said Giulia, laughing at Sydney's startled face. "It's a door, a second exit from this place. It leads to what was once a gun emplacement, connected to the tower by a tunnel. I'll show you when we go out, but we won't go down it now. We are not dressed for guerilla warfare."

Outside, Giulia led the way around the curving wall of the tower and stopped.

"See?"

She pointed toward a flat metallic disc about three feet in circumference, set in concrete, that gleamed dully among the plants and grasses. "That can only be opened from the inside. It covers a circular dug-out area where they had a gun — the edge is serrated, very strong, so it was possible to close it off. They made it out of the turret ring of a French tank. But you have to be careful here, because all is not as it seems. Look."

Giulia picked up a stone and threw it. The stone disappeared.

"Trenches. Overgrown trenches."

"*Esattamente.* The stone walls are covered with flowers and plants, almost two feet of them in places."

Sydney walked forward. Close up, it was comparatively easy to see the opening of the trench nearest to her, in spite of about two feet of ivy, ferns, and a small plant that looked like a miniature cream-coloured lupin. A cultivated rose from the garden of the original house on the property had gone wild, covering the native growth with deep pink double petals, now past their prime. A flash of movement overhead made her look up to see a wraithlike white bird flying silently overhead, its long legs trailing behind its body.

"Heron," said Giulia. "You don't see them too often. Like a ghost bird, no?"

A line of poetry that Gil once quoted to her floated into Sydney's mind. *The sedge is withered from the lake, and no birds sing.* His beautiful voice that could caress as well as castigate. She'd forgotten she had been wooed by more than the money. She had loved him once. Hadn't she?

"But now, we can forget about all this."

"Where are we going?" Sydney asked.

"You like jazz? That's where we go — and to give you another surprise, I think. *Avanti!*"

It smelled right. It smelled like the *boîtes* on the Left Bank she had loved when she danced with the Paris Opera Ballet, the bistros and clubs of Milan when she guested at La Scala, a blend of smoke from Gitanes and Camel cigarettes, the vinous bouquet of wine and the dark golden aroma of cognac and whisky, the faint but sharp undertone of humanity: a tinge of sweat, threads of perfume. A gust of nostalgia for her lost dancing days engulfed Sydney as she and Giulia Vannoni went down the steps beneath an illuminated sign that read "Le Grand Saracen." Drifting up from below came the sound of music — bass, drums, but mostly piano. The tune was a standard: Cole Porter's "In the Still of the Night."

The room they entered was dimly lit, with a cavelike quality suggesting both a return to the womb and something faintly sinister. There was nothing remarkable about the decor, which mostly consisted of a variety of posters from art exhibitions, jazz concerts, and stage shows against dark walls. As they entered, the music ceased, and there was a smattering of applause. The place looked full.

"Well, look who's here! Giulia Vannoni, *la bella donna senza pietà*!"

The speaker was a dark-haired woman about the same height as Giulia, but of a different build, slender to the point of almost emaciation. She was dressed in the de rigeur black of the avant-garde, with a pair of huge earrings not unlike the chandelier in Giulia's *castello*, kohl-rimmed eyes and a slash of carmine on her long, thin mouth.

"*Saluto*, Deb. Meet Sydney."

The two women shook hands, the dark-haired woman frankly appraising Giulia's companion.

"Oh, yes, now I've got it — you're the wife of —"

"I'm Sydney Tremaine."

"Okay." The dark-haired woman smiled, as if she understood the subtext. "I'm Deborah Duchemin. Welcome to the Grand Saracen. Let's find you a table before they start playing again. Giulia drinks red wine — and you?"

"The same."

Sydney watched Deborah Duchemin leave. "Why did she call you the pitiless beautiful woman?"

"Oh." Giulia pulled off her heavy jacket, and around them, heads turned.

The clientele was a mix of very young men and women — a tube top, singlet, and jeans crowd — and a fair number of middle-aged couples still clinging in garments and ponytails to their golden hippie age. A couple of men in business suits seemed to have wandered in after a long day at the office. There were other women on their own or in groups, particularly among the younger set, but no one greeted Giulia, or even acknowledged her presence. She may have been recognized, but she clearly was not a local.

"She wants us to be — what do you Americans say? — an item."

"And you're not interested?"

"Of course. But Deb is a complicated woman — *capricciosa*. She is not for me."

As Sydney turned round to put the art director's jacket over the back of her chair, she glanced toward the little platform on which the jazz group was reassembling. There was a bass player, percussionist, pianist. Through the mists of cigarette smoke the pianist looked vaguely familiar.

"Is that — ? No, it can't be. Can it?"

"It can. That's the surprise. I recognized him when I saw him this morning. The group is called Les Fénions — which is, so I'm told, island French for do-nothings. *La dolce far niente*, no? Sometimes they have a sax player. The policeman plays piano. Interesting, don't you think? The same man and yet one must be so different from the other."

Sydney looked again. The policeman was wearing a white shirt, open at the neck. She could see a jacket and tie hanging over his chair, and she wondered if he'd come there straight from work. Bent over the keys, a slight smile on his lips, he seemed absorbed in what he was doing as if he were on his own. On a desert island. At this moment, the drums and bass were listening to him as he set up the melody of another Cole Porter standard, "I've Got You Under My Skin," with a pure simple sound that gradually began to swing as the other players took up the harmony and rhythm. As the notes became more intricate, the piano player's body moved slightly, his hands flying over the keys swiftly and surely, free and yet in control. The buzz of conversation quietened.

When the piece came to an end, the pianist turned to acknowledge the applause with the other players. For a moment he looked almost startled. Then he grinned and reached up for a glass that stood on top of the piano.

"*Bello,* no?" said Giulia.

"It's an interesting face," agreed Sydney. "Lean, and just a tad mean. The camera would love him, I think."

"Deb tells me he has an interest in the club, and the restaurant upstairs. His father owned them."

"I heard him speaking Italian this morning."

"His father was Italian, his mother a Guernsey woman. She rescued him or something, I don't know. Something to do with the war."

"It sounds romantic," said Sydney. The piano player looked up from his keyboard, and at that moment he saw her.

"I think he's seen me," she said. "And he's looking more than a tad mean right now. He's coming over."

Detective Inspector Moretti was heading across the room, briefly sidetracked from time to time by friends and well-wishers at intervening tables.

"Ms. Vannoni — Mrs. Ensor —" Moretti turned to Sydney.

"Tremaine," said Sydney. "Sydney Tremaine."

"Ms. Tremaine," said the piano player. Her correction seemed to have annoyed him further. "Your husband has reported you as missing."

"I'm off-duty, Detective Inspector. Aren't you? I'm Ms. Tremaine when I'm off-duty, so do I call you Detective Inspector when you're supposedly off-duty?" *I'm already slightly drunk*, Sydney thought.

"It doesn't matter to me. I thought you should know."

"Thank you. Now I do. He is missing me, but I am not missing him. You can call off the search parties, Detective Inspector Moretti."

Moretti said nothing more. As he turned to leave, Giulia put a hand on his arm.

"Do you take requests?"

"It depends on the request," he answered.

"'Mack the Knife,'" suggested Giulia Vannoni.

Her smile challenged him.

He did not respond, but for a moment Sydney thought the piano player would become the policeman, as his expression moved from annoyed to thunderous. He seemed to be on the verge of saying something, but instead he shrugged off her hand that still held his sleeve, turned away, and went back to the tiny stage. She watched as he said something to the other musicians, sat down at the piano, and started to play.

Why can't you behave — oh why can't you behave?

Opposite her, Giulia started to laugh.

"The policeman has a sense of humour. Is there a message for us, do you think?"

"Perhaps he thinks the message was for him. Or maybe it's just Cole Porter night," said Sydney.

But Giulia's flippant request disconcerted her. Was there a message for her, let alone for the policeman-piano-player? Was she being a complete fool? Possibly. In her experience, the only way to blind yourself to sense and sensibility was to get drunk, and it seemed she was not yet drunk enough. She reached across the table for the bottle of wine.

* * *

Moretti saw them laughing as they left, arm in arm, and his anger returned. The clear night sky outside the club, the sound of halyards clinking against the masts of the hundreds of boats in the Albert and Victoria marinas, the clean bite of the air usually enhanced the tranquility of mind he found in the smoke-filled, half-lit womb of the jazz club. This time he had taken his preferred escape route, only to find reality there ahead of him.

They stopped to say goodnight to Deb Duchemin at the door, and it looked as if Giulia Vannoni was having to hold her companion up, to keep her on her feet.

He thought of the uncontrollable anger of Gilbert Ensor, of the professional consequences for himself if he walked away — which was what he wanted to do, because he was bloody tired, and the whole point of coming and playing a set with the band was to forget about the case and Sophia Maria Castellani, whoever the hell she was, for an hour or two — and the personal consequences for this silly woman with her luminous good looks and her wasted talents. He followed them into the small, well-lit car park, where Giulia Vannoni had left her pricey Ducati.

"Ms. Vannoni —"

He could see from Giulia Vannoni's eyes she was not sorry to see him.

"You're not seriously thinking of putting her on the back of that machine, are you?"

"I was going to get a taxi for her."

"This is not New York or Rome. You'd have to wait. And Gilbert Ensor is an explosive man, Ms. Vannoni. It would be best if she checked into another hotel for the rest of the night until she has sobered up. I will let her husband know she is safe — I'll say she was visiting friends."

"Friends? Here?"

"I'll come up with something."

"I understand." Gently, Giulia Vannoni disentangled herself from Sydney Tremaine. "Perhaps it would be better."

Moretti thought she had fallen asleep. She sat beside him in the Triumph, her head dropped on his shoulder. He felt her shift on the seat, heard her sigh.

"I'm drunk, aren't I?"

"Yes."

"What's your name? I mean, your first name. Detective Inspector is too — difficult, when you're pissed."

"Ed, I'm called. My full name is Eduardo."

"Oh right, Italian. Did you know, Eduardo, that Giulia says I can only learn to read in Florence if I become a nun?" Her voice was completely serious.

"Ah," said Moretti.

There didn't seem to be anything else to say.

PART TWO
The Shoot

chapter six

The Police Station in Hospital Lane had at one time been the workhouse, although it had never been called that. It was a fine mid-eighteenth-century building, L-shaped around a spacious quadrangle, more reminiscent of an old public school than "La Maison de Charité," as it had sometimes been known. Hospital Lane itself had once been called Rue des Frères, as the original track had led to the old friary, now Elizabeth College.

The police force had relocated there in the mid-nineties, and Moretti had only worked on the island after the move. As he turned the Triumph into the quadrangle that night, he looked up over the elegant old wrought-iron entrance gate, at the stone bas-relief of a pelican feeding its young with drops of blood from her own breast. The white-painted carving that had in the past given the building its popular nickname, the Pelican, gleamed dimly in his headlights as he went through. In this light, he could not see the drops of blood.

* * *

In Moretti's opinion, one of the few pleasures of working at the Hospital Lane headquarters at night — the *only* pleasure of working at Hospital Lane at night — was the amount of work you could get through. The place was quiet, he could play Peterson or Brubeck or Ellington without interruption on the small stereo he kept at the office, and there were very few distractions, apart from some of his colleagues on night duty who dropped in from time to time to hear what was going on in a murder inquiry that involved the kind of exotica rarely found on the island.

And, on the subject of exotica —

Moretti pushed back the pile of papers, got up from his desk, and stretched, feeling the lack of sleep in his back and his leg muscles as well as his tired eyes. Brubeck and his quartet were playing "Audrey," the sound of saxophonist Paul Desmond's composition pure and sweet in the stale air of the room. He was caught up now, his reports up to date, ready for Chief Officer Hanley the next day, and he remembered he wanted to take a closer look at the murder weapon. He flicked off the stereo, went down to the duty officer, picked up the key to the incident room, signed for it, and made his way back up the stairs.

Lying there on the tabletop, with its razor-sharp blade exposed, the bevelled centre glinting under the fluorescent light, the dagger looked more lethal than it had buried up to the hilt in the chest of Toni Albarosa. The overall length was marked on the label attached — twelve inches — of which the handle was probably about three inches, intricately carved. Gingerly, Moretti picked it up and took a closer look.

The central part of the hilt was embossed with vines, bearing what looked like grapes, and there was a crown on the pommel. Running across the hilt was either a thick cord, or a branch of some kind, cut in the metal.

"Interesting."

His voice echoed in the silent room. Near the murder weapon were the two other weapons: the dagger used to slash the costumes, and the dagger thrown onto the hotel patio. They were identical.

Now, he thought, *I have to decide — does this all mean something, or did the murderer purchase whatever he could get hold of?* He had asked Liz Falla to see if she could track the design, but the possibilities were endless, ranging from the websites that sold similar weapons, to any number of shops and boutiques in Italy or, possibly, France.

"Sleep on it," he said out loud to himself.

Which was easier said than done, since he would have to sleep in his office. Still, Chief Officer Hanley should be impressed, finding him here as soon as he arrived in the morning, with all his paperwork up to date. Or, at least, he should be impressed, as long as he didn't find out what the chief investigating officer on the case had done with the drunken wife of Gilbert Ensor.

Left her in his bed, sleeping like a baby.

"Evening, Inspector — or should I say morning? What *have* you got there?"

Moretti had started off by taking Sydney Tremaine to one of the hotels closest to the Grand Saracen. It was a five-star establishment, comparable to the Héritage, which meant that it would be at Sydney Tremaine's level of comfort, and that it would still be open, with someone on duty all night at the front desk. Not only would he be able to book her in for the night, but Moretti wanted to be sure that no one got near her — whether it was her husband, or whoever the dagger thrower was. Whoever had killed Toni Albarosa, Moretti believed, had probably been on their way to kill someone else. Oh, the arbitrary quality of life — you're on your way to carry on your extramarital affair, and you get murdered! But you're *not* the intended target.

Or are you? Was this indeed all about sex, as Liz Falla surmised? Were the daggers merely exotic red herrings, after all? The weapon that came to hand? Somehow, Moretti didn't think so. Anyway, he had taken on the responsibility for Gilbert Ensor's wife, and now his port of call in a storm was turning out to be anything but.

Les Le Cheminant, the night manager at the St. Andrew's Hotel, had been there as far back as Moretti could remember, which was another reason he had chosen this particular resting place for his burden. If he could have counted on anyone to take Sydney Tremaine in her present state, no questions asked, it should have been Les Le Cheminant. But the position of night manager involved dealings with drunken arrivals in the small hours more times than Les cared to think about and, as he explained to Moretti, "I get the blame for them waking up the other guests and heaving up their guts all over the new carpets or doing unmentionables wherever takes their fancy — no, not even for you, Inspector. She's not even a registered guest and she's in a bad way — why don't you just put her in one of your cells for the night? Isn't that what you usually do?"

"Yes, but —"

"Not a local, is she?" The night manager gave Moretti a conspiratorial look and a knowing smile as he glanced across at Sydney, whom Moretti had deposited in one of the armchairs in the hotel lobby. With sinking heart, Moretti realized the impossibility of his task, and faced the inevitable.

"Come on, Ms. Tremaine."

He pulled Gilbert Ensor's wife up from the upholstered depths of the chair. She didn't resist, but leaned against him, featherlight, half-asleep, as he half-carried her back to his car.

The streets were by now deserted, and he could be fairly sure that no one would see them together in his car. There would be no all-night staff at his cottage, but she should be safe enough there on her own. He could not guess how Sydney Tremaine would react on discovering where she had spent the night, and Moretti decided he would be well advised to cover himself by signing in at Hospital Lane and staying until daylight.

Particularly if Gilbert Ensor found out.

He pulled the Triumph up in the small cobbled courtyard outside his home, thanking the gods he had no neighbours close by, extracted his by now sleeping companion and, grateful that she was a lightweight, got her up the stairs to his room. As he opened the door, Sydney Tremaine's shirt slipped away from one shoulder, and he saw a key on the twisted gold chain she wore around her neck.

To what? he wondered. It didn't look like any hotel key he'd ever seen, and it looked too solid for a key to a suitcase, or a safety deposit box. But these were not the clothes she had worn that morning, so presumably she had borrowed them from Giulia Vannoni — hadn't someone said she had a place of her own? On the interview sheets, she had given the hotel as her address.

He carried Sydney Tremaine over to the bed, where he laid her down, her backless gold mules falling off her feet. *She is the most exotic creature this room has ever seen*, he thought, looking at her spectacular hair spread across the blues and yellows of the bedspread quilted by his mother. Beneath the black spandex tights he could see the long, strong muscles of her calves and thighs, reminding him that her appearance of physical fragility was deceptive. In her own way, she was as fit as her Amazonian escort for the evening.

Why can't you behave?

He thought he knew the answer to that.

Moretti closed the door quietly behind him — although by now it would have taken a major earthquake to awaken her — and went through to the bathroom, where he took a clean blue shirt down off the shower rail. Then he went back downstairs, took a sheet of paper from his desk, and wrote:

"Ms. Tremaine: you are in my house. Your husband will be told you were invited to spend the night with friends in town — I leave you to work out which friends. I strongly suggest you stick to that story. I have left you a shirt to use in the morning, if you wish. The phone number of a reliable taxi service is on a list over the phone in the kitchen." He hesitated a moment, and then signed it, "Ed Moretti."

He went back upstairs, cautiously opened the door, put the shirt on a chair, and the note on the bedside table.

Chief Officer Hanley was not a Guernseyman. He had been brought in to head the police force after a major reassessment of the island's financial regulations and, not surprisingly, his appointment had been viewed as demonstrating a lack of faith in the local talent, a judgment not tempered by his uncommunicative and lugubrious disposition. Which was probably why he had gone overboard in his congratulatory remarks toward Liz Falla, overcompensating and thus further antagonizing a section of his subordinates. Moretti himself had less of a problem with Hanley's temperament than some of his colleagues, since he preferred withdrawal over warmth in his superiors. Warmth, in his experience, could be more misleading than reserve.

However, Moretti knew that distrust and hurt egos made the chief tread very warily around certain issues and certain personalities. And members of certain classes — such as the one to which the Marchesa Vannoni belonged.

Chief Officer Hanley looked up from his desk with his habitual lack of bonhomie. He had a face perfectly suited to melancholy, long and thin, with heavy shadows under his eyes and a downturned mouth framed by two heavily etched lines.

"Good morning, Morettti. I see you have your reports with you."

"Yes, sir, good morning. Just wanted to let you know where we stand — the details are all in here."

Briefly, Moretti outlined the events of the past three days.

"Would it be fair to say that we have so far got nowhere?"

"Well, I —" Through a haze of sleeplessness, Moretti finally absorbed that what he had originally taken as Hanley's usual lack of affect was something more abrasive. Like actual, seething, irritation.

"Since I arrived here this morning — which is only about half an hour ago — I have personally been bombarded — well, there have been three calls from a Mr. Gilbert Ensor, and I have to tell you, Moretti, you could have stripped paint with the man's language. I gather he thinks his wife is missing and could be in danger, that he informed you of this yesterday, and that you have done nothing. Is this true?"

"It is true, sir, that he told me yesterday Mrs. Ensor was missing. But she is alive and well, and safer where she is for the moment than with her husband. She will be returning to the hotel today, so I am informed."

Oh please God may she, Moretti prayed silently, *and please may she have the sense to keep her silly mouth shut.*

"Are you saying he is a suspect in this killing?"

"He has no alibi — but then, most of them don't, sir, not for the small hours of the morning. Which is why progress is slow at this stage."

"I see. My prime concern, of course, is with our residents who are caught up in all this — the Marchesa Vannoni, for instance. I trust I will not be receiving calls from her of a similar nature to the literary gentleman's."

"I hope not, sir. In fact, there's no love lost between the marchesa and Gilbert Ensor." Moretti described to Chief Officer Hanley the marchesa's attack on "the literary gentleman."

"Good gracious!" exclaimed the chief officer. "The marchesa has always struck me as a very self-contained sort of person — quite unlike the usual idea of the hot Latin temperament."

"I think she's from Florence, sir. They tend to be very different from a Neapolitan or a Sicilian."

"Oh, right — you're half Italian, aren't you?" said Hanley, as if something was suddenly explained to him. *Possibly the piano playing,* thought Moretti.

"Do you think piano playing in such an environment advisable, Moretti?" he had once asked, and Moretti had replied, "I wouldn't do it if I didn't, sir." And had taken his superior's confusion and half-completed sentence — "Well then" — as a go-ahead.

"What are your immediate plans?"

"DC Falla and I are going back to the manor this morning, sir. Anna Albarosa, the marchesa's daughter — the widow — is due to arrive today. I want to speak to her as soon as possible. Given Mr. Albarosa's reputation, it is perhaps fortunate for Mrs. Albarosa that she was not on the island. But I will not be taking that for granted."

"Good. So he was a lady's man, the murder victim? Could this be a crime of passion, you think?"

"Oh, I think it's a crime of passion, sir, but what passion precisely I am not sure."

"I see," Chief Officer Hanley responded, sounding as though he did not. "Keep me informed, won't you?"

"So, Chief Officer Hanley got an earful from Mr. Ensor," said Liz Falla, shifting gears with a subtle flick of the wrist. "I had a word with the Ensors' driver, Tom Dorey — he lives near my parents — and he says he's as nasty a piece of work as he's driven in a while. Says he feels sorry for his wife, having to put up with him."

"Did he express an opinion as to whether Ensor might become violent? To his wife, or to others?"

"I asked that. Said it was mostly running off at the mouth, as far as he could see."

"That's my feeling too. Here we are, and I think they're waiting for us."

As they pulled up in front of the main door to the manor, it was opened. The marchesa stood there, with her son on one side, and Monty Lord on the other. As Liz Falla put out a hand to open her door, Moretti stopped her.

"DC Falla — what I want you to do this morning is watch these women, particularly the widow. I don't think I need explain what I mean, do I?"

Liz Falla looked at him gravely. "No, sir," was all she said, but there was something in her eyes that suggested irritation.

"I don't want to say feminine intuition, but I do mean impressions, that kind of thing, right?"

"Right." Liz Falla looked toward the waiting group. "Well, I'll tell you right now, Guv, that the waiting committee looks set to repel all boarders. Talk about a united front."

The marchesa's heavy handsome features were sombre, and she was dressed in black — not peasant black, but something chic that suited her well. She still wore the hefty necklace of the day before but, as if responding to the solemnity of the occasion, her black-grey mane of hair was pulled back in a heavy chignon low on her neck. Like his partner, Moretti had the impression of forces marshalled, loins girded, the putting on of public faces. The marchesa spoke first.

"Good morning, Detective Inspector. You are here to see my daughter. She is waiting for you."

"My sister is distressed," said Gianfranco Vannoni, in Italian. "You will remember that, Inspector."

"Oh, he'll remember that," added Monty Lord in his impeccable Italian.

They stood side by side in the doorway and, for a moment, Moretti wondered if he and DC Falla would have to charge the trio and break through their line of defence. Then the marchesa moved back into the house and the others followed, with Moretti and his constable behind them. Somewhere in the house someone was playing a Chopin mazurka. It sounded inappropriately frothy in contrast with the joyless trio who had confronted them.

Anna Albarosa was seated at a grand piano in the dining room close to the main reception room in which Moretti had first interviewed Monty Lord and the Vannonis. She stopped playing as soon as they came in, and rose to face them.

Toni Albarosa's widow had not inherited her mother's good looks, nor her imposing height. In front of them stood a small, overweight woman, probably in her late thirties, wearing glasses and no makeup, whose short hair was already going grey, and whose clothing was so commonplace that Moretti had difficulty remembering afterwards if she had worn a dress, a skirt, or pants.

What stuck in his mind, however, was that she wore pastels, and not black, like her mother. He introduced himself and Liz Falla, and expressed, in Italian, their sympathy at her loss.

"Thank you." Anna Albarosa replied in English. If she were indeed distressed, as her brother claimed, then she was concealing it magnificently. "Your Italian is good, but I speak English. I spent some time there, at university." She turned to the phalanx at the door, speaking this time in Italian. "I can manage, thank you."

The marchesa looked taken aback. As she opened her mouth to speak, her daughter went forward and kissed her on the cheek. *"Grazie, mamma."* As the trio turned and left, the marchesa turned and gave a last warning look at Moretti.

"She's only trying to protect me, you know." Anna Albarosa's smile gave her plain face an individual warmth and charm, if not beauty. "So difficult being a mother — you never know what to do for the best. To hold on, or to let go. In my mother's case, she has always opted for complete control, and never doubted she was right. As in the case of my marriage to Toni. Please sit down."

Anna Albarosa indicated two chairs near the window, and sat down on a sofa opposite. She seemed quite calm, completely self-possessed.

"You are a mother also?" asked Moretti.

"Yes. I have a boy of ten and a girl of six. I am glad to say that my daughter has inherited her father's looks." Her smile contained no rancour, no bitterness that Moretti could see.

"I must ask you first of all, Mrs. Albarosa, to confirm that you were not on the island when your husband was killed."

"I was at my home in Fiesole, Inspector. I have witnesses up to about midnight, which I imagine would cover even the use of a private plane." Anna Albarosa suddenly leaned forward and said, "You may have noticed that I am not crying, or emotional, Detectives." Behind her glasses, her eyes seemed mildly amused. "In fact, you should check out my alibi carefully, or put me at the head of your list of suspects."

"Why is that?" asked Moretti, although he was sure he knew the answer.

"Because I know where Toni was probably going — or coming from — that night. The poor, stupid man!" There was now some emotion in her voice, but it sounded more like anger than grief.

"I see. Did someone tell you?"

"Oh, I watched him at the party that was held to greet the cast and crew in Florence, lining up Vittoria Salviati in his sights. It was how he usually operated: arrive, reconnoitre, stalk, and then in for the kill. Only this time, it was Toni who got killed." Anna Albarosa's laugh had none of the attractiveness of her smile. "I had become quite used to it. I did feel some pity for the girl, who bought Toni's sweetness and light act. Just as my mother and I did, ten years ago."

"Did you challenge him at any point, ask him if he was having an affair?"

"Not anymore. After a while, I didn't care. I had got what I wanted out of the marriage — a name that equalled my own, two children I adore, and the pleasure of being made love to from time to time by Toni Albarosa. In many ways he really was a sweet man, you know, and a good and kind father. Only he just couldn't keep his pants on."

"You saved your mother from hearing all this. How much did she know?"

"Not as much as she thought she did," was Anna Albarosa's cryptic reply.

"Your father and mother live apart, I believe?"

"What has that to do with Toni's death?" Moretti had a sense of guards going up, shutters closing.

"I don't know that it has anything to do with your husband's death, but at this stage of the investigation we try to build up a complete picture." Abruptly, Moretti changed tack. "So what do *you* think, Signora Albarosa? You say you should head our list of suspects. You were not here, so — if not you — then who do you think killed your husband?"

Toni Albarosa's widow frowned. "At first I assumed it was a jilted lover or a cuckolded husband — there are any number of those in Toni's past — but it's not as if he was in Italy when it happened. Then I was told about the attack on the writer and the business with the costumes. Now I simply don't know."

"Can you think of any reason why these daggers have been used?"

At this question, there was one of those flickers of expression across Anna Albarosa's face that reminded Moretti of Sydney Tremaine's reaction to Giulia Vannoni's arrival at the murder scene.

"No," she said. "None."

"Thank you." Moretti stood up and Liz Falla followed suit, pocketing her notebook. "I gather you are not directly involved with the making of *Rastrellamento*?"

"No. It was really my father's suggestion they could film here."

"Why? He doesn't live here, does he? Do you know?"

At this, Anna Albarosa started to laugh. "To annoy my mother, perhaps? You'd have to ask him."

"Perhaps I will. Will he be coming to Guernsey?"

"No, not unless he is required to do so. You'd have to go to him, Inspector."

As they walked to the door of the dining room, Moretti thought of something Anna Albarosa had said earlier in the interview. "You said, Signora, that Albarosa was a name that equalled your own. What exactly did you mean?"

"That the two families are of equal standing in Italian society. Let me show you something."

Instead of turning toward the front door, Anna Albarosa went toward the principal reception room and a short distance along a side corridor. It opened into another smaller reception room with a huge stone fireplace that dominated the space, and above it hung a coat of arms.

Beneath a gold coronet was a quartered shield, holding a device in each quarter: a stylized olive branch and a bunch of grapes across the top, a snake and arrowhead across the bottom. The quarters were enclosed in a wavy border made up of what looked like vines and initials.

"This," said Anna Albarosa, "is the combined family crest of the Vannoni and Albarosa families. It was not combined for my marriage, I assure you, but many years ago, when Vannonis and Albarosas first united in matrimony. It is quite usual in Italy — I don't know about other countries — particularly when a father has only a daughter to whom he can leave his fortune and property. If the woman brings that wealth and land into her husband's family, part of the two original crests is combined, with the woman's heraldic devices on the sinister side — the left side as you are wearing it, or carrying your shield, but the right as you are viewing it."

"Interesting."

Moretti watched Liz Falla's mouth open. He looked at her. She closed it again.

"Just one last thing, Signora — it is clear from this that your mother has immense pride in her family traditions and still thinks of herself as Italian. Why on earth is she in Guernsey?"

Again there was the flicker in Anna Albarosa's eyes. "The separation from my father was very painful. Family, you understand. So important in my country. Loss of face. I don't know. And something to do with money, I think. My mother never talks about such things."

She sounded stilted, her English no longer fluid, and Moretti sensed she was regretting the impulse that had taken her around a corner to give him a look at the crest. She moved ahead of them and led the way back to the main foyer, where the marchesa erupted from her study at the sound of their approach.

"I hope you have been considerate of my daughter's feelings. This has been a great shock to her."

"Mother, I'm fine. It is in all our interests that the detectives do their job."

"Of course." The marchesa looked irritated at the patronizing tone in her daughter's voice, and Moretti decided to ask a provoking question while the woman's lofty sang-froid was shaken.

"Marchesa — why do you think your husband suggested the filming of *Rastrellamento* at your home?"

He expected anger, or outrage at his *lèse-majesté*, and he got it all. Moretti felt lucky those long nails were not scoring his face, as they had Gilbert Ensor's.

"What has this to do with the murder of my son-in-law? My feelings about the filming here are none of your business, Detective Inspector, and if you try to drag my family's good name into this inquiry, I shall insist you are taken off the case. The lieutenant-governor is a good friend of mine."

There was something else in the marchesa's face, besides anger. *She's frightened*, thought Moretti. *Something about the question terrifies her*. Unfazed, intrigued, he replied. "Your family's good name is already dragged into this enquiry, Marchesa. It was dragged in when your son-in-law got killed on the grounds of your home at four o'clock in the morning. We can only hope that the mainland press don't pick up on this too swiftly, but inevitably they will. The murder has already been reported in the *Guernsey Press*, on BBC Guernsey, and Island FM, but the death of a location manager is not quite as newsworthy as one of the stars would have been. We will do our best to help you avoid the mudslinging a murder like this attracts."

Moretti could feel the heat from the marchesa's eyes burning holes in his jacket as he and Liz Falla returned to the car.

"Want my first impression, Guv? She really hates her husband."

"I've no doubt she does, DC Falla, but that's not what that was about."

"I nearly said something when we were looking at that shield, but I saw your face. It's got something to do with dagger handles and that shield thing, you think?"

"Well, I want to keep that to ourselves for a bit. There's a family aspect to all this we've not got a handle on yet — sorry, bad pun. Signora Albarosa showed us that coat of arms of her own accord, and then, suddenly became — or, was it suddenly?"

"She changed her mind, didn't she? Wished she hadn't."

"Yes. When I asked her what her mother was doing here when she's so proud of her roots. Roots — hold on. I've just thought of something. We can drop the car off at Hospital Lane, and walk down to Blondel's."

"The grocer's, Guv?"

"We'll pick up a bottle of olive oil from the Vannoni estates. I know Blondel's carry the Vannoni olive oil."

Blondel's Grocers were the top such establishment in town, catering to the carriage trade. They stocked most of the luxury products the island uppercrust might require, including a superb range of vintage wines and fine spirits and cigars in their off-licence. Over the years the business had expanded into a couple of supermarkets and more than one joint project with leading banks, such as Barings, but the family had retained the original store between a jewellers and a bookshop on a small street called the Pollett near La Plaiderie.

Moretti and Liz Falla walked down the hill past what had once been the townhome of the De Saumarez family, and was now Moore's, one of St. Peter Port's most central hotels. Moretti caught his partner's wistful glance up the narrow steps that led to Moore's patisserie.

"Hungry, DC Falla? Me too. We'll take a break after this."

"We're in luck, Guv." Liz Falla pointed at the window of Blondel's which was just across the narrow street. "I think there's a Vannoni bottle in the display."

The window's theme was labelled "Harvest Riches." There were bunches of convincingly realistic plastic grapes, their fabric vine leaves entwined around bottles of wine and various exotic vinegars, and jars of black and green olives, some with the contents spilled out across the space. Among the olives were bottles of olive oil, some of them gigantic, their colour varying from yellow through lime to almost-green.

"There it is, the Vannoni bottle — we're looking at the shield, right?" said Liz Falla, pointing at one of the more modestly sized bottles.

"Right. There's one on every bottle — I use their brand. I've noticed that much but, like most things one sees everyday, I've never really taken a good look at it."

"From here," said Liz, her nose almost touching the glass, "it looks just like the one we saw at the manor."

"From here. But I think not. Let's take a closer look"

Inside the shop, the warm, complex smell of cheeses, fruit preserves, chocolate, and coffee, mixed with the hospitable fragrance of wines and spirits, reminded both of them they were hungry.

"There you are, Guv. There's one on the counter." Liz picked it up. "Looks the same to me. Crown on top, grapes and olives and — just a second, that's not a snake, is it?"

"No. A dagger."

"Brilliant, Guv," said his partner. "Fancy you remembering that."

"I didn't, not really, but the quarters up at the manor seemed different to me. Sometimes these heraldic symbols are far from clear — take the balls on the Medici coat of arms, for instance. The French in the sixteenth century spread the rumour they represented poison pills, but nobody really knows what they are."

Liz Falla nodded sagely. "How come the bottles are different from the shield up at the manor?"

"Remember what Anna Albarosa said about the addition of another coat of arms, when the woman brings her name and fortune into the family? This is what happened here — this shield we're looking at now is almost certainly the Vannoni coat of arms without the Albarosa addition. And remember what I said about how, like most things you see every day, I'd never really examined it. That, I think, is why Anna Albarosa made the mistake of drawing our attention to the family crest, and then why she got cold feet."

"Right." Liz Falla waved across at a well-fed white-coated lady slicing off thickly cut chunks from a succulent roast of pork for an equally well-endowed customer. "Where does this get us? I mean, we have to work out, don't we, what all this has to do with the attempt on Mr. Ensor, a rack of damaged costumes, and a dead location manager? Sorry, Guv, perhaps you already have."

"I wish! But we now know for sure that the dagger is not just idiosyncratic or purely decorative. It's significant. And, second of all — I don't know. I haven't yet worked it out. Hello, Mike."

Mike Le Page, the manager of Blondel's, was approaching with the look of someone anxious to please, while at the same time hoping to keep any unpleasantness at bay, or at least away from public scrutiny. He was a middle-aged man with the dark hair and eyes that marked his Norman ancestry and, in the midst of constant temptation to overindulge, had managed to keep impressively slim.

"Can I help? Is there a problem? Hello, Liz."

"None," Moretti reassured him. "We needed to take a good look at one of the Vannoni olive oil bottles."

"Terrible business." Mike Le Page said, shaking his head. "The kitchen staff up there told my delivery man all about it. But why are you looking here?"

Moretti waved a vague hand in the air. "We look into all angles at this stage of the investigation. I imagine you sell the Vannoni brand as much because it's good as because the marchesa is on the island?"

"Oh yes. We have no dealings with her, but we've had some with her niece. She came in and put on a tasting for us once — first time I've had as many males as females for a sampling, once word got around. She's a fine-looking lady, that one. Only, if the stories I hear are true, they were wasting their time. The lads, I mean."

Mike Le Page gave a knowing laugh.

As Moretti was paying for the bottle of olive oil Mike Le Page said, "Tell you what, Ed, there's someone who knows more than I do about that lot up at Ste. Madeleine. Dan Mahy. His wife was employed by the family right after they bought the manor. He worked here for years — goes back to the days when we did deliveries by bicycle — but he's been retired a while now. He lives out at Torteval. Hang on, I'll get his address for you. We still ask him to our staff get-togethers, although he doesn't come any longer. But they tell me he still puts in an appearance from time to time at the manor — course, it's much closer to where he lives than we are. They give him a bite to eat and send him on his way"

Out in the street, Liz Falla said, "Dan Mahy might be a waste of time, Guv. Nutty as a fruitcake, my mother says. Never got over the death of his wife."

"Talking of fruitcakes, DC Falla, I think we should get some lunch."

On the other side of the street, a Labrador retriever with his leash fastened around a lamppost began to bark at an approaching collie.

"Dogs, dogs," said Moretti. "Why didn't the dog bark in the night?"

"Sorry, Guv, I'm not with you."

"You know — Sherlock Holmes," said Moretti, leading the way up the steps past the huge mural painted on the wall of the house adjoining the patisserie. They each ordered a prawn salad and coffee in the restaurant and made their way back outside on to the wide terrace that looked down on a cluster of financial buildings and their closed-circuit cameras.

"Sherlock Holmes, Guv?" asked Liz Falla, pulling in her chair under the shade of the green and white table umbrella advertising Grolsch beer. The cerulean background of the mural behind her nicely complimented the darker blue of her suit. *Gamine*, thought Moretti, looking at her short dark hair, cut in wisps around her face. *Yes, I suppose she is.*

"Sherlock Holmes, DC Falla. This afternoon, I want you to go back to the manor and check with the security people if there was any unusual behaviour from any of the guard dogs on the night of the murder. Also, get someone to check our records, and see if there has been any sort of complaint or report of trouble from the Vannoni family in the past few months, however trivial it may seem."

The salads and coffee arrived, served by a cheerful red-aproned waitress with an Australian accent.

"What are you expecting to find, Guv?" asked Liz Falla, after the server had left.

"That's just it. I don't know, and I want you to stay open to anything, even the apparently inconsequential." *The coffee is excellent, almost as good as my own,* thought Moretti. "Now, about those two women. Apart from your feeling the marchesa can't stand her husband, was there anything else that struck you?"

His partner inspected a large prawn impaled on the tines of her fork as though it pleased her mightily.

"Yes, but it's difficult to put into words — ones that make much sense, that is. There's something going on, but I have the feeling that neither of those ladies are entirely sure themselves what it is — see," said Liz Falla, examining the crustacean as though it had the answer to the mystery, "I got the weirdest feeling from them — that they both know something, but they're neither of them sure if the something they know is the something that caused the murder and the other stuff, and they're darned if they're going to say anything in case they let slip something that may have nothing to do with the murder but they don't want to be public knowledge."

Moretti watched her silently for a moment as she demolished her plateful of prawns.

"Believe it or not, DC Falla, I understood every word you said."

Her laughter startled a nearby sparrow, waiting hopefully on the back of an empty chair.

"Thanks, Guv. And thanks for asking my opinion. I never said, but I'm really grateful for the chance to work with you. I've felt at a bit of a loss up to now, but your asking me my impressions really helped."

"Good." *I'm feeling less at a loss myself,* thought Moretti — about the partnership at least, if not the case.

A drop of rain splattered on to the umbrella above the table.

"One other thing, Guv." DC Falla speared a last piece of radicchio. "I get to call you 'Guv,' but you have this mouthful to say every time. DC Falla, or Detective Constable Falla —"

"I can't say your first name," said Moretti. Had a small joke and a moment of laughter led to distressing personal requests, unprofessional familiarity? She was giving him that look of hers again.

"And I wouldn't dream of it, Guv. That's all we need, gossip among the lads."

"What then, DC Falla?"

"How about just 'Falla,' Guv."

"Very well, if that's what you'd like."

"I would. And I'll tell you something else I'd like —" His partner stood up and attracted the attention of the waitress. "If we've got the time, I'd like a piece of their Dobos Torte. I'll burn it off in the pool at the Beau Sejour Centre tonight before I have my rehearsal."

"Rehearsal?" Moretti didn't know why he should feel surprised. After all, he knew nothing about Detective Constable Liz Falla. "Are you a member of the Island Players like your uncle?"

"God, no!" Falla seemed to find this funny. "I'm a member of a group. We call ourselves 'Jenemie.' A Guernsey word, but don't ask me what it means. We just liked the sound of it."

"Group? You mean you're a musician, Falla?"

"Not like you, Guv. I play some guitar — acoustic — but mostly I'm a singer."

"I didn't know."

There was the old-fashioned look again. "Why would you, Guv? I don't go around Hospital Lane singing my little folkie heart out."

"So you're a folk singer."

"More like — do you know Enya's music? A New Age folkie singer. Sort of like that. My real heroine's a

Canadian called Loreena McKennit."

"Interesting," said Moretti. It was his favourite fallback word. This time he meant it, although whenever anyone said "New Age" he usually ran fast in the opposite direction. "I think I will go to Torteval after all, have a word with Dan Mahy. Oh, and Falla, next time you're in touch with Benedetti, perhaps you could ask him to see what he can find out about this person. No rush." Taking out his notepad, Moretti wrote down the name "Sophia Maria Catellani," added a couple of details, tore out the page, and handed it to Liz Falla.

"Okay, Guv." His partner looked at the paper, but she asked no questions. He liked that.

"Rain's starting," said Moretti, standing up and putting the notebook back in his pocket. "They said it would by afternoon. You enjoy your cake, and I'll see you at the manor."

No need to tell Liz Falla he was making a stop on the way to see if his overnight guest had left his bed.

Rastrellamento. *It's all in there somewhere*, Moretti thought. *I've got to talk to Gilbert Ensor again*. Rain was now pattering steadily against the windshield of the Triumph.

I thought about you.

Miles Davis's version of the Johnny Mercer standard played in his head. In his mind's eye Moretti saw the auburn hair of Sydney Tremaine burning against his pillow, her backless gold mules slipping off her feet.

She was gone, as he had expected. On the note he had left she had written, "Thank you. I took the shirt."

He felt a pang of something that felt disconcertingly like regret, got back in the Triumph and set out to Torteval.

chapter seven

People have long memories.

But was it a long memory that Dan Mahy had? Or none at all? Was everything he said the product of delusion?

Torteval, on the south coast of the island, was a parish divided by another parish, St. Pierre du Bois. Dan Mahy lived in the western portion in one of the cottages once used by the families of the Hanois lighthouse-keepers, that had been his parents' home. The cottages had fallen into disrepair during the German occupation, as every piece of timber had gradually been removed from the homes and used for fuel, and after the war there had been plans to rebuild them and make them fit for use again. This had not yet happened, and probably never would, but Dan Mahy had refused to leave.

Moretti's route took him past the airport. As he drove past the Happy Landings Hotel a small private plane was coming in to land, and he made a mental note to himself to get someone to check the comings and goings of private planes over the past two or three days.

He thought about his next move when he returned to the manor to meet Liz Falla. Should he see the marchesa and her son again, push a little harder. Dig a little deeper into the past?

No, he thought, *leave them alone. Don't tip your hand, not yet.* He had little enough to go on, and at this stage he'd prefer the family to have no idea he suspected some past secret quite as much as some present indiscretion for the murder.

But if Toni Albarosa was not the intended victim, then who was? For it seemed much more likely that the murderer, knife in hand, was en route to a preplanned target rather than merely lurking about the manor on the off chance of finding someone to stick a dagger in. The most likely candidates were the marchesa or her son — if his theory about the murder were correct, that is.

And the most likely perpetrator? Well, if you took the usual elements of investigation into account — motive and opportunity — the list would include most family members, and some of the crew. Moretti felt reasonably safe at this stage ruling out the cast: they were chosen by the producer and the director, and thus were not proactive participants. Family motives would include jealousy and revenge — and it might still be a crime of passion in the usually accepted sense, after all. He must beware of getting too clever about the whole business. As for the crew, director Mario Bianchi was a prime suspect; he was responsible for the rewrites and he was Italian. And, for the moment, the most likely candidate was Italian. Which would be a great relief to Chief Officer Hanley.

If, that is, he was right about the war and past events being the motive for murder. As Sydney Tremaine had pointed out, there was a lot of volatility on a movie set. It could be that the art director, Piero Bonini, and the co-designer, Eddie Christy, hated Betty Chesler's guts, and decided to sabotage the project. It could be that *anyone* hated Gilbert Ensor's guts and decided to sabotage the project.

Ahead of him, shrouded in a misty grey drizzle, Moretti could see what remained of the Hanois cottages. The lighthouse itself could not be seen from this point, because of the towering granite slab around which the coastal road wound itself, but on that rocky platform, in the days before radio and telephone, the lighthouse keepers' wives used to send messages to their husbands with flags. Now, the summit was empty, and only traces remained of the massive shelter and the tank traps erected by the occupation forces.

He brought the Triumph to a halt and got out. Because of the miserable weather, the place was deserted and silent, except for the sound of the sea on the rocks below the point. Gulls wheeled overhead, their cries suddenly climaxing in a raucous cacophony, and Moretti could hear the piping shriek of an oystercatcher somewhere, looking for the winkles and barnacles exposed by the low tide. He experienced a moment of suspension in time, as a past embracing all those hundreds of ships lost on the Hanway rocks, the earthworks thrown up and the great guns and powder magazines mounted to fend off Buonaparte on this vulnerable coastline, the debris left behind by a more recent enemy, hung in the swirling fog, tangible as the pebbles beneath his feet. Which past, indeed, did Betty Chesler mean?

"Wharro! Lookin' for me?"

A small gnome-like creature materialized through the mist in front of Moretti.

"Dan Mahy?"

"Don't look so surprised, lad. I got second sight, me, but I also got a phone!"

The gnome cackled.

"Can we have a word?"

"Why you came, innit?"

On closer inspection, the gnome was not so small after all. His back was nearly bent double, and his broad-featured face was the colour of mahogany. The weathering of time and climate made it difficult to judge his age, but he appeared to be in his eighties. He took Moretti's arrival with the calm of one who had faced enough of life's calamities and contretemps not to find anything extraordinary.

"Mr. Le Page says you're the one to talk to about the Vannonis at the Manoir Ste. Madeleine."

"Did he now? That would be because of my missus, God rest her soul."

"That's right. She worked there."

"So she did. Became very friendly with that poor old lady they brought with them."

"What poor old lady?"

"Patrizia, she was called. Italian, of course, like them. Oh how she wanted to go back again, that one! Didn't speak much English, but she used to cry about it to my missus, she did. Died here, poor woman. Never got back. Mind you, she told Aggie they could never."

"Did she say why? I thought they did go back from time to time."

"Oh, not to Italy, she didn't mean. She meant to the house and the place where she was born. I know what that's like." Dan Mahy looked around him. "Always want to be here, me, and now I got a little windfall, I have." The old man chuckled and rubbed his hands together with a sound like the rasp of sandpaper. "Put it away in my *pied-du-cauche*."

"That's nice," said Moretti. "Wouldn't it be safer in the bank than in the toe of your sock?"

"Huh!" Dan Mahy snorted and spat. "Not for me, and no St. Peter Port, or St. Andrew, no thanks. Social Services keep at me, to get me out. Here, where I was born, this is where I'll die."

"So," said Moretti, gasping hold of the direction of the conversation and wrenching it back to the matter in hand, "Patrizia said they had to leave a house? A place?"

"Right. You're Emidio and Vera's boy, aren't you?" Dan Mahy suddenly said, looking at Moretti as if he had seen him for the first time.

"I am. Now, about the Vannonis and the old lady —"

"But you should know, lad. Your father now — he couldn't go back, neither, could he?"

"My father?"

Moretti felt as if he had trodden on one of the old fortifications and uncovered a rusty mine beneath the surface. It still happened, from time to time.

"Just like Patrizia used to say about the Vannonis. That she couldn't talk to anyone about her old home because of the bad things. No one talked about it, the house."

"What house?" *Scramble through it*, thought Moretti. *Stick with his train of thought, or we'll both get lost*. And at the moment, he seems to know what he's saying, though God knows what he's saying.

"She said she always had to remember the bad things didn't happen. Like they told her."

"Did she ever tell your wife where this place was in Italy?"

"Don't remember — like I said, she didn't speak much English. But Aggie brought old Patrizia out here to visit many times, that I do remember. She'd sit and look at the sea and say the same thing, over and over again. Then one day my missus told them back at the manor. Told them what the old lady had said, asked them what it meant. She never came no more."

"What was it she said — do you remember?"

Dan Mahy screwed up his eyes and mouth. After a moment he said, "Pretty it was. Stuck in my mind, it did. Let me think — ah, got it. Said she could smell the sea again, that it did her good. Bury the past, she said. Then she said, '*Maledetta Maremma, maledetta Maremma.*' Chanting, she was, like it was a prayer, over and over."

"*Maledetta Maremma, maledetta Maremma?*"

Dan Mahy cackled appreciatively. "That was just like her saying it, *ma fé*! Just like your dad, you."

Moretti decided to risk changing direction. "Why, Dan, should I know how Patrizia felt? You say my father could not return to Italy. But he did, from time to time."

Not often, thought Moretti.

"Well, *mon viow*, it was more the running away for him, eh? Mind you, lad, there was many of us as would've run a mile or two for your mother. Nobody blamed him."

"Blamed him?"

Suddenly, the old man became a child. "I'm tired. I want my dinner. *Fiche le camp*, Emidio."

"Eduardo."

But Dan Mahy's moment of sanity — if that indeed was what it had been — was over. He turned on his heel and walked away from Moretti back to the home of his childhood, his oversize boots dragging on the wet road.

"Your eyes betray you, Contessa — I know them so well by now. Tell me where he is. Do not go on with this dangerous game, I beg of you!"

Before the Panavision cameras in the principal reception room of the Manor Ste. Madeleine, Gunter Sachs was sweating heavily, and regretting the self-indulgences of a month in the south of France that had added body fat to burn beneath the great arc-lights that lit the set. Although it was still early in the afternoon, it had already been a long day. Outside, the sun shone on a rain-soaked landscape, but in the manor it was night, blinds and curtains closed over the windows set in the gold-brocaded walls. Mario Bianchi had decided against using available light and had opted to set one of the pivotal dramatic scenes of the book and the movie on a hot July night in 1944 so he could use the magnificent candelabra and chandeliers in the room.

After much discussion in two languages about light levels and other technical details between the cinematographer, an American called Mel Abrams, who often collaborated with Monty Lord, the art director, Cosimo del Grano, the director, Mario Bianchi, and the head cameraman, the actual shooting of the scene finally got underway.

"Ah, Ricardo, *mio*. This is no game we play."

Behind the cameras and lights, in the dark recesses of the great room, Monty Lord and Mario Bianchi smiled at one another. In one sentence, with one inflection of that magnificent voice, Adriana Ferrini reminded both men why they had paid a king's ransom to get her for *Rastrellamento*. Later, the rushes would give them further proof, if they needed it, of the soundness of their decision.

Adriana Ferrini was a legend in the world of cinema — not just in Italy, but anywhere there was a movie house and people saw film. From her poverty-stricken roots, through her rise to screen goddess, to her present incarnation as model mother, faithful wife, and generous colleague, she had moved into the realm of icon. Good genes, good habits, and great cosmetic surgery had maintained the beauty of her youth into her fifties. To watch an Adriana Ferrini close-up was to see the cliché, "the camera loves her," become reality.

Gunter Sachs, perspiring in his German commandant's uniform, was only too aware of her charisma. His role was a gift, a chance to portray a character usually shown as a bumblehead or a bully — or worse — as a sensitive, cultivated man caught in a moment of history not of his making. Gilbert Ensor's creation of Commandant

Reinhardt Ritter was one of the most admired and praised elements of the original book, and the integrity of the character had been maintained through the various rewrites of the script. Although the other actors grumbled that this made his task easier, what they overlooked was the effect that the changes in character of those around him had on the delivery of a line.

Take, for instance, the complete turnaround in the character of the housekeeper, who now stood in the shadows beyond the lights, waiting for her scene. Hers was not a big role, but many of his own scenes began with some sort of conversation between the two of them — in a sense, she was the go-between in the love affair of the commandant and the contessa. It made one hell of a difference to even "Good evening, Anna," when he was greeted by the steely glare of a gaunt, black-clad harpy instead of the conspiratorial giggle of the rosy-cheeked rotund actress with whom he had originally exchanged such pleasantries.

Then there was the priest, with whom he had some major scenes. Overnight, the cadaverous skeleton of an actor who had been the very epitome of a brooding, Macchiavellian hound of God had disappeared to be replaced by a jolly, plump leprechaun of a man who played the role as a kind of cute, comic Friar Tuck.

At least Clifford Wesley's head hasn't rolled — yet — he thought, thankful for small mercies. The British actor was a studious, reserved type — what his countrymen called "a decent bloke" — and his acting talents came from some intellectual and intestinal Gordian knot deep inside him. He was the one sympathetic personality in the group, in Gunter Sachs's opinion; he had even read Goethe, which was more than could be said of most Germans these days. The scenes the commandant had with the British prisoner of war, Tom Byers, were now mostly "in the can," and they would be spared reshooting them all.

Presumably.

Nothing was for certain in the make-believe world of *Rastrellamento*, and even the luscious Vittoria Salviati had expressed her insecurities to him that morning, as they waited together for their call. Of course, it now appeared she had been carrying on a clandestine affair with the murdered Toni Albarosa, and was afraid she might be the next target. Gunter Sachs's own insecurities made him uncharacteristically spiteful.

"Your fears are probably justified. Jealousy is, in my opinion, the most powerful of emotions. A primitive passion."

He watched her dark eyes grow wider, and chided himself for his cheap victory. However, from her next remark it was clear he had misinterpreted her reaction.

"That's how I saw it, first of all. But now I wonder, Gunter. The last time I was with Toni — just before he died — he was really upset because of something that happened over a location he suggested."

"To whom? What location?"

"I don't know — he wouldn't say. But it was something to do with the family, that much I know."

"Have you told the police?"

"No. What is there to tell? I'm scared enough already as it is, without giving anyone *another* reason to come after *me*."

The conversation had stopped at this point, when they were called for their scene together, and the only thought Gunter Sachs gave subsequently to Vittoria Salviati's dilemma was that fear and loss had greatly improved her acting abilities. *Access to the emotions*, he thought, as he watched her character, Maddalena, weep at the commandant's cold anger. *That's what it's all about. Though in real life, it can play havoc, God knows.*

"Cut! Print!"

With relief, Gunter Sachs moved away from the heat of the lights and loosened his collar. The scene with Adriana Ferrini had gone well, and would require no more takes, thank heaven. One of the dressers was waiting for him to take his jacket and to hand him a bottle of mineral water, which he drank thirstily.

"Hot work, sir."

Gunter Sachs's eyes adjusted to the light and he saw it was the detective inspector with the good bone structure he had seen the day of Albarosa's murder. They had not spoken before, because his statement had been taken by one of the other policemen.

"Detective Inspector Moretti, sir. I am in charge of this investigation. Could I have a word? I am told by your director you are not needed for a while."

"Of course. We can go to my trailer."

Gunter Sachs's trailer was a comfortable haven of leather armchairs, thick rugs, a sofa bed, and a heavy teak table piled with books and magazines in German and English.

"A drink, Detective Inspector? No? Then I hope you won't mind if I have a beer. Please, sit down."

"You do a lot of reading, I see," said Moretti, picking up a copy of *Rastrellamento* from among the books on the table.

"There's always time to do that on a movie set, no matter how major your role."

"So I am beginning to realize. You are not staying in the manor, I believe."

"No. I am at the Héritage. I prefer my independence. I ordered room service late the night of Albarosa's murder, but I have no real alibi for the time itself, I'm afraid."

"Like many others. But I actually wanted to ask you about this." Moretti held up the copy of *Rastrellamento*. "I see you are familiar with the original work, which is helpful, because I gather there are changes to the role played by Adriana Ferrini. From what I remember of the story, that should affect you — am I right?"

"Yes. Reinhardt Ritter is in charge of the prison camp set up in what was once an orphanage in the town, where the contessa's family, the Cavallis, have ruled the roost for centuries. He is an educated, sensitive individual, ill-suited to the task expected of him — which is to run the camp after the departure of the Italian troops in 1943, and to recapture the prisoners who escaped at that time. What starts off as hostility between the contessa and the commandant develops into a warm friendship — she calls him 'Ricardo' — that could have changed to love. Only Hitler is defeated, and the commandant is arrested by the allies. Strangely enough, the changes to the contessa's role have made little difference to my own. They have built up Adriana's role in relation to the other characters — for instance, the housekeeper and the priest. And that's where the problem lies for me — not in the size of their roles, but in the interpretation."

"Can you think of any reason why they would have built up her role vis-à-vis rather minor characters?"

"You'd have to ask Mario that question, but I think the quick answer is that it's Adriana Ferrini." Gunter Sachs smiled and shrugged his shoulders. "She's a huge box-office draw, as you probably know."

"Of course. The time span of the original novel was about a year and a half, I believe — from just before the arrest and internment of Mussolini in July 1943 to just after the fall of Rome in 1944."

"That much hasn't changed. What has changed, it seems to me, is proportion. There is more emphasis on the contessa, her entourage, her relationship with the fascists and partisans in the town, and less on the love affair between the daughter of the family and the escaped British prisoner of war. Or else both elements have been balanced out, you might say."

"If I remember the book correctly, one of its strengths was Ensor's ability to convey the complexities of human nature — in other words, there was no clear-cut bad guy, or good guy. Has that changed at all, particularly with the rewrites?"

"I hadn't really thought about it before but, now you ask me, I think so. How can I put this — things have become more black and white. Perhaps that is what cinema audiences want today, and certainly that is Monty Lord's strength — giving them what they want. Mario is the genius, and Monty the facilitator."

"Who does the rewrites? Not Gilbert Ensor now, I gather."

Gunter Sachs laughed. "God, no! Mario does them."

"The director? Is this usual?"

"If you're Ingmar Bergmann or Woody Allen, yes — Kubrick would even rewrite a scene while the actors were before the cameras. Mario is that kind of director."

"One more question, Mr. Sachs, and then I can leave you in peace. You say things are now more black and white. In your opinion, who is the bad guy?"

Gunter Sachs got up and fetched himself another beer from the small fridge. For a moment, Moretti wondered if it was a diversionary tactic; he wanted to see the expression on the actor's face when he replied. However, Gunter Sachs turned back, the open bottle in his hand, and the only expression Moretti could read was one of uncertainty.

"Now, there's the strange thing. The only bad guys I can see from all this rewriting are both women; the contessa and the housekeeper. Then there's the priest — and here things become even stranger. He's a caricature, and he's so — cozy. But the way the script reads, you wouldn't trust him to christen your children, let alone take your confession."

"Because he doesn't keep his mouth shut?"

"Exactly."

"Does he betray partisans? Fascists?"

"He's a turncoat. Many were, of course. At that time, in Italy, survival often depended on being in the right camp at the right time in the war — you must know that, you being a Guernseyman. The stories I have heard since I've been here! But you take the *carabinieri*, for instance. In *Rastrellamento*, when the Germans arrive in the town, they take their orders from them. It is a situation familiar to many of my own countrymen. I wouldn't have agreed to take this role if there had not been an understanding of motivation, what makes people betray. What makes them evil."

"So the contessa is now evil?"

"She is driven by a desire to preserve the status and position of her family into — yes — evil decisions."

"Such as — ?"

"The betrayal of her own daughter."

"In the book, the escaped prisoner of war, Tom Byers, survives to marry the daughter."

"Not in the movie. They both die. But that change was in the original script. Mario has always liked unhappy endings."

"Is that good box office?"

"If the survivor is Adriana Ferrini, probably. Besides, Detective Inspector, think of Romeo and Juliet. There won't be a dry eye in the house."

Moretti held up the copy of *Rastrellamento*. "May I borrow this?"

"With pleasure."

Moretti stood up and held out his hand. "You've been very generous with your time. Thank you."

"Tell me, Detective Inspector," said Gunter Sachs as they shook hands, "do you think the murder and the other attacks are to do with the plot of *Rastrellamento*?"

"It is certainly one of the many angles we are exploring, sir," said Moretti, falling back on convenient procedural cliché. "People have long memories."

"Ah, that is so true."

It was only after the policeman had left his trailer that Gunter Sachs remembered what Vittoria Salviati had told him. He thought of calling Moretti back, or contacting him, then dismissed it. For the life of him he couldn't think how a movie location could be of any importance at all in the death of Toni Albarosa.

Liz Falla was sitting on a curved stone seat between two massive pots of hydrangeas writing in her notebook.

"This is a big place, Guv. Good thing you phoned on your mobile or we could have looked for each other the rest of the day. It's got seven bathrooms, so they tell me. I found the security people and the feller who was covering this part of the premises —" Liz's arm swept over the expanse of terrace, "— says there was no unexpected behaviour from the dogs that night. Everything was quiet."

"Which is exactly why the behaviour *is* unexpected. Whoever stabbed Albarosa had to be on the grounds — as you say, this is a big place — and I'm presuming the security staff's rounds would be frequent enough to coincide with the murderer, concealed in bushes or among trees. Were the dogs allowed to fraternize with any of the cast and crew?"

"Yes. Usually that's not the case, but because this is a private home, the dogs had to know who they should expect to find in the grounds. They didn't have to be big buddies with them, just had to be familiar with their smell, apparently. I got a list." Liz Falla consulted her notebook. "The marchesa and her son, Mr. Albarosa, Monty Lord, Mario Bianchi, and three cast members who are staying here: Miss Salviati, Ms. Ferrini, and Mr. Wesley."

"Good work, Falla." It came naturally, to Moretti's relief. "We'll need to look more closely at all of them, but I want to start with Mario Bianchi." Moretti went over his interview with Gunter Sachs, concluding with his theory about the rewriting of the script. Liz Falla raised her eyebrows.

"Really, Guv? Then I don't have to be a genius to know why you want to check into Mr. Bianchi. He's directing the film — and the plot."

"Yes. It should be easy enough to run a background check on him, because he's a celebrity. I'll get records to run his name through the computer and give us everything they come up with — everything. I want all the gossip, all the dirt, even from unreliable sources, like the tabloids."

"Do you know what you're looking for?"

"I'm hoping to find something about his family. He's too young to have been around at the end of the war, but at the back of my mind is a feeling I've read something about him that has something to do with the political situation in the thirties and forties."

"What now, Guv?"

"Back to headquarters. I want to see if anything has come up about any kind of an incident involving the Vannonis."

There was a sudden burst of noise, and a small but voluble army of technicians came round the corner. Moretti stood up.

"We've been displaced, Falla. The world of make-believe is taking over while we go back to reality."

Back to reality. The phrase kept recurring in Moretti's mind on the drive back to St. Peter Port. Back to the reality of the war years, when the uniforms and the dresses in Betty Chesler's lodge and the military vehicles in the car park that looked so quaint and picturesque were part of an actual and threatening landscape in which real people lived, and lost, their lives.

chapter eight

"Bitch — you bitch."

"Hypocrite — you hypocrite. Just because you think I slept with Giulia Vannoni, you're oh so *upset*!"

"Giulia Vannoni? Christ almighty! Giulia Vannoni! Whose fucking shirt is that then? Hers? I thought you said it belonged to that policeman!"

"It does. But the black tights don't come from *his* wardrobe — hadn't you noticed them? Funny, my legs have always been such a turn-on for you. My strong point, in more ways than one — right, sweetie?"

"Bitch — you *bitch*!"

"You just said that, darling. Are words failing you? Dear me, I hope not, or why should I stay with you? I'll go be someone else's muse."

"*Muse*? If you'd taken a minute out from examining your own navel over the past few weeks you might have noticed I haven't written a bloody word — be it good, bad, or indifferent. You're no muse, woman, you're a — a — pestilence, bringing death, disease, famine of the imagination and writer's block. Damn you to hell!"

Sydney winced. "Don't scream. Hysteria doesn't suit you — you sound like a cross between a hyena and a eunuch."

"Doesn't suit your hangover, you mean. So the great detective thinks he can screw my wife on the job, does he? I'll show him! I'm getting on to that prissy-mouthed Chief Officer Hanley and letting him know that one of his officers has compromised a murder investigation!"

Gilbert Ensor crossed to the phone.

"Oh, I'm so scared! Please, Gil, you'll have to do better than that."

Sydney Tremaine did not feel as calm as she hoped she sounded. Unable to resist turning the tables on her husband, she had revealed much of the previous night's events, with some added embroidery that involved much more than merely abandoning Ed Moretti's suggested version.

As Gil picked up the phone she added, "If you do this, I shall tell them I spent the night with Giulia Vannoni, and your accusation is vindictive and groundless." Sydney placed herself in front of Gil, hands on hips. "Do you want the whole world to know that the wife of superstud writer Gilbert Ensor is having an affair with one of the highest-profile lesbians in Italy? I'd quite enjoy that, myself."

"Fucking bitch."

Gilbert Ensor's hand fell limply from the phone that crashed back on its cradle. She had him by the proverbial short and curlies and he knew it. Screaming had got him nowhere this time. Usually in their relationship, she screamed back and eventually surrendered one way or another — sexually or emotionally. Gilbert Ensor was a bastard, but he was a highly intelligent bastard, and he knew that something had changed in the balance of power. He decided to try pathos.

"Syd, darling, do you really hate me that much? Do you want revenge so badly you'd go against your nature to make me suffer?"

His unrepentant wife gave a short, sharp laugh laced with sarcasm. "Which nature is that, my darling? My heterosexual one, or my lesbian one? When it comes to navel-gazing, you know nothing about my nature because it has never interested you. Anyway, may I remind you that last night — I did *both*!"

With a theatrical toss of her auburn hair, Gilbert Ensor's scarlet woman turned away from him and started unbuttoning the accursed blue shirt that hung loosely over her slim torso. "I'm going to soak in a bath," she said.

As the shirt fell from her shoulders, Gilbert Ensor saw she was wearing yet another shirt underneath. The slippery fabric gleamed a luminous green in the sun slanting in through the window, making her look like a mermaid washed up on the island's shore, to hurt him and to haunt him with her bedtime stories.

"Bitch," he said again, weakly.

"That's right," she called back over her shiny green shoulder. "Bitch in heat. That's me."

He could hear her humming as she closed the bathroom door; she had a pretty singing voice. He recognized the tune: it was Snow White's theme song, "Someday My Prince Will Come."

Gilbert Ensor collapsed into an elegant gilt chair that squawked beneath the sudden arrival of his dead weight. So preoccupied had he been with her disappearance from the manor and her subsequent reappearance at the hotel, smelling of another woman's perfume and another man's cigarettes, he had not got around to telling Sydney about Monty Lord's visit.

This, he thought, *has to be one of the worst days of my life. So far.* With a promiscuous wife, an unbalanced director, and a nutter on the loose with a knife, who knew what fate might yet have in store for him!

When there had been a rap on the door at about nine o'clock that morning, he had assumed it was Sydney. Rage filled him, accelerating his heartbeat and filling his mouth with spittle and venom.

"Where the fuck have you been, you whore?" he spat through the door.

"Gil?" said a surprised voice. "It's Monty Lord. Is Sydney not there?"

"Monty?"

Shit, he thought. *Now he knows my wife stayed out all night. I'll be a laughingstock.* A second or so later he admitted a concerned-looking Monty Lord.

"Hi, Gil. What's happened to Sydney?"

"Oh —" Gilbert Ensor made a valiant attempt at nonchalance and failed miserably. "She'll turn up — she always does. Night on the town, I should think."

"You knew she left the manor with the marchesa's niece?"

"The one with the motorbike?"

"Yes. Giulia Vannoni."

"Oh." Gil's relief was palpable. "Girls' night out — she'll like that, Syd will."

Monty Lord looked mildly amused. "Yes," he said. "So will Giulia."

A nasty suspicion crossed Gil's mind, but faded swiftly into insignificance when he heard Monty say, "I didn't want to do this on the phone, but in person, Gil."

"Christ almighty, not another rewrite."

"No, no. In a way, this will interfere less with your original work."

"This? In what way can *any* change interfere less? At least, I presume that's what this is about — another change."

"No, Gil — you know, and I know, that we're both fortunate to have Mario Bianchi on board for this project. The man's a genius, with an instinctive sense of what works on the screen." Monty Lord gave a little self-deprecating laugh. "When he says 'jump' — creatively, that is — I say 'how high?'"

"Do you? I don't. And it makes no difference who's on board, as you put it, if the ship's the frigging *Titanic*! We should all be jumping, or looking for bloody lifeboats."

The tone of saintly patience left Monty Lord's voice and it became undisguisedly unpleasant. "You can sink a project by talking like this — is that what you really want, Gilbert?"

"I'm beginning to think I do, Monty — I mean, hell, what's left of my work?"

"Everything. Never doubt it. This is *Rastrellamento* by the incomparable Gilbert Ensor. But it became clear to Mario when he started shooting the scenes between Clifford and Vittoria that the movie needs another deus ex machina, as it were."

"As *what* were? Why doesn't Mario have the balls to tell me this himself?"

"Look, Gilbert —" Monty Lord took Gil by the elbow and guided him to a nearby sofa. "— I'm going to have to share this with you, I should have done before. In confidence, this is a very fragile man."

"*I'm* a very fragile man, for God's sake!"

"You're not fighting a serious drug habit and you're not under the permanent care of a psychiatrist, are you?"

"Is Mario — Jesus Christ!"

Monty Lord sighed. "We've both paid the price for my choice, I grant you. But I must tell you I agree with the changes to the script. They have made this a stronger movie without compromising the integrity of your original vision."

"Bullshit, Monty. And, may I add — bollocks."

"I don't think so, Gilbert. I think what we have here is a rare cross between an art-house movie and a blockbuster. I've been in this business in Italy and the States for years, and never have I been so excited about the creative *and* the financial aspects of a project. Need I remind you that you will make ten percent of the gross — besides that humongous fee we paid for the rights to *Rastrellamento*?"

Greed, thought Monty Lord. *Appeal to "what's in it for me?" and even this so-called creative genius becomes a mere mercenary. Just like me.*

"Deus ex machina, you said. Will Tom Byers be rescued by his guardian angel, flown in on wires?"

Monty Lord laughed. "Perhaps in the sequel? No, seriously, Mario has dreamed up another character who will interract with the two principal groups: a schoolteacher, not originally from the village. An outsider who observes the unfolding drama and finds himself drawn into the web of events."

"Jesus *wept*! Shambolic — it's a fucking farce, that's what it is. An utter shambles!"

In an instant, the mercenary was replaced by the writer, and Monty Lord realized he was in for the all too familiar scene of Gilbert Ensor in a rage. Only this time, Sydney Tremaine was not here to control her husband. All he could do now, as producer, was resort to the use of legal ultimatum. Raising his voice above the noisome stream of continuous obscenities that poured from Gilbert Ensor's lips he shouted, "Need I remind you, Ensor, that under the terms of the contract I don't have to get your permission for this kind of change? None of your original characters have been removed, as per our agreement. The teacher is in — get me?"

"You Yankee swine! We'll see what my lawyer has to say about that! We'll see what difference it makes to 'as per our agreement' when it turns out the director is a junkie and should be in the nuthouse! We'll see!"

"If you want to waste your time and money, feel free, Gilbert, but directors with a drug problem are a dime a dozen — really *good* directors with a drug problem are as rare as rubies."

Who can find a virtuous woman? For her price is far above rubies.

The biblical echoes of Monty Lord's choice of simile reminded Gil of his missing wife. Sydney's show of independence was new in their relationship — oh, she fought with him, but in the end it was all sound and fury and signified nothing. Her unexplained absence had shaken him, and now Mario Bianchi was at it again.

"Tell Mario I'll fight this one — no, I'll tell him myself," he said, and burst into noisy sobs.

Not a pretty sight, thought Monty Lord, as he surveyed the blubbering figure beside him on the sofa. He stood up. "I'll see myself out," he said.

As the door closed behind him, Monty Lord heard a scream from inside.

"Sydney!"

Like Marlon Brando screaming "Stella!" thought Monty. As theatrical. As desperate.

As he left the hotel, a taxi drew up. Inside he saw the red hair and Dresden profile of Sydney Tremaine, returning home from her night on the town.

"Well, what do you think, Guv?"

"Think?"

Moretti looked up as if he had been miles away, thought Liz Falla. In fact, he had been years away.

He couldn't go back, either.

Dan Mahy's words kept running over and over in his head. Drip, drip, drip. That and "*Maladetta Maremma*." All he knew about the Maremma was that it was an area in Italy where the marshes had been drained, but more than that he didn't know.

"Does any of this have anything to do with the death of Toni Albarosa? A place like this sometimes has trouble with prowlers, doesn't it?"

"True. But two things are interesting about these reports. First, there's the business with Dan Mahy. I'm not sure I'd have seen that as significant if I'd not just spoken to him. Let's go over what we have."

What they had on the table in front of them at the Hospital Lane headquarters were three incidents at the Manoir Ste. Madeleine; two incidents had taken place within a month of each other in April, the third just after the arrival of the film crew. In the first, one of the live-in staff was making sure the fire was out in the marchesa's sitting room at about eleven o'clock at night, when she saw someone peering through the window at her. She ran screaming from the room and, apart from her lurid description of the prowler's eyes as "glowing like living coals" — which might well have been inspired by her task and not based on observation at all — she could not even be sure if the prowler was a man or a woman. She *assumed* it was a man.

In the third incident, the guard dogs in the grounds "set up a racket" at around midnight, according to one of the handlers. When he checked he found skid marks on the ground near the lodge, and thought he heard the sound of a motor in the distance, out on the road. There were signs that one of the locks had been tampered with. The security staff thought the tire tracks were made by a motorbike.

"A Ducati, perhaps?" suggested Liz Falla.

"They don't say. But why, in this case, did the dogs bark? If it was Giulia Vannoni? They must have been familiar with the sound of her bike, I would think, let alone her presence. She's a regular."

"Maybe they always bark at night."

"Except they didn't, did they, when Albarosa bought it? Anyway, why would the marchesa's niece need to creep around at night? She had a perfect right to be there. No need to draw attention to herself — even if she was on her way to kill someone. But it's the second incident that's really interesting."

It appeared from the second report that the local station in St. Andrew had received a phone call from Toni Albarosa himself at about midnight. Sounding somewhat agitated, he'd said that one of the staff thought the prowler was back, and could someone come. The police officer who arrived on the scene made a search of the grounds where the intruder had been spotted, and found Dan Mahy, crouched down against the wall of one of the old stables that now served as a garage. Toni Albarosa identified him, and vetoed the suggestion he should be taken in for questioning. In fact, he now seemed eager to dismiss the whole episode.

"The officers assumed it was because the prowler turned out to be Dan Mahy, who tends to hang around the place. But now I wonder," said Moretti. "From the report it looks as if the old fellow told the officer he had met someone on the grounds — a friend, who wanted to hear about the old days."

"The old days," said Liz. "Keeps coming back to that, doesn't it? Looks like your feeling about the old days is beginning to hold water, Guv."

"Doesn't it, though? And here's the second thing that's interesting — why did no one in the family mention any of this? I'm not thrilled this wasn't brought to our attention by the St. Andrew's people, but surely it must have occurred to at least *one* of the family that it might have some bearing on the death of Albarosa?"

"Right. It's not so much they're lying as they're keeping their mouths shut. About something."

"A conspiracy of silence. I think so. I'm going to take another look at the statements by the marchesa, her niece and her son in particular, because these incidents change the time frame of the investigation. And I have to talk to Gilbert Ensor about his novel — whether *Rastrellamento* had not only its time period rooted in historical fact, but its storyline."

At this point they were interrupted by the arrival of a young constable almost hidden behind a mass of paper spat out by the computer about Mario Bianchi. Refusing his offer of help — "Don't know what we're looking for ourselves, PC Le Mesurier" — Moretti split the pile in two and handed one half to Liz Falla.

"Anything in Italian, throw it over to me. Unless you feel you can manage?"

Liz Falla smiled. "What are we not looking for then, Guv?"

"Anything that might give Mario Bianchi motivation to kill — not just Albarosa, but anyone in the two families. And anything that might link him in any way to events that took place during the war."

So much of what we do is dull as ditchwater, thought Moretti. As boring as being the accountant, or lawyer, his parents had wanted him to be when he had graduated from university in London. Between his hands lay the life of a star in the creative firmament, and it would have made interesting reading in other circumstances. *So far are we from the truth*, he thought, *that the key word for the search is "anything."*

"What about this, then?"

Liz Falla's finger stopped suddenly in mid-page. "*Fasciti*. That's 'fascist,' isn't it? Read this, Guv." She passed the sheet over to Moretti.

It was a report from about five years earlier in the

Italian newspaper, *Nazione*, about the career of Mario Bianchi, which went into his background in more depth than the usual piece of journalistic puffery. The writer described what he called "the cultural roots of the Bianchi phenomenon," attributing the film director's writing ability and social conscience in large part to his father.

"This is what I was trying to remember, Falla," said Moretti. "His father was Antonio Bianchi, a famous war correspondent for — here it is — *Corriere della Sera*. He's probably best known for a book he wrote in secret, *Il Giorni Avanti*, which was published in 1944, saying that Hitler was evil and that Mussolini had corrupted the high ideals of fascism. He was shot to death about ten years after the war ended — says here no one was ever sure if it was murder or suicide. And look at this."

Moretti held out a photograph of Mario Bianchi, apparently taken from some tabloid, with a short article beneath it in gigantic letters, studded with exclamations:

THE PRESSURES OF GENIUS! YOUNG MEGA-DIRECTOR MARIO BIANCHI PICKED UP IN DRUG RAID! POLICE SOURCES REVEAL THE AWARD-WINNING DIRECTOR IN POSSESSION OF HEROIN AND COCAINE!

The same information, in more restrained print and tone, appeared in the *Nazione*, and a later excerpt told readers that Bianchi, a first offender, had been given probation, as long as he underwent treatment for his addiction.

"Well, well," said Liz. "It would certainly make him a likely candidate for blackmail. I wonder if that director, Mr. Lord, knew about it."

"We'll ask him. My feeling is that this kind of thing is so common he probably isn't that concerned as long as Bianchi can do his job. And I suppose we didn't pick it up here, because he doesn't have a record."

Moretti and Liz Falla ran through the rest of the information but, apart from a growing list of movie achievements and awards, and the fact that Bianchi had married quite recently, there was no further mention of drugs, or idealist fascist fathers.

"Interesting," said Moretti. "If you look at the dates of his films, there appears to be a bit of a drought before *Rastrellamento*. Perhaps he was just writing, or enjoying his newly married state."

Before Liz could respond, the telephone on the desk between them rang. Moretti picked it up and gave his name.

"Detective Inspector Moretti, this is the Marchese Paolo Vannoni. I am told you are in charge of the murder inquiry into the death of my son-in-law?"

The voice was cultured, the English heavily accented but fluent, a dry brittle quality to the tone, like sandpaper against wood.

"You are phoning from Florence?"

Moretti scribbled the marchese's name on a piece of paper and held it out to Liz Falla, who raised her eyebrows and whistled noiselessly.

"Yes."

"Would you prefer to speak in Italian?"

"It would be better, yes." They switched languages. "Time is passing, Inspector, and I am told that no one has seen fit to keep the family informed as to how the inquiry is progressing. No explanations, no information as to when we can bury Toni. Nothing. What do you have — anything? A suspect, at least, I hope."

As the language changed to Italian, the sandpaper changed to steel.

Moretti thought of Giulia Vannoni's flippant request at the Grand Saracen, Sydney Ensor's game-playing, the marchesa's arrogance, both his and his partner's feeling that *something* — God knows what — was being withheld. He counterattacked.

"Marchese, you cannot expect me to discuss our

inquiries with you over the phone. This is a complicated business, since there is a possibility that your family and the Albarosa family have been targeted for some reason. And, sir, as to being kept informed, there have been incidents involving a prowler at the manor, and not one member of the family has seen fit to tell us about them."

From the other end of the line came a rusty chuckle, suggesting years of disuse.

"Detective Inspector, forgive me. You should understand I am very much regretting my decision to encourage the making of *Rastrellamento* at the manor, and I am sure that Toni's death and the previous events to which you refer are all connected to a wild and dissolute element in that unstable and corrupt world. Why you think the family has been targeted I cannot imagine. Nothing like this had ever happened until I gave permission."

Let's be conciliatory, thought Moretti, *and see where this is leading — see why this distant, disconnected aristocrat picked up the phone to speak to me.*

"You may be right, sir. But can you think why your son-in-law would be the target? I was under the impression that until the making of this film, he had *not* been part of that unstable and corrupt world, as you call it?"

"Detective Inspector Moretti —" the marchese too was sounding conciliatory, his tone almost confiding, "— Toni's marriage to Anna was a great mistake, encouraged by my wife, in spite of my misgivings. It has caused a permanent rift between us. My daughter was crazy about him and, in fact, became pregnant by him. The family is a good one, so I gave my permission."

"Would permission have been necessary in this day and age?"

"If Anna wanted to remain in the family and to receive her share of the property and inheritance, yes."

"I see. Why, sir, *did* you give permission for the filming of *Rastrellamento*?"

"Well — money, of course was one of them. *Vannoni Vigneti e Boschetti* is doing very well, but our way of life is increasingly expensive to maintain. The other reason was the talent of the director, Mario Bianchi. Which is ironic."

"Ironic? How?"

"I feel he is a bad influence for my son, Gianfranco, who has no willpower and little backbone, and I regret it deeply if I have opened the wrong door — which I may have done. Mario has brought an unsavoury element along with him."

This time, Moretti waited.

"Drugs."

Droghe.

Across the desk, Liz Falla leaned forward in her chair.

"You are saying then, sir, that in your opinion this could be a drug killing?"

"Drug related, yes."

"Do you have any evidence to support your theory?"

"It is the only one that makes sense. It is your job to find the evidence."

"Why then use daggers?"

"Detective Inspector, I cannot see into the mind of some hop-headed addict."

Moretti changed direction. "I understand you are close to your daughter, Anna. Yet you say the marriage distanced you from your wife. You never come here, I believe, and she rarely returns to Italy."

The marchese was back to sandpaper and steel again. "What any of this has to do with Toni's death I cannot think. All this is a waste of time, an unnecessary intrusion into people's lives."

"Nothing is private, Marchese, in a murder investigation, as I told your wife."

Moretti expected anger, but now there was a sadness in the marchese's voice.

"Life has not been kind to my daughter, Detective Inspector."

"She has health, wealth, a renowned family, and two fine children, she tells me. Many would say she was fortunate."

"In a world where beauty matters, she has none. In a world where fidelity is dismissed with a shrug, she fell in love and was betrayed. Again, and again, and again. If anyone wanted to see Toni Albarosa dead, it was me. I'm glad he is dead, but I didn't kill him."

It was a passionate speech, delivered cold and hard, in the marchese's sandpaper rasp. Moretti felt chilled.

"I presume you have read *Rastrellamento*, Marchese?" he asked.

"Yes. It is not my kind of literature, but Mario told me there would be many changes."

"What do you dislike about it, sir?"

"I am not one for harking back to the past, Detective Inspector. Life goes on. And now, speaking of life going on, I must go."

"Thank you for getting in touch with us, sir. Of course we will let the family know as soon as we have any solid information."

"*Grazie.*"

Before the word was completely out of Paolo Vannoni's mouth and he had a chance to hang up, Moretti broke in.

"One thing, Marchese. About the manor — it is yours, I believe?"

"Yes."

"And you live in Florence all year round?"

"Yes. Why?"

"Is there another property in the family? Besides the Albarosa villa, I mean. Another house?"

For a moment, Moretti thought the marchese had hung up on him.

"No. No."
Then the line went dead.

"There's a turn-up for the books, Guv. Fancy him calling all the way from Florence. Now why would he do that?"

"Did you pick any of that up?" Moretti asked, scribbling furiously. "I want to get it down before I forget."

"I caught the word 'drugs,' and I think I heard him say something about the director and his son, didn't I?"

"You did, Falla. You did indeed. One brings an unsavoury element with him and the other has no backbone."

"Then he hung up on you when you asked him about a house. I don't get it."

"Hold on and I'll tell you what Dan Mahy said."

Moretti finished writing and filled Liz Falla in on his rambling interview with Dan Mahy, leaving out the comments about his own father and mother.

"I might have thought it was all the ravings of someone gone soft in the head, if the marchese hadn't reacted to my inquiry as if I'd accused him of murdering his son-in-law himself. Not that he'd have minded, because for that he's off the hook."

"Why would he take a powder about another house?"

"Whatever the reason, Paolo Vannoni is prepared to throw the reputation of not only Mario Bianchi, but also his own son, to the wolves. He handed us two suspects on a plate: Gianfranco and Mario. That's why he phoned, Falla — to divert our attention from the internal affairs of the family itself. But I think we should double-check the two statements, anyway."

"I'll pull them, Guv."

"It's getting late, but I want to return to the manor and ask the marchesa why she said nothing about the prowler.

Perhaps she will be a little more forthcoming — and I want to see her reaction to her husband's comments."

This time Donatella Vannoni was graciousness itself. She offered coffee, tea — even a beer — and made sympathetic noises about the length of their day. Gone was the defensive, hostile woman of the morning. As soon as Moretti saw her face, he knew the marchese had phoned her, and that any element of surprise he might have hoped for was gone. The enmity between husband and wife was not going to play into his hands, as he had hoped. The marchesa was even prepared to agree that her encouragement of the relationship between Toni Albarosa and her daughter had been "a terrible mistake."

"And as to the prowler, Detective Inspector, why would I tell you? The housemaid in question is unreliable, given to hysterics — she probably imagined the whole thing."

"And Dan Mahy?"

"Who? Oh, that poor man — senile, I'm told. Lives in squalor, I believe, on the coast somewhere — his wife was on staff here. You knew that? He still hangs around the place, and we do what we can for him."

Outside the door of the marchesa's private sitting room, Moretti and Liz Falla stood and looked at each other.

"Nothing like a threat to the dysfunctional family to make all its members suddenly remember they are in complete accord about everything," observed Moretti. There was a faint smell of expensive cigar in the passage, and he was longing for a cigarette.

"That was the most frustrating —" began Liz Falla.

"Signor! Signorina! A moment of your time?"

A figure was approaching them down the long stretch of corridor with the bravura and élan of a luxury ocean liner, the floating skirt of her gown creating an ivory wake around her.

"Wow! Adriana Ferrini!" breathed Liz Falla, starstruck.

"Yes! That's me!"

Ferrini's rich laugh preceded her. She was dressed as if for a garden party in a floor-length chiffon and satin creation, her sumptuous mouth, flashing eyes, and almond skin perfectly made-up, her bronze-tinted hair arranged in carefully casual disarray around her internationally celebrated face. Where the marchesa wore gold so heavy it still bore the appearance of the nugget from which it came, Adriana Ferrini's choice of ornamentation was diamonds, sparkling imposingly in her ears and against the luminous satin of her gown.

The door of the marchesa's sitting room opened.

"Adriana. I was just about to ring for —"

"Donatella darling, I must speak to these two officers. Later."

Moretti's sixth sense, numbed by the previous half-hour's stonewalling, sprang to life. Standing between the two women, he could almost feel the animosity vibrating in the air as they exchanged their apparently innocuous banalities.

"My suite is on the next floor, officers — we could talk there."

Adriana Ferrini occupied a splendid set of rooms that faced the front and one side of the villa. The windows of her sitting room overlooked the far end of the long terrace, well away from the scene of Toni Albarosa's murder, and the noise, bustle, and lights of the film set. Motioning them toward two brocade-covered gilt chairs by a low marble table, she sat down on a matching sofa opposite.

"Would you prefer to speak in Italian?" Moretti asked.

"Of course, I heard you were fluent. No, no. I've spent much time in America. It would be better for the signorina, I think?"

The marchesa and the actress were built on the same scale — imposing women, with strong bones, long legs, and generous breasts. But there the resemblance ended. Where the marchesa's dark eyes suggested banked fires kept rigidly under control, only to erupt in anger when she felt threatened, Adriana Ferrini's emotions constantly bubbled to the surface during the course of the interview, her body moving to the rhythm of her mood, her hands constantly in motion. If ever, thought Moretti, one wanted to show Chief Officer Hanley the difference between a Neopolitan and a Florentine, one would only have to place the two women side by side.

"So," she began, "is it a compliment or an insult that neither of you have interviewed me yourselves?"

Before either Moretti or Liz Falla could respond, she threw her head back and roared with laughter, tossing her meticulously tousled mane of bronze hair. Even the lobes of her ears were magnificent.

"Am I not a suspect?"

"In a murder investigation," Moretti replied, "everyone without an alibi is suspect. But you are certainly not at the top of our list. We have, of course, read your statement. You asked to speak to us — is that because you wish to add to that statement?"

The amusement left Adriana Ferrini's face as swiftly as it had appeared, to be replaced by what looked like apprehension. "Do police officers give any importance to feelings, forebodings — what I can only call atmosphere? I cannot add any facts to my statement, but I need to give you my impressions."

Liz Falla thought of Moretti's instructions to her that morning and her own chilly frisson in the manor lodge, smothered as swiftly as it had been born.

"Impressions, Signora, can be crucial to an investigation. In my experience, women are particularly good at picking up the clues that lie in a smile, a frown, the way someone looks at someone else," Moretti replied.

Like whatever it was I sensed between you and your hostess, he thought to himself.

"I'm glad you feel like that. Because, even before Toni was killed, I had the feeling something was going to happen. Behind all this, someone is pulling the strings — only I don't know why."

"Pulling the strings — are you talking about the changes in the screenplay?"

"Among other things. When we first arrived here, everything was sweetness and light, but that has changed. I really don't know what Mario is up to, or why. Movie scripts get rewritten all the time, as I know only too well, but there is a feeling of — oh, I don't know — a hidden agenda to these changes. Mario and I were good friends, then he hit a bad patch, and now he's pulled out of it. Or so I thought. His wife is a lovely person, and he had everything going for him again."

"Have you asked him about the changes?"

"Yes. He talks about creative freedom and so on and so forth."

"Perhaps that's what it's all about."

"Look, Signor." Adriana Ferrini leaned forward, hands on her knees. "I'm not a member of any artistic elite. I'm not a contessa or a principessa or a marchesa. I come from peasant stock, and I came up the hard way. Now I have diamonds and furs, and homes in three countries, but I also have my sound peasant common sense. I know soft soap when I hear it, and bullshit when I smell it."

"So," said Moretti. "Give us your theory, Signora. Use that sound peasant common sense of yours. What, in your opinion, is the hidden agenda?"

"Family." It was said firmly, without hesitation. "Mario is under pressure from someone in the Vannoni-Albarosa family to make changes to the script — and now you're going to ask me why, aren't you? Well, I don't know. But if I had to put my money on anyone, it would be on Donatella. She spends a great deal of time with Mario and Monty Lord, apart from general get-togethers at mealtimes and cocktails and so on. She is manipulative and cold — a combination I detest."

"Then why are you staying here?"

"Because I can get more privacy. Not that anyone on your island has bothered me, but a few paparazzi appeared on the hotel doorsteps and were disappointed. Besides, the atmosphere has changed since I arrived."

"Then who do you think murdered Toni Albarosa — and why?"

"Why is easier. He was two-timing a member of the Vannoni family, right here at the manor. Who? Donatella? Gianfranco? Giulia?"

"Signora —" Liz Falla's tone was tentative, until Adriana Ferrini turned and smiled at her. "We were under the impression the marchesa was unaware of her son-in-law's affair."

Adriana Ferrini snorted and tossed her head. "Monty is such a romantic — he told you that, didn't he? Donatella has the poor naive man believing she is in need of protection from the wicked world, when it is Monty who should watch out for his virtue, and his heart."

"In your opinion," Moretti asked, "has the film been compromised? Is it in jeopardy? Is someone trying to stop it being made?"

"Are either of you married?"

Adriana Ferrini's unexpected response had both Moretti and Falla speechless for a moment and then they answered in unison.

"No."

La Ferrini gave one of her celebrated, throaty laughs. "*Che peccato*! The reason I ask is not to embarrass you, but because there is often a time in a marriage when the husband or wife says one to the other, 'I don't know what it is, but something is not right, I am not happy — and I can't put my finger on it, but it's not your fault, darling.' That's how I feel about all this, and I have even wondered if Toni's death has absolutely nothing to do with Mario's games with the script. I told you I could only give you impressions."

"This has been very useful, Signora, and we are grateful you have given us the time." Moretti stood up, and Liz Falla followed his lead.

"Oh, by the way — have any members of the family ever spoken about another house, apart from the manor?"

"Another house?" Adriana Ferrini thought a moment, and then shook her head. "No, not another house. But I know the Vannonis are not originally from Florence or Fiesole — one of my maids told me that when she heard about *Rastrellamento*. There's Anna's house in Fiesole, the marchese's apartment in Florence, and this place. I wouldn't know about Gianfranco — not my favourite character. Perhaps they had a place that was destroyed during the war — have you asked them? Is it important?"

"Possibly not. They say there is no other house."

"Ah." Adriana Ferrini stayed seated on the couch and extended her hand. "I hope I have not wasted your time."

"Far from it."

"They tell me you are a pianist, Signor Moretti. A jazz pianist. I must come and hear you play sometime."

"It would be an honour, Signora."

Moretti and Liz Falla were at the door when the actress called after them.

"Officers — if what my maid told me is true, you are

not dealing with Florentines here. It might be useful to remember that."

Outside the manor, night had fallen.

"What did she mean about them not being Florentines, Guv?"

"I think, Falla, she was talking about passion."

"You don't just mean sex, do you?"

"No."

Inside the police car, the phone started to ring. Liz Falla got in and answered it.

"The results are in from the post-mortem, Guv. No surprises. Estimated time of death about four o'clock in the morning, a single stab wound to the heart, massive internal bleeding, and little external bleeding. No signs that Albarosa put up a fight, no cuts to his arms or hands. Oh, and the blow was upward, suggesting the attacker was shorter than his victim."

"Or her victim," said Moretti. "It could have been a woman — a woman he knew from the sound of it."

"It doesn't rule out too many people, because Albarosa was tall. What now, Guv?"

"Home, Falla. No need to go back to the station. We'll drop off at your place first and I'll take the car on home. Do you live with your parents?"

"That would cramp my style, Guv," said Liz Falla cheerily, putting on the headlights and heading out of the courtyard. "I've got a flat out at La Salerie, on St. George's Esplanade by the old harbour. Used to share it with a feller, but I ditched him and kept the flat."

His partner's unself-conscious insouciance about her love life was light years away from the *sturm und drang* Moretti had gone through with Valerie. Maybe it was a generational thing — she certainly made him feel like Methuselah.

"Nice pub out there — watch out."

A dog appeared in the headlights, his eyes glowing red.

"Ooh, very *Hound of the Baskervilles*," said Liz Falla, hitting the brakes. "And there's his handler."

A uniformed figure emerged from the shadows, and Moretti rolled the window down and identified himself. The man called the dog to heel and waved them on. In the wing mirror, Moretti saw him watching them until they were out of sight.

Instead of heading out to the coast and taking Val des Terres back onto the Esplanade skirting the harbour, they came back into St. Peter Port by La Charotterie and Le Bordage, down the steep slope of Fountain Street, with the town church on their left. As they turned the corner onto the North Esplanade, Moretti said, idly, his thoughts elsewhere, "You brought us back in along La Valée de Misère, Falla. The Vale of Suffering."

His wandering mind snapped briskly back into the present as, beside him, his partner shuddered violently.

"Don't say that." Her voice was ragged, and she sounded angry.

"I'm sorry." Surprised, Moretti turned to look at her, but all he could see was her profile against the window of the car, the lights along the harbour wall flashing as they passed. "This was a nasty part of the town, but it was a long time ago, Falla. Four hundred years or more. Is that what's bothering you?"

"Yes, Guv. Sorry I spoke to you like that. Blame my grandmother, Guv, and her stories."

"Did she give you nightmares when you were a child?"

"Yes. More than that, she says we are descended from the Becquet family — you know the ones."

"Becquet? Weren't a few of them executed in the sixteenth century as witches?"

"More than a few. The family died out, but my grandmother insists that's who we are. My dad says there's no proof whatsoever, and she just likes to dramatize everything."

"Like your uncle Vern."

"Right." At least he had made her laugh. "Why anyone would want to claim that lot as ancestors beats me."

"Perhaps she needs them for some reason."

"Perhaps. Here we are."

Liz Falla brought the car to a halt alongside the sea wall on St. George's Esplanade. Moretti opened the car door and was assailed by the pungent smell of salt and seaweed from the bay beyond. The moon was almost full and he could just see on the horizon the dark humps of the islands of Herm and Jethou. He got out, walked across the pavement, and leaned over the sea wall. The tide was on its way out, leaving behind rock pools edged with acorn barnacles, dog whelk, and coralweed, quivering with the hidden lives of lugworm and shore crabs, long strands of thongweed floating in them like hair. He heard Liz Falla shut the door of the car, then the click of her heels as she walked around to join him.

"I live just across the road," she said. "I like it here. It's not spectacular, or postcard-pretty, mind you, but that's what I like. It looks, feels, and smells real."

"It's pleasant," Moretti agreed. "Why did you want to be in the police, Falla?"

"Me?" She sounded surprised at the question. "I didn't want to sit at a desk in Lloyds Bank or the Crédit Suisse. I needed excitement, but I wanted to find my excitement in the here and now, not in claptrap about four-hundred-year-old satanists." She shivered, but this time it was with mock fear. "How about you, Guv?"

How to encapsulate in a few words, as she had done, the twisting path that had brought him to Hospital Lane?

That would mean disclosure, exposure, confidences. His fault, he had asked the first question.

"Much the same reason as you. I'm not a desk person."

She must have sensed his withdrawal, because she immediately turned away from him.

"Goodnight, Guv. The keys are in the car."

Moretti watched her run lightly across the road and waited until she had unlocked the door of one of the terraced houses that curved along St. George's Esplanade. In the night silence he could hear the clack of the door closing, shutting off the light in the passage beyond.

chapter nine

By the time Sydney woke up, it was late afternoon. Much of her hangover had dissipated, but she was incredibly thirsty. She pulled on her kimono and padded on bare feet to the adjoining bathroom to splash her face with cold water, then returned to the bedroom. There was no sign of Gil, and she wondered if he was on the patio.

Surely not, she thought. But she had seen little of him since the murder of Toni Albarosa, so maybe he had got over his fear and returned there. The very fact he had been advised not to do that would have been spur enough.

In the bedroom, she removed a jug of ice water from the fridge, poured herself a glass, and drank it. Refilling the glass, she took herself through to the sitting room. There was no sign of Gil there.

"Gil?"

No answer. Sydney shivered, the glass frigid against her fingers. Across the stretch of Turkoman carpet on which they had last made love she saw the closed doors to the patio, and just above the backrest of one of the chaise lounges she could see the top of Gil's head, tipped to one side, motionless.

"Gil!" she called again.

There was no response. A chill of terror struck her, turning her stomach to ice. Dropping the glass on to the coffee table, Sydney ran to the door and threw it open.

"Gil!"

She flew across the patio and around the chair to face whatever was waiting there.

"Jesus Christ, woman! You scared the fucking daylights out of me."

Puffy-faced with sleep, her husband looked up at her. The striations left by the marchesa's nails were only just beginning to fade.

Sydney threw her arms around him. "I thought you were —"

"I'm not," he interrupted her. "Sorry to disappoint you."

"Don't say that." Overcome with relief, Sydney rested her face against his. "I was scared. What in the hell are you doing out here, anyway?"

"Trying to sleep before I was so rudely interrupted. It was stuffy inside, and I couldn't work out how to unlatch the damn windows." A lifetime of being picked up after and waited on had left Gil hopeless at many of the simpler technical manoeuvres that cropped up in everyday life.

"You should have come and woken me."

"Be it far from me to disturb your post-coital slumbers. Besides, you'd locked the bedroom door."

Sydney looked at her husband's bloated, scratched face with concern. The Gil she was familiar with would have screamed and banged on the door, battering it down if necessary.

"What's happened?" she asked. "Have you been out here all afternoon?"

"That I have not, and that's why I'm shagged out. I got a limo and went out to the manor, to see Mario."

"About the changes?"

"Right. I didn't have the chance to tell you about Monty's visit — just before you returned from your night of debauchery it was."

"It wasn't — I didn't —"

"Belt up, baby. I've got bigger problems than whether you had it off with superwoman and supercop."

The ice in Sydney's stomach felt the same as the minute before, melting the tenderness of her relief at finding him alive, but this time it was the old familiar chill of a relationship on the rocks.

"Baby'll belt up with pleasure on that subject. What problems?"

The chaise tipped perilously to one side as Gil swung his feet down. "Problems as to what the hell is going on."

"Going on with what? Surely it's just a question of a superstar director with a big head and big ideas? Maybe we should go home and let them get on with it — you know what it's like for writers on a film set."

"No."

There was something about her husband's unaccustomed gravity that made Sydney realize Gil was not off on one of his ego trips. "Mario seems — well, scared. Maybe he's back on the hard stuff again, I don't know. I had a hell of a time getting him on his own, then I cornered him in his trailer. He went all spiritual on me, told me he was being *guided* into the decisions he was making — went on about higher forces and trusting to other voices. It was like talking to a bloody yogi. When I tried my usual yelling and browbeating approach, he broke down, and next thing I know Monty's sidekick, Piero Bonini, comes rushing in and orders me off the set. But I'm not leaving it there, and I think I've finally made that clear. *Something* is going on."

"You're paranoid, honey. What could be going on? What happened — out here — is making you imagine things."

A cool wind was blowing in off the cliffs, and Sydney trembled in her flimsy wrap.

"Come inside, Gil. You shouldn't be sitting out here."

"Don't patronize me, Syd. I'm right, I know I am. Besides, I gotta reason to hang about a bit longer, and I ain't talkin' script changes now."

He was leering at her, but she knew the lechery in his eyes was not for her.

"Christ, I'm dying for a cigarette and a drink. Be a good little wifey, will you, and pour me a Scotch?"

He followed her inside, fumbling in his pocket for his cigarettes, humming to himself. *All, or nothing at all. A spectacularly inappropriate choice*, she thought, pouring a large Scotch into a large glass.

"I'm going back to bed," she said.

"I'll be going out again."

"I'd figured that out," Sydney said. "Research."

"Clever kitten. Don't you want to know who's my research assistant?"

"No."

"Pity. We could make it a threesome. Her idea — what a vixen! Vroom vroom! She likes you, sweetie-pie."

Sydney poured herself another glass of water, threw it in his face, and went back to the bedroom.

It was dawn when she woke and he still was not back. Sydney went across to the bedroom door and locked it. Then she went back to bed and cried herself back to sleep, swearing as she did so that she would never, ever humiliate herself that way again. She woke up again at eight o'clock, phoned room service, and ordered breakfast.

"Coffee, grapefruit, whole wheat toast. For one."

At nine o'clock, she began to worry.

Gil had stayed out on the tiles longer than this, many times, but ever since she had once — out of spite — reported him missing in Los Angeles and the press had got hold of it, he had taken to calling her and telling her his whereabouts. Gil had never been averse to a little gloating, anyway, and besides, he was not one for hanging around the morning after. Maybe, under the circumstances, she should be letting someone know.

Sydney got showered and dressed, then took a man's blue shirt out of the bedroom dresser. From the top pocket she pulled out a scrap of paper and dialed the number on it.

"Moretti."

The live voice startled her. "I thought I'd get an answering machine."

"Is that Ms. Tremaine?" It was said with incredulity.

"Yes. I took your number off your phone when I was —"

"I'm writing up my report before going to the station. That's how you got me. What is it?"

"It's Gil. He's been out all night. I didn't want it spread around the police station and the island, so I thought I'd —"

"Is this unusual, Ms. Tremaine?" She heard the tentative note in his voice.

"Ever since I reported him missing once and we had every tabloid in the States on our doorstep, he's let me know he's okay. It's unusual."

"I'll be right over. Don't open your door to anyone until I get there — it'll take me about fifteen minutes."

She heard him hang up the phone. Twenty minutes later he was with her, and Sydney was astonished at the wave of relief and pleasure she felt on seeing him.

"Sorry. It took me a little longer than I thought. My partner has gone out to the manor to see if anyone there knows anything, or has seen your husband."

Moretti came into the suite and closed the door. "Let's sit down, Ms. Tremaine, and go over what happened before your husband left you last night."

Carefully he took Sydney through the events of the evening. When she got to Gil's final remarks to her, she faltered, close to tears. Moretti leaned forward and took her by the hands. It was a gesture that surprised him quite as much as her.

"Now, Ms. Tremaine, I've got to get this straight. First, your husband reports *you* missing, and I find you at the Grand Saracen with Giulia Vannoni. Then you report *him* missing, and if it weren't for the fact this is a murder inquiry, I might wonder if this isn't a game you both play. Is it? You played games, didn't you?"

"Yes. Gil liked games. He needed them, he said, for his books. Research, he called them. When I said he needed them to cure his whisky droop, it was the only time he hit me."

She removed a hand from Moretti's and put it up to her face, remembering.

"Was it generally known that he — liked games?" Moretti asked.

"Oh, yes. That was part of it for Gil. Being the centre of attention, the rest of the world as voyeur."

"Who do you think he's with? Have you any idea?"

"That's just it — I think he may have taken his revenge by — oh God, I can't believe she'd do it, but then, what do I know about her?"

"Are you saying," said Moretti, "that your husband told you he was going to see Giulia Vannoni?"

"Not in so many words." With difficulty, Sydney repeated her last conversation with Gilbert Ensor. Then she wept against his shoulder, and Moretti put his arms around her, and tried not to think about Chief Officer Hanley.

* * *

It was cool out, and Sydney was glad she had brought a jacket. Beside her in the Triumph, Moretti was silent, his eyes on the road.

"You're a great pianist," said Sydney, "with a style of your own. Have you ever thought of turning professional?"

"Often. But I've always woken up in time. How about yourself? Have you ever thought of going back to the stage — to dance, or to act?"

"Sometimes. I too have always woken up in time. Reality bites."

Moretti nodded, but kept silent.

"This is nice," Sydney said after a while. "Yours, I guess, not an official car."

"Yes. My partner picked up the police car."

"She's pretty. Kind of Audrey Hepburnish."

"Is she?" He sounded surprised.

"You hadn't noticed? I guess I can't call you Ed, can I?"

"You already have. Well — Eduardo. You also told me you'd have to be a nun if you wanted to learn to read."

"Jeez, did I? Just at the moment, that doesn't seem such a bad idea."

"Learning to read?"

Her laughter dissolved as the Martello tower came into view.

"Oh God, Ed —"

"We don't know they're here. We only know that the marchesa said her niece was at her place at Icart. I just want us to sort this out quietly, so we can get on with the investigation. I'd like you to stay in the car — please, Ms. Tremaine," Moretti added, as she started to open the door. "Lock yourself in and wait for me here. I'm going to climb over the gate."

Sydney watched as Moretti straddled the gate and jumped over. Through the bars she saw the door of the Martello tower open. She saw Moretti walking up the path, and then she saw Giulia Vannoni coming down to meet him. A moment later, Giulia was running toward the car, with Moretti behind her.

"Sydney! *Idiota! Che stupidità!*"

There were various other epithets, but those she understood. She got out of the car and waited for Giulia to open the gate. She expected to be hugged, but instead Giulia took her by the shoulders and shook her.

"You — you —! Do you really think I'd do that to you? *Dio mio!*"

"Well, then." Moretti's quiet voice broke into Giulia's angry outcry. "Ms. Vannoni is on her own and has been all night. It would seem your husband was trying to get back at you. Both of you."

At that moment, Moretti's mobile rang.

"Okay, Falla. We'll be right over."

He put the phone back in his pocket and took Sydney by the arm.

"It may be nothing, but the dogs have picked something up."

"Dogs?" Sydney asked, bewildered.

"The dogs with the security firm — they know your husband's scent, of course." Moretti decided not to tell her that Liz Falla had picked up a piece of clothing from the hotel suite and taken it to the manor. "They are waiting for me. I suggest you stay here with Ms. Vannoni until I contact you."

"No. I'll come with you."

"I'll follow," said Giulia. She locked the gate again and left them, running back up the path with her powerful stride.

* * *

There was quite a crowd gathered around the entrance to the bunker. Monty Lord, Gianfranco Vannoni, Piero Bonini, and two of the actors. Moretti recognized Gunter Sachs, talking to a younger man whom he presumed was Clifford Wesley. There were also a couple of security guards and an excited dog, the only member of the gathering showing any animation. Liz Falla was by the door, and she left the group as soon as she saw Moretti. She looked warily at Sydney Tremaine.

"Mrs. Ensor, perhaps it would be better if —"

"What have you found?" Now beyond weeping or hysteria, there was a stillness about Gilbert Ensor's wife.

"Nothing — that is, the dog is indicating there is — something — in the bunker. We were waiting for you, Guv," said Liz Falla, turning to Moretti.

"Okay. Let's get this crowd away from here," Moretti said to one of the security guards, "and get hold of some lights — torches, flashlights, lamps, whatever." The guard spoke into his mobile and started marshalling the onlookers in the direction of the terrace. It was with relief that Moretti heard the arrival of the Ducati from the direction of the road, and watched Giulia Vannoni rounding the corner of the manor. He took Sydney Tremaine by the arm and led her away from the entrance.

"You stay with Ms. Vannoni for now — that's an order."

"I hear," said Giulia, pulling off her helmet. "We can stay here, Sydney, until *signor pianista* comes to get us."

Moretti was aware of two pairs of green eyes — one hostile, one haunted — watching him walk toward the dog handler.

"Tell me what happened."

The handler held out the linen jacket he was holding. "I took the dog round the grounds first — nothing. But when we got to the top of the path —" he waved in the direction of the two waiting women,

"— he led me straight down here, and he's been at this door ever since. Mr. Lord gave me a key, but the officer said to wait for you."

"Here they come with the lamps," said Liz Falla.

The darkness behind the steel door was palpable, thick as the smell of mould and decay in the airless space. The pressure in Moretti's chest eased as he saw the steady beams of light splitting the blackness ahead of them, motes of dust and moisture hanging in the air.

"You go ahead," he said to the handler, who held the jacket to the dog's nose. The animal whimpered excitedly, and pulled at his lead, heading for the nearest entrance, his paws slipping on the greasy stone.

"The command room," said Moretti. "I saw this with Mr. Lord."

Moretti, Liz Falla, and one of the security officers came around the corner after handler and dog and, at first sight, nothing appeared to be out of order. The retriever padded around the desk, followed by his master, and started to worry at something on the floor, whimpering and yapping.

"It's a shoe, sir," the man called. "A slip-on type. And the phone's been pulled down off the desk."

Before the rest of the search party could enter the room, the dog moved past them, pulling the handler along with him, heading farther along the corridor away from the entrance.

The ground sloped beneath their feet, taking them even farther down below the surface. The rays of light from their torches illuminated entrances and alcoves in the walls, the remnants of wires, cables, and pipes hanging on to the concrete. Rivulets ran in the gutters hollowed out of the concrete floor, humidity dripped from the curved brick ceiling overhead. The air was foul, and Moretti remembered stories he'd been told of how the Organisation Todt had sent down prisoners overnight as guinea pigs, canaries in these concrete pits, to see if they could breathe. Sometimes they died.

He was beginning to think they would have to break off the search until they could get some kind of breathing apparatus, when the handler called out, "There's an air shaft here."

They stood beneath it, gratefully inhaling the fresher air, but the dog was restive, pulling away from the group, anxious to move on.

"What do you want to do, sir?" his handler asked.

"Continue as long as we can."

Beside him, Liz Falla sneezed and rubbed her eyes.

With the dog leading the way, they stumbled along the narrow passage, which was suddenly intersected by another, wider passage, with the remnants of a light railroad track running down the middle. They all stopped abruptly at this point, as the dog hesitated a moment, and then turned to the right, accelerating rapidly.

Ahead of them and above them was a huge shaft. A glimmer of daylight shimmered down, faint but unmistakable. Leading up to the surface was an iron ladder fastened to the wall, its rungs rusted to the colour of lichen-covered rock. And at the foot of the ladder lay what looked like a heap of abandoned rags, but which they all knew was the body of Gilbert Ensor. The retriever sniffed at him and lay down beside him, his task completed.

He was dressed to kill, in a suit of navy wool and cashmere, a pale blue silk shirt with gold cufflinks in the sleeves, a gold tie clasp holding a paisley-patterned tie against his bloodied chest. He was curled up on one side, face hidden, the shirt buttons across his corpulent belly pulled open, revealing blood-soaked body hair, and he was wearing one shoe over one dark blue sock. The other sock lay close by.

And as he looked at the body curled up on the floor, all Moretti could think of at that moment was the memorial in the Underground Hospital: "This memorial is dedicated to the slaveworkers who died in Guernsey for Hitler's Organisation Todt." Gilbert Ensor was only the last of many hundreds who had lain dying on that floor, and other similar floors.

Just beyond the body something glinted in the diffuse light from the shaft. Treading warily around the edges of the space, Moretti picked his way around the body and bent down to see what it was.

It was a dagger — another dagger, but this one was not medieval. He had seen others like it in the display cases at La Valette, alongside the numbered arm bands worn by the workers, the picks, the bull whips. It was a storm trooper's dagger with a curved hilt, bearing the legend, "*Blut und Ehre.*" Blood and iron, Bismarck's grim axiom about Germany's survival.

For just a moment, the search party stood there looking at Gilbert Ensor, speechless. Then one of the security guards said, his voice shaking, "What in the name of all that's holy was he doing down here? We had the devil's own job getting him to stay inside a trailer, for God's sakes, when we wanted to run security checks. Said he couldn't abide confined spaces, but I suppose he was just being bolshie as usual."

Liz Falla walked across, bent down, and peered closely at one of the gold cufflinks on Gilbert Ensor's sleeve.

"*Cherchez la femme*, Guv?" she said to Moretti, and then sneezed again.

chapter ten

September 17th

The two women stood at the top of the path, waiting. It had started to rain and seeing them through the light mist, Moretti thought of the Widow's Walk at Saumarez Manor, the railing around the centre of the highest storey, as on some old houses in New England facing the sea. Sydney Tremaine would never again have to pace and wait and wonder where her husband was. This time he had set out on an adventure that had cost him his life. As he started to walk up the slope, she moved away from Giulia Vannoni and came toward him.

"He's dead, isn't he?"

She looked like one of the women beloved of the Pre-Raphaelites — Ophelia drifting in her watery grave, her skin bloodless, waxen.

"Ms. Tremaine — Sydney." He took her by the arm, and she did not resist as he led her to his car. He opened the passenger door, and she got in and sat there, obediently, like a child going on an outing. Moretti got in the other side and sat down. Her hands were folded in her lap, and she did not look at him.

"Yes. Your husband has been killed in the bunker, Sydney. A knife was used, but not the same type of knife. That doesn't matter now. I shall want you to tell me again every word you can remember of what he said to you last night. If we go into the manor, can you manage that?"

"No." She turned to look at him, and he could not read anything in her eyes. They seemed as blank as a painted surface. "Not the manor. I shall never go in there again."

"Then we'll go to the station, or back to the hotel, if you'd prefer. But for now I'd like someone to be with you. My partner, DC Falla, would —"

"Betty Chesler — I'd like Betty."

She was weeping now, tears falling on her hands.

"I'll get her."

Strike while she's vulnerable, he told himself. *Forget about the lipstick stain on your pillow, the faint scent left on the sheets that was probably dreamt up by your overheated imagination. Remember, this woman is not frail.*

"Who was on the cliff path, Sydney?"

"Giulia. Giulia running." She turned to look at him and this time he could read the expression in her eyes. She seemed angry. "She knows something. They all know something. About the daggers, Ed. It's all about the daggers."

Then she wept again, and when he put his arms around her this time he did not care about the onlookers, and gave no thought at all to Chief Officer Hanley.

When the SOC crew had taken over, Betty Chesler had left with Sydney Tremaine, and reinforcements had arrived to take statements, Moretti and Liz Falla went into the manor.

Giulia Vannoni was waiting for them in her aunt's sitting room. She was dressed in black: the black leather pants she had worn when Moretti had first seen her, a black shirt of some kind, and a black leather jacket that fastened over the firm disks of her breasts with one large leather button. The only note of colour was her scarlet lipstick that flamed against her tanned skin. Beneath the plucked arch of her eyebrows and the fringe of heavy black mascara her green eyes glittered with what looked like contempt.

"You wish me to accompany you to the police station, no? Trust the great minds of the police to go for the obvious."

"We have some questions to ask you in connection with the death of —"

"Gilbert Ensor. Are you going to handcuff me?"

"You're not under arrest, Signorina."

Which was, of course, true. So why would a highly intelligent woman be carrying on as if they were about to accuse her of murder? Maybe she saw herself as some sort of a decoy, running ahead of us and dragging her wing so that we'd follow her instead of — whoever and whatever it is in her family we should be following. *So let's do that,* he thought, *and see what happens.*

"Would you like to call a lawyer?"

"I will. Later. Let's get this farce started, and see how far it goes."

Giulia Vannoni walked between Moretti and Liz Falla, towering over the policewoman, her head about level with Moretti's eyes. *She must be nearly six feet,* he thought, *and her shoulders are about as wide as mine.* She said nothing during the journey, but her physical presence in the back of his car was as potent as the perfume she had worn the first time he met her.

*And she is capable of causing uproar, with her
connections. We'll have to tread damn carefully, or
Hanley will have me on the carpet, thought Moretti. I'm
sure he's hoping our murderer is some benighted foreigner
on the film crew who did this, and not a member of a
prestigious local family.*

Their arrival at Hospital Lane did not go unnoticed.
Giulia Vannoni strode through the building as though
she owned it, returning the stares of those passing by
with a parting of her scarlet lips that was more a rictus
than a smile. Once in Moretti's office she sat down on a
chair without waiting to be directed.

"Signorina —"

"How is Sydney?"

"Not good, as you can imagine. She asked for a
member of the film crew, Betty Chesler, to be with her."

"So she is safe with Betty? Of course, since you
suspect me, you would think that, wouldn't you?"

She gazed around Moretti's office as though the decor
offended her sensibilities, her eyes washing over him in
contempt, and Moretti knew he must establish his control
over the interview or she would run it, and him. Which
was how they were all here together, instead of back at
the scene of the crime, or interviewing Mario Bianchi —
which was what he had originally intended. He slammed
his hand down on the desk, and saw Liz Falla start, taken
by surprise at her Guv'nor's uncharacteristic outburst.

"Signorina, your arrogance is helping no one,
least of all yourself. We are in my office, not in an
interrogation room, and there is no tape recorder. You
are a smart woman — Mr. Lord calls you the cleverest
of the Vannonis — and yet you have deliberately drawn
attention to yourself as a possible suspect. Why did you
not tell me you were out running on the cliff path near
the Héritage Hotel when the first attempt was made on
Gilbert Ensor's life?"

"So. Sydney told you."

"Yes, but she waited until today. Did you ask her not to tell us?"

"Of course not. I suggested to her that maybe she wished whoever it was had not missed."

"What was her reaction?"

"Confused. That was some love-hate relationship, that one. Most are, in my experience." Giulia Vannoni leaned back in her chair, and Moretti sensed that her act of bravado — if that was indeed what it had been — was over.

"Do you have an alibi for last night?"

"No. I was alone in my *castello*. You accuse me of drawing attention to myself, but this is the fact. I am a suspect."

"Yes. But there is something more, Signorina, than your lack of alibi, or your presence on the cliff path. From the beginning I have felt a conspiracy of silence around these three episodes — from the apparently trivial incident of the damage to the costumes to the death of these two men. And I am certain that you, among others, could tell me a great deal more than you have. Why is that, Signorina?"

If I could capture the reactions of the Vannoni family to that kind of question, thought Moretti, *and bottle them, the contents of those bottles would all look exactly the same*. The sudden stillness of Giulia Vannoni's body was unmistakable, the sense of withdrawal palpable. Like the regret of Anna Albarosa for drawing attention to the family crest. If Giulia Vannoni could have hung up on him, as her uncle had done, the line would now have gone dead.

"I accused you of pursuing the obvious, Detective Inspector. I was wrong, it seems. You also pursue flights of fancy — or is it that you are more paranoid than I thought? A conspiracy theory now — what next!"

She laughed scornfully but she was rattled, Moretti could see it. He remembered why Hanley had been so keen to get him back. *You speak Italian.* In this investigation, it would take more than his knowledge of the language to uncover the truth; it would take an understanding of his father's people.

La famiglia, for instance.

For a man who rarely returned to his roots, his father talked a great deal about the importance of the family in Italian society — not in such grandiose and abstract terms, but it permeated his conversation about his native land. In spite of a growing divorce rate, a dropping birthrate, and the perennial problem of unfaithful wives and husbands, lovers and mistresses, that ancient institution remained the crux, Moretti knew, of the most profound and significant elements in Italian society. Its hold on the loyalty of its members was as tenacious as ever, the basis of much that was precious and good — and some that was bad.

This woman had talked about love-hate relationships, which was how his father had spoken about family: family loyalty, family obligation. He could only hope that the element of surprise would work with Giulia Vannoni where bullying or reasoning would be so much wasted breath. He asked his next question without preamble or explanation.

"This house, Signorina. The one near the sea. Where is it, and what does it have to do with these murders and *Rastrellamento*?"

He heard the intake of breath, and then she said, "What is all this crap? I want a lawyer."

Without another word, Moretti picked up his phone and handed it to her.

"What a ball-breaker, eh, Guv!"

"Bit of a misnomer in her case, Falla, but I know what you mean."

"What with one thing and another, I forgot to tell you — Giorgio phoned last night. He's found the birth. Sophia Maria was born in Pistoia to Maria Colombo. Father unknown."

"Pistoia was my godmother's home town. Father unknown? Then where does the name Catellani come in?"

"She was adopted by a Franco and Rosa Catellani. Now he's checking on the whereabouts of Sophia Maria — the Catellanis' home town was given as Montecatini, near Pistoia and it seems she's still alive — or at least, there's no record of a death."

So his godmother had given birth to a child out of wedlock. And had kept silent, a silence only broken after her death. A complete human life, obliterated by silence.

"Please thank him for me." He had completely forgotten about Sophia Maria Catellani. "We're going back to the manor, but first I want to see if any of the crime-scene investigators have returned."

As Moretti and Liz Falla came downstairs, some of the crew were just coming into the building chattering like magpies, the adrenalin still pumping from the scene in the bunker.

"Hey, Moretti. We've left everything like you said, but there's a problem."

"Problem?"

Of course there's a bloody problem, thought Moretti. *There's a mountain of problems, a bunkerful of problems. There's a family conspiracy problem, and the fact that I may be pursuing a chimera anyway. A red herring of a house. Because, above all, there's a change of dagger motif problem. The roots of this business may well be right here on the island, and not in Florence, or Fiesole, or the Maremma after all.*

"Yes. The medico says there may be trouble establishing time of death, because of the temperature and humidity down there — Christ, what a hellhole! He may call in a pathologist from the Met for a second opinion."

"I see. Could he at least establish if death was immediate — as in the case of Albarosa?"

"Of that he's sure. It wasn't. There was a struggle — Ensor fought back. And that's not all. There's a possibility the dagger wasn't the cause of death. Seems the victim crawled to where he died. And the doc thinks there's a chance he died of suffocation. Or fright. He'll get a preliminary report to you tomorrow."

"That confirms one thing for us, Falla," said Moretti as they crossed the courtyard together, "Toni Albarosa was probably surprised to see whoever it was on the terrace, but was not aware he was in danger. Gilbert Ensor did not see the person he expected to see, and knew immediately he was in trouble."

"Couldn't he have been forced down there?"

"Possibly, but I think he was lured there, and I'm sure you're right — he thought he was going to an assignation. From something he said to his wife I think he was expecting some sort of erotic thrill — maybe having sex in that fake command centre — I don't know. For a man like Gilbert Ensor, sexual experimentation was as necessary as — as —."

"A good single malt, Guv?"

Moretti looked at his colleague, who was backing the Mercedes out of the narrow parking space with practiced ease.

"I was going to say bread and butter, but that's certainly more accurate in Ensor's case."

"Guv —" Moretti sensed that his partner was treading delicately, "— isn't it possible his wife has something to do with this? I mean — I shouldn't be saying this as a police officer, but can you blame her? And couldn't she and Giulia Vannoni be in this together?"

"Which is why I've arranged for a police guard on the door of her hotel suite. And since there is also the possibility she herself is in danger, the guard serves a double purpose. As for the signorina, it's more likely she was the decoy for someone other than Sydney Tremaine. When we get to the manor, park around the back, Falla. We are going to obey the Vannonis' commands, and go in through the tradesmen's entrance."

"May I ask why, Guv?"

"Because the only mini-break we've had on this case came from a contact of the Vannonis' servants. I want to see if we get lucky again."

Security had obviously been beefed up since the discovery of Gilbert Ensor's body in the bunker. As Liz Falla brought the car to a halt alongside a jeep and a row of motorbikes, they were immediately approached by one of the private security staff, who peered into the car, acknowledged them with a touch of his cap, and moved on. The back door of the manor was locked, and Moretti rang the ponderous iron bell pull alongside it. The sound reverberated inside the house.

"You'd expect a zombie or something to answer that, wouldn't you, Guv?" said Liz Falla with a theatrical shiver.

The door was opened instead by a tiny black-clad woman, who fixed them with a baleful glare.

"Yes?"

"Police," said Moretti, pulling out his identification.

"You go front," she said, starting to close the door.

"Signora, come sta? Italiana?"

"Si." Cautiously, the door opened a little wider.

"Mi chiamo Eduardo Moretti. Mi padre era Italiano — da Pistoia."

"Ah — Pistoia!" The door opened wider again.

Still talking, Moretti eased himself into the hallway, with Liz Falla close on his heels.

Where the passage of time and the outlay of money had bestowed a mellow richness and a warm and mature patina on the formal and family areas of the Manoir Ste. Madeleine, the servants' areas of the building were in need of, at the very least, a fresh coat of paint. The corridor in which they stood had a general air of neglect, with faded wallpaper peeling off the walls, and some rather ratty linoleum underfoot.

"Signora, your name is —?"

"Teresa Stecconi. I've been housekeeper here longer than I care to remember. Oh, what a business this is! That poor man, and the poor signora and her fatherless children!"

"Indeed. You know Anna Albarosa?"

"Of course. I've known her since she was a little girl. I came here with them, to help them move, and I never went back. They are my family — I have no one else."

"So you knew Patrizia."

"Of course. Now, *she* knew the marchese *and* his father when he was a little lad — such a wild one, the marchese's father, she said. Who would have thought he'd become such a pillar of society!"

"So he was wild, but aren't all young ones wild? Like the marchese's son, Gianfranco, for instance?"

The old woman snorted. "Ah, Gianfranco! He is *signor perfetto* compared to the marchese at his age. Mind you, that was just boyish wildness, not the crazy madness that Patrizia used to speak of. But that's all gone now. Still waters run deep, she used to say. Who would have guessed?"

"Crazy madness? This would be when the family were still in Florence, or Fiesole?"

"No, no, before that. But I wasn't with them then."

"So," said Moretti, hoping that he sounded reasonably interested but not interrogatory. "This would be when she was with them at the other house."

Teresa Stecconi looked sharply at Moretti. "You know about that? That's the past. Bury the past, I always say, with its dead."

"But now there are dead in the present, Signora, and perhaps the reason for that lies in the past."

Moretti watched the shutters come down. The old woman turned away from him.

"We are here now," she said. "I have left the memories — the bad and the good — behind me. Patrizia should have done the same thing, always moaning about how much better it was — there. *Buona sera, ispettore.*"

She turned and, with a speed that took both Moretti and Liz Falla by surprise, she zipped off down a side corridor and out of sight.

"So, where does that leave us, Guv?" asked Liz Falla, peering after the spritely octogenarian.

"I'm tempted to say in limbo, but that's not quite true. What she told me was interesting, because she more or less confirmed there was another house. And something more than that — something happened in that house that was so terrible everyone has been sworn to silence."

"I must ask you, Detective Inspector — where have you been? The security guard says he saw you into the house about half an hour ago!"

Flushed with anger, gold chain rattling, the marchesa faced Moretti across the broad expanse of the main salon, which was still encircled with lights and cameras. Beside her sat Monty Lord, holding her hand. He looked haggard and worn.

"Marchesa — there has been another murder, as you know, and part of my responsibility is to check the security of you and your family."

"There was no need to disturb my domestic staff — and we have private security for that."

"Need I remind you they were unable to save the life of your son-in-law, Marchesa."

Thank heavens Monty Lord is here, thought Moretti. *He seems to have a calming influence on her.* The producer sat staring at them across an elaborate malachite table, as though hoping for some kind of miracle.

"This is a disaster, Detective Inspector Moretti. A tragedy. I got in from the shoot only to hear that Gil was missing. Selfish as it may sound, I must tell you that I have been on the phone to our lawyers to check we are covered for such an eventuality, that we may go on filming *Rastrellamento*. It would help nobody and serve no useful purpose if the whole project went up in smoke."

"And are you?"

"Covered? Yes. Death is covered — the nature of it is not significant. If you understand what I mean."

"Of course. You say you were on the set — the shoot, you called it?"

"Yes. This morning we were filming some of the action scenes out at L'Ancresse. Mario was not with us, he needed a rest, he said. So much of the war stuff is logistical, and his associate director had plenty to be getting on with."

"Where is he now?"

"Sedated." It was the marchesa who answered. "He was very upset."

Moretti decided to leave that for now. Instead he turned his attention to Monty Lord.

"I understand you went to see Gilbert Ensor yesterday morning."

"Yes. I wish now I'd kept an eye on Mario, because I knew how angry Gil was. But I'd no idea he'd get up the energy to come here and that they would run into each other when Mario returned from checking the bunker."

"Checking the bunker?"

"Yes. We had planned to start shooting there in the

next few days. Now, of course, it's yet another scene of the crime, isn't it?"

"I'm afraid so. When you took me down there, Mr. Lord, the door was locked. Was it always kept locked?"

"Supposedly."

"Who had keys?"

"Myself, Mario, and I think there was a key in the house — wasn't there, Donatella?"

"Yes. When this happened, I went to make sure it was still there and it was."

"Where was 'there,' marchesa?"

"In a drawer in my bedroom. I had two copies made for Monty and Mario."

"I see. Was anyone around when Gilbert Ensor and your director had their confrontation?"

"I was. It was unbelievable." The marchesa was disturbed enough to get up from her seat by Monty Lord and start pacing. "I thought Gilbert was going to attack Mario physically — hit him, I mean, not just scream at him. We were all getting used to that."

Spoken with the contempt of one who has conveniently forgotten her own assault on Ensor after the first murder, reflected Moretti. "Did he have to be restrained?" he asked.

"Yes. By me. He was out of breath from just the screaming. It wasn't difficult."

I believe it, thought Moretti. *A very strong woman, this one. Like her niece.*

"Then what happened?"

"Piero Bonini came in and ordered Gilbert off the premises. He told him he would get an injunction to keep him away from the shooting, if he did not do so voluntarily."

"Where did all this take place?"

"Out on the terrace."

"So any number of people saw what happened?"

"Yes. It was disgraceful. Mario tried to reason with him, explain the nature of the changes, talk about his personal philosophy of filmmaking, but he was shouted down."

"Did you see Signor Bianchi leave, Marchesa?"

"Yes. It was I who took him away when he broke down, and I made sure he got something to eat and a rest before he went into town. He had an appointment."

"With whom, do you know?"

There was an exchange of glances between the marchesa and Monty Lord, and it was Monty Lord who replied.

"Mario has regular appointments with a psychiatrist, and we were able to make a similar arrangement for him here. I imagine you know he has had problems with substance abuse in the past."

"And those problems are, you are sure, part of the past?"

"I'm certain of it."

Moretti stood up. "If Signor Bianchi has taken sedatives, there is little to be gained by questioning him now. We will come back."

As they left the room, Moretti looked over his shoulder. The marchesa had her head on Monty Lord's shoulder and he was patting her hand. Beneath the shining dome of his shaved head, the expression in the American producer's eyes was panic-stricken.

"Now, are you sure you'll be all right?"

Betty Chesler thumped the pillows behind Sydney Tremaine's head and tugged at the bedcovers with the grim determination of someone erecting ramparts around a threatened and vulnerable keep. The two women had met on the Pavlova movie and had kept in touch with the odd letter and card over the years.

"Thank you for coming with me, Betty. I'm so grateful. I'll be fine now — I'll take one of the sedatives you put by the bed and get some sleep."

"You know, pet — it's hardly the time to mention it, but you should think of getting back into the swing of things. You have so much to offer."

"Oh, Betty, honey, I couldn't dance professionally again!"

"I don't see why not, but I was thinking of how well you worked with those children on the Pavlova set with their dancing. It's been a while, but people still remember you. You should take advantage of that while you can."

"Oh Betty, I don't know —"

But the thought lingered after Betty Chesler had left. Sydney heard her speaking to the police guard outside the door, and then there was silence.

She leaned over the side of the bed, fingered the bottle of sleeping pills, and shuddered at the thought of sleep. The last thing she wanted to do was sleep, perchance to dream. She got out of bed, took a shower, and made herself a coffee.

For the first time in her relationship with Gil she was grateful he was an only child and both his parents were dead. In the past, she had thought that being a much-adored child had only made matters worse when fame arrived on the scene, because it had prolonged his indulged childhood into a self-centred manhood. Gil expected to be worshipped. She couldn't bear to think of where he was now, and what would happen before he could be laid to rest — a new state of being, or non-being for Gil. Laziness came naturally to him, but not restfulness.

Sydney forced her mind away from the thought of what had to be done over the next few days, and concentrated on what Betty Chesler had said. Once or twice she had suggested to Gil she might like to put her talents to some use, only to be discouraged. *No*, she thought, *not just discouraged. Derided*. Gradually, the fragile flower of hope and belief in herself had withered and, she had thought, died. It would be ironic if it took the death of her husband to bring it back to life again.

Sydney finished her coffee, went into the bedroom, and pulled out a leotard from a drawer. She changed into it, went through into the sitting room, and put some music on the stereo. Slowly, with a sense of strangely unbroken continuity rather than that of a return after an absence, she started to put her body through the sequences followed by every classical dancer anywhere in the world.

About an hour later, she stopped. She went back into the bedroom, put on a tracksuit over her leotard and a pair of running shoes, and made a phone call. Then she unlocked the door of the hotel suite.

Outside the door of the suite sat a very young policeman. Sydney smiled at him, prettily.

"Thank you for watching over me. I'm just going down to the lobby to buy cigarettes — I'm gasping."

The constable jumped to his feet, eager to help. "I'll get them, miss. What kind do you want?"

"Oh no!" Sydney looked at him in alarm. "I can't — I just can't stay here with no one outside. I just can't." She allowed a note of hysteria to enter her voice.

"Then I'll come with you."

"And leave this place unattended? After what happened out on the patio I could never relax again, even if you *searched* it. Please — just stay watching for me, will you? If I'm not back in five minutes, then, of course, I'd expect you to come after me — okay?"

"Five minutes." The young constable looked worried and confused.

"Right — thanks!"

She ran down the corridor, waving as she went.

Five minutes. *Please God*, she prayed, *may the taxi get here in five minutes.*

The lobby was quiet, with only the desk clerk in attendance.

"Mrs. Ensor — should you —?"

"I'm going in to the police station — they're sending a car. The constable is staying to watch over my suite."

Beyond the revolving doors, a taxi was pulling up. Sydney whisked through the doors and into the car.

"The tower on Icart point."

As they exited through the gates of the hotel, she saw the young police officer standing in the doorway with the desk clerk.

She had no problems unlocking the gate, and the key worked easily in the lock of the Martello tower door. There was no sign of Giulia's Ducati on the terrazzo by the door, and the place was in darkness. Feeling for the switch, Sydney found it and put it on, feeling relief at the sudden brilliance that flooded the space. She didn't need a cigarette, but she needed a drink, badly.

In Giulia's small kitchen she found the Aperol and poured herself a glass. It did not produce instant cessation of pain, but it did give an illusion of pleasure.

About fifteen minutes later, she heard a key in the door. Giulia appeared, pushing the Ducati ahead of her. She started when she saw Sydney and her hand went to the pocket of her leather jacket.

"Don't kill me. All I took was a little Aperol. A large Aperol."

"What are you doing here? You should be under guard somewhere, not tempting fate. *Idiota*!"

"You called me that before, I remember. Okay, so you didn't sleep with Gil, but you did keep your mouth shut about — whatever it is that's behind all this. About that I am no idiot, Giulia."

Giulia paused, sighed and took off her jacket. "*Bene*.
I'll tell you about the past, but don't think I have the
answer, because I don't. I'll have some of that also."

They carried the drinks into the living area and sat
together on a sofa covered in soft black leather.

"The past, Giulia — how can this be about the past?
Gil only spent time in Italy when he was researching
Rastrellamento. Why kill him?"

"*Rastrellamento* is about the past. Do you know if
he based the book on any actual events?"

"Not as far as I know, but Gil didn't talk much
about the process of writing — at least, not to me.
Knowing Gil, I think he'd have preferred the world to
feel *Rastrellamento* was entirely a product of his genius.
His imagination."

"Perhaps it was, but I think he stumbled on to
something. And I know that clever policeman feels the
same way — that's where I've been, at the police station."

"Clever policeman — Ed Moretti?"

"You are on first-name terms?" Giulia raised her
eyebrows.

"Yes — well, I am, anyway, and I spent a night in his
bed, and none of this is as it sounds."

"Pity. You could do worse."

"I did. I married Gil." Sydney put down her empty
glass. "So far I've answered most of the questions,
Giulia. Tell me about the past. Your father, I guess, was
a Vannoni."

"My grandfather. My mother was not married,
and she herself was the child of rape — no, don't say
anything, not yet." Giulia got up, went into the kitchen,
and brought the bottle back with her. "These things
happen all the time, yes, since the beginning of time,
and this was wartime. The man who was actually my
grandfather was probably not a German, and possibly a
partisan, but I don't know. It was a small village, and one

of the agreements between my grandmother and the man who married her and became father to her child was that she would never say, never talk about it. I imagine she was quite happy to go along with the deal, no?"

"I'm sure. So a Vannoni made an honest woman out of your grandmother? Forgive me, Giulia, but with what I know about your family, I find that hard to believe."

Giulia threw back her head and laughed. "*Cara*, you know us well in so short a time! There were what the lawyers call mitigating circumstances: first, my grandfather was the younger son, and second — and much, much more significantly, he was almost certainly what was then called a degenerate. A homosexual. He had shown no desire to marry and had never been in the least interested in women. Given how things were then, it is unlikely he got much further than that. Oh, there was talk, and he was told by the family to silence the gossip. So he married my grandmother, who had been a close friend since schooldays, and was a sweet and kind husband to her and father to my mother. My mother was a wilful and wild woman, quite unlike her mother and stepfather — there is a lot of her in me. She became pregnant and refused to name the father — there is a chance she didn't know who the father was — and so I was born, and kept the Vannoni name."

"So, by blood, you're not a Vannoni at all. Is your mother alive?"

"No. She died when I was eight, and I was raised by the marchesa. Donatella is a difficult, proud woman, but I will always have a place in my heart for her, because she was good to me, and treated me like family."

Sydney reached out and poured herself another glass of Aperol. "I'm trying to work out how Gil's death — and Toni's — could have anything to do with your unknown father and your grandfather."

"Maybe so, maybe not, but I think it has to do with another mystery in the Vannoni past. Not about my step-grandfather, but about his sister, Sylvia Vannoni, the eldest child. I didn't even *know* there was a sister; I thought there were just two brothers. But about ten years ago, I decided to look into my past." Giulia's smile had more of pain than pleasure in it. "At that time I was facing up to the fact that I preferred girls to boys, *cara*, and that made me wonder if my grandfather Vannoni was indeed gay, and if he was, in fact, my real grandfather. It turned out that he was probably gay, but that he was *not* my grandfather."

"How did you find this out?"

"Not from records. It was much easier to conceal the truth during wartime, and records were often not kept, or were inaccurate. I talked to every old family retainer I could find — there were more of them around ten years ago. And the woman who told me about Sylvia once lived at the manor. Her name was Patrizia. So the chances are that someone else on the island knows about this — and that is how your clever policeman friend asks the questions he asks."

"Giulia," Sydney stood up, feeling her legs shaking beneath her with stress, anxiety and Aperol combined, "shouldn't Ed Moretti be told anything that would help him catch Gil and Toni's killer?"

"But what do I know, in fact? Will any of this help him catch the man, or woman?"

"Woman?"

"It could be. I think your policeman friend has even wondered if you and I are together in this." Sydney sat down again, and Giulia gave her a wry glance. "And you come here, no, is that what you're thinking? Family honour is just as important to a woman, and this is about honour, of that I'm sure. Patrizia told me that Sylvia died, and that she was forbidden to speak about her, or even to remember she had ever lived."

"But that's terrible! Wiping out the memory of a

human being's existence from the face of the earth! I still don't understand why you won't tell the police."

"Because it's a mystery no one in the family will talk about. Because when I tried to talk to Donatella about Sylvia, for the first and only time in my life I was afraid of her. She threatened to throw me out of the family and, more importantly, out of the family business. I love what I do, and I would be lost without my professional life. In a toss-up between Donatella and Eduardo Moretti, Donatella wins, hands down."

"You say all this goes back to the war years — could it have anything to do with the war?"

"I think so. In *Rastrellamento* there is a love affair, isn't there, between the daughter of the house and an escaped British prisoner, and I wonder if that is what happened to the unknown Sylvia. Did she have a child by the prisoner? Did she die in childbirth? Did the child survive?"

"Where did all this happen? Couldn't you get some answers from people living in Fiesole or Florence?"

"If that's where it happened. But it didn't. It happened, I think, at another house. A house that no one talks about, because they say there never was another house."

"Who says there *was* another house?"

"Patrizia. She said it was closer to the sea, and claimed that she first worked for the Vannoni family in the Maremma, where she came from."

"Then it must be there."

"Unlikely, at that time. The Maremma then was a wild, uncivilized place. Patrizia may well have come from the Maremma, but any great house must have been on the edge of the area, to the north or to the east."

"So, Gil was killed because he told a fiction he thought his own, that was a fact about your family. What about Toni?"

"Ah, Toni. An oversexed son of a bitch who would have sold his soul for the right price. I have asked myself whether he gave away something to — oh, I don't know, somebody working on the movie — for forty pieces of silver."

"Who, Giulia — who?"

This time it was Giulia who stood up, towering over Sydney. "Who. The big question, yes. I think — I think it could be Donatella. Oh yes, I think it could be. Not on her own, perhaps, but with the help of someone else. Gianfranco perhaps, although I think he has not enough courage. I think you, but especially Mario and Monty, should be careful."

"Shouldn't you warn them?"

"And have Donatella find out? That is why I cannot tell Moretti and you must not. He will have to work it out on his own."

"Why daggers, Giulia? It could be someone crazy."

"Oh, they are crazy all right — crazy enough to use a specific weapon, because they are saying something to those in the know. Come on." Giulia pulled Sydney to her feet. "Let's get you back to your hotel before the police send out a search party for you. And you know what is the only thing worth remembering from this conversation?"

"To keep my mouth shut?"

"That whoever it is, is crazy. That's the only thing worth remembering, Sydney. Carry the key I gave you, always. No one in my family has keys to this place, and no one knows that you have one."

Night was falling when they left Giulia's castello. Against the darkening sky the Martello tower took on a more sinister aura as its shadow against the ground reached out to touch the two women walking the Ducati to the gate. Sydney could hear the sound of her own breathing, swift and shallow with tension. Beside her, Giulia lengthened her stride.

chapter eleven

"**S**he fooled you all right, PC Brouard — Mrs. Ensor doesn't smoke. Fortunately she got safely back, and we know where she went because of *how* she got back. On a Ducati. We've also had her destination confirmed by the taxi driver."

The morning sun filtered in through the windows of the crowded incident room at Hospital Lane. The place was full and there was electricity in the air, which had something to do with the sensational nature of the investigation and more to do with the anticipated arrival of Chief Officer Hanley at any moment, and the real possibility of a clash of personalities between Moretti and the head of the forensics crew, Jimmy Le Poidevin.

Jimmy Le Poidevin was a heavy-set man in his forties, short of both fuse and stature, given to bombast. His outbursts were usually because he objected to having his forensic conclusions and insights questioned by anyone, and because he tended to step out of his own field of expertise and interpret the medical evidence. Although Moretti knew this was tempting because there was no coroner on the island, he always attempted to rein in Le Poidevin's flights of forensic fancy.

Most officers at Hospital Lane tended to back off and leave him alone because he was good at his job, but Moretti saw that as no reason not to push from time to time. And Le Poidevin, being an emotionally volatile extrovert himself, had assumed that Moretti's customary reserve hid a docile and acquiescent nature. Discovering in one spectacular confrontation that he was wrong did not stop him repeating the behaviour.

Moretti transferred his attention from the mortified PC Brouard to Liz Falla, who was sitting beside him, her notepad open on the table in front of her. "DC Falla's inquiries confirm that Gilbert Ensor took a taxi to the manor at about eleven-thirty, and the driver dropped him near the trailers used by the film crew."

"Yes." Liz Falla took over, and Moretti was again aware of the depth of her voice. "The driver says he was, I quote, 'Full of himself and on and on about himself.' He doesn't seem to have said anything too specific about what he was up to, but the driver got the impression he was meeting a woman. When I asked him why he said, 'You don't get in the state he was in about a bloke.'"

There was a ripple of laughter in the room, quickly suppressed as Moretti held up his hand. "Because of the large number of people involved in this film project and the number of alibis and statements we have to check, I have Chief Officer Hanley's permission to get some extra help. My main concern is that information we have withheld stays that way, which is why I have called this meeting. The second dagger, for instance. Go on, DC Falla."

From under her notebook Liz Falla pulled a handful of papers. "These are printouts of various Internet websites selling daggers of all kinds. The one used in the Albarosa murder, and the hotel patio and costume incidents, is a copy of a seventeenth-century Italian dagger in the Wallace Collection in London — almost. It is described as 'designed for the thrust and is often viewed as the favorite of assassins,' and it looks as if the attacker had these specially made for him, or her. The dagger in the Ensor murder is the genuine article, carried by some members of the Hitler Youth in the war, and that gets trickier. Not everyone selling something like this is that keen on publicizing it. I've checked with the Underground Hospital, the Occupation Museum, and La Valette Museum, and there's nothing missing from their display cases. Nor has anyone made inquiries about purchasing a similar dagger. I was reminded more than once that there may be others in private hands on the island." Liz Falla turned to Moretti, who took over.

"Apart from the fact that DC Falla had to make inquiries about the Hitler Youth dagger, we have withheld that information and I want it to stay that way. As you know, the murder of Gilbert Ensor has attracted attention, and we have a few members of the mainland press on the island. Now, PC Brouard, a chance to redeem yourself — you're a computer buff, I'm told, so I'm giving you the task of going through every site you can find, anything you can find, about daggers made to order. Possibly in Italy."

Moretti picked up Liz Falla's papers and held them out to a stunned PC Brouard, who took them without comment.

"PC Roberts, PC Le Mesurier, PC Clarkson — divide up all the statements between you and go through them with a fine-tooth comb. What are you looking for you're going to ask me, right? The answer is — I don't know. There are dozens of people without alibis because both murders took place at night. But watch out for inconsistencies, discrepancies, stories that seem too pat, or stories that seem too alike. Okay, Jimmy," The tension in the room went up, "go over the basic nuts and bolts stuff from the murder scenes — similarities, differences, that sort of thing."

Jimmy Le Poidevin raised an eyebrow. "You want me to tell you what you already know, Moretti? We've been over this, and you got my report, didn't you?"

Moretti smiled. His smile made Liz Falla think of an old children's fable in some book she'd had as a child. Something about a crocodile smiling. "Humour me, Jimmy. Perhaps it will suddenly transmogrify into new and important revelations."

"Well, for a start, there's little similarity between the two crime scenes, for all that both murder weapons are daggers."

"Go on," said Moretti.

"First of all, the Albarosa death looks like it was either accidental or opportunistic and — either by luck or good management — it was quick and clean. The Ensor murder, on the other hand, is clearly premeditated — I mean, it must be, mustn't it, or else how did they both get down there in the first place? And whoever did it must have underestimated the victim, because he fought for his life the length of that corridor to where we found him. We're still waiting for the final results, but the P.E.H. medics are of the opinion it was death by vagal inhibition."

Here we go, thought Moretti.

"In layman's terms, he died of fright — like suffocation, really." Jimmy Le Poidevin turned and faced the assembled officers, as if he were in a lecture hall. "The vagus nerve sends a signal to the brain that makes the heart stop beating. Mind you, he'd have bled to death in the end, anyway — he had one hell of a slash in the belly. Time of death is estimated at between midnight and two a.m."

"I thought they were getting a second opinion on that," observed Moretti quietly. Jimmy Le Poidevin turned away from his audience.

"P.E.H. think they can take care of it themselves," he said, his face reddening.

"Then I'll talk to them myself. What I want from you are the forensic details from the two crime scenes —"

"Nuts and bolts, I know. I'm sure most of the officers here have no need of a frigging forensic kindergarten class" — a dramatic pause — "even if you do, Moretti."

The crocodile smile again. "Don't tell us, Jimmy. Show us. You say Ensor fought his way along the length of the passage. How do you know that? Coded messages written in the dirt? Second sight? A voice from beyond the grave? Give us a frigging forensic kindergarten class, Jimmy. That's what you're here for."

"Jesus Christ!" The red in Le Poidevin's face had deepened to an ugly purple. "Don't tell me what I'm here for, you arrogant bastard!"

The door opened, and Chief Officer Hanley joined them. He surveyed Moretti, Jimmy Le Poidevin, and the assembled staff with a melancholy sweep of the eyes.

"Good morning."

There was a muttered ripple of "good morning, sir"s around the room, and silence fell as everyone waited for him to speak.

"I trust I didn't hear what I just heard," he said, fixing his chief forensic officer and Moretti with the gloomy stare of one who knew only too well what he had just heard. "We have enough problems to be going on with without pitched battles between senior officers. But I'll deal with this another time, not in public in the incident room. DI Moretti — you have, I trust, explained just how — stalled, this investigation is. We need results, and we need them fast, or we will have Scotland Yard here before you can say —" Here, Hanley himself stalled, and Moretti bit his tongue on filling in "— eagle-eyed, sir?"

"— Bob's your uncle," Hanley continued. "So, on the principle that six or seven heads are better than one —" this with a reproachful glance at Moretti, "— I have given DI Moretti some extra help. I realize it may be too much to ask, but it would be most welcome if some sort of advance could be made before my scheduled holidays. Now, are there any questions?"

"Sir," PC Clarkson had his hand up first, "this second dagger — do you think this has anything to do with the Occupation?"

"It certainly opens up that particular can of worms," Moretti replied.

"Then, shouldn't we ask questions locally — I mean, wouldn't it help?"

"We may have to do that eventually. But not right now."

"Surely, Moretti, we must now accept the fact that there may well be a Guernsey connection?" asked the chief officer, his irritation barely concealed, to Jimmy Le Poidevin's undisguised relish. "I'm reluctant to do so, but I feel we should be exploring local possibilities in the light of this last weapon. Old enmities, and all that."

"Possibly, sir, but I'd rather hold on to that information a bit longer." Moretti stood up, and Liz Falla followed suit. "I have arranged to speak to the film director this morning — if you'll excuse me, sir."

Outside in the corridor, Liz Falla exploded — a *sotto voce* explosion. "What a *prat* — just because the murderer was selfish enough to endanger Mrs. Hanley's holiday in Torremolinos or whatever — sorry, Guv, but what a wally!"

"That's enough, Falla. He's not the only wally in this station, but he's right about one thing," said Moretti. "What he said about old enmities — he's got that right."

"So you think this might have a Guernsey connection then?"

"No, I don't. But I want to keep quiet about the dagger that killed Ensor, because you never know. I've got to cover all bases, but I still believe it's a red herring. That's why Hanley and PC Clarkson and the others in there —" Moretti jabbed his thumb in the direction of the incident room door, "are on a wild Guernsey goose chase, looking busy and keeping the chief officer happy."

The dying man lay on the dirt floor, life ebbing slowly from him. He was young, in his mid-twenties, slightly built, his nimbus of blond hair in stark contrast to the cloud of dark hair around the agonized face of the girl who cradled him in her arms. Suddenly, with what was left of his strength, he raised his face to hers and kissed her, then fell back.

"No!" The girl's frantic cry echoed in the silence.

The camera crept in noiselessly to catch the agony in Clifford Wesley's eyes, the blood caked on his clothing, as the boom of the mike was lowered to pick up his final words.

"Cosa fatta, capo ha."

A thing once done has an end.

"Cut!"

Mario Bianchi turned and looked at Monty Lord, who stood beside him. There were tears in his eyes, slowly spilling over onto his cheeks.

"Magnifico."

A brief spattering of applause from the assembled crew dissipated the tension, bringing everyone back into the present.

Clifford Wesley got up from the ground and gave Vittoria Salviati a hug.

"Terrific, Vicky. One take and we gave it to 'em."

"What Mario wanted, *si*."

Mario Bianchi's well-known preference for the immediate reaction, his dislike of repeated takes for scenes of emotional intensity, put tremendous pressure on his actors, and Wesley, with his stage experience, was at an advantage over Salviati. There was no doubt, he mused, as he allowed the dresser to peel his blood-soaked shirt off him, that Gunter was right. The murder of Toni had opened some emotional floodgate in the beautiful body and limited mind of Vittoria.

Well, it's an ill wind, he thought. *She may have lost a lover, but found her centre. Who knows?*

And who cares? he added to himself. *With that scene in the can, I can get out of here. Take the money and run, before the arrival of this extra character dreamed up by Mario.* Rumour had it that they were casting an Italian soap star, and Clifford Wesley smiled to himself as he imagined what Gilbert Ensor's reaction would have been. He'd have gone ballistic, no question. Shame, really, that particular scene would not be played out. He used to enjoy Gil's histrionics. They reminded him of his father inveighing drunkenly against the fates in his penniless Liverpool childhood, with a luxuriance of language and epithet intensified by hardship and deprivation.

Pulling on the dressing gown offered by the wardrobe assistant, Clifford Wesley retrieved his glasses and started to make his way across the tangle of cords and leads that brought life to the cameras and lights. Monty and Mario were deep in some sort of confabulation together and, from what he could hear, the discussion was not friendly.

Second time in two days, he thought. *I'm well out of this.*

Outside his trailer, he saw the lean figure of the detective inspector, waiting for him.

"Mr. Wesley?"

"That's me. You want to talk to me? Come on in."

He ushered Moretti over the threshold into an extremely untidy space, filled with discarded garments, glasses, newspapers, and books.

"Sorry about the mess, but I can't stand having strangers mucking about with my belongings. I prefer to wallow in my own filth." Wesley pushed a pile of magazines off a chair and motioned to Moretti to sit down.

"Now, how can I help you? I've nothing to add to my original statement. The body count continues to go up, eh?"

"Indeed. I understand this is your last day."

"Too bloody right it is. Thank God."

"Does your feeling have anything to do with the changes? Do they affect your own role, or its prominence in the film?"

"Prominence!" Clifford Wesley laughed with what sounded to Moretti like genuine amusement. "Look — Detective Inspector, isn't it? — let me explain something to you. I'm twenty-eight years old and I stumbled into this business by accident while I was at university on scholarship, living hand to mouth. I spent four years in repertory theatre, making peanuts, absolutely *no* money, and then some agent sees me in a play in the middle of nowhere and next thing I know I'm in the West End, and the *next* thing I know I'm in *Rastrellamento* making more money than my dad made in his whole working life. It's a hell of a role, and apart from cutting it out altogether, there's little they can do to alter that. By the time I've finished with them there won't be a dry eye or a dry seat in the house. Fuck the schoolteacher. Fuck prominence. I'll take the money and run, thank you."

"Schoolteacher?"

"That's the newest addition."

"I see. I'd like to find out more from your point of view about some of the circumstances surrounding the making of *Rastrellamento*."

"Happy to help if I can. Gil was a bastard to his wife, but he was a hell of a writer."

"In my opinion also. Why then do you think they were making all these changes?"

"This is my first film, Detective Inspector, but I know this kind of thing happens all the time, or so Gunter tells me. However, you have to hope in this case that Mario's decisions are being dictated by his cinematic skills and not by little packets of white powder. You know about that, I imagine. Some of the changes don't make sense."

"Really? Then I wonder why Monty Lord would agree to them?"

"That's another reason I'm glad to be leaving. All is not sweetness and light any more between those two, and they used to be thick as thieves."

"Oh?" Moretti watched as Clifford Wesley got up from his chair and went across to a counter at one end of the trailer.

"No. Over the last day or so they've had words, hot and heavy ones. Want some?" He was holding up a kettle and a jar of instant coffee. When Moretti declined, he grinned. "Didn't think you would. As Gunter says, I have depraved tastes. Can't get used to the real stuff."

The young actor plugged in the kettle and, when the water had heated, put a spoonful of brown powder into the mug and added water. A malodorous smell filled the trailer. Two heaping spoonsful of sugar and a similar amount of powdered creamer were added to the mix, and Wesley returned to his seat. After a couple of sips he said, "They had a loud argument the day before yesterday, in Monty's trailer. I'd been over to Betty Chesler's lodge for a fitting and was coming back to the manor when I heard raised voices. I couldn't hear what they were saying, and not being that interested I just kept on my merry way. Besides, they were speaking in Italian."

"You're sure it was Monty Lord and Mario Bianchi?"

"Yes, I'm certain."

"Did you hear anything at all that might have given you any idea what it was about? Had anything happened in the last few days that might have caused an argument?"

"The only thing I could think of was the new character. The schoolteacher."

"How did you find out, and were you told anything about the new character?"

"Piero Bonini told me. He said Monty was concerned I'd be worried about my impact in the film, so I asked him — *should* I be worried? He laughed it off, saying they'd be crazy to alter the tragedy of the two lovers in any way. My opinion exactly."

"Thank you for your time, Mr. Wesley." Moretti stood up. "I'll leave you to enjoy your coffee in peace. I shall look forward to seeing you in *Rastrellamento*. Don't get up — I'll see myself out."

"Oh —" Clifford Wesley gestured toward Moretti with his coffee mug, "you asked me if I knew anything about the new character. All I know is they've apparently cast some big Italian soap star in the role. A bloke called Tibor Stanjo, or something."

"Stanjo? That doesn't sound Italian. Or British, or German, come to that."

"Nope. Slovak originally, so Bella tells me. Probably cast him for his mass appeal, and for no more sinister reason."

"Sinister? That's an interesting choice of word, sir."

Clifford Wesley shrugged his shoulders. "Isn't it. Possibly all those fake *feldgendarmen* and *repubblichini* getting to me. That's the trouble with this business, Detective Inspector, illusion becomes more real than reality itself. Probably also my imagination that Donatella and Monty are no longer as chummy as they once were — a certain coolness there now, in the last twenty-four hours. Breakfast this morning was a frosty affair."

"Interesting. Did you get any impression of who was angry with whom?"

"Donatella was icy and giving a fawning Monty the cold shoulder. For what it's worth, I've never believed there was ever really anything going on between those two — she enjoyed the admiration, and he was making sure his bread remained buttered."

"A wise move, I would think. Thank you again."

"Hey, don't mention it. I tell you, they're a colourful lot, these Vannonis. Even the murders on their property are exotic — do you know the writer, Jan Morris? Yes? She's written some lovely stuff about Florence." Clifford Wesley took off his glasses and put down his empty coffee mug. "*If there is crime, it is gorgeous crime, all daggers and secret poisons.*" His beautiful actor's voice filled the trailer. "A romantic, foreigner's view, wouldn't you say? Twenty-first-century Florentines seem like a practical bunch to me."

"An original viewpoint, sir. Safe journey home, Mr. Wesley."

"Safer than staying around here appears to be. Good luck, Detective Inspector."

I'll need it, thought Moretti. A piece of sheer, utter luck. Clifford Wesley was right, there was something fake or stagey about the murder weapon. A dagger. Now why in the name of all that's sacred, or profane, would a Vannoni attract attention by choosing part of their own coat of arms as an instrument of death?

"Guv!"

Liz Falla was walking even more briskly than usual toward him from the direction of the manor. Given the current stagnant state of the investigation, her eager-beaverness was more than welcome.

"Any luck?"

"Oh yes. Guess who's the head gardener!"

"An ex-boyfriend."

"Right!" Apparently unaware of any satirical subtext, Liz Falla continued. "Brad Duquemin. We used to go out together when we were still at school, so I haven't seen him in years. He's been here now just over a year, and he's got the housekeeper in his pocket, so he says — well, he's a good-looking bloke. Got a way with words, among other things. They have a little tipple in the evening before he goes home, and she's told him quite a lot about the family."

"Such as?"

"No, the marchesa is not having an affair with Mr. Lord. Yes, most people knew about Miss Salviati and Mr. Albarosa. And — get this, Guv — Giulia Vannoni *isn't* a Vannoni!"

"Isn't?"

"Not by blood. In the housekeeper's opinion, that's why she's what she calls 'different.' Interesting, eh?"

"Very. Did she explain who she is if she's not a Vannoni?"

"No, or not that he could understand — there's a problem with the language. Oh, and she told Brad there was a fight between Mr. Albarosa and the marchesa on the night of his murder. He asked her if it was about Vittoria Salviati and she laughed and said something like 'too many, too many,' which Brad took to mean that kind of thing happened all the time. But she said something that sounded like 'tradition' — *tradimento*, he thinks. She said it more than once."

"*Tradimento*," said Moretti slowly. "Not tradition, Falla. Betrayal."

"And she also kept on about honour — he understood that. So he asked her if it wasn't to do with a woman, what was it? And *she* said —" Liz Falla paused for effect, "'With an *esterno* for the film.'"

"Did she mean 'location'?"

"That's what Brad thinks. Because when he said he didn't understand, she said 'house.' And that's when she dried up. Tapped the side of her nose, said '*basta*,' got up and left."

"Good work, Falla. This is all useful stuff. There's just one problem — well, there's a whole slew of them but the one that keeps hitting me is that the Vannonis may think a deep, dark family secret is at the back of these murders and be terrified of exposure. And that the damn thing, whatever it is, has absolutely nothing to do with it."

Liz Falla looked at him. "One thing they — well, some of the fellers at the station — told me when I was to be your partner, Guv. They said, 'He's got the best instincts of any of the DIs. Never puts a foot wrong when he trusts them.' I don't know about you, but I personally am going to trust them if that's all right with you."

Before Moretti could respond to her revelation about the fellers at Hospital Lane, Liz Falla pulled out her notebook. "About the bunker key in the marchesa's bedroom — her door isn't always locked, even with some of the film people staying. One of the cleaning ladies was around, and she says they can usually get in without asking the housekeeper. And I had a word with the head of security, as you asked. Mr. Ensor's arrival by taxi was noted by one of the security staff, who saw him near the entrance to the bunker. He offered to escort him to the manor and was told to bugger off — Ensor's words. The guard watched him walk as far as that path that leads to the entrance and, as he thought, turn toward the terrace. Since he knew there was a regular patrol in that area, he decided to do exactly what Ensor had suggested."

"And he saw no one else?"

"No. Of that he's sure."

Moretti looked at his watch. "We're still too early for Bianchi. Come on, Falla, let's take another look at the scene of the crime."

* * *

The SOC tapes were still across the entrance to the bunker, but the police guard and the incident van had been removed from the immediate vicinity and placed at the main gate to the manor. Moretti took the key obtained from the marchesa out of his pocket and turned it in the lock. The damp and moisture seeped out immediately, and he felt the familiar tightness in his chest. Behind him he heard Liz Falla shiver.

"First, the film set."

"Lights, Guv?"

"They leave one by the door — here — it's been fingerprinted."

"There wasn't a key on him, was there?"

Their hushed voices echoed around them.

"No. He must have been let in, or the key was removed by the murderer."

For Moretti, there was less a sense of a terrible past in that ersatz, reconstructed room than in the dank, collapsed tunnels, the brick-filled alcoves, the deserted, echoing corridors. The phone had been left on the floor, but the single shoe had been removed to the SOC lab.

"Perhaps he thought it was connected," said Liz Falla, resisting the temptation to rub her eyes.

"Desperately hoped it was, I'm sure," said Moretti, bending over to look at it. "He would have been sitting at the desk when he reached for it. I imagine this was where he hoped to have his rendezvous with whoever." He looked at the bunk bed. Its grey blanket cover was smooth, unrumpled. "He didn't get any farther than here, I think. As soon as he saw who it was coming in through the door, he knew he was in trouble."

"How did he get past the murderer and out of the room?" asked Liz Falla. "The doorway's quite narrow." She reached up and touched the top of the opening.

"I've been thinking about that. There must have been some sort of discussion before the murderer tried

to kill Ensor. He probably tried to reason with him or
her — after all, words were his stock-in-trade — and the
murderer was probably equally anxious to say why he
was going to kill him. He or she may have come around
the side of the desk to get at Ensor, who then took off
around the other side, and out into the corridor. SOC
found no signs of a struggle near the door, where Ensor
would have been cornered, so he must have headed
down the corridor."

"Why? Surely he knew there was no way out?"

"Desperation? Or did he know about the tunnel
that's supposed to come out in the manor? Come on."

The single shaft of light from the lamp peeled back
a narrow central strip in the darkness along the corridor,
and Liz Falla stumbled as she followed Moretti.

"Take my arm, Falla. This light's not too good." He
felt Liz Falla's grip on his elbow.

The beam wasn't as strong as Moretti remembered
from his visit with Monty Lord. Every few feet he
swept the light to one side and the other, examining the
entrances and alcoves in the walls. They stopped briefly
by the ventilation shaft for some air.

"Where did SOC say the blood started, Guv?"

"Just about here — they marked it — there we are.
This is where the murderer either caught up with him, or
chose to start stabbing."

Circles were chalked on the floor, some of them
surviving the moisture that ran down the gutters and
over the surface. Some moved in the direction of an
entrance, or a recess in the wall.

"Like following a trail of breadcrumbs, isn't it?"
Moretti could hear a note of hysteria in his partner's giggle.

"Much the same. Ensor left us a route map of the
end of his existence with his lifeblood. You can see where
he looked for a way out — the tunnel to the manor. And
it takes us, of course, to the escape shaft."

Moretti swung the beam to the right and together they lurched over the corroded rail tracks. Ahead of them lay the chalked outline of Gilbert Ensor's body, indistinct, but still visible.

"And here we have the answer to one of the problems, Falla. How the murderer got away without being seen by anyone. Getting away from the scene of the crime is one of the most difficult of a murderer's tasks, and this way there's no need to risk the door."

Above them loomed the iron ladder, rung upon rung, disappearing into the distant darkness beyond the beam of their light.

"Not out the door? Someone went up there, Guv?" Incredulously, Liz Falla looked up into the void.

At this point the light went out.

"Shit," said Liz Falla, and sneezed. Her grip tightened on Moretti's elbow.

"Okay, Falla — give me a moment." Fumbling in his pocket, Moretti extracted the disposable lighter he had not yet disposed of.

"I didn't know you smoked, Guv."

"I'm supposed to be giving up, but I've not quite succeeded."

"Thank God, is all I can say."

Together they made their cautious way back through the noisome, dripping darkness and into the light outside.

Neither of them spoke for a moment as they refilled their lungs with fresh, clean air. Liz Falla looked at her watch.

"Just about time for the interview, Guv."

"So it is," said Moretti. "But first I want to take a look at the outside of that escape shaft. Mr. Bianchi can wait a moment for us — heaven knows he's made us wait for him."

The bank that covered the bunker was overgrown with holly bushes, honeysuckle, pennywort, and stinging nettles. A couple of elderberry bushes had grown into flourishing trees. Clearly this was one area of the well-tended property allowed to stay wild, and Moretti noticed that he and his partner left clear evidence of their progress.

"There it is," said Liz Falla, pointing to the apex of the mound.

The escape shaft was well concealed by the plants and grasses, and would have been as treacherous as Alice in Wonderland's rabbit hole if it had not been covered by a solid piece of grating. Moretti bent down and pulled at it. It shifted in his hand.

"See — it's been prised loose. And the plants around here have been trampled down by someone. Whoever it was came and went in that direction."

They both stood up and looked toward the lake. Through the light mist that hovered over it they could see the naked torso of a green-blue woman, bathing in the water.

"A statue?"

"I hope so. She's got no arms. We'll go down that way, and take the path around the lake back to the house."

They passed the woman dreaming in the lake, and the sight of her there, head bowed, motionless, flooded Moretti with a morbid awareness of his own impermanence.

chapter twelve

They were met in the marchesa's sitting room by someone Moretti knew well, but had not expected to see: Reginald Hamelin.

Reginald Hamelin was the senior member of one of the oldest law firms on the island. Known as the silver fox because of his magnificent head of hair and his cunning in litigious matters both matrimonial and commercial, he was officially retired, but was brought out of mothballs from time to time for certain clients who believed that anyone under the age of sixty or so wouldn't know a tort from a tart.

"Detective Inspector —"

"Advocate Hamelin. Where is Mr. Bianchi?"

"He will be with us shortly. I wanted to speak to you first, privately."

Moretti thought about protesting, but decided to appear acquiescent — for the moment. When pushed into a corner, the silver fox tended to show some of the less attractive characteristics of his namesake. He sat down in one of the two chairs placed opposite the marchesa's little desk, and Liz Falla followed suit, pulling out her notepad.

"Off the record?"

"I can't promise that, Advocate Hamelin, as you well know, but DC Falla will take no notes at this stage. We have had enough problems trying to interview Mr. Bianchi, as it is."

Reginald Hamelin watched Liz Falla put away her notebook and turned his attention back to Moretti. "I have managed to persuade Mr. Bianchi to come and talk to you without his psychiatrist, which is what he wanted to do. Frankly, the last thing I wanted was for my client to have two handlers — and besides, I pointed out to him that it did not help his situation if he looked incapable. Unbalanced."

"I see," said Moretti. "What did you want to tell me, off the record?"

Reginald Hamelin leaned across the desk, looking with what was intended to be disarming earnestness at both police officers.

"I must talk to you about Mr. Bianchi's former drug problem. As you may or may not know, my client had a minor relapse about two years ago, and was hospitalized. I wanted to clear that up first, before you brought the matter up with him. I can assure you Mr. Bianchi is not on drugs now, and thus there is no question of his former habit having anything to do with these dreadful events. He is clean, Detective Inspector, and I told him I would deal with that before he came. He'll submit to tests if necessary. It was the only way I could persuade the psychiatrist not to be here. He warned me there is a possibility of a complete mental breakdown if he is rigorously questioned about his past drug habit."

"I see," Moretti repeated, making a token response so that they could at least get started. "We shall have to hope things don't lead in that direction, won't we? And if you could persuade your client to make an appearance, we won't have to move this to an interrogation room at Hospital Lane."

Reginald Hamelin picked up a mobile phone sitting on the desk in front of him.

"Donatella? Ask Mario to come now, would you?"

They could not have been far away, because almost immediately the door opened and Mario Bianchi came in.

The Italian director's long hair was loose on his shoulders and around his face, giving him a biblical, almost Christlike appearance. He looked tired and drawn, but Moretti recalled that when he first met him he hadn't exactly looked the picture of health. The deep-set dark eyes above his prominent cheekbones looked haunted, and there was a nervous tic in the corner of his mouth that even the heavy moustache failed to hide. One would have had to know him years ago, thought Moretti, to know if it was the struggle to be free of drugs, the effect of the drugs, or the sensitivity of a highly creative human being that made Mario Bianchi look as if nature had made him a particularly vulnerable creature.

Bianchi sat down alongside Reginald Hamelin, and looked across the desk at Moretti.

"We can speak Italian, if you prefer, Signor Bianchi."

"English is fine. I'll tell you if not. Better for Signor Hamelin."

"Very well. Signor Bianchi, I want to ask you first about your father."

"My father?"

Mario Bianchi was clearly not expecting Moretti's opening line of questioning and, from the look on his lawyer's face, neither was he. "I thought you'd want to re-check my alibis, that kind of thing."

"Not much point to that, sir, since most people at the time of both deaths were asleep. You are far from the only one without an alibi. For the moment, I'd like to explore other areas of investigation with you."

"How can my father have anything to do with these deaths?" Mario Bianchi's hands went up to the open collar of his shirt with a gesture Moretti recalled from their first meeting.

"I don't know if he has anything to do with it. Yet. Your father was a prominent member of the fascist party before and during the war, wasn't he?"

"Yes, but he was an intellectual. A writer, a journalist. He didn't go around bullying, torturing, and killing people, if that's what you're suggesting."

"I was not. But his writing may have made others do so — the pen being quite as powerful as the sword. Wouldn't you agree?"

"Of course I do, as a writer myself. It is difficult for us now to understand the forces that drove men like my father to support fascism — there was much political corruption in Italy, and a real fear of the spread of communism in Europe. Many who supported Mussolini in the early days quickly became disillusioned when he joined forces with Hitler. Although my father died when I was very young and I don't really remember him, I don't intend to sit here and revile him. Especially since I don't see what this has to do with the deaths of Toni and Gilbert Ensor over three decades later."

Mario Bianchi's hand dropped from his collar on to his lap, and Moretti saw that the unexpected direction of his questions was having the effect he hoped for. In spite of his emotional support of his father, the director's body settled more easily into the chair, his spine relaxing against the high padded back.

"Am I right in thinking he spent much of the war in and around Siena?"

"You've done your homework, Inspector. Yes, it was safer than Rome, particularly after the fall of Mussolini."

"You must have been fascinated by the plot of *Rastrellamento*, with your family background. Did you approach Monty Lord, or did he approach you?"

"He came to me. I'd just gone through a — a bit of a lull. It was a godsend, not just a make-work project. I now have a two-year-old son, a family. I'd have taken almost anything, but this was wonderful."

"You say you met Toni Albarosa while on holiday in Venice, and that he was the first member of the Vannoni-Albarosa family whom you met. I'm presuming you already had been approached by Monty Lord about *Rastrellamento* — am I right? Did you suggest filming in Guernsey? I was under the impression it had been arranged between Monty Lord and the marchese."

"Yes. The preliminary groundwork had been done, but Toni did much to smooth the way for us."

"That surprises me. I got the impression the marchese was not enamoured of his son-in-law."

Mario Bianchi laughed. "Paolo wasn't, but that doesn't mean he wasn't anxious for him to find some sort of job with us. Appointing Toni as location manager did much to win over the marchesa to our invasion of her home, of that I'm sure. Besides, you'd have to have met Toni to know just how charming he was — it really was difficult to dislike him."

"So he could charm his way around most obstacles, get people to give way and agree to various requests. That must have made him very useful as a location manager."

"It did indeed. I said to you when I first met you that he opened doors for us, and that was literally true."

"But isn't it true that, just before his death, he had tried to get permission for a location that the family vetoed?" *Let's give it a shot*, thought Moretti, *see if it's game over*. Basta, *and a tap on the side of the nose*. But Mario Bianchi only looked surprised.

"You heard about that? See, I don't know if the family vetoed the request, or even if Toni lived long enough to make it."

"From the information we have, he and the marchesa had a falling-out about a location on the night of his death."

"Really?" Mario Bianchi's surprise seemed genuine. "That's news to me, and the marchesa has never said anything about it."

"I presume you had needed another location — where, and for what?"

"It was for a crucial scene I had not planned to shoot until toward the end of our schedule — a flashback. We needed a broken-down church in a much wilder location than the island could offer us, and preferably on a hill. I wanted ruins, if possible, that I could use in the exterior shots. Toni became quite excited, said he knew just the place, but he would have to check with the Vannonis. Apparently it was some place his wife had mentioned, many years ago."

"Near Florence, or Fiesole?"

"No, much farther south, and closer to the coast."

"Was he more specific than that?"

"Well yes, and then *I* became quite excited, because it was close to Siena and I know the area well. He said it was a small village, now deserted, between Siena and Grosseto. There were the remains of a church, he said, because his wife had mentioned an abandoned church."

"Did he say anything about a house?"

"Not specifically, but he said there were ruins."

"Are you pursuing the location?"

"It's been put on hold for the time being. We may have to compromise with the setting, because all this has lost us valuable time."

The directions the questions were now taking had made Mario Bianchi return to his nervous tics, and

Moretti saw that his forehead glistened with sweat. The inconsistency was puzzling — surely he had just said he was excited by the proximity to Siena? Why was he disturbed all of a sudden? Was he lying about the reasons for dropping the location?

"Time is valuable, you say, Signor Bianchi. Haven't the numerous changes to the script and the recent addition of an extra character also lost you valuable time?"

Mario Bianchi's head jerked forward, a curtain of hair concealing his expression. For the first time in the interview, Reginald Hamelin intervened.

"These are artistic matters, aren't they? Surely Mr. Bianchi does not have to justify himself for adapting a book for the screen?" The lawyer laughed lightly, dismissively, as if to dissipate his client's obvious tension.

"It could be useful," Moretti replied. "One of the lines of inquiry we are working on is that there is some connection between the political aspects of the script and the murders. Why, Signor Bianchi, have you and Mr. Lord had a disagreement? Is it about the character of the schoolmaster? And why cast a Slovak in the role?"

"Oh, for God's sake, who said I had any disagreement with Monty?" Mario Bianchi's hysteria bubbled close beneath the surface. "There is stress, yes, because of the money. One of our investors is a bank, and banks don't like murders in what for them was a speculative undertaking in the first place. I should have thought it was obvious why we have cast Tibor — box office, Inspector, box office. We are lucky he is available."

Mario Bianchi broke off abruptly and turned to Reginald Hamelin. "I've had enough of this. They are waiting for me on the terrace. I can't sit here any longer."

Moretti stood up, followed by Liz Falla, taking the initiative from lawyer and client. "Thank you, Signor Bianchi, for your time. We may of course have to speak to you again."

Reginald Hamelin extended his hand to Moretti. "We will make ourselves available," he said magisterially, affirming his presence in any interrogation.

Moretti and his partner had just reached the door when Mario Bianchi called after them. "*A proposito*, Inspector — Tibor Stanjo is not a Slovak. Common mistake. He has lived in Italy since he was a small child. Came when his father had to come — like you and your father here, no? He is a Slovene."

Outside the manor there were sounds of activity from the direction of the terrace.

"Between Siena and Grosseto," said Moretti. If he'd been a police dog instead of a policeman, he'd have been whimpering with excitement and pulling on his lead. "Whatever it was happened there. Between Siena and Grosseto. And the schoolmaster becomes even more interesting as a Slovene, rather than a Slovak."

"I have to say, Guv," admitted his partner, "I get all confused with those parts of the world. Slovene, Slovak — I'd have thought they were the same. Why more interesting?"

"Because there was a forced evacuation of Slovenes before the onset of the war. I remember my father talking about it — many were transferred to Italy against their will. I thought they were mostly put in northern towns, like Parma and Milan, but a schoolmaster might well have to move farther south, to a more remote region, to find employment. I'm sure this schoolmaster is not in *Rastrellamento* on some idle whim. He's there for a reason."

"Bianchi says the reason is money, the investors."

"Box office? Think about it, Falla. It doesn't really hold water. You don't have to be an expert to know the big money to be made with this film is in North

America, where you can be certain they've never heard of Tibor Stanjo."

They were now in the courtyard near where most of the trailers were parked. Betty Chesler and her assistant, Eddie Christy, were making their way across the yard chattering away nineteen to the dozen, carrying between them a large box of German helmets. When she saw the two policemen Betty Chesler twisted around to speak to them, leaving most of the weight in the hands of her punier colleague. With a plaintive cry, he staggered and lowered it awkwardly to the ground.

"Sorry, Eddie, love, but I wanted to have a word — I'm so glad I saw you. I was about to call the police station, actually."

"More trouble at the lodge?" Moretti asked.

"No, thank God. But I wanted to have a word with you." She looked around her, and at her assistant. "I'd — rather not talk here."

"Tell you what," said Liz Falla in her firm, take-control voice, "I'll give you a hand with those, shall I?" She hoisted up one end of the container with impressive ease. Eddie Christy took the other side, and together they walked off in the direction of the terrace.

Betty Chesler waited until they were out of earshot and turned back to Moretti. "It's about Sydney Tremaine. We can talk in Clifford's trailer, I've got a master key. He left this morning."

Clifford Wesley's trailer was still showing signs of its former occupant and Betty Chesler tut-tutted as they went in. "Dear me, what a pigsty. I do apologize. But he was such a *nice* young man. I just hope stardom doesn't spoil him."

"You think *Rastrellamento* will make him a star?"

"Oh I think so. I've seen so many get started, and you get to know what to look for. That seriousness and those glasses might make you think otherwise, but on camera he's just gorgeous — oh, he made me cry buckets yesterday when he died. In the film, I mean. The way things have been around here you've got to say that, haven't you?" Betty Chesler gave a little shudder.

"You wanted to talk to me about Ms. Tremaine."

"Yes." Betty Chesler sat down and Moretti took a seat opposite her. With great earnestness she leaned forward and patted his knee. "Now, dear, I know you're a police officer — well, a detective — but I'm going to be quite straightforward."

Nonplussed, Moretti replied, "I hope you will, Ms. Chesler. It'll make a pleasant change."

"Very well. I know from what Sydney has said that she's taken a shine to you."

"A — shine?" Moretti stared at Betty Chesler's solemn face.

"You've been so kind to her. She's not used to the man in her life being kind to her." She was now giving him a stern but motherly look.

"Now, Ms. Chesler — I don't know what Ms. Tremaine has said to you, but I am far from being the man in her life," responded a now dismayed Moretti.

"She told me you're a real gentleman — even gave up your bed to her, and never laid a finger on her. She's not used to that. Don't worry — Sydney and I have known each other a long time, from the Pavlova film. She's not told anyone else, with one possible exception, and that's what I wanted to talk to you about. Or who, rather."

"Giulia Vannoni."

"You know! Oh, I'm so worried about her friendship with that woman! Sydney can be so naive about life — dancers are often like that. They live in a cocoon, you see, from about the age of ten, and they go from barre to the ballet to bed at night and that's it. Sydney seems to have complete confidence in her, and in my opinion she's just as likely to have been the culprit as anyone. Those muscles!

Have you seen the key Sydney's wearing around her neck?"

"I have. Is it the key to the tower on Icart point?"

"If you mean what she calls Giulia Vannoni's castello, yes. She says it's where she'll be safe and I'm to tell no one. It could be a trap. It could mean her death!"

Betty Chesler's emotional style was reminiscent of early silent films, all clasped hands and tortured looks, but her anxiety was clearly genuine.

"Has Ms. Tremaine told you anything about their conversations? Anything at all that might be useful to our inquiries?"

"I don't know if it's useful or not, but she told me that Giulia thinks the murders have something to do with some old family secret. It all sounded highly unlikely to me."

"Was she more specific about the secret?"

"Something to do with how she was close to the marchesa, but how just once she had been frightened of her. She asked the marchesa about a sister of her grandfather's she found out about, and the marchesa threatened to throw her out of the business, so she said. It all seemed a bit farfetched to me — to think that it would have anything to do with the murders. That woman can turn nasty at the drop of a hat. I've seen it."

"A sister," said Moretti. "She didn't by any chance give her a name, this sister?"

"Yes, she did, and I remember it because of that old folk song." Betty Chesler broke suddenly and unexpectedly into song in a melodious voice, heavy with vibrato. "*Who is Sylvia? What is she, that all our swains commend her?*" She beamed at Moretti. "Not bad, eh? I used to sing with a dance band when I was young. Best days of my life, they were."

"So," Moretti confirmed, "the name was Sylvia?"

"I'm sure of it. My main concern is for Sydney's safety, so I've no scruples whatsoever about sharing her confidences with you."

"You saw her this morning?"

"Yes, at the hotel. She said she was coming here."

"Did she? She told me she never wanted to come near this place again."

"I could understand that, but she wanted to have something to do, and I said she could help me. *De mortuis* and all that, Detective Inspector, but she's better off without Gilbert Ensor. I've been talking to her about getting on with her life."

"I'm glad to hear it. Anything more? I've got to find Monty Lord, if I can."

"That's about it. Monty's in the manor, because they're shooting on the terrace today. You should be able to catch him when they break for lunch."

Together they walked back to the lodge, where Liz Falla was waiting for him. Moretti watched Betty Chesler disappear up the steps and into the lodge, closing the door behind her.

"Anything useful, Guv?"

"I think so, but I'll tell you later. I don't want to talk about it here. Let's go back to the manor. We'll wait for Mr. Lord in the foyer."

Somehow, the end of summer seemed more palpable in the Manoir Ste. Madeleine. The air was cooler, almost damp, and the once light-filled interior was now shadowed and dim. The entrance hall was deserted, and Moretti and Liz Falla were just sitting down on a pair of high-backed mahogany chairs when Bella Alfieri came down the stairs. She was wearing the same severe suit, and her swept-up hairstyle gave her a retro fifties look.

"Can I help you?"

"Perhaps you can, Signora," said Moretti. "We are waiting to speak to Mr. Lord. Is he on the set? We understood they were shooting here today."

"They are, but Signor Lord has left the set now. He is doing some paperwork in his bedroom upstairs. He didn't return to the trailer, because they all break soon for lunch."

"Could you show us the way?"

Bella Alfieri looked doubtful. "We are not supposed to disturb him, Detective Inspector."

"Signora Alfieri, this is a murder investigation."

"This way."

With an alacrity that took both officers by surprise, Bella Alfieri turned and made her way back up the stairs into a second floor hallway that overlooked the ground floor. Monty Lord's room was right at the top of the stairs. Bella Alfieri knocked and an irritated voice replied, "*Chi è?*" The tiny interpreter turned to them, and smiled, lovingly.

"He speaks beautiful Italian, you know. Not a trace of an accent. And, by the way, it's 'signorina,' and not 'signora.'" She called through the door. "Monty, it's Bella. The two detectives are here to speak with you."

From inside the room came the sound of papers rustling and drawers and cupboards opening and closing. Then Monty Lord called out, "Come in, come in."

The producer's bedroom was sizeable, with plenty of space for an elaborately carved desk that was either Renaissance, or a very fine copy of a Renaissance piece. No utilitarian steel and aluminum construction for this piece of furniture, unlike the desk in his trailer, and Moretti was again struck by the marked difference between the servant quarters and the rest of the manor.

The producer was in his customary black, his shaved pate glowing white in contrast. He was standing up, a sheaf of papers in his hand, all smiles, his irritation apparently over.

"Please forgive my churlish greeting, officers, but we are under the gun — an unfortunate choice of metaphor in the circumstances, I grant you, but that's how we all feel." He turned to Bella Alfieri, who threw him a glance of undisguised adoration. "Bella, sweetie, could you tell the marchesa I may be a little late for lunch, and not to wait for me?"

Bella sweetie's expression now became a complex blend of adoration, eagerness, and unvarnished loathing. "Of course, Monty."

Monty Lord blew her a kiss and she blushed and giggled like a young girl as she closed the door behind her.

"Sit down, officers. How is the investigation going?"

"Slowly would be a polite way of putting it, Mr. Lord," said Moretti. "I wanted to ask you a couple of additional questions — about matters that have arisen since the murder of Mr. Albarosa. First of all — has there been a disagreement of any sort, a cooling-off between yourself and the marchesa? I am told there has."

Rather than being offended or disturbed by the question, Monty Lord looked saddened. "Ah, Detective Inspector, there has, there has. I blame myself entirely, and I'll be honest with you. After the agreement with Paolo, I had to win Donatella over, and I think I overstepped the mark. I think — how can I say this without sounding conceited? — she became too fond of me. I am reaping my own whirlwind, and I can only hope we can remain civil with each other until the filming is over."

"So you are saying the marchesa expected more of you romantically and personally than you could give her?"

"Delicately put, if I may say so. Yes."

Remembering the hopeless devotion on the face of Bella Alfieri, Moretti modified somewhat his first impression of Monty Lord as a decent fellow.

"I see. So the disagreement between you has nothing to do with the changes to the script and to the storyline of *Rastrellamento*?"

"Good God, no!" Monty Lord looked taken aback at the idea. "I doubt we've exchanged more than a couple of sentences about the contents of *Rastrellamento*, and that would be mostly about the hold-ups in the shooting schedule. But there is a compensatory clause in the contract: we will have to pay the Vannonis more money if we do not adhere to the original plan, so they are not as bothered as we are."

"I see. As you probably know, we had a meeting with Mario Bianchi and his lawyer a short while ago."

"Yes. I've already spoken to him."

"Did he tell you anything about the nature of the interview?"

"Some. I gather you were more interested in his father than in his drug problem."

Monty Lord got up from behind his desk and walked over to one of the windows that overlooked the terrace. He pulled it open, and a breath of cool air blew in from outside. "See? Time is passing, we're way behind, and the weather could break at any moment. They tell me it can storm like crazy in the fall here." He turned back to them and asked, "What is all this, Detective Inspector? Why are you examining the past for an answer? Toni was utterly charming and a shit; Gil was hugely talented and a shit. Both fooled about, and it cost them their lives."

"That's interesting, sir," Moretti observed. "When I suggested at the onset of this investigation that philandering might be the answer, you felt it unlikely, given the nature of film sets, film actors, and film crews. Have you changed your mind? And, if so, why?"

Without warning, Monty Lord slammed his hand down hard on a small round table near him. The slap echoed through the room, like a warning shot from a starter's pistol.

"Christ almighty, guys! I've changed my mind because I have to believe that none of this has anything to do with Mario, or his past — or his present, come to that. I have to believe the changes he's making are based on sound artistic judgment. I have to hope we can keep him going until we call this a wrap. And I must tell you that the one good thing about Gil's death is I no longer have to play monkey in the middle between the two of them — and if that makes me a prime suspect, so be it!"

Moretti responded calmly, as though the outburst had escaped his attention. "Bear with me a little longer, sir, would you? Let's suppose for a moment the two murders do indeed have something to do with the plot of *Rastrellamento*. As a man who deals with storylines, fiction, creations of the imagination — who then would be the most likely suspects, in your opinion?"

"*Dio mio*, guys — you want me to do your job for you?" Monty Lord came back to the desk and sat down. The flare-up seemed to have left him exhausted. He ran his hand over his bald head and took a moment before replying.

"Okay, let's play whodunnit. If your theory is correct — and I still think you're barking up the wrong tree — then it has to be a member of either the Vannoni or Albarosa families, doesn't it? The killer is far more likely to be one of them than Mario. And, you know, you asked me if Donatella and I had talked about the changes, and we haven't. But I know she and Mario have talked about them. Not that I'm saying it's Donatella, mind you. But she may well have told another member of the family."

"Such as who?"

Monty Lord got up from his desk and picked up a navy baseball cap from the quilted satin bedcover. It had EPICURE PRODUCTIONS printed on the front, and Moretti had seen other crew members wearing them. "Well — knowing them all as I do, my money would be on two of them. Long shots in my opinion, but hey, you asked for my opinion, so here it is, for what it's worth. Paolo or Gianfranco. Or perhaps both in combination. Gianfranco would do just about anything to get back into his father's good books. " He put the cap on his head. "And now, if you'll excuse me, I'm going downstairs for lunch."

Moretti and Liz Falla followed him downstairs. When they reached the hallway, Moretti could see through the windows that other members of the film crew had started to gather on the terrace. Cosimo del Grano, the art director, was talking animatedly to the cinematographer, Mel Abrams, Betty Chesler and Eddie Christie, and Piero Bonini was sitting with Gianfranco Vannoni, who was drinking a glass of wine and gesticulating languidly with a long ivory cigarette holder. Mario Bianchi was sitting next to Adriana Ferrini.

As they followed Monty Lord out on to the terrace, the producer turned to Moretti and said, "I trust you are not going to say anything about the opinions you elicited from me?"

"No, sir."

They walked on to the terrace just as the sun came out from behind a cloud and bathed them in light. There was a startled murmur at their appearance, and Moretti realized it looked as if they had Monty Lord under arrest. Obviously, the same thought occurred to the American producer, for he stepped forward from behind his escorts and announced, "Relax, ladies and gentlemen — appearances are deceiving. See — no handcuffs!" He held out his hands in front of him to a ripple of relieved laughter and a babble of comments.

At precisely that moment, Sydney Tremaine came around the far corner of the terrace beyond the cameras and cranes of the film set, walking slowly toward them. She was wearing a long sheath dress in ivory satin with a flared skirt that undulated around her as she moved. There were ruched bands of black chiffon tied around her slender arms and twisted in her hands was a black chiffon stole that trailed on the ground. Her red hair was piled up loosely on top of her head, tendrils falling

around her pale face, against which her lipstick looked
almost black.

There was a gasp from the assembled company, a
group appreciative of dramatic entrances and theatrical
gestures. Moretti heard Eddie Christie say, "Ooh,
gorgeous. It's her Christian Lacroix."

"Yes." Betty Chesler moved forward. "Gil got
it for her in Paris, as a peace offering after one of his
sordid little adventures. Hardly the outfit for an al fresco
luncheon, but that's the point I would think. Sydney —"

She started to move toward Sydney, who put out her
hand and stopped her, like a traffic policeman. With a
final swirl of her skirt, Sydney came to a halt before her
startled audience and began to speak.

"Ladies and gentlemen, here I am, the grieving widow,
come to be the spectre at your feast." Her voice was quite
strong enough to carry across the space. "Isn't it strange
to think that, among the group I see in front of me, is the
person who killed my husband. I have a message for that
person: I know now why Gil died. And I will find you."

The last two sentences were delivered slowly, clearly,
deliberately rather than dramatically.

Standing beside Moretti, Monty Lord started to clap
his hands.

"Magnificent! *Brava*!"

At the table farthest from the self-proclaimed spectre
at the feast, Mario Bianchi put his head down on his
hands and started to sob uncontrollably.

Moretti went up to Sydney Tremaine and, as he took
her by the arm, she looked defiantly at him. He could feel
her trembling. Anger and exasperation filled him and he
controlled his voice with difficulty.

"Ms. Tremaine, it's best you leave with us." He felt
her resist, start to pull her arm away from his grasp.
"Come on, Sydney," he said gently, "There is nothing
more you can do here."

chapter thirteen

Nothing was said in the police car. Liz Falla drove in silence, her eyes fixed on the road. Moretti, for his part, was making decisions. The rustle of Sydney Tremaine's dress and the faint perfume in the air distracted him from time to time. What perfume, he wondered. Certainly not Fracas. There was a haunting sweetness about it, a vulnerability and a sadness.

At the Héritage Hotel he said to his partner, "Stay here, Falla. I'll escort Ms. Tremaine to her suite."

She said nothing as they crossed the foyer and went down the corridor, passing a couple of startled hotel guests who stared as the haute couture vision floated by. Sydney gave them her sad, submerged Ophelia smile, and Moretti thought of the armless beauty navel-deep in water lilies in the manor lake.

At the door of the suite he asked her, "Where have you got your key in that getup — or have you?"

"Of course. In my arm band."

She extracted the door key from one of the ruffled

chiffon ties, opened the door, and they went inside.

"Ed, I want to explain why —"

"Explain later. Don't move from here, don't open the door. If you are gone when I come back, I'll put out an all-points bulletin to have you picked up, and I'll put you in protective custody."

"I can't just sit here! I went with Betty to the hospital to identify Gil and I lost it."

"I'm with you on that. And you won't just be sitting here. Pack a suitcase with enough clothes for about a week. If you want something to eat, get room service, but don't tell them you're leaving."

"Where am I going?"

"I'll tell you when I come back to get you."

Sydney Tremaine flung herself down on a nearby sofa, her skirt rustling expensively around her, giving Moretti a glimpse of the highest and skinniest pair of heels he'd ever seen in his life.

It was a reassuring return from the unreal to the normal to see Liz Falla waiting for him by the police car in her conservative dark blue suit and her sensibly heeled shoes.

"What a scene, eh, Guv! Like something out of a film was what I thought."

"Contrived, yes, but no less effective — and stupidly dangerous — for all that. Which is why I have to talk to you, Falla, and not at headquarters. I'm going to ask you to use your personal phone for this, so let's go to the Salerie Inn and get something to eat."

"Okay, Guv."

She looked at him questioningly, but said nothing, for which he was grateful.

The coastal area called La Salerie is part of St. Peter Port, but north of the main shopping section of the town, the marinas, and docks. The name describes its old function as a salt manufactory, and the curve of the coastline embraces a wide stretch of bay emptied twice a day by the thirty-foot tides of the island. Echoing the contours of the coast are a row of eighteenth-century houses, some with small front gardens, some built flush along Glategny Esplanade, their walls bending around Salerie Corner, and it was in one of these that Liz Falla had her flat.

They drove down Val des Terres into town, past the Guernsey Brewery and the bus terminus. To the right, beyond Castle Cornet, Moretti saw that the islands of Herm and Jethou were obscured by mist, and the windshield of the car was spotted with moisture. Past the bottom of St. Julian's Avenue, the hoardings around what had once been the Royal Hotel, one of *the* places to see and be seen, now a hole in the ground. On past more hoardings and boarded up buildings, all scheduled for renovation. No risk of them remaining as they were, crumbling and becoming ruins and rubble — too much money now on the island, and these would soon be cleaned and painted and prettied up once more, home to some of the businesses associated with the offshore island boom.

Liz Falla manoeuvred the Mercedes into a narrow parking space outside the Salerie Inn. Moretti glanced across the road at the old careening hard, the exposed area of beach near the jetty where his mother's ancestors had brought their boats up for cleaning, three or four hundred years ago. The tide was on the turn, and a lone cormorant was fishing out in the bay. Overhead a tern shrieked and dived into the water, then swooped off followed by an irate gull.

"I live quite close, Guv. Do you want to use my phone now?"

"Let's eat first."

The inn was painted blue, not navy or marine blue, but the blue of the sea below the cliffs over Saints Bay on a summer day. There were hanging baskets and window boxes of petunias and geraniums the length of the building and through the broad glass windows Moretti caught a glimpse of the splendid brass fittings of the inn's old lamps. He had once asked how old they were and was told "old."

The section on the right of the door was quiet, and they sat down at one of the round polished wood tables beneath the patterned Lincrusta ceiling. A collection of blue and white plates sat on a rack just below ceiling level near the dartboard, where they were safe from random darts. Nobody was using the dartboard, and there was only one other couple at a table across the room — not locals, because they were studying the ubiquitous tourists' friend, *Perry's Pathfinder*, the route map and town plan of the island, with the zeal of military leaders planning a campaign.

"Been thinking about it ever since we passed the brewery — I could use one of their Special Creamy Bitters. What can I get you, Falla?"

Liz Falla stuck to coffee — "they do good cappuccino here"— and they both decided on fish and chips. Moretti gave their order at the bar, which boasted more of the "old" brass fittings with fine horses' heads on them, and returned to the table. Liz Falla's usual expression of sunny insouciance was gone, he noticed.

"What I'm asking you to do is — irregular, Falla, so you are free to refuse. I'm going to ask you to cover for me."

"And what will you be doing, Guv?" She was cool; he liked that.

"Leaving the island."

At that moment their meal arrived, and Liz Falla waited until the server had gone.

"You'll be somewhere between Grosseto and Siena, right?"

"Right." Moretti took a long draught of his beer.

"I'm supposing you have a plan for this, so why don't you tell me what it is first."

Actually, he didn't really have a plan. Yet. And what he did have depended on the co-operation of DC Liz Falla. "I'm leaving Sydney Tremaine at my place and you are the only one who is to know that. That's the first thing. After we've done what we have to do here, I shall pick up some supplies, go back to the hotel, and pick up Ms. Tremaine. We will leave by the patio exit and meet you out on the road. Okay so far?"

"Okay so far."

"I don't believe in coincidence, but I do believe that, just occasionally, you get lucky. And our biggest break is that Chief Officer Hanley is going on vacation. I know he won't cancel it."

"How do you know that, Guv?" Any misgivings she might have were not affecting his partner's appetite, Moretti noticed.

"Because I shall shortly be making a phone call to reassure him with news of a major break in the investigation. It will not be a lie, because that's exactly what has happened."

"Okay so far, Guv. But how am I going to cover for you? You're not going to be available for — how long?"

"Don't know. About a week, maybe less if I get lucky. It'll have to be something to do with the case, and I'm more concerned about any civilians finding out than I am about Hospital Lane finding out. But if you could avoid saying anything at all about Italy, I'd be happier."

"I've got an idea." Liz Falla drank some of her cappuccino. "You've got a roomful of officers back at headquarters thinking this may have something to do with the Occupation, right? Well, how about me saying you're on Alderney."

"Alderney?"

On a clear day you could just see Alderney, lying beyond Herm and Jethou. It was the third largest of the Channel Islands, lying only about six miles off the coast of Normandy.

"What would I be doing on Alderney? Taking a break?"

"Looking for clues, Guv. Remember, there were some really bad things happened on Alderney during the war?"

Liz Falla was right. If the story of Guernsey's occupation was one of hardship, deprivation, and moments of sheer terror, Alderney's war years were unremittingly hideous. The whole population had been evacuated in 1940, leaving the island to be used as a self-contained concentration camp in the hands of sadists, and the true horror of those years was a story that had never been fully told.

"I could say something about certain leads pointing to Alderney and you having to go there."

"It might work." Moretti's respect for the resourcefulness of his partner was growing by the minute. "You'd be best keeping it vague."

"You're telling me! Being indefinite is usually best when you're pulling the wool over somebody's eyes — at least, in my experience." Liz Falla laughed, dipped a last chip in ketchup, and ate it. There was a small gap between her two front teeth that made her look even younger than she actually was. "What do you think, Guv? Or do you have a better idea?"

"No, I don't, so we'll go with yours."

"When will you be leaving? Is that why you wanted to use my phone?"

DC Liz Falla appeared to be taking his irregular proposal in her stride, and Moretti felt it had more to do with his partner's breezy insouciance about love and life in general than any starry-eyed admiration of his brilliant stratagem.

"No, but that might be a good idea also. I want *you* to use your phone — I'll go and buy some stuff and come back and pick you up — and this is what I want you to do."

Draining the last of his bitter, Moretti outlined the rest of his plan.

"I'm not going back to the States. If you put me on a plane, I'd only come right back here."

"I know. Anyway, you're a material witness. You're not going anywhere, and the only trick is to make sure you stay alive."

"That's why I'm here."

"That's why you're here. I presume your claim to know the reason for your husband's death was just window dressing?"

Moretti and Sydney Tremaine were in his sitting room, her suitcase on the floor between them. She was wearing jeans and a white turtleneck sweater, but she still looked far too exotic for her setting. Now that she was standing there, her spectacular red hair backlit by a coral-shaded standard lamp, surrounded by his parents' furniture, Moretti began to have severe doubts about his course of action.

"Yes. I've gone over and over anything and everything he ever said to me about *Rastrellamento* and I can come up with nothing. Does anyone know I'm here?"

"Only my partner, DC Falla. These are her phone numbers — her mobile and her home phone. She'll check up on you from time to time, but she won't come here unless it's absolutely necessary. Don't ever pick up the phone yourself if it rings. She'll leave a message, and you call her right back."

"Why? Where will you be?"

"Not here."

At which Sydney Tremaine sat down on the sofa and started to cry.

"I can't be left on my own, Ed. Please stay with me. I won't get pissed, and I won't be a pain in the ass, and I'll even stop calling you 'Ed' and start calling you Detective Inspector. Please."

Moretti sat down beside her. "I can't stay here, Sydney, even if you call me Detective Superintendent, but maybe you shouldn't get too pissed. Still, there are a couple of good reds in the kitchen, and I put some white wine in the fridge, and there's plenty of food and plenty of books and CDs. There are also some videos. When did you last eat?"

"I don't remember." She put her arms around his neck, and he wondered why it was that some people looked like hell when they cried, and some people actually glittered with tears in their eyes. He removed her clasped hands and stood up, pulling her up with him.

"Come on. I'll show you where everything is, and I'll make you an omelette." She followed him through into the kitchen.

"Look at that — a harvest table! Just gorgeous. I love antiques."

"Is it? That table's been in this place as long as I can remember." Moretti went over to the fridge and took out eggs, butter, cheese, and a bottle of white wine, which he opened first. "Here — have some of this. I've got some questions to ask you."

"And the first is why in the hell did I set myself up."

"It wasn't, but since you've brought it up —."

"Guilt, I guess. Gil was a shit sometimes, but he didn't deserve to die, and I think I may have helped matters along by taking off with Giulia."

"It's possible, but I don't think so. I think your husband brought it on himself. Tell me why you went to see Giulia Vannoni."

What Sydney told him was precisely what she had told Betty Chesler. *Nothing new there*, he thought, putting the grated cheese into the omelette and flipping it over. "Cut us some bread, will you? I'm going to draw the curtains and put on another light. We are going to eat, and you are going to tell me about your dancing career. I saw you once."

"Oh God — in which movie?"

"No. On stage. Guesting with the Royal Ballet at Covent Garden. Les Sylphides."

"One of my all-time favourites. The last act — I get goosebumps just thinking about it."

As they sat together at the kitchen table, it occurred to Moretti this was the first time he had invited anyone to eat with him — man or woman — since he had returned to the island. He poured both of them another glass of wine, and watched the colour come back into her face. Suddenly she put down her glass and for a moment he thought she was going to cry again.

"How can I be feeling like this? My happiest moments on this island have been drinking Aperol in Giulia's castello, and being here with you. Isn't that just terrible?"

"Terrible, no. Honest, yes. And sad. Sad that your husband did not leave you with happier times to remember. You said it yourself, he didn't deserve his death, but he also didn't deserve for you to falsify your emotions. He certainly never disguised his own — from what you told me, he always satisfied his own emotions and desires, however hurtful that was to you. I have wondered whether that played any part in your instant friendship with Giulia Vannoni."

"At first, yes, it was for revenge. But now I like Giulia for herself. Maybe I need the example of a strong woman who has carved out her own way in life."

"With some help, in her case." Moretti stood up.

"We all need some help, which is why you are going to stay here until I get back."

"You're leaving?" Sydney pushed back her chair and came around the table. Moretti took a step backwards and she smiled. "Are you afraid I'll lure you like some fairy spirit, to betray yourself, dance you to death?"

"That would be tricky. I don't dance very well."

"But you play piano like an angel. Be an angel and play for me before you go."

He played "Sweet Georgia Brown," and "Easy To Love," "Just One Of Those Things," and "Night And Day." And, feeling the need for parental guidance, he finished off with "Roses in Picardy."

"Nice," she said. "You're a romantic, I'd guess. And I'd also guess you're coming off a bad relationship. Am I right?"

"I don't know about bad, but I'm coming off one, as you put it — yes."

"Giulia is celibate. She says it makes life simpler. Does it, Ed?"

"Yes." *And harder. And emptier,* he thought. He got up from the piano. "I've got to go."

"Kiss me goodbye, Ed."

So he kissed her, picked up his bag and left, hearing her lock the door behind him.

They were used to doing without the piano player when there was an investigation underway, so they were surprised to see him at the club. Lonnie Duggan, the bass player who was also a bus driver in the summer, asked, "Shouldn't you be looking for clues? What the hell are you doing here?" Duggan was a big slow-moving man with blindingly fast fingers.

"Cooling off. What do you want to open with?"

"We have a tenor sax tonight, so 'I Fall in Love Too Easily.' Okay?"

"Perfect," said Moretti. "Garth is coming?" Garth Machin was with one of the international banks on the island, and spent long hours making millions for his clients in one of the financial buildings in La Plaiderie, not far from Hospital Lane. Classically trained, he was gifted enough to have made a career out of his saxophone, but he had opted for the security of money-making rather than the uncertainty of music-making. The angst induced by this decision gave his playing a delicious, melancholy edge.

"Yup, so he said."

"He'll be here." Dwight Ellis gave his serene smile.

Dwight Ellis, the percussion player, was one of only a handful of island residents from the Caribbean. Trinidad, in his case. He had ended up on Guernsey after drifting around the world, playing his drums, and now worked in a restaurant in St. Peter Port that served Afro-Caribbean food. He was of an optimistic, sunny disposition that, somehow, never cloyed. Once, Moretti had asked him if he encountered more racial discrimination on such a white island than anywhere else, and he had replied, grinning, "No more, no less, man, eh? I just add 'eh' to everything I say, and everyone think I'm real Guernsey. I call it protective colourin', eh?"

Garth Machin walked in, swearing away as usual, dragging on his cigarette and looking as far removed from his pinstripe persona as he could contrive. He used more obscenities than the rest of the Fénions put together, and Lonnie was of the opinion it was a public-school-boy's effort to bring himself down to their level. Moretti read it as an outward manifestation of inner frustrations.

"Come on you lazy buggars, get up off your arses and let's get this sodding show on the road." He looked in surprise at Moretti. "Thought you were occupied, Ed. Heard you had other things on your mind — such as escorting beautiful Broadway broads to hotels." He leered, and started to open his instrument case.

So, *that* little episode had got around. God help him if the world found out he had installed the beautiful Broadway broad in his home.

"Fuck off, Machin." A casual, scatological response was best. Machin loved to needle, and denial would only give credence to his throwaway insinuation.

After a brief exchange of similar pleasantries, the Fénions got their sodding show on the road.

With the sound of Garth's sax floating around him, Moretti walked north on the Esplanade, past St. George's Hall. Once, people had danced there. Once, the Red Cross parcels that had saved the life of many islanders in the dying days of the war had been distributed there. Now it was empty and deserted, waiting for another life. He let himself in to the small hotel in which he was staying the night, grateful that he had whiled away a few of the hours. Sleep would not come easily, he knew.

PART THREE
The Wrap

chapter fourteen

Beyond the stretch of its gravel courtyard the ochre length of the Pitti Palace, the Florence headquarters of the carabinieri, seemed to have absorbed more heat than the rest of the city. The lowering storm clouds overhead presaged thunder, and the late summer humidity hung heavy in the air.

Moretti had taken the first morning flight out of Guernsey to Gatwick, then transferring to an Alitalia flight that got him into Florence at one o'clock. He picked up his rented Alfa Romeo at the airport and drove straight to the Pitti Palace.

Giorgio Benedetti was waiting for Moretti in the entrance hall. He was at the same level of seniority as Moretti, but was somewhat younger — about mid-thirties, Moretti reckoned. They had briefly met at the drug symposium so they recognized each other, and it was easy to see what had attracted Liz Falla. Benedetti had dark hair and dark eyes and was as tall as Moretti, but there the resemblance ended: the carabinieri had an outgoing manner, a twinkle in his eye, and was quick to touch an arm or pat a shoulder.

"*Buon giorno,* Moretti! You made good time, and I know you have little of it, so let's get down to business. We'll go to my office, where I've got someone waiting to meet you who knows more about the part of the world that interests you than I do. A stroke of luck, really."

"I need a few of those. Who is he?"

"A colleague of mine, Emilio Ruggero. His home town is Grosseto, and that's where he's planning to retire. I told him what you wanted to know, and he thinks he can help you."

Emilio Ruggero was a short, stockily built individual who was only too happy to talk about his home town.

"I'm counting the days," he told Moretti, his wine-coloured cheeks growing ruddier at the thought. "I visit my family there all the time, so I know the area like the back of my hand." He held out one massive paw. "You wanted to know about a deserted village on a hill north of Grosseto, with a ruined church, and at one time a leading family who owned much of the land around — a family who may have left suddenly at the end of the war."

"Yes. Any ideas?"

"There was one village to the north of Grosseto in the old days, high on a hill, where most of the villagers left some time after the war, moved away. It had something to do with the principal landowner taking off, if I remember rightly. Some sort of a feud or something."

Moretti could feel his pulse quickening. "Do you remember the name of the family? Could it have been Vannoni?"

"I don't remember a name, and by my time they were all long gone. You'd have to talk to the older generation for that, the ones who are still alive, that is."

"I will. You don't by any chance remember the name of the village?"

"San Jacopo — yes, that'll be your village, I'm sure. And the church was the Chiesa San Jacopo. There was a fire there, I heard, so that'll be your ruin."

Emilio Ruggero chuckled and rubbed his hands together, pleased with himself. "Now, let's take a look at the map, and I'll show you the best way to get there."

Half an hour later, Moretti was saying goodbye to Giorgio Benedetti on the steps of the Pitti Palace.

"Sunday is a good day to drive — there'll be no transports or trucks on the autostrade." Benedetti gave an exclamation and put his hand into his pocket. "I nearly forgot — I have some more information about Sophia Maria Catellani here." He extracted a sheet of paper and handed it over to Moretti. "I don't suppose you'll be doing anything about her now, but when you do, look me up again and we'll have dinner together — agreed?"

"Agreed, and I am very grateful to you for taking the time, Giorgio."

"Anything for Elizabeta! *Che gioiosa ragazza*!"

Moretti folded the paper and put it away in his inside jacket pocket without looking at it.

The Alfa Romeo cleared the outskirts of Florence fairly swiftly, heading south down the autostrada. Adrenalin, and the excitement of the chase, were helping Moretti forget he was short of sleep, and he was anxious to make as few stops as possible. He had already arranged accommodation in Grosseto with the help of Emilio Ruggero, and he hoped to make just one stop on the journey.

At Poggibonsi, about fifty kilometres outside of Florence, he encountered his first major holdup with a stream of tour buses heading off to see San Gimignano's

fifteen medieval towers. With a supremé disregard for
other smaller vehicles, they travelled two and three
abreast, like sharks in shoals, jostling for supremacy
amongst each other. He decided to stop in Siena, which
was about thirty kilometres ahead.

He arrived only to discover that cars were not allowed
in the centre of the city. The air here was clearer and
cooler than in Florence so, leaving the car just inside the
old city walls, he made his way to the Piazza del Campo,
the lovely square outside the cathedral of Santa Maria.

Sitting in a little trattoria facing the white, green, and
red marbles of the duomo's facade, beneath an awning
the colour of the pigment that came from the rich, brown
earth of the city, Siena's great gift to painters, Moretti
ordered a glass of chianti and some taglierini pasta
with porcini. As his hand went to his pocket he felt the
paper Benedetti had given him, but instead he pulled out
the small map Emilio Ruggero had drawn for him and
took a look at it. Given that it was an unmarked, unlit,
deserted village he decided, reluctantly, that he would
have to wait until the next day to look for it.

The sky above the majestic roof of the Palazzo
Sansedoni was blue as the walls of the Salerie Inn. Moretti
looked at the fifteenth-century fountain that dominated
the open centre of the square, trying to remember its
name. *Fonte Gaia*, that was it. The fountain of joy. It
hit him like a bolt from that blue sky over him that he
was feeling as happy as he had in months. Years. He
wondered if it was the thrill of the chase, or the thought
of Sydney Tremaine. He suspected it was a bit of both.

The Hotel Airone in Grosseto was a recent structure,
built principally to serve the professional community
and to attract conventions and therefore business to
the city. It had satellite television and fax machines and

conference rooms, and was the sort of hotel to be found in any reasonably prosperous city. What it lacked in individuality it made up in amenities. And it had good security; even the parking was patrolled.

By the time Moretti checked in, it was early evening. He decided not to eat in the hotel, but to take a brief look at the town. Along the Corso the lights of the boutiques and the artisans' stores sparkled, and many of the locals were out taking a stroll in the cool, evening air. He found a pleasant-looking place near the Piazza Dante and sat outside to eat, and the scarlet petals of a climbing rose fell from time to time on to his table and into his Brunello di Montalcino.

Emilio Ruggero did indeed know his birthplace like the back of his hand. The map he had drawn for Moretti was precise in every detail, noting helpful landmarks and estimating the distance to the tiny lane, hardly a road, that led to San Jacopo. It was early in the morning when Moretti drove out of Grosseto, and the sun was only just coming up over distant hills, clearing the last shreds of morning mist from the valleys. The road was dotted with farmhouses and small settlements and beyond was the familiar pattern of the hill towns, rising straight up above the terraced fields. There had been rain in the night, and alongside the road the grapes on the vines glistened with moisture.

Moretti knew that he had to look out for the small town of Pagánico and head west in the direction of the Massa Maritima, but even with Emilio's map, the turn to San Jacopo took him by surprise and he almost missed it. The entrance to the lane was overgrown with bushes, vines, and briars, obscuring the shrine that Emilio told him he'd find in the remnants of an old stone wall that marked the corner. Moretti pulled the Alfa Romeo over to the side of the road and got out to take a look.

Yes, she was there, a battered porcelain Madonna concealed in greenery, protected for countless generations in her niche beneath the overhanging wall. Only vestiges of the cobalt blue of her gown remained, and the worn, hollowed-out bowl for offerings must have been empty for decades. Moretti picked a handful of wildflowers and placed them before her. Then, remembering something he had seen his godmother do, he kissed his fingers and placed them for a moment on her time-worn, serene face.

He considered leaving the car at the bottom of the lane and continuing on foot, but decided against it. He had deliberately chosen a powerful car, but it was a conspicuous one, and he was going to have enough trouble explaining his trip to Chief Officer Hanley without having the department budget stretched to replace an Alfa Romeo. The road was overgrown but passable, as far as he could see, and it looked like there had been some clearing of the underbrush. In fact, on closer inspection, it appeared to have been originally a fairly substantial thoroughfare, certainly wide enough to take cars.

"Good. Reassuring," he said out loud. If the house he was looking for was in San Jacopo, then there had to have been an approach from the road that was more than a cart track. He got back in the car and turned it on to the side road.

The hill climbed steeply and the road curved frequently, like a skier turning to cut the danger and speed of the slope. On each side lay neglected olive trees with dead, dangling branches, and the low stone walls were almost obscured by thickly growing ivy. A week or two of the rains of approaching autumn had spurred them on in their unchecked career, free of human hands. As Moretti moved further away from the main road, the land took on a wilder aspect, and he could see caves and tunnels cut into the hillside. They were almost certainly

Etruscan, and would have been used by San Jacopo's more recent inhabitants for storage of all kinds: wine, oil, livestock.

Moretti turned the steering wheel and took the Alfa Romeo around the next corner, then came to a sudden halt. Ahead of him was a narrow, hump-backed bridge that took the road over a small stream that rippled noisily over pebbles and boulders. He sat in the car and pondered the pros and cons of risking a bridge that looked as if part of it dated back to the Etruscans, and certainly had not been maintained for half a century. The cons won. He got out of the car, not bothering to pull it in to the side of the road. It was not likely to be obstructing anybody and, if it did so, so much the better in the circumstances. If he was on foot, he would just as soon any new arrival was as well.

The bridge marked the intersection of three roads: a continuation of the road he was on, and a smaller path that cut across it. He decided to keep going up the hill, toward what must have been the centre of the community of San Jacopo, for ahead of him he could see the first of the houses — more a tumbled pile of brick than any kind of dwelling.

The going was rough and steep, and Moretti was glad he'd brought solid boots with him. To each side of him lay the crumbled debris of San Jacopo, relics of lives lived, the shells that had once been homes for a vibrant, established community. Little, twisted pathways led off between the ruins, disappearing into the grey distance. It looked as if a storm was coming.

The steepness of the grade was dropping off gradually, and Moretti's lungs were grateful for it. Making yet another mental resolution to keep off cigarettes, he climbed one last little hillock in the flattening terrain.

And there it was. Suddenly, ahead of him. Just like that. As dramatic as that.

Silhouetted against the thunderclouds of the approaching storm was a house. No, not a house. A mansion. A palace. The Villa Vannoni. He was as certain of it as if it had its name up in lights, or carved in stone over the front door.

Not that he could see a front door — or many windows, come to that. From the towering bulk of its colossal central turret to the extremities of the two great wings to each side of the central block, the entire structure was smothered in wisteria. Tendrils of it shivered in the freshening breeze, reaching out toward him as he stood there, staring. Not even Columbus on the shores of the new world, nor yet Schliemann uncovering the remains of Troy, could have felt greater elation, he was sure.

The crumbled masonry of stables and buildings of various kinds lay around the great house, choked with undergrowth, beyond which Moretti could see what once must have been a formal garden that had encircled the villa, its topiaried evergreens and tended rose bushes now returned to nature. Ahead of him was the entrance and courtyard, and he could see the remains of cobblestones, thick with weeds. He walked slowly forward and stumbled over something solid, lying on the ground beneath a layer of long grasses and ivy.

It was what was left of a massive wrought-iron gate, which presumably had marked the entrance to the inner courtyard of the villa. Moretti bent down and pulled away handfuls of grass and ivy, tearing at them more feverishly as he cleared the pattern in the rusted *ferro battuto*. Scrolls and curlicues, elaborately detailed, surrounded a giant, ornate letter V.

There was a sharp, clacking sound from the house and Moretti jumped, feeling his heart thump against the wall of his chest. He stood up and moved back against a portion of a wall that remained more or less upright. A window on the ground floor seemed to be clear of creeper, and its wooden shutter, hanging on one hinge, had caught the strengthening wind. Even from where he stood, the creeper looked as if someone had cut or pulled it back. There was no point in looking for cover to approach the villa, there was none, so Moretti cautiously advanced across the cobbles. If someone was indeed waiting for him in the ruin with a knife, he hadn't much chance, unarmed as he was.

"What the hell," he said out loud, quickening his steps.

What was left of the massive front door lay on the cracked shards of black and white ceramic tiles in the entrance hall. Much of the wood had rotted, but someone had cut away chunks of the healthier sections — Moretti could see axe marks on what remained. From one of the shadows a scorpion scuttled across his boot to disappear back into the shadows again, and there were animal droppings on the filthy floor.

There were also signs that something or someone had been in the house in the not too distant past, for there were tracks across the dead leaves and dirt on the tiles. Moretti bent down to examine them. They were, unmistakably, the tracks left by a motorcycle. He followed them farther into the villa. From the look of the ceilings above him, cracked and covered with mould, he was more likely, he thought, to be crushed than knifed to death.

The tracks led him into what had once been the stateroom, the central salon of the house. A gigantic fireplace dominated the far wall, and the area around it looked as if it had been swept or cleaned at some time — certainly since the death of the great house. Swaths of faded flowered wallpaper hung like peeling skin from the damp walls, and strips of dingy white plaster trailed from the magnificent ceiling centrepiece that had probably surrounded a chandelier. And, faint as a ghost hovering above his head, was the indistinct outline of an angel painted on the ceiling. Moretti could see the wings, the flowing robes, and something held in now-effaced hands.

A trumpet or a lyre? Possibly. But this could also be an avenging angel, and what he held in his invisible hands was a sword, or a dagger. There may once have been other angels watching over the Vannoni family, but this one spirit was now all that was left of the unknown artist's design for the stateroom of the Villa Vannoni.

So that was where the wood from the door had ended up — in the fireplace. Moretti went over and touched the ashes and charred remains, although he was sure the visitor to the villa was long gone. Of course, it could be vagrants living rough, or locals who used the place as a shelter. But even as he reasoned with himself, Moretti knew in his heart of hearts, with every fibre of the instinct his partner had told him was admired by his fellow officers, that he was looking at the campsite of the killer of Toni Albarosa and Gilbert Ensor. Beyond the broken shutters the sky was getting darker. Taking out the flashlight he had with him, Moretti went back into the hallway.

The stairs that led to the upper floors had almost entirely rotted away, so it seemed unlikely the intruder had gone upstairs. Moretti confined the rest of his inspection to as much of the ground floor as seemed safe. In some rooms, the ceiling had fallen, and Moretti could see through to the sky above non-existent stretches of roof. Nowhere else was there any sign of recent habitation. Nowhere was there any sign of the family who had once lived there, not a fragment of furniture or decoration or personal belonging. The place had been completely, utterly stripped. Or ransacked.

When he had reasonably satisfied himself there was little more to be learned from the great wreck of a villa, Moretti took himself back out into the yard. Now he had to find the church — a more difficult proposition, since it had apparently burned down.

The likelihood was that it had been quite close to the home of the ruling family of San Jacopo, so Moretti started by checking the tumbled-down masonry around the abandoned garden. One of the pathways between the wreckage had a used look, as if something or someone had passed that way in the last little while; the weeds were less flourishing above what was left of the gravel, and there were traces of motor oil on the ground. Moretti found himself on the outskirts of the ruins in the immediate vicinity of the villa, looking across a small copse of ilex and chestnut and some blackened, charred masonry. So little was left standing that it had not been visible from the road.

The fire had been devastating enough to leave very little of what had been a solidly built structure, and Moretti wondered if he should just go back to the car. He could hear thunder beginning to rumble in the distance, and the setting made it seem more foreboding, heavy with menace. But he pushed on through a thicket of blackberry bushes and found himself in what probably had been the nave, the main area where the congregation of San Jacopo had been seated. Only a low outline of masonry marked where the walls had been.

Suddenly, Moretti felt chilled. Afterwards, he would tell his rational self that it was the storm front bringing in cooler air. But his sixth sense would know that what he experienced that day in the church of San Jacopo was not meteorological. It was an awareness of evil, a place that still held between its burnt-out walls the memory of a terrible act. He turned to leave and, as he did so, he saw something on the ground.

Candle wax. Someone had been in the church lighting a candle. Who — and for whom? Moretti had a sudden vision of the priest's costume and the dressmaker's dummy from which it came, ripped and slashed. Like a massacre, Betty Chesler had described it. Spooked,

Moretti got out of the ruin, made his way back across the blackberry thicket, and hastened down the hill to his car.

Just before he descended the slope that hid the villa from sight, he turned back. The dark clouds behind the massive turret of the villa were suddenly slashed open by lightning, as the first drops of rain began to fall.

By the time he got back into the car he was wet, trembling with cold and with emotion. He was also starving. Collecting his thoughts, he decided to get something to eat on the way back, and to pay a call on the questura, the local police station in Grosseto, to make inquiries. There had to be someone there who knew the local scene, although carabinieri were moved around far more than their British counterparts.

Moretti stopped at a roadside restaurant near the small hamlet of Batignano, just north of Grosseto. The place was quiet, as it was still early for lunch, and the proprietress welcomed him effusively and exclaimed at his wet clothes.

"The rain has stopped now. Give me your jacket, and I'll shake it out and hang it on the line to dry until you've finished your meal. The choices for today are up on the board over there."

She bustled away, leaving her pretty daughter to take his order: *zuppa di fagioli*, the traditional Tuscan bean soup, followed by a plate of grilled vegetables. Moretti drank his wine and waited for his meal to come, feeling his body gradually relax.

Over apricot tart, he struck up a conversation with the young woman.

"I've been hiking north of here — that's how I got so wet. Found an abandoned villa in what looks like it was once a village. Do you know it?"

The daughter, who appeared to have been hoping for a more flirtatious conversation, shrugged her shoulders and said, "San Jacopo? Yes. There was something happened there, something to do with the war. I don't know, really, but I think my mother does. *Mamma*!" Her mother came back out from the kitchen. "The signor found San Jacopo. He was wondering what happened there."

"Ah!" Her mother threw up her hands and shook her head. "Such a tragedy. The war brought us such destruction here, with Grosseto being bombed, and no one knowing at the end of it all who was the enemy and who was not. Let me think — the Vannonis, yes, that was the family. I was only a small child, of course, but I remember my mother talking about it."

In the end it is as simple as this, Moretti thought. *She knows what happened, and she's going to tell me.*

"I have an interest in local history," he said. "Can you take a moment and tell me about it?"

The proprietress needed no further invitation. She wiped her hands on her apron and sat down opposite him.

"Bad years they were, those last two years, after Mussolini was overthrown. People turned on the *fascisti* here — they were beaten up or worse, some of the leaders were arrested, and some joined the army to fight against the allies. The air raids started — it was terrible in Grosseto. Then the Germans arrived — I remember that, the tanks and armoured cars. They came looking for the prisoners of war who'd been held by the *fascisti* and then released, and were all over the countryside here. Quite in the open, often, until the Germans came."

"In the open, you say — you mean, the British prisoners?" Moretti asked.

"All kinds — Americans, Canadians, South Africans, even Turks were here. But yes, the British. After they got out they helped on the farms. My mother said everyone was sorry when they had to go into hiding."

"Where did they hide?"

"In the hills, some — like the partisans, the young men who'd run away to fight for freedom when the fascist militia started up again. Some tried to get to the coast, to Livorno. And some were hidden by families like the Vannonis."

"Looks like it was big property," interpolated Moretti. "Were they important?"

"Important?" His hostess's ample body shook with laughter at what was clearly an understatement. "They were *everything*, Signor! They owned land nearly to the coast, and had fifty or more tenant farmers on their property — my father was one of them. *Mezzadria* — you know about that?"

Moretti nodded. He knew enough to know it was the traditional farming system, now fallen out of favour in Tuscany, where the farmer had his own farm, shared his produce with the owner of the land, who made all the decisions about which crops to grow, but provided equipment and even financial help in hard times. In other words, a patriarchal, feudal system quite like the one that used to exist in Guernsey.

His hostess continued. "They were good proprietors, the Vannonis, my father always said. They took care of you, and when the war came they took care of all those kids whose parents were in Turin and Milan, where the bombs were falling. There were at least twenty little ones out on the property, evacuees, being looked after by the daughter."

"The daughter?"

"Sylvia. Lovely girl, my mother said — oh, not in looks, you understand, but in character. There was a saying in these parts: beauty goes to the Vannoni boys. So it was, in this case. And, of course, there was the British prisoner of war they hid, right there in one of the stables."

"So what happened? How was it they left the land and the villa?"

"Well, the story goes that the daughter fell for the British boy, head over heels. They used to meet in the church, so my mother told me. And she also told me the marchesa did not want Sylvia to marry — not just the soldier, but anyone, if you can believe such a thing. She was supposed to stay home and help *mamma* and *pappa* in their old age. It happened in those families, my mother said, and Sylvia was the eldest, not even that young when she met the British soldier. So they kept it a secret from her mother, and she was betrayed."

"Who by — do you know?"

"The priest, my mother said. But there was someone else who was also betrayed. The schoolteacher."

"A schoolteacher — where did he fit in?"

"He was the go-between, and that was what finally did them in. He was a Slovene from the north somewhere, a cripple — something wrong, so he couldn't fight. The children really liked him, but he was suspected by some as being secretly in the pay of the local fascist party. When the marchesa found out about her daughter from the priest — God rot his soul! — she told the partisans that the schoolteacher was a traitor. They found him in the church with the British soldier, asked no questions, and killed them both. It was how it was in those days."

"Good God." Moretti sat silent for a minute. "But why abandon their ancestral home? Why give it all up? Doesn't make sense to me."

"Ah, everyone wondered about that. To be sure, poor Sylvia killed herself, but it came as a shock when they moved right out of San Jacopo. Lock, stock, and barrel. Cleared all their possessions out of the villa and walked away."

"The daughter killed herself?"

"Yes, in the church. At night. She set fire to it, and then she killed herself." The storyteller crossed herself. "There are ghosts up there, they say. Lights in the church and the sound of wailing — not that many people go near anymore."

"I can imagine. Did anyone stay to look after the property? A housekeeper, for example?"

"Not that I know of. Most of the servants went with them, even though it meant leaving their families. But the farms around here were badly damaged during the war, and the Vannonis were good to the people who worked for them. Many of them came from families who'd been with the Vannonis for generations."

The little restaurant was beginning to fill up, and the proprietress smiled apologetically. "I must go back to the kitchen, Signor. And don't forget your jacket."

"I'm very grateful for your time." Moretti got up.

"Oh —" the proprietress stopped and turned back to him. "You mentioned a housekeeper?"

"Yes. I wondered if they'd left anyone behind as a caretaker."

"Funny you should say 'caretaker.'" The woman laughed. "That's what she did, once the truth about the daughter got out, and her lover was killed. My mother said Sylvia Vannoni was made a prisoner in her own home, never leaving her room. And the person who took care of her was the housekeeper. Scarpa, I think, was her family name — they're still around, run a souvenir store on the Corso in Grosseto. In these parts they called the housekeeper 'the jailer.' Only one day the prisoner escaped, and killed herself in the church where her lover and her friend were betrayed, and died."

The marchesa, the German commandant, the priest, the housekeeper.

Moretti saw again in his mind's eye the mutilated costumes in the lodge at the Manoir Ste. Madeleine, stabbed through the heart.

chapter fifteen

September 21st

The questura in Grosseto's Piazza Roselli was an imposing structure, the front facade curving gently around a large pool with a fountain in the centre. Moretti parked the Alfa Romeo in the forecourt and went into the building. About an hour later he came out again, little wiser than when he went in. There were no officers left from the years when Emilio Ruggero started his career in the carabinieri before being posted elsewhere, and many of the present police force came from other areas. They had little or no knowledge of local conditions around Grosseto, particularly of events that occurred over fifty years ago.

But one thing was certain. Without exception, every officer he spoke to confirmed that a crime could easily be covered up in the circumstances that prevailed at the time. One young officer who was a history buff was happy to talk to him about the events of the time.

"My grandfather was in the carabinieri during the war. He refused to take the oath of loyalty to the Republican government after Mussolini's downfall, fled to the woods, and joined the partisans. But his brother didn't. My grandfather said that, in those last years of the war, all hell broke loose. You had men wandering the countryside, many claiming to be other than they were — prisoners of war who were *not* prisoners of war, but could have been many things, like Austrian deserters from the German Army, or spies for the *fascisti*. You had communist partisans and anti-communist partisans, who hated each other's guts. You had corpses alongside the roads and bodies buried in the woods. Easiest thing in the world, to cover up a murder. Death was everywhere."

Death was everywhere. No point then, thought Moretti, *in spending hours unravelling red tape so he can go through old records of ancient crimes*. Because there would have been no crime reported; no one would have recorded the execution by the partisans of a fascist sympathiser and a prisoner of war who got in their way. And Sylvia Vannoni had taken her own life.

Or had she? Was her death the reason the principal family in the area had pulled up centuries-old roots and moved their lives so far away? Among all the question marks in the case, one thing was certain: the killer knew, or had uncovered, a great deal about what had happened in San Jacopo.

By the time Moretti left the questura it was late afternoon, and the storm had cleared the air, leaving behind the promise of a beautiful sunset. He decided to go back along the Corso and see if he could find the souvenir shop run by the Scarpa family. Perhaps he could pick up a small token of appreciation for DC Falla, he thought, though heaven knew what her tastes were.

It didn't take too long to find the store. It turned out to be one of the oldest established in the area, and a generous donation to a local panhandler gave him the answer.

"Scarpa? Souvenirs? Just ahead of you, Signor. Thieves, all of them. Genuine antiques, fresh from their factory in Milan. Take my advice, don't waste your money, Signor. *Grazie mille!*"

The mendicant's judgment was a bit harsh. The boutique was selling copies of Etruscan pottery and artifacts, some of them quite well done, none of them pretending to be other than they were. The owner was a man in his forties, long-haired, in jeans, with an earring, and a tattoo of a rose on his bicep. He acknowledged Moretti's presence with a nod, and went on reading his book. Moretti noticed that it was a war story of some kind, with a picture of war planes on the cover. Picking up a small statue of a cat, he went over to the counter.

"Local history, is that? They tell me there were air raids on Grosseto during the war."

The shop owner looked up from his book reluctantly. "Not local, but it's a good one. Yes, Grosseto was bombed. I wasn't around, of course, but it's a story my grandparents never tire of telling — you know, like most of that generation who lived through it."

Moretti laughed. "I know. As a matter of fact, a woman out in the country just north of here was bending my ear about some local drama that happened during the war — sounded highly unlikely to me. About a family called Vannoni, and a daughter called Sylvia who killed herself, because she was in love with a British prisoner of war they were hiding. Said she was kept a prisoner by the housekeeper. They called her the jailer, she said, around here. Are you from Grosseto yourself?"

The shop owner was now looking more interested. He put his book down on the counter and said, "Yes, I'm local, and the story's true, as far as I know. The woman she called the jailer was a distant cousin of my father's or my grandfather's, I don't remember which. Luisa Scarpa. She was a midwife, which is how she got involved, or so it was always told in my family."

"Midwife?" Moretti felt as if he were frozen to the floor.

"Yes, didn't she tell you that part? Mind you, nobody talks about it much from that generation, because there's no doubt someone got away with murder."

"There was a baby? The baby was murdered?"

"I don't know whether it lived or died, or even what sex it was. Two guys were murdered, I think — a wartime thing. Traitors, I gather."

"I'm amazed the woman I spoke to didn't tell me about the baby."

"I'm not. There's people like my grandparents who want everyone to know what they went through in the war, and people like Luisa Scarpa who'd just as soon everyone forgot. I think it was some sort of deathbed confession, and whoever was told passed it on to my mother. Compared to some of the stuff that happened around here, it was nothing special."

"I suppose so."

Moretti paid for the cat and left the shop. He didn't stop for a drink, because he no longer felt thirsty. Instead he hurried back to the hotel and up to his room. There he put in a call to DC Falla's home number, leaving a message on the answer-phone as arranged. He then ordered a drink and something to eat from room service, and waited.

About an hour later, after he had finished his meal, the phone rang. It was Liz Falla.

"Am I ever glad to hear from you, Guv. There's a lot to tell you. How's it going?"

"Better than I could have hoped. You go ahead, Falla."

"First of all, the son has done a bunk."

"Gianfranco?"

"That's the one — but don't worry, Guv, because we know where he is — he's in the nick. He's in Florence, being held on morality charges. He was picked up in a sweep in the — hang on a tick while I check this — Sant'Ambrogio area. Using the services of underaged prostitutes."

"Christ. So he did a bunk because he is a pervert, and not because he is a murderer, maybe."

"Maybe — but he wants to do some sort of deal, which is how we know where he is. Says he knows something. The police in Florence got in touch with us, and I told them you're on your way." Liz Falla gave him the address of the questura where Gianfranco Vannoni was being held, and there was a chuckle on the other end of the phone. "They'll be amazed at how quickly, won't they?"

"I'll head back there now — it'll be quieter driving at night. Anything else?"

"Yes, PC Brouard got lucky with his Internet search, and he's found where the daggers were made. Not the Hitler Youth one, but the others."

"Fantastic! Where?"

"Pistoia, believe it or not."

"Really?" said Moretti, "Give me the details."

"I'll give you a shortened version of PC Brouard's saga, he's that full of himself. Seems there are all types of arts and crafts going on in Pistoia and he found a small forge where they're still making all kinds of artifacts. Of course, they didn't speak English, but we managed to make ourselves understood. He asked them if they'd ever made daggers that matched the description he gave them and they said yes."

"Then they must know who ordered them?"

"It was a Signor Baza, and he mailed them a cash advance."

"How many, and where did they send them?"

"Four. And they didn't send them, Guv. Someone picked them up."

"Signor Baza?"

"No. It was a woman. They never got her name, but she paid the balance, and they described her." Liz Falla paused.

"Well, go on."

"All they could remember was that she was thin and red-headed."

"Oh God," said Moretti. "Did they say whether she had an American accent?"

"I asked him to ask that, and they couldn't remember — she didn't say too much. Don't worry, Guv, Mrs. Ensor's not going anywhere. I told her there'd been a threat made against her, sent to the station. But I think what's working best is what I told her about you. That you're for the high jump if there's a cock-up."

"That just about sums it up, Falla. Now let me give you my news, which is for your ears only, by the way."

She listened in silence and then she said, "Oh, Guv, that poor woman and that poor little baby. It's just terrible. To kill those two men is bad enough. But to kill a *baby*."

"Oh no," said Moretti. "I don't think so. I don't think that baby died. I think, Falla, he or she is very much alive."

Gianfranco Vannoni looked a mess. He was wearing the clothes in which he had been arrested, and his pale wool jacket and pants had not responded well to being slept in. He also had a black eye and a fat lip.

As Moretti looked over the charge sheet, he saw that the injuries were not as a result of police brutality, but had been inflicted by the thirteen-year-old in the car with him, who had objected to what the report described as "certain services required of her by Signor Vannoni," and had fought him off. It was her noisy resistance that had attracted the attention of the arresting officers and, from the report on the victim, it was likely the disagreement had been over the financial arrangements. The victim was undoubtedly one sad, street-smart little girl who had long ago lost not only her innocence, but the luxury of objecting to any demand made by men like Gianfranco Vannoni.

"Well," said Moretti, looking up from the report. "This is a sorry state of affairs, Signor Vannoni. I understand your father has refused to put up bail. What about your mother, the marchesa?"

"My father is a bastard, and my mother has little spare cash. My father makes sure of that." Gianfranco Vannoni winced as he spoke — clearly his split lip was painful. Moretti thought of the neglected behind-the-scenes areas of the Manoir Ste. Madeleine.

"You wanted to talk to me?"

"Yes. I would like to spare my mother and sister the pain of seeing this — stupid indiscretion of mine reported in the papers. You look like a man of the world, Inspector — I'm sure you understand how a man might want a little excitement from time to time?" Risking his split lip, Gianfranco Vannoni smiled conspiratorially.

"If a little excitement means having paid sex in a car with a child, Signor, then no, I don't understand. Let's cut the bullshit and get to the point. It does you no credit that it has taken fear of exposure to make you divulge information possibly relevant to two murders."

"But I didn't know it was, until my mother told me you were questioning people about the other house. Then I did some thinking, and realized what might be going on."

"Which was —?"

Gianfranco Vannoni removed a large white silk handkerchief from his pocket and mopped his damp forehead. "What reassurances do I have that we can forget the — matter in hand?"

"None. But we can add the charge of obstruction to the list, if you like. Best you talk to me."

The story Gianfranco Vannoni told was, in the beginning, essentially the story Moretti had heard twice already that day. What was interesting about Gianfranco's version was where his sympathies lay: unequivocally, uncritically, with his family. Never once in the telling was there the slightest suggestion that anyone had done anything wrong.

Except Sylvia Vannoni. In fact, most of the account concerned the reputation of the Vannonis in San Jacopo: how beloved they were, how respected — and how the selfishness of the woman who had been his aunt had changed everyone's lives. Moretti thought it was a particularly unpleasant example of how subjective both history and fact really arei. And what added to the unpleasantness was the irony of this unprincipled decadent talking about honour and duty on the heels of his own unsavoury conduct. Impatient with the ongoing moral rhetoric, Moretti attempted to speed things up.

"So, you feel that someone is taking revenge on your family for the indiscretion of your aunt and her subsequent suicide? You have told me she, to use your words, 'behaved improperly.' Let's be more specific: she had an affair and became pregnant."

"That is correct." It was startling to watch just how difficult it was for Gianfranco Vannoni to say even that much. He flushed, and his pricey calf brogues from which the shoelaces had been removed, shuffled loosely on the floor.

"You speak of the goodness of your family in San Jacopo during the war. They hid a British prisoner of war, you tell me."

"Yes! At great risk to themselves."

"And he was the father, I presume."

"Oh, no."

"No?" Moretti sat up. It had been a long night, and he had been drifting into a semi-somnolent state, since the story was now so anticlimactic.

"No. They used him as cover. They met when my aunt Sylvia went out to take him food, and she lied about going to church as well. Said she was going to mass and confession, when she was meeting her lover."

"Let's back up a little. They? If not the POW, then —?"

But Moretti knew, even before Gianfranco Vannoni gave him the answer.

"Some son of a bitch from Slovenia, hired as a schoolteacher when all the real men were fighting for their country. A coward and a lecher. He was her lover."

"The schoolteacher," Moretti repeated.

"Him. And now Mario is trying to add a schoolteacher of some ethnic persuasion or other to the cast of *Rastrellamento*. I have never seen my mother so angry. You've seen my mother in action, so you'll know just what a stink she's been raising. That's why I had to get away — she leans on me, you know, and I just had to escape for a while. But it makes you think, doesn't it?"

"But your mother is not a Vannoni."

"That has nothing to do with anything. When she married the Marchese Vannoni she became the keeper of the family honour, who knew all the secrets. She was a Vitali. Her family owned the jeweller's stores of the same name."

So the marchesa's family were in trade, albeit the luxury trade. The Vitalis owned one of the boutiques, Moretti knew, on the Ponte Vecchio, and he'd seen others in Rome and Milan.

Gianfranco Vannoni kept talking. "When the family moved away from San Jacopo, they settled at first in Florence. The marriage between my father and my mother was, to all intents and purposes, an arranged marriage, combining property, wealth, and name. We children in the family were told about Sylvia, and sworn to secrecy."

"Why tell you? Why not let it rest?" Moretti asked.

"Because vicious and inaccurate lies are still being told about San Jacopo, and the family thought it best we hear the truth."

"The truth," Moretti repeated. "I assume this is why your mother is in Guernsey. To escape what you call vicious lies."

"Yes, partly. About ten years ago, there was someone — we never knew who — asking questions in the region, stirring things up again. Sylvia may be dead, but the damage goes on. I have begged my mother to break the silence and put an end to her exile, but she won't hear of it. She says she only married my father for his name, and he married her for her family's money, and she's damned if she's going to end up without the one thing she wanted: a title with an unblemished reputation. My mother's social life was ruined by the stories, and it helped bring about the end of my parents' marriage. Can you blame her for hating my father for what his dead aunt has done to her life?"

Moretti did not respond. Bracing little homilies about the difference between good and evil, truth and lies, would have no impact on Gianfranco Vannoni, and really didn't matter, as far as the case was concerned. "So, your great-aunt had an illicit relationship with a Slovene schoolteacher in San Jacopo, and they used a British prisoner of war as a go-between, or as cover. The Slovene had pro-fascist sympathies, and was shot by the partisans, along with the Briton. Later, Sylvia killed herself. Is that substantially correct?"

"Yes," Gianfranco Vannoni agreed. "Could I have a cigarette, by any chance?"

As Moretti took out his packet of cigarettes it occurred to him he hadn't smoked in over twenty-four hours. Across the table, some of the swagger returned to Gianfranco. He drew deeply on the cigarette and attempted to straighten his bedraggled jacket.

"So, Detective Inspector, what is happening about my present situation?"

"If the girl does not press charges — and it is highly unlikely she will — you will be released — but that is only because you are a material witness in a murder investigation, and should return immediately to Guernsey. That is what I have told the arresting officer, and also that I will be leaving with you." As Moretti looked at the battered face of Gianfranco Vannoni across the table, it struck him that this debauched piece of pond life was providing him with an alibi for his own Italian adventure.

"Before we attend to the paperwork, there is one part of the story you have not completed for me. What happened to the baby?"

"I don't know — I swear to you that's the truth. I don't even know if Sylvia miscarried, if it was a boy or a girl, or even if the baby survived."

"The answer to that," said Moretti, "is yes." He stood up and gathered together the papers from the table between them. "Yes, I think we can safely assume the baby survived." He left the room, ignoring the outstretched hand of Gianfranco Vannoni.

It had been an unpleasant journey back to the island. Lack of sleep and the repellent proximity of Gianfranco Vannoni at his elbow for the two-and-a-half-hour flight to Gatwick, plus another hour on to Guernsey, made Moretti feel a desperate need for a hot bath or a swim in the ocean. Thankfully, DC Falla had arranged for the

Guernsey flight to be held for fifteen minutes, so Moretti was spared sitting at Gatwick for about two hours making small talk with his unwelcome flight companion. There must be some puzzlement at Hospital Lane as to how he had got to Florence from Alderney and back with such speed, but with any luck, such minutiae would have faded from the collective memory by the time Chief Officer Hanley returned.

This time, as he walked from the plane with Gianfranco Vannoni and saw DC Falla up on the observation deck, Moretti felt only relief.

She was waiting for him as they came through customs, with two uniformed officers.

"Good morning, sir. The officers here will take Mr. Vannoni with them to the station."

"I'll go along —"

"No, sir."

Startled out of his semi-somnolent state by such *lèse-majesté*, Moretti watched as his partner took hold of Gianfranco Vannoni by the arms and held them out for the handcuffs carried by one of the constables.

"I'll explain in a minute, sir."

As Vannoni and his escort disappeared through a separate entrance from the other passengers to the waiting police van, Liz Falla said, "Sorry, Guv, but I couldn't say in front of Vannoni. There's been another knifing."

They were walking briskly toward the exit doors of the airport. "Who? Not —?"

"Ms. Tremaine is at my place."

"Your place?"

"She's fed up with your selection of videos. I told her she'd probably see you later on today. No, the victim is Dan Mahy. He's dead."

"Mahy. Dear God, poor old devil. I should have got him moved into town."

"He'd never have gone, Guv, you know that."

"Who found him? When?"

"Someone from Social Services. This morning. We're going out there now."

"How did the Alderney cover story go?"

They were in the police Mercedes, heading south. Rain was falling steadily, and the wind whipped leaves and small twigs against the windscreen.

"Iffy. But everyone now thinks it was a cover for tracking down Vannoni. When asked questions, I just looked inscrutable. DCI Hathaway says there'll be some explaining to do about not reporting."

"There's more to add to the story I told you on the phone, Falla, but I'll go over it when we get to the station. How did your other inquiries go — at the airport, I mean?"

"I confirmed that the airport is closed between the hours of nine at night to nine in the morning for all flights. Even private planes can't operate during those hours, because the tower is closed. But — a funny thing. About a week ago they found one of their jackets — those lime-green sleeveless ones worn by personnel? — down beyond one of the administrative buildings, just lying on the ground. It was one of the ones worn by the terminal duty officers, and they're stored in a room down between the customs area and the public toilets. They swear the room is always kept locked, and don't know how it got there. I took a look while I was waiting for you — there's a sign up: NO UNAUTHORIZED PERSONS BEYOND THIS POINT."

"Interesting. Clearly *some* unauthorized person managed. Here we are."

Ahead of him, Moretti could see through the heavy mist a cluster of police cars and vans, the cordon of tape cutting off the path that led to the old cottages. It was only six days, in weather just like this, since he had spoken to the old man.

"A stupid, dumb oversight."

"What is, Guv?" Liz Falla brought the Mercedes to a halt just outside the cordon.

"My failure to grasp the importance of Dan Mahy. I was so caught up with the damned Vannoni family, I never even thought he might be in any danger. I thought a lot of it was the ramblings of old age."

"Who was to know, Guv." Liz Falla got out of the car, and swore under her breath as her heels sank into the soft, soggy turf.

"I should have known. That's my job. Where was he killed?"

"In his cottage. The SOC people are out here, of course, but I've told them to touch nothing till you got here."

They stumbled down the sharp incline to what was left of the Hanois cottages into the wind that whipped in off the sea below them. Moretti could hear it crashing against the rocks. Most of the cottages looked like something out of the village of San Jacopo, but the one that presumably had belonged to Dan Mahy still looked like a place of possible habitation. The heavily mossed roof was intact, and there were curtains over the windows, whose glass was still in one piece. He remembered the sensation he experienced on his last visit, as the years coalesced into one single suspended moment. Which past, indeed, had brought about the murder of Dan Mahy?

"Morning, Moretti."

"Jimmy. Hi."

Jimmy Le Poidevin stood in the entrance of Dan Mahy's beloved cottage, his official garb a stark anachronistic statement against the ancient weathered door.

"The body's in here. Also the medico. No fancy dagger this time — looks like a common or garden kitchen knife. In my humble opinion, that is."

The front door led straight into the main living area, which looked as if it were indeed the only living area for the occupant. There was a couch close to the fireplace, a battered metal stove in a far corner, an equally battered wooden table with two chairs. Stuffing was coming out of the padded back of the couch, which was heaped with a couple of blankets and a large, stained, uncovered pillow. Two oil lamps, one by the stone fireplace, the other on the table, seemed to have provided the only illumination. The sole decoration on the walls, which bore the remnants of a faded, flowered wallpaper, was what looked like old family photographs. There was a faintly fetid smell in the air of unwashed clothing, mould, and drains.

Dan Mahy was lying in the fetal position on a piece of faded, scorched rug close to the fireplace. His heavy boots were by the door and he was wearing slippers on his feet, and he would have looked quite comfortable were it not for the knife protruding from his upper back through the dark oiled wool of his Guernsey. Moretti bent down and looked at the old man's face. In death it appeared calm, his thin pale lips curved in a half-smile. Moretti looked up at the doctor.

"Dr. Lawson, isn't it?" Lawson was one of the duty doctors from Princess Elizabeth Hospital Moretti liked working with. He was young, sharp witted, and yet far from opinionated.

"That's right, Detective Inspector."

"Any idea when this happened?"

"From the state of the body, I'd estimate probably about twelve hours ago. Early evening yesterday, say."

Moretti turned back to Le Poidevin. "Any sign of a break-in?"

"No. The door was open."

"So he let his visitor in."

From the corner of the room Liz Falla said, "And from the looks of it, made his killer a cup of tea." She pointed to two chipped mugs and a battered metal teapot on a wooden table against the wall. There was also the remains of a loaf of *gâche* — the yeasty, raisin-filled Guernsey bread still made on the island.

Moretti stood up, feeling as he did so the unpleasant combination of fatigue and shock dragging at his leg muscles.

"What's been taken out of the drawer, Falla?" He pointed to a collection of small objects, scattered on the table surface above a half-open drawer set in the side of the table.

"Looks like a collection of Occupation memorabilia, Guv." Liz Falla pulled out a pair of latex gloves and pulled them on. "Ration books, old cinema tickets, that kind of thing."

Moretti joined her at the table. Piled on its stained, pitted surface was a hoard of wartime island ephemera, most of it the worse for wear: mildewed newspapers, recipes for everything that could possibly be made out of kelp and carrageen, tattered leaflets of various kinds in both English and German. There were some coins, one or two medals, and a couple of rusty penknives. Moretti picked one up. The German manufacturer's name was still faintly visible on it.

"Well," he said, looking across the table at Liz Falla, "I think we can safely say we now know where the murder weapon in the bunker came from."

"Can we?" His partner waved her hand over the motley collection in front of them. "There's nothing nearly as valuable in this lot, is there?"

"No, but Dan Mahy told me he had a windfall in his *pied-du-cauche*."

"You think he sold it to the killer."

"Who then killed him when we appeared to be getting closer. Why *is* Ms. Tremaine at your place, Falla?"

Liz Falla shot a meaningful look in the direction of Jimmy Le Poidevin, who was standing in the cottage doorway oozing impatience and hostility. "I'll tell you on the way back to the station, Guv," she said.

chapter sixteen

It was only twenty-four hours since Moretti had left, and the Alderney alibi was beginning to sprout as many holes as her uncle Jack's old wreck of a tub that he kept in St. Sampson harbour and refused to get rid of, although Liz Falla's aunt Doreen called it the bottomless bucket. By the evening of the first full day after Moretti's departure, she had parried questions from Detective Superintendent Hathaway, who was in charge in Chief Officer Hanley's absence, bitten her tongue and ignored insinuations of incompetence from Jimmy Le Poidevin, and fobbed off the heavy-handed witticisms of some of her colleagues about the disappearance of Ed Moretti after only eight days of partnership with her.

Eight days, she thought, as she drove herself home in the early evening. *It seems more like eight weeks, and that has nothing to with Moretti.* If there was one plus in the whole sticky situation, it was that she liked working with the guy. *Now there is a surprise*, she reflected, as she brought the Mercedes to a halt alongside the seawall opposite her flat on the Esplanade. And the biggest surprise of all was the presence of Sydney Tremaine in the Guv's cottage. Still waters run deep, as her grandmother always said.

As she went into her sitting room she saw that the light on her answer-phone was flashing. Given the current state of her love life it was either a member of the Jenemie group, her mother, that bloody DS Hathaway again — *oh please*, she thought, *not him, please* — or Moretti's glamorous guest. She pressed the "play messages" button.

The first message was from Nick Le Page, Jenemie's keyboard player.

"Liz, it's Nick. We've got a gig at the weekend — the Petit Moulin. Rehearsal tonight at my place."

Liz Falla grinned. So like Nick to assume she could make it, not being a nine-to-five man himself — *correction*, she thought, *not being an in-any-way-employed man himself*. An aging and charming flower-child who had survived the excesses of the sixties, he still did not believe in toiling and spinning, if he could possibly help it. He left that to his schoolteacher wife.

The second message was from Sydney Tremaine. Liz had checked in with her already a couple of times, and both times she had sounded fine when she picked up the phone after hearing Liz's voice on the answer-phone. This time was different.

"Liz — please call. There's something — I'm scared. Liz — please call."

There was panic in her voice, and she sounded close to tears. Liz picked up the phone, waiting impatiently for Moretti's voice on the tape to say, "I'm not here. Leave a message at the beep."

"Ms. Tremaine — it's Liz Falla. What's up?"

She had barely completed the final word before the phone was picked up and she heard Sydney Tremaine.

"Thank God — it's going to be dark soon and I don't want to spend another night here. I'm leaving." Her voice was ragged with tension.

"Don't go anywhere. I'm coming right over. It'll only take me about five minutes — promise me, don't move till I get there. Then, I promise, I'll get you out of there."

Liz Falla hung up without waiting for Sydney Tremaine to reply.

Sydney Tremaine was not normally a nervous woman. Life in the performing arts had given her nerves of steel — she did not count stage fright as evidence of emotional weakness — and the slings and arrows of an outrageous husband prone to frequent temper tantrums and with unsavoury sexual proclivities had further hardened her.

His murder had changed all that. She was rattled. She was prepared to believe that her imagination might well be working overtime in the circumstances, but she simply could not endure another night on her own at Ed's place.

At first it had been fun. Shamelessly, she had poked around, examining all Moretti's records and the truly antediluvian player he used. She checked every book in his bookcases and came to the conclusion that anyone who shelved Robert Ludlum and Ovid's Metamorphoses in the original Latin cheek by jowl was much too clever for her. She had not gone through the contents of the wonderful old keyhole desk, but she *had* taken a peek at a letter or two left on the writing surface. Well, more than a peek.

One was from someone at Scotland Yard, who had some interest also in jazz, and was about to retire. He spoke of his first meeting with Ed Moretti: "This skinny young law student who sat down at the piano and played himself into a part-time job with the rest of us pick-up players. I still have feelings of guilt, Ed, that it wasn't the music that seduced you, but my métier. Has it been worth it? From the defence of innocence or the prosecution of evil to a profession that has been called the blind eye of history?"

The other was from a woman called Valerie. Sydney read only the opening sentence: "The house is sold, finally. I can't wait to shake you and the dreck of yesteryear from the soles of my Mephistos."

Holy Hanna, she thought, putting it down. *What happened, Ed?*

Most of the videos were old black-and-white movies — *Casablanca*, some Greta Garbo, some European stuff with which she was not familiar. She played his records, watched some of the movies, read an early Iris Murdoch, and drank too much wine. Then the noises started.

Swish-swish-swish. They seemed to come from above her, on a level with the upper floor. At first she was not particularly bothered. When she arrived she noticed that the high walls on each side were thick with plants and growths of various kinds, and she assumed it was the wind blowing them around, or the ivy that grew on the cottage walls. But even through the haze of too much soave she realized they were strangely rhythmic, systematic, almost. Just as she was beginning to feel jumpy, they stopped. It started to get dark, and she went into the kitchen to get herself something to eat.

As she came through the doorway she was aware of a movement outside the kitchen window that looked onto the lane at the back of the property. Shaken, she stood a moment in the doorway, then pulled herself together. *Come on*, she told herself — *it's probably nosey small* ragazzi. She crossed the room and looked out. She could see nothing, only the heads of the fuschia nodding on the walls around the little courtyard, and the lane stretching away into the dusk. Somewhere in the distance she could hear the sound of a motor, and the sound reminded her of what she had heard outside the Héritage Hotel after the dagger was thrown at Gil.

Baloney, Sydney told herself — *since when have you been able to tell the difference between the noise of one engine and another?* She drew the curtains firmly over the windows and started to prepare her meal.

Later, much later, the noise outside started again. Like someone, or something, shuffling through a thicket. She put on the television very loudly and watched a couple of sitcoms and a talk show. She drank more soave and then some gorgeously ripe Burgundy, and the resultant headache sent her to bed early. When she woke up in the small hours and thought she heard the sound of someone laughing — high up — she was able to convince herself it was overindulgence and overimagination.

But by five o'clock the next day, as the wind got stronger and the sun sank beyond the walls of the cottage, her nerve failed her. She phoned Liz Falla. Her relief at hearing the sound of the policewoman's strong voice was only surpassed by the relief she felt when she saw the police Mercedes finally come into sight, stop in the courtyard, and Liz Falla step out.

"Ms. Tremaine —"

"Sydney, please. How long does it take to be on first-name terms in Guernsey? Takes forever in Britain."

"Takes a while here too," said Liz Falla cheerfully, closing the cottage door behind her. "You sounded —"

"— spooked. I'm hearing things. D'you want some coffee? Something stronger?"

"Better not. I'm off to a rehearsal. What are you hearing?"

"I'll tell you in the car. I'm coming with you — yes I am, honey, or I'm taking off back to the hotel."

So Liz Falla found herself driving to Nick Le Page's in Vale with Sydney Tremaine alongside her.

* * *

Vale is a parish in the north and northwest corner of the island, sliced in two by a pie-shaped wedge of St. Sampson. It has a church that was once cut off from the mainland, and whose parishioners rowed to worship at high tide, the ruins of a castle alleged to have been built by the father of William the Conqueror, whose barracks have served as public housing, the remnants of many disused quarries, and some fine megalithic dolmens.

Nick Le Page lived in a modest bungalow chosen by his wife so that she could be close to the school where she taught. He was always careful to stress this to first-time visitors, who might otherwise have been bemused by the discrepancy between the fifties architecture and decor and its John Lennon look-alike occupant.

"Nick can play virtually anything you hand him," said Liz to her passenger. Sydney Tremaine, clad in grey sweats, asked, "Such as?"

"Anything with a keyboard, for instance — organ, piano, accordion, even. And he plays a balalaika pretty well too. Here we are."

Liz Falla brought the car to a halt outside a modest bungalow of off-white stucco. Beyond a low wall the small front garden consisted of gravel and coloured pebbles, a more effective ground cover than grass against the salt-sea air. It was topped by a row of pots under the bay window of the bungalow containing some sparsely flowering pelargonium in subdued colours.

They were let into the house by Brenda Le Page, who was on her way out to visit her sister, as she usually did when invaded by Jenemie. A woman of as subdued appearance as her pelargonium and of few words, the appearance of Sydney Tremaine shook whole sentences loose.

"I saw you as Anna Pavlova! Oh, you made me cry — are you here to do some singing with them?"

"Perhaps. If I'm asked."

They sang together most of the evening — Sydney, a

dazzled Nick, singer and guitar player Stewart Newton, still a teenager, whose parents hoped that performing with Jenemie would get "it" out of his system — as Liz told Sydney in the car, whereupon they both laughed — and Liz.

"Greensleeves," "Plaisirs d'amour," some Celtic music that was new to Sydney, Irish and Scottish folk songs. Liz Falla's true, resonant voice floated above the cut moquette sofa and the wall-to-wall carpeting, out beyond the stuccoed walls and the gravel ground cover, drifting across the marshy fields and the old saltwater ponds, carried on the wind like her Becquet ancestors when they flew on their brooms to dance at le Catioroc.

At ten-thirty, Brenda returned home on the dot, as always, and the rehearsal was over. Liz pried Sydney loose from the prolonged goodbyes of Nick and Stewart and ushered her into the car.

"Take me to a hotel, Liz — any hotel, but I'll not go back to Ed's."

"Okay." Liz started the engine and eased away from the curb. "But I think we should pick you up some gear, don't you? I'll be there, and I'll come in with you."

"It won't take long. I've already packed my bag."

They were not followed to Moretti's place, of that Liz was sure. Behind her, cars and motorbikes approached, and then departed down other roads, turned away down other lanes, and there was nothing behind them as they drove up the lane that led to the cottage. Sydney seemed relaxed, sleepy, talking little, humming under her breath.

So it was odd that, just as she brought the Mercedes to a halt in the courtyard, Liz Falla was engulfed by what she could only describe as a panic attack. Heart jumping, palms sweating, skin crawling, the hairs on the back of her neck prickling against the collar of her jacket — *by the pricking of my thumbs.*

Then she saw the movement. Something was moving along the top of the wall. A cat? Possibly. She reached across Sydney and made sure the door was locked.

"What?" The American woman was wide awake now.

"I'm not sure. Where's that bag of yours?"

"Near the door. I nearly brought it with me. I should have brought it with me. You saw something."

"Probably a cat. You stay here. Give me Moretti's key. I want to check inside."

Liz closed the front door behind her, leaving the lights off in the house. It seemed intrusive, impertinent to be in her partner's home without his say-so. All she could hear was the hum of the refrigerator in the kitchen and a tap-tap-tapping sound coming from upstairs somewhere. Grabbing a heavy walking stick from an umbrella stand by the door, she fumbled her way across the room to the staircase, feeling for the bannister. Please God, let her have done the right thing, leaving Sydney Tremaine outside, please God, whoever it was still preferred daggers to guns.

There was a small landing at the top of the stairs. She stopped, listening. The tapping was coming from behind a closed door to her left. Liz Falla felt her way along the landing, stopped by the door, and shoved it open. It shot back, the moon outside creating a pathway of light along the floor. The window was open, wide, the curtain pull tap-tapping against the window frame. A small chair to the right of the window had been knocked over. But the room was empty.

Liz Falla shut and fastened the window, but she left the chair as it was. She made a brief inspection of the second bedroom and the bathroom, then went downstairs. She checked the kitchen, made sure the back door was securely fastened, returned to the living room and retrieved Sydney Tremaine's bag. She put the stick back in the stand, then took it out again.

The moments between relocking the front door and getting back inside the car seemed interminable. As she flung the bag in the door of the car she thought she saw something, a dark shape on the top of the wall against the moonlit sky.

"You saw it, right?"

Sydney Tremaine was shaking. She grabbed hold of Liz Falla's jacket.

"A cat. Could be a cat."

"Too fucking big for a cat. Oh, God. Start the engine."

Liz was only too happy to do as she was told.

"Did you leave a window open in one of the bedrooms?"

"You kidding? I had everything sealed up tight as a drum. Which bedroom?"

"The one on the left at the top of the stairs."

"That's where I was. Oh, God. Take me to a hotel, take me to your police cells — take me anywhere."

"Okay."

"And that, Guv, is how Sydney Tremaine ended up sleeping on my sofa bed," said Liz Falla as they turned into the courtyard on Hospital Lane.

Luck was again in Moretti's corner. DS Hathaway, the officer left in charge in Hanley's absence, was in a meeting, and had left a message for Moretti to report to him as soon as possible. Ensconced in his office, Moretti and Liz Falla went over the details of the tragedy in San Jacopo. Liz Falla cupped her hands around her pointed chin, and looked thoughtfully at Moretti across the desk.

"So what you're saying, Guv, is that the baby survived, and was farmed out or adopted, found out the truth, and is now seeking revenge. The dagger was to let the Vannonis know that all this was about Sylvia and the scandal. But why kill Toni Albarosa? He wasn't a Vannoni, and neither was Mr. Ensor."

"I think the killer's hand was forced," said Moretti. "I don't think those murders were planned, but had to be carried out because the avenger's real, long-term, long-planned design would have been thwarted by the actions of Albarosa and Ensor. In Albarosa's case it is still possible he or she was on their way to kill another member of the household when they ran across Toni Albarosa on the terrace."

"What was the long-term plan, do you think, Guv? Was the avenger, as you call the person, going to wipe out the whole family, or what?"

"I think the making and completion of *Rastrellamento* was a crucial part of the revenge. Therefore, Mario Bianchi's cooperation was essential. I'm not saying he knew the reason, but someone fed him the ideas and he went along with it. I also feel the ultimate gesture would have been the death of at least one principal member of the family: the marchese or the marchesa, or both of them."

"Shouldn't we be giving them a more specific warning, then?"

"About what? About a scandal they deny ever happened? To a woman they deny ever existed? You can be sure that Gianfranco is not going to tell anyone he spilt his guts to me. Even his adoring *mamma* would no longer protect him from the wrath of the marchese."

"Okay. So let's say we know why. Do we know who?"

"I think so. There are some problems, but it seems certain now there are two people involved."

"The woman who picked up the knives, you mean."

"Yes, and there's something else I've been thinking about ever since Ensor was murdered. Remember what you said?"

"*Cherchez la femme,* you mean, Guv?"

"Right. So who was the woman? See, Falla, it had to be a woman who got him down there. Ensor didn't have email at the hotel, and he had no office here. Don't tell me it was by letter, so it had to be by phone. Let's take a look at the statements again."

"Which ones, Guv? The officers went through them with a fine-tooth comb."

"I'm sure they did. Sydney Tremaine, Giulia Vannoni, Monty Lord, Mario Bianchi, and Adriana Ferrini."

"Adriana Ferrini?"

"She's about the right age, and I believe her mother was unmarried, so we'll include her."

About an hour later, Liz Falla said, "Okay, these three —" pointing at the statements taken from Giulia Vannoni, Mario Bianchi and Adriana Ferrini, "— have no good alibi for any of the three incidents. Sydney Tremaine has an alibi for the Albarosa murder, her husband, but he's dead. Isn't Giulia Vannoni too young to be the baby?"

"She is, but her mother and unknown father would have been the right age. We haven't checked out the story of her parentage. And she has a motorbike — whoever was prowling outside the manor about a month ago, and whoever was at the ruined villa, had a motorbike."

"Monty Lord couldn't have got back from Rome in time for the first murder, could he?"

"Couldn't he? He's an expert pilot and flies solo. Did you check his arrival at the airport?"

"Yes. They have him clearing customs at just after nine a.m."

"They do? I've been rethinking his alibi since you mentioned the airport jacket."

"I wondered about that, because the tower has no record of giving him clearance to land. But it was a busy morning, apparently, and they were snowed under with private and corporate planes coming in for some sort of a conference. Still — he's an American," said Liz Falla.

"Why not Italian-American?" Moretti suggested. "There are thousands — millions — of them. He's the right age, and he's the person most likely to have fed the new script ideas to Mario Bianchi."

"You're not saying Ensor's wife helped Monty Lord, are you, Guv? He was a shit to her, but I don't believe that for a moment."

"Ah, but there is another woman close to him, a woman who would do anything for him. Her alibi may be watertight, but she wasn't the one committing murder."

"Bella Alfieri. Ensor would never have gone into a bunker for her, Guv. Oh, I know, she'd have used the telephone, but he'd have known her voice, wouldn't he? It's sort of squeaky, as I recall. And besides — an Italian with a name like Monty Lord?"

"Many people in show business change their names," Moretti reminded her. "We don't know if it's his real name. I know who might know: Sydney Tremaine." He leaned across the desk and picked up the phone. "What's your number, Falla?"

He waited as the answering machine picked up and started to speak.

"Sydney? It's Ed Moretti."

Across the desk Liz Falla was giving him one of her looks.

"Ed!" He had forgotten how pretty her voice was. "Where are you?"

"At police headquarters."

"You heard what happened?"

"Yes. I have something to ask you about Monty Lord. Did you and your husband spend any time with him when you were discussing *Rastrellamento*?"

"We did. Many drunken luncheons and dinners. Why?"

"Did he tell you much about himself?"

"Quite a bit — *in vino veritas*, honey. What did you want to know?"

"Did he ever tell you whether he had changed his name?"

"Never mentioned it. As far as I know, that's his real name."

"I see." Moretti felt disappointment tamping down the euphoria of hearing her voice.

"But it's an amazing success story. He was a stuntman, you know."

The rush of excitement Moretti was now feeling had nothing to do with Sydney Tremaine's sweet tones.

"No, I didn't. A stuntman?"

"Few people know. Many actors move into producing and directing, but Monty came up the hard way. He said stuntmen get little respect, so he doesn't mention the past too much. He was pretty drunk when he told us about his time in Italy before he started producing spaghetti westerns. Some of the tricks he performed would make your blood curdle!"

"Such as?"

"Oh, you know, jumping off tall buildings and through fire, that kind of thing. But he had two specialities. One was bike-riding. Like Evel Knievel — if you wanted anything extraordinary done that involved a motorbike he was your man."

"And the other specialty?"

"Climbing. He had absolutely no fear of heights, and he could climb up a skyscraper or the side of a mountain. They used to call him *Il Ragno* — the Spider."

"And his assistant, Bella Alfieri — what about her? Was she around in those days?"

"Yes. Bella was in show business and she had a specialty of her own. She did the voices for many of the characters in Italian cartoons. They met in Rome, I believe. Monty always says he doesn't know where he'd be without Bella, and she's devoted to him."

"I'm sure that's true. One more question: did your husband carry a phone?"

"Why yes, he did — odd for a guy who was a technodinosaur. He got over that where the cellphone was concerned, because it meant he could bug Mario and Monty. It drove them nuts."

"I can imagine."

Moretti said goodbye and put down the phone. His head was spinning from lack of sleep and the elation of having the last pieces of the puzzle put in place by the woman who, only a short time before, he thought might be a piece of the puzzle herself.

chapter seventeen

September 22nd

The wind was gathering strength by the time Moretti and Liz Falla got out to the Manoir Ste. Madeleine, and Moretti was grateful for the showers and chill that lifted the drowsiness assailing him after he and Liz Falla snatched something to eat. It had already been a very long day.

Liz Falla pulled in alongside a battered-looking 1940s staff car with bullet holes in the doors, and attracted the attention of a security guard who was chatting with one of the extras, disconcertingly dressed in blood-drenched overalls.

"We need to get in the back entrance," said Moretti, showing his identification.

"The front is open. They are shooting in the main salon today. I am instructed to —"

"And I am now instructing you to let us in the back," said Moretti. The security guard shrugged his shoulders, went over to the back entrance they had used before, and let them in.

"What's the plan, Guv, if we see Mr. Lord first?" Liz Falla sounded nervous.

"Tell him we've come to see Mr. Bianchi — which we have — but we make it appear we are taking him in again for questioning. Hopefully Monty Lord is in his office, and hopefully we can pull Bianchi off the set before his producer knows it."

All was silent backstage at the manor, apart from the drone of a vacuum cleaner somewhere. So connected was the manor now in Moretti's mind with the unreal world of *Rastrellamento*, that it was the reminder of day-to-day living that seemed unreal.

Rastrellamento: the examination of the past for ancient evils. That was how he had once explained the significance of the title to Liz Falla. How perfectly apt the novel must have seemed to Monty Lord when he read it, the ideal medium for his message. Perhaps he had originally intended to leave the plot as it was, but had been unable to resist the temptation to link it more closely to the past. After all, he had discovered, or known, that his director was an easy target for blackmail. If luck was on their side they would be able to break Mario Bianchi's silence before Monty Lord was aware they were on the premises.

The passage they were in came to an abrupt end at a pair of doors that seemed to have some sort of hectic activity going on beyond them. From the sound of the voices, speaking in both Italian and English, there were a number of people involved. Liz Falla tried the doors, but they were locked. She knocked vigorously, in an effort to be heard above the noise. Finally, someone responded, calling through the door.

"Who is it? You know you're not supposed to come this way!"

It was the voice of Betty Chesler.

"It's the police. Can you let us through?"

The door was opened by a frazzled Betty Chesler. "Well," she said on seeing them, "at least it isn't some of those extras playing the fool again. Did security send you the wrong way? Can I help you?"

The room was clearly an ante room to the main salon, and it was full of actors dressed as *contadini*. For a moment, time was suspended, and Moretti saw the villagers of San Jacopo as they must have looked before a tragedy beyond their control or comprehension changed their lives forever.

"Sorry to interrupt. We're on our way through to see Mr. Bianchi, Ms. Chesler. He's on the set in the drawing-room?"

"That's right. He'll be all of a tizzy today, I warn you. This is a very upsetting scene, and Mario always tends to identify with the actors — and besides, there have been some late changes again."

"This is an upsetting scene, you say."

"Yes. Maddalena — that's the daughter in the film — kills herself. Vittoria's doing a lovely job, I must say, and as for Adriana, she's fabulous, as you'd expect. I just saw the rehearsal and when she stands there, looking at her dead daughter, you can see it all!" Betty Chesler clasped her hands in front of her in her now-familiar, overcome-with-emotion gesture.

"And what can you see? What does the director want her to convey?"

"Love and hate," said Betty Chesler, simply. "Both love and hate. That's what I saw when I watched Adriana's face, Inspector." She pointed to a door to one side of the room. "That will take you out into the area behind the set and the lights. You can wait for Mario there."

On the other side of the door, Moretti and Liz Falla found themselves suddenly in darkness. Ahead of them bathed in brilliant light, were Adriana Ferrini and Vittoria Salviati. The young actress was lying on a couch, as if asleep, with Adriana Ferrini standing over her. Just in front of them, silhouetted against the light, Moretti could see the head of Mario Bianchi with its distinctive ponytail. There was complete silence in the room, and the cameras were moving around the two women. There was no sign of Monty Lord.

"Aaaah — !"

The silence was broken by Adriana Ferrini's savage cry of grief, the sound thundering from her with an operatic resonance.

"No man is worth it, Maddalena — don't you understand? No man!" The actress crossed the set, the cameras tracking after her. "Die for your country's honour, die for your family honour — but oh, my daughter — never, *cara figlia*, die for love."

"Cut! Print!"

The applause was more than the usual pro forma smatter of sound heard around the set of *Rastrellamento*. There were whoops and shouts of "*brava!*" and some members of the crew were hugging each other.

"Well, it's a wrap, certainly for the interior scenes."

It was Eddie Christie who spoke, standing next to them in the darkness.

"A wrap?" Moretti asked. "You mean the film is virtually finished? I thought a new character was added."

"Apparently Mario is rethinking the schoolteacher," Eddie Christie replied. "We've been told to put any costume plans on hold."

Liz Falla was almost left behind by Moretti's abrupt departure, and hastened after him as he pushed his way through the laughing, chattering throng toward Mario Bianchi. Unseen and unnoticed by either of them, Bella Alfieri moved from the shadows and slipped out the door through which they had come.

* * *

"Signor Bianchi, is there somewhere we can talk?"

Far from being in a tizzy, Mario Bianchi was looking as calm and collected as Moretti had ever seen him. *Almost serene*, he thought to himself. *Let's hope it's artistic satisfaction at the successful conclusion of the scene and not the effect of some mood-enhancing substance or other.*

"Of course. We'll go to my rooms."

It was said acquiescently, almost as if Bianchi had been expecting them. There was no mention of either lawyers or psychiatrists. Liz Falla shot a surprised look at her partner as they followed the director through the crowd to the main door to the salon — the door through which Moretti and Liz Falla had come on their first meeting with the Vannoni family and Monty Lord.

Mario Bianchi had a bedroom and small sitting room on the second floor overlooking part of the terrace.

"I thought you would want to see me." The director's smile was that of a man at peace with himself. "You have heard about the removal of the schoolteacher from the script."

"Not until we arrived today." Moretti went straight to the point. "I think it was Monty Lord who forced your hand over the changes that so infuriated Gilbert Ensor."

"Correct." Mario Bianchi flung himself down on one of the brocaded sofas that proliferated throughout the manor and pulled out a packet of Gauloises. As he lit up, he continued talking.

"This morning I did something I should have done long ago. I told Monty to take his schoolteacher and shove him up his ass." He smiled beatifically at the two policemen. "I feel like a new man."

"What brought this about? Surely whatever hold he had over you did not disappear? I presume he was blackmailing you in some way?" Moretti asked.

"Yes. Just over two years ago I — well, I went back on drugs and I was caught. At the time my wife was out of the country in Switzerland, about to give birth to our son in a clinic there — she was having a difficult pregnancy — and I managed to keep it from her. I spent only a short time in jail in return for naming my supplier, a major dealer whom the police had been after for a while. The few people who were in the know made it difficult for me to get a new project — my supplier was also their supplier, so not only did their source dry up, but they were scared shitless he would name names. He didn't, served his sentence, and is now back in business again. Monty found out — he has all kinds of contacts in Italy — but he still came to me with *Rastrellamento*. At first it seemed like a gift, because there was no mention of changes. All that started once we were underway, and when I objected, he told me I was in no position to make trouble, unless I wanted my wife to find out."

Mario Bianchi took a last drag on his cigarette and stubbed it out on a cut-glass ashtray the size of a dinner plate. "I don't know if either of you are married, but I can't imagine life without my wife and son. We broke up once, just after we met, because I was taking cocaine and she found out, and when she came back to me, she told me, no more chances. But during this last week, when Monty made this final addition, I knew I couldn't go on. *Rastrellamento* is my chance to make it back to the top of the heap, and I just couldn't go on compromising my artistic integrity. So I risked everything and phoned my wife."

"How did she take it?" Liz Falla asked.

"Like an angel — an angry one, when she heard about Monty. So, with her blessing, I told him the schoolteacher was out. The strange thing was how calmly he took it."

"When did this happen?" asked Moretti.

"Only yesterday. I told the crew and I told the marchesa."

"Why the marchesa?"

"Because she had come to me the day before in distress, asking me why I was making the script changes, and I told her it was Monty. She said he was playing games with her — cruel games, and that *Rastrellamento* was being used to get at her family. For the life of me I couldn't understand how the storyline of the film could affect Donatella, but I let her know as soon as I made my decision about the schoolteacher."

"Signor Bianchi," said Moretti, "we believe Monty Lord is responsible for the deaths of Mr. Albarosa and Mr. Ensor. You may be in some danger yourself."

Mario Bianchi looked dismayed. "Are you sure?" He got up and moved to the window. Around the corner of the building, Moretti could just see part of one of the Skycranes. "Monty was quite zen about the whole thing yesterday, and I cannot see any reason for him to kill anyone, let alone me."

"There is a reason, believe me," Moretti assured him. "Is Mr. Lord on the premises at the moment?"

"As far as I know, he's in his trailer — at least, that's where he said he would be. Are you going to arrest him?" Mario Bianchi was now looking his former worried self again, his fingers pulling nervously at his collar. "We need him, and we need Epicure Films Italia. Without him the money dries up, and we're not finished shooting yet."

"I don't think you need worry about the money, Mr. Bianchi," said Moretti, as he crossed to the door. "Your chance for a return to the top is quite safe, of that I'm certain. Much of his original plan has gone wrong, so there is nothing Monty Lord wants more at this moment in his life than the completion and the success of *Rastrellamento*."

Sydney Tremaine put down the phone and stared into space. "You bastard, you manipulated us, didn't you?"

she said out loud. Jesus, how could she have forgotten? That was the trouble with booze — there was not only truth in it, but oblivion. How Gil would have hated knowing that his precious *Rastrellamento* had only been a vessel, a vehicle for another man's hatred!

She picked up the phone, dialed. She had no specific plan in mind, but she knew she couldn't go on sitting in Liz Falla's flat, charming as it was, waiting for something to happen. It had felt so good when she walked out on to the terrace and challenged the killer, taking the initiative for the first time in God knew how long. Why she didn't know, but she wanted to avenge the death of a husband she wasn't sure she had ever loved. With Gil her life had been sometimes wonderful, but more often godawful, fights and fur flying followed by expensive peace offerings, all of it fuelled by too much whisky, or wine, or champagne. Or all three. She wasn't even sure it was Monty Lord they were after, but she was damned if she was going to let him get away with it.

The line was ringing.

"Monty Lord." There was a new sound in the producer's voice, but she was not sure what it signified.

"Monty?" she said, controlling the tremor in her own voice. "You killed Gil, and I am going to make sure that *Rastrellamento* never gets made, never gets distribution. I can do that, and you know I can. And don't think you can get at me to stop me, just like you stopped Gil. You've already tried, I know. But this time I am going to be where no one can get at me, and I am going to wait there until the police have taken you in and charged you. They're on their way, Monty, right now."

"I know," said the calm, detached voice at the other end. "Bella just told me." There was a click as the line went dead. She may not have been sure a minute earlier, but now she had her answer. Hands trembling, Sydney made another call, this time to Giulia's castello, leaving a message on the answer-phone.

"Giulia, it's Sydney. I'm on my way to your place. Ed Moretti just phoned and asked questions about Monty Lord. It's Monty, Giulia — Monty killed Gil and Toni. I just phoned him, told him what I knew, and that I would stop him. But I'll be safe at your place. Be careful, Giulia. Be careful."

Sydney hung up and made one more call.

"Taxi — yes, right away. To the tower on Icart point." She told the driver where she was, and went to wait by the door.

Monty Lord looked at the body of Bella Alfieri, lying on the floor of the trailer. *So much for complete devotion*, he mused. Without him, her life would have been nothing, and yet she came bursting in the door, pleading with him to give himself up! "They are talking to Mario now. It's gone too far, Monty — I'm scared." The sight of her crying disgusted him, but he wouldn't have touched her if she hadn't turned back to the door and said, "I'm going to them, Monty, telling them how I helped you. I'm doing it for your sake, just like I helped you, for your sake."

It gave him no choice but to stop her. He got up and went around his desk, smiling, his arms extended, and she walked right into them. Holding her close — she was so tiny against him — he removed the knife from his pocket and she never felt a thing, of that he was sure. Not like Ensor — who would have thought that bloated lecher would have so much fight in him!

Pity about Toni, because anyone who made the Vannonis suffer was a prince in his books. But Donatella was being difficult: first of all, he had no desire to sleep with her, and second of all, she was asking questions. It was time to deal with her because she was beginning to make noises about the script changes, and who should he bump into on the terrace but Toni, the tomcat. He'd pulled his knife, and Toni had taken fright and switched on one of the film lights. "What the hell are you doing, Monty?" he asked, relieved, all sunshine and smiles, and then he'd seen the knife, and that was it. Too much of a risk. Couldn't have him saying over rolls and coffee the next morning, "Guess who I bumped into on the terrace last night carrying a knife?"

Monty Lord checked out of the window of the trailer, stepped outside and locked the door behind him. This was the tricky part, crossing the open space between the trailer and the motorbike he kept among all the other motorbikes and bicycles in the courtyard behind the manor. He'd dealt with the problem of security guards in the area by making a quick call, telling the head of security to move all his men to the front of the manor.

Walking unhurriedly, as though he hadn't a care in the world, Monty Lord made his way through the bikes to his Moto Guzzi. There was no sign of any security guards, and fortunately, no sign of actors or crew. No one was standing around in the drizzle for a chat or a smoke.

Not that it mattered now. *Almost over, Stefano, almost over*, he told himself. Just stop this crazy red-headed babe from derailing *Rastrellamento*, and then off to the airport, and on to Florence. He'd have to settle for one Vannoni, instead of two.

Rastrellamento was *his* masterpiece, not Ensor's, his show and tell. What did Ensor's wife care about that abusive son of a bitch of a husband, anyway? This was probably more about money than anything else, but he couldn't risk it. It wasn't about love — not that he'd ever felt love himself. But then, he'd never looked for it, not after learning the truth. Not after learning the price paid by Sylvia and Stefan.

Monty Lord opened the throttle on his Moto Guzzi and let it rip, almost immediately cutting it back again. No need to rush — it wasn't far. Nothing was far on this island. He knew where she'd be holed up — hell, it was so obvious she might as well have told him. The cop had no idea where he was headed, so it was unlikely there'd be a reception committee waiting for him. Ideally, the marchese should have been his first target, anyway, and it now looked as if he was going to have his wish.

His physical skills had been useful when setting up his alibi for what was intended to be his first strike, Donatella's death. He could move through dense traffic like a shark cutting a shoal in heavy seas, travelling at speeds no car could maintain in similar circumstances. That was how he'd moved between Rome and Florence, using the skill and nerve required in his career as a stuntman. Yet many of the stunts he used to perform required limited skills, relying more on nerves of ice and what the Latins called *cojones*. He had both, and they had come in very useful, even when he transferred to a more respectable area of the profession. Anyone involved with the financing of movies was well advised to have both guts and balls.

Guts and balls: he'd done some stunt flying in his early days, and landing on the darkened runway was not as difficult as he'd feared. Besides, there were always some lights still on, and he'd made careful note of their position on previous trips. With the airport closed there was no danger of collision with other planes, and he had the place to himself. You needed *cojones*, but you also needed luck, and whoever left the keys in the door of the storage room for the safety jackets added that ingredient to his undertaking. On an earlier visit he was waiting for the arrival of the new actor taking the role of the priest, went to the toilets, and there they were. He was in and out before you could say *vendetta*, the jacket's fluorescent lime green concealed under his own jacket.

And he had needed it. The only hairy moment had been when he saw someone — presumably airport security — in the doorway of the building closest to where the small private planes were parked. With a confidence born of the years following his quest for the truth, he waved and sauntered on toward the club building, round the corner, and out of sight. Then he ran across the field beyond the airport property, cutting across through a garage and into the car park of the Happy Landings Hotel, where he had left his Moto Guzzi. The manor was only about five minutes away, and the roads were deserted at that hour.

A fine plan it had been, using legitimate business as cover, only to be thwarted by Toni Albarosa's latest amatory exploit. He had returned to the airport, which was part of his original plan, left his bike again at the hotel, cut across to where he had left his plane, dumped the jacket, re-entered, and checked in through customs as soon as the airport opened. Only the flight tower would know he had not landed when he said, and here again he had been lucky. At nine o'clock the air was full of Trislanders and Britton-Normans and sexy little private jets jostling for a landing slot.

So she was going to be where she was safe, was she. Silly bitch. The world was going to see *Rastrellamento*, and nothing was going to stop *Il Ragno* now.

The rain was coming down steadily by the time Sydney arrived at Icart Point. She paid the cab driver, pulled the hood of her anorak over her head, and jumped the gate. Running across the rough open field, heart pounding, she reached the door, unlocked it without difficulty, and locked it behind her.

Safe as houses. Safe as you could possibly be in this fortress. She awoke the vibrant colours of Giulia's castello with a flick of the switch by the door, and pulled off her wet jacket. Across the room the answer-phone's light was flashing. She picked it up and heard her own voice, telling Giulia to be careful.

"What now?" she asked out loud.

"A good question. Want the answer?"

Sydney thought her already-shaky legs would give way beneath her. The breath left her body as though she had been punched.

Monty Lord was standing on the iron staircase. When she made a move toward the door he was on her in a flash, his hand like a vice on her arm.

"Oh my God. How did you get in?" she found the breath to stammer out.

"I climbed the wall, Rapunzel. Not up your pretty hair, but you'd be surprised how many footholds you can find on even a Martello tower, if you're good at that kind of thing. And I am. And then in the window I came, ready to greet you."

Sydney looked at Monty Lord in horror. She had forgotten the width of the windows on the upper floor, never imagined for a moment that this man could even scale the sides of a Martello tower. With his customary black he was wearing a watch cap over his shaved head that altered his appearance entirely, making his eyes seem paler and more intense than usual. The eyes of a madman was the chilling thought that crossed Sydney's mind.

"You killed Gil."

"Yes. With a different knife, because he wasn't family."

"Why throw a dagger on to the patio?"

"Waste of one of my special daggers, I know, but I was hoping it would shut him up, even persuade him to leave the island. It didn't."

Sydney moved slightly and his grip tightened on her arm.

"Don't try anything, Sydney. I have one dagger left, and I can have it out and into your beautiful bod before you know what's hit you."

"Try what?" Anger was giving her courage. "*I* don't have a concealed weapon."

"Don't you want to know what this is all about?"

"You're going to tell me."

"I think you should know — I want you to know — hell, I want someone to know. I'm in no mood for sweet talk or listening to reason. Reason and I parted company a long time ago. Sit down, honey and don't try to tell me to give myself up and all that shit. Like Bella did."

"Bella? Oh, dear God, not Bella."

"Yes. Such a pity, stupid broad. But hey, Syd, anyone who stands in my way!"

At that moment the telephone rang. Sydney started, and in a flash Monty Lord had a dagger in his free hand and against her throat.

"Don't move."

Across the room she heard the sound of the machine clicking as it recorded the message, and then she heard Ed Moretti's voice as it was played back.

"Pick up the phone next time it rings, Mr. Lord. We have to talk."

"Ed!" She called out his name and Monty Lord lowered the knife from her throat.

"Ed? You're on first-name terms with the cop?"

"He's my lover. He'll be going crazy." It was worth a try, and she had very little else at her disposal.

"You're a fast worker, baby — and I thought it might be Giulia! Revenge against that *bastardo* you married — I can understand that. Perhaps we could do a deal. When the phone goes, answer it."

It rang again. Moving cautiously, Sydney walked over to the phone and picked it up.

"Ed, it's me."

"Are you okay?"

"I'm okay. Ed, he's got a knife."

"Put this on speaker-phone, Sydney, so Mr. Lord can hear me."

She found the button on the phone, pressed it, and Ed Moretti's disembodied voice filled the room.

"Mr. Lord, *Rastrellamento* is almost finished, and I know Ms. Tremaine will not stand in the way of its release when she hears your story. You have done what you set out to do in making it and, in the end, even if you get away from here, you will be caught. Why not give yourself up now?"

"That, of course, is a possibility." Monty Lord spoke coolly, as though he were giving serious thought to the matter. "Only one problem, Moretti. It's the logical thing to do, and I have lived without logic all my life. As an ending, it does not appeal to me. It lacks the grand gesture."

"Then let Ms. Tremaine go. She's not part of your storyline."

"Hey, don't blame me for that." He sounded angry now. "She wrote herself into the script, and I don't like bit players directing the action. I must have control — what my parents did not have in their brief lives. I've got to hand it to you, you managed to find out in a short time what it took me years to discover. Just how much do you know?"

Sydney Tremaine listened in silence while Ed Moretti explained, as engrossed in the narrative as her captor.

"I know that your mother was Sylvia Vannoni, the eldest daughter of the family, and that your father was a Slovene schoolteacher in the village of San Jacopo, where the Vannonis lived for centuries. That they fell in love, and used Sylvia's comings and goings to look after a British prisoner of war on their property to carry on their love affair, and that they were betrayed by the priest. That the Vannoni family set the schoolteacher up to be killed by the partisans, who also killed the Briton, who, presumably, happened to be on the scene. That Sylvia gave birth to you in secret, guarded and midwived by the family housekeeper, Luisa Scarpa. And that your mother set fire to the church where she had been betrayed, and killed herself there. That the Vannonis then left the area, to settle in Fiesole and Florence, taking many of the family retainers with them. What I don't know is how the Vannonis managed to get you out of Italy and into the States, completely hushing up that part of the story."

"That's not all you don't know, Moretti. But that's pretty good, I grant you. I want to tell you and your current squeeze here something about my father — what little I know about him, anyway. His name was Stefan. I have been unable to find out his last name, because the people who remembered him had known him by his first name only. His last name was difficult, unpronounceable for Tuscans. One thing is certain: he was not a fascist sympathizer, because that was the very reason he left the village, near Parma, to which his family was moved before the outbreak of war to escape working in the offices of the local fascist party. He couldn't fight because of a limp — a club foot, I think."

"Your real name, then," interjected Moretti, "is not Monty Lord."

"My real name?" Monty Lord gave a bitter laugh. "I don't know my family name, but I was named Stefano by my mother, after my father, and that was the name I took to the States, when Luisa Scarpa took me there, with some of the other evacuees whose parents died in the bombing."

"So that was how they got you out of the country."

"Yes. Easy to hide a baby among other babies. An orphan among other orphans, when the world was in chaos, and there were hundreds and thousands of similar children. I was adopted by an Italian-American family, the Romanos. I spent the first part of my life as Steve Romano, in New York City."

"But Luisa Scarpa made some sort of confession on her deathbed, and said nothing about the baby being adopted."

"Ah, so you also found the guy in Grosseto selling fake Etruscan shit, did you?" At this point, Monty Lord got up and started walking around almost as if he had forgotten Sydney's presence. "I didn't leave it there. As soon as I heard her called *la guardia carceria*, I thought she probably had been in on my birth."

"Monty —" Sydney broke in gently, afraid to draw attention back to herself and find a dagger at her throat. But she wanted Ed Moretti to hear her voice, to know that she was coping. "How did little Steve Romano from New York City find out he was a Vannoni?"

"From my adopted mother." Monty Lord turned and smiled at Sydney, the knife still in his hand, as though they were exchanging casual chit-chat over cocktails. "See, I always knew I was adopted, a war orphan originally from Italy. But I was blond and light-skinned. I wondered if I might have been the child of rape — an Italian woman by a German soldier — so I asked my mother when I was about sixteen. She saw I was distressed by the idea and told me some more of my story, which she had been asked to keep from me. She said that Luisa Scarpa told her that, out of all the orphan children, I was the one in whom the Marchesa Vannoni was personally interested. I had to be well placed, with a good family — and I was. I have nothing against my adoptive parents. Luisa Scarpa told my American parents that I was the love child of an Italian girl and a British soldier. It took me a while to discover my father was the schoolteacher, and not the British prisoner of war."

"That was the first story I heard." It was Ed Moretti's voice again. "How can you be sure?"

"Only reasonably sure," Monty Lord replied. He was still walking around the circular space, reliving the years of his search. "But that's what I found out from Patrizia."

"Patrizia?" Both Sydney and Moretti said the name in unison. Moretti added, the surprise clear in his disembodied voice, "You've been here before, haven't you? Patrizia's been dead a long time."

"Oh yes. I came here a while ago, when I discovered that some of the old servants were still alive and had been taken by the marchesa to Guernsey. They're all gone now, except Teresa Stecconi, and she knows no more than I now do. I risked discovery a couple of times when I came here a month before we started shooting, scouting my own personal scenarios — I had an earlier try to get at the costumes, and I talked to an old guy I found hanging about the grounds. He yammered on about Patrizia, but he didn't tell me anything I didn't know before."

"Dan Mahy. You killed him."

"Sure, had to. He was out of his tree most of the time, but even he might eventually remember the guy who gave him a small fortune for his SS dagger."

"A helpless old man who had nothing to do with any of this."

"Come on now, I did him a favour. Put him out of his misery in that shack he called home before the do-gooders had him out of there. Anyway, let me tell you about Patrizia — now, that was exciting, exhilarating, because she heard the sound of my father in my voice. She was almost blind, you see, and sound was everything to her. She said I reminded her of the schoolteacher in her old village, whom all the children loved, even though the Vannonis said he was a fascist. The sound of my voice triggered a whole bunch of stuff and it just poured from her. She said she never believed he was a fascist, because he and Sylvia got on so well, and Sylvia didn't like the fascists. They worked together, looking after the children, she said. See, Patrizia prepared the meals for *la guardia carceria* and her charge. She never saw the baby, but she heard him — me — crying. And she heard my mother crying when I was taken from her."

He held her life in his hands, but at that moment, Sydney wanted to put her arms around him. Monty Lord looked at her and saw the pity in her eyes.

"And now you know why I could not let Gil stop me, and why I cannot let you stop me. This has been a long time in the making and you know what they say about revenge: a dish best eaten cold. And this dish is very, very cold. For years I put the pieces together, and I thought of challenging the Vannoni family, but I knew there was something more I wanted. Only I didn't know what. Then I read a new novel by the acclaimed British writer, Gilbert Ensor, called *Rastrellamento*. And hey — I'd even scouted the locations!"

"I can understand why you'd want revenge." Sydney's voice was puzzled; in spite of her fear the story had caught her attention. "But I don't understand why, after all this time, the Vannonis are so paranoid about keeping the story quiet, with everyone sworn to secrecy. Why move, give up their ancestral home? Why such a conspiracy of silence?"

"Good question, honey. I think I finally found the answer — quite by chance — after I hired Mario for the movie. I was in Siena, doing some research on the fascists and partisans in the area with some of his family contacts —"

"I knew about his father," interjected Moretti.

"You dug deep, didn't you, Inspector? Well, one elderly ex-partisan said to me, 'Vannonis? Sons of bitches, the lot of them. Blamed us for their own killings.'"

"Their own killings?" Monty Lord's audience again spoke in sync.

"Local partisans swore they'd never laid a finger on either man, and that the story about my father being a fascist sympathizer was fabricated by the Vannonis themselves, to discredit him after his death."

"So," said Moretti, "you are saying the marchese or the marchesa, or one or both of their sons, killed your father. And, in all probability, then had to kill the British prisoner of war because he saw them."

"Right on the money, Detective. The Vannonis are murderers."

"And thieves."

Another disembodied voice. For a moment, both jailer and captive were thrown. Monty Lord spun around, holding out the dagger, staring into the air as though expecting a phantom to materialize. But Sydney, turning in shock toward one of the silk wall hangings, knew where the voice was coming from and who it was. Giulia was standing there.

chapter eighteen

"*Vacca*! How did you get in?"

Instead of going for Giulia, Monty Lord grabbed Sydney and held the knife against her throat. She wanted to cry out, but she couldn't breathe. Monty Lord spun round, holding Sydney across his body. She could now see Giulia. She looked tough, dressed in her motorcycle leathers, but she didn't appear to be carrying any kind of weapon. Then she saw that Giulia was laughing, actually laughing.

"This is my place, Signor Lord. I know every nook and cranny. There are some alcoves in the Martello wall."

"How the hell did you get past me?"

"I was already here, and I'd picked up Sydney's message on my machine — I screen all my calls. I heard you break the window upstairs, Monty, and then come down the stairs. Before I could do anything, Sydney was letting herself in the door, so I hid. You set me up as a suspect, didn't you?"

"Sure, it was convenient you rode a motorbike and took your runs near the hotel. And Bella does — did — your voice very well. Created some confusion with the local constabulary. But don't tell me you're going to do something heroic for this baby — she's got the hots for the cool-cat copper."

"So she told me." Giulia smiled at Sydney, shrugged her shoulders and turned back to Monty Lord. "Hey, Stefano, don't you want to hear the rest of the story? Why they didn't want your mother to marry anyone, let alone your father, a penniless schoolteacher?"

"Of course I want to know. Don't play games with me." Monty Lord brought the knife up to Sydney's throat again, and she couldn't repress a cry of fear. Ed Moretti must have heard, because he called out, "Tell him, Ms. Vannoni — do what he says, for God's sake."

"I will." Giulia looked at Sydney and smiled again. Her eyes darted toward the bronze sculpture on her white translucent cube. "But first you have to let Sydney go. Put her over by the statue — looks a bit like her, doesn't it? — where you can watch her, and I'll tell you."

Sydney felt Monty Lord's arms relax around her body. He pushed her toward the statue, and her legs almost buckled under her as she went over to it. She rested her body against the cube, thinking desperately about the door in the black wall. All Monty Lord's attention was now on Giulia Vannoni, but she remembered another of the skills he had boasted about to her and to Gil at one of their drunken dinners: his brief sojourn in a travelling circus performing a knife-throwing act. She prayed Giulia also knew the story, but it was unlikely.

"Why?" Curiosity and eagerness filled his voice.

"The oldest, most sordid, reason in the world, Monty. Money, money, money. *Soldi, soldi, soldi.*"

Giulia Vannoni moved slowly toward the black leather sofa that was between Monty and Sydney. "I'm going to sit down — okay?" she said and did so. Monty Lord watched her.

"What's all this about money?" he asked.

"Sylvia was a girl, but she was the eldest child. She was therefore entitled by Vannoni tradition to a sizeable dowry and, above all, land. A nasty habit grew up in comparatively recent years of cheating the eldest daughter out of her inheritance by ensuring she didn't marry, therefore keeping the money and property intact for the sons. This wasn't so hard in the days when you could virtually lock up your daughter and make sure she didn't meet marriageable men. It was also not too difficult to do when the looks in the family went to the males. Of course, if Sylvia had met someone wealthy, things might have turned out differently. No one objected to an amalgamation of fortunes — that is why Donatella married Paolo, and how Toni married Anna. But a penniless schoolteacher!"

"Ah." Monty Lord's sigh was full of pain. "I could never understand why they wouldn't let her marry him — a woman beyond her first youth, beyond any chance of the kind of marriage that would enhance the family's fortune or position." He fixed his intense pale eyes on Giulia.

"When did you become Monty Lord, and why?" Giulia asked.

"After I started my quest, because there was always the chance someone in the family would know who Steve Romano really was. Monty Lord doesn't sound Italian, but it is. No one remembers my Slovene father's last name, but Patrizia remembered the Italian village near Parma where he came from: Montealloro."

Monty Lord's attention now moved from Giulia to the telephone on the table near the sofa. He called out, "Detective Inspector Moretti, are you still listening?"

"I am." Moretti's voice hung in the air, incorporeal but comforting to Sydney's ears.

"You've been to San Jacopo, haven't you?" Monty Lord did not wait for a response, but continued. "There is an angel on the ceiling in the room where I camped on more than one occasion. Once I had found it, I used to make a pilgrimage there, every year, to light a candle for Sylvia and Stefan in the church. That angel on the ceiling holds a sword in her hands. I thought of her as an avenging angel. I thought of myself as an avenging angel."

"Bring them to justice." It was Moretti again. "Would that not be the ultimate revenge?"

Monty Lord laughed derisively. "Come on now, Moretti. Who are you kidding? You know as well as I do I've got about as much chance as a water drop in hell of proving any murder from that time." Suddenly, he was weeping, his free hand running over his shaved head and his face, the dagger held down by his side.

"Have you ever heard of the *sepolti vivi*? It's what they call cloistered nuns, buried alive of their own free will and choosing. During the war that's what they called the Jews, opponents of the government, all those who were hidden away in sealed-off rooms with no access to the world. Cloistered and imprisoned even before she met my father, even before her pregnancy and his murder, that was my mother. A *sepolta viva* all her life."

He rubbed his hand over his eyes and Giulia screamed. "Run, Sydney, run — now!"

This time the adrenalin pumped strength into her legs and she ran, darting around the side of the cube. Behind her Sydney heard another scream, a scream of rage from Monty Lord, a clattering, tinny noise, and the sound of bodies crashing to the floor.

The door behind the sculpture opened smoothly and closed with a heavy thud. On the other side the air was damp and fetid; it was also pitch-black. Sydney could hear the sound of her breathing, like bellows in the dark silence. She stumbled forward, hands stretched out, feeling for the sides of the tunnel. *Please God, may there be only one passage to the exit,* she prayed. She started moving forward, feeling pebbles and debris shifting beneath her feet. At one point, her head scraped against the top of the tunnel hard enough to make her wince with pain. She crouched and stumbled on, terrified at the thought of someone coming after her in the darkness.

"Oh Giulia, Giulia," she said out loud. She heard what sounded like panting behind her, but realized it was the sound of her own breath echoing around the hollow space. Over and over in her head rattled the words of Monty Lord. *Sepolta viva, sepolta viva.* Buried alive — would that be her fate? Death by fear or suffocation in darkness instead of a dagger in the light.

Suddenly the tunnel took a sharp turn, and Sydney flung out her hands to each side of her, panicked at the thought that she might have to decide between one passage or another. But there appeared to be only one direction in which to move, and she took it. It led into a wider area where she could no longer feel the sides of the space. Disoriented, she looked up and saw a glimmer of light, a faint sheen of metal. With a cry of triumph she recognized the metallic disc and serrated edge of the gun turret. Time now to be thankful for the low height of the tunnel, because she had to stand on her toes to reach the catch, and use all her strength to unfasten it from the bar that held it closed.

The cover was heavy. Frantically, she pushed against it, and felt the load abruptly lifted from her. A pair of hands appeared around the rim near the catch and a voice said, "That you, Sydney? Liz here — hang on, I've got it."

The lid was flung back and rain fell on Sydney's upturned face. A moment later and she was hauled out, half-winded, on to the wet grass. She heard the cover slam shut behind her.

"Come on." Liz Falla was pulling her up, and dragging her away from the tunnel exit.

"Watch out," Sydney croaked, her voice coming back to her. "There are trenches everywhere."

"I know, we hid in them — see."

From the tangle of ferns, ivy, pennywort, and rambling rose peered a number of heads.

"Backup," said DC Falla, holding on to Sydney's arm, hastening them both along.

"Ed — where's Ed? He was on the phone and he —"

"Breaking down the front door, now we know you're out."

"How did you know where I was?"

"Ms. Vannoni phoned the station when she got your message."

"Giulia? How is Giulia?"

"Don't know — let's keep moving."

"Giulia!" Sydney broke away and started to run toward the front door of Giulia's castello, fear and anxiety spurring her on, with Liz Falla at her heels.

The heavy wooden door was on the ground, a splintered mess. Several police vans, lights spinning, were parked at a distance up the lane. Uniformed policemen wearing bulletproof jackets and carrying guns stood in the entrance. Most were looking inside. Sydney pushed through, and was held by the arms as she got inside the door.

Giulia and Ed Moretti were kneeling down, crouched over the body of Monty Lord on the ground. At the disturbance in the doorway, they both looked up and Giulia sprang to her feet.

"Sydney."

"You killed him?"

"No, *cara*, he killed himself. He threw the dagger at you, but it only damaged Arethusa." She pointed at the sculpture. Sydney could see a gash on the bronze surface. "We can only be thankful he was crazy enough to stick to daggers."

Sydney walked toward the crumpled body of Monty Lord. His agonized face looked up at her, a yellow froth caking his contorted lips.

"He took poison." It was Ed Moretti who answered her unspoken question. He pointed to a tiny vial on the floor by the body.

"He spoke before he died," Giulia said. "'*Cosa fatta, capo ha.*' A thing once done has an end."

"Gil used that in *Rastrellamento*."

"Yes," said Moretti.

Running through Moretti's head was the beautiful voice of Clifford Wesley.

If there is crime, it is gorgeous crime, all daggers and secret poisons.

He looked at the tiny vial by Monty Lord's side, lying on an emerald dragon with a dagger in his ivory throat. It was the kind the beggar on the Corso said was sold as genuine in stores like the one close to the town walls of Grosseto. But Moretti felt certain this one was for real, found by Sylvia and Stefan's son in an Etruscan cave, on the road to the deserted village of San Jacopo.

"*Rastrellamento* will be made?"

"Oh yes. I shan't stop it, and I never intended to. There's a clause covering not only the death of the writer, but the death of the producer. And there is very little left to do."

Sydney and Giulia sat together on the black leather sofa, drinking Aperol. Two days after the death of Monty Lord, the door was back up, the window on the upper floor repaired, and there was no sign of the drama of forty-eight hours earlier. Sydney pointed to the sculpture, the mark still visible on her faultless thigh. She noticed for the first time the outline of a dolphin swimming in the translucent depths of the white cube.

"Who is — was — Arethusa?"

"A water nymph. Legend has it that she dived under the sea to escape the attentions of a river god. She emerged again as a freshwater spring in Sicily."

"You have your castello back together again, Giulia." Sydney looked around the glowing cavern of light and colour.

"I don't think so, *cara*. Time to move on. My space has been invaded, violated. It will never seem the same."

"I'm sorry."

"Me too. I was happy here, in my *castello isola*, but I should be rejoining my community in Florence — one cannot run away for ever. And I love my professional life. I have that, after all."

"Yes," said Sydney. "You have that." She put down her glass and stood up. "I should be leaving now — I've got an early morning meeting with Mario. He has made me an assistant producer — a grand title, he tells me, for a dogsbody, but even gophers do something useful."

Giulia looked up at her speculatively. "And *are* you the policeman's current squeeze?"

"Ah," Sydney replied. "One can but hope."

October

The last, dwindling days of late summer were gone, and it was raining when they drove out to Montecatini together.

"Tell me again, *caro Eduardo*."

"Sophia Maria Catellani is now a widow and she lives with her daughter and her son-in-law, who owns a restaurant and bakery in the town, and her two grandchildren, a boy and a girl."

"And she is —?"

"I think she's my half-sister. My father's child by my godmother, Maria Colombo."

"You never knew. Do you think your mother knew?"

"I don't think so — at least, not in so many words. She was not a fool, she may have guessed and decided to let the past alone. According to her adoption papers, Sophia Maria Colombo was a war orphan. Her true identity was buried to protect the unmarried mother. The birth certificate says 'father unknown.'"

"But what makes you think you share the same father?"

The same gut feeling, he wanted to say, *that made me pursue a past drama as the motive for murder. Masculine intuition.* Instead, he said, "Here we are. It's the best restaurant in town, they tell me."

The restaurant was in a pretty stucco building with geranium-filled window boxes, green shutters, and small wrought-iron balconies that curved around the upstairs windows. Moretti and Sydney Tremaine were received by the owner, a strongly built man in his early twenties. The place was busy, but he found them a table near the window. The dull light beyond the glass took on a brighter gloss against Sydney's hair, the cranberry colour of her cashmere sweater.

They ordered their food and ate without much conversation, small talk not being the lingua franca of their particular country, a landscape across which they moved together in physical harmony. Not words; there were few words. She picked up a grape and put it in his mouth, and Moretti felt his body tremble as the world shimmered and spun around him with the touch of her fingers.

"So, are you going to ask —."

Before Sydney could answer, a middle-aged woman came through from the kitchen, carrying a small child in her arms, and Moretti felt a chill run through him. He was looking at an older, female version of himself, with the dark eyes of his godmother.

"My God," Sydney said.

Moretti watched the woman sit down with a middle-aged couple at a nearby table, handing over her grandson to be admired, watched her laugh and talk with them.

Moretti thought of another so-called war orphan and his father and mother. Stefan and Sylvia Vannoni, the father murdered, the baby wrenched from the *sepolta viva*, raised in a foreign land. Wouldn't Steve Romano of New York City have been better off not seeking his true identity? *Truth*, thought Moretti, *is not always the best thing, not always the right thing.*

"Well," said Sydney, "are you going to do anything?"

Across the room, Sophia Maria held out her arms for the child. A line of Dante's came to Moretti from *The Divine Comedy* — one of the few works he had read in Italian. *Non ragionam di lor, ma guarda, e passa.* Let us not speak of them, but look, and pass on. He did not remember committing it to memory, and it seemed to him like a sign.

"What are you going to do?" Sydney asked again.

"I'm going to take you back to Florence and spend the night with you," he said.

He stood up and held out his hand for Sydney.

"What do you think happened? How did it happen?"

Her hand was warm against his shoulder. Moretti picked it up and kissed it. The dawn light was just filtering through the curtains of the bedroom. Beyond lay the Uffizi and the Bargello, the candy stripes of Brunelleschi's Duomo. One day he would come back and explore his father's country, but for now the world was here, in her green eyes and her long dancer's limbs and her red hair.

"It's possible they really *did* believe she was a war orphan. My father disappeared, and even his own family didn't know where he was or what happened to him. So my godmother gave up her child, and gave up on Emidio Moretti, and moved away. He came back after the war, she had moved, and he'd fallen in love with my mother." *Como un fulmine, Eduardo*. He could hear his father's voice.

"Enough about me. Tell me more about this movie."

She sat up, and he could feel the excitement in her body already distancing her from him.

"It's about Marie Taglioni — she was one of the great Romantic ballerinas of the nineteenth century, daughter of a Milanese dancing master. She changed the look of ballet — Bournonville created *La Sylphide* for her. When I went to meet the director and producer, what I had in mind was to be an expert consultant on the dance of the period. What they had in mind was to cast me as Taglioni. I was amazed."

"I can't think why."

"I'd lost faith in myself. Some people are not — good — for you. Or maybe I'm not good for some people."

"I'm trying to read between the lines."

She turned to him. "Ed, my sweet tender Ed, at the risk of sounding trite, I have to find myself before I commit to anyone else again. Remember Giulia's statue? She is Arethusa, a water nymph who dived into a river to escape a river god and came up again as a freshwater spring in Sicily. God, I'm getting confused here, but what I'm trying to say is —"

"You don't want to metamorphose into a freshwater spring in Guernsey."

"Something like that."

Moretti saw the armless woman bathing her blue-green body in the lake at the Manoir Ste. Madeleine. Sydney's underwater Ophelia smile was gone. Immobility and immutability were only good for statues, and that was what commitment could do, if it was one-sided. The irony was not lost on him.

"I understand," he said. "Something I keep meaning to ask you — the name of your perfume."

"*Je reviens*, Eduardo."

Together they laughed at the apposite name, the triteness of the cliché.

The ATR was bringing them in across the harbour. No clear blue sky this time, but the soft grey light of approaching winter on St. Peter Port below. How could he have thought that Castle Cornet still looked like an eighteenth-century print? The old tower on the engraving was long gone and facing the sea was the great concrete rampart of a German gun emplacement, built on earlier foundations.

One saw what one wanted to see. Monty Lord had clearly seen a sword in the hand of the angel on the ceiling at San Jacopo. *But the hands were no longer there, and it could just as well have been a lyre, or a harp*, thought Moretti. Soon they would pass over the military underground hospital, the manor with its hidden bunker. *Festung Guernsey*. A world buried beneath the rock of the island. War buried many things: crimes, past passions, motivations.

He thought about his father. Had the discovery of Sophia Maria changed how he felt about him? Theirs had been a relationship both abrasive and tender, his mother often the buffer between them. Now all he remembered, all he felt, was tenderness. After what Emidio Moretti had been through, and survived, how could he pass up the chance to live his life with the woman he called his angel of mercy?

Como un fulmine, Eduardo.

* * *

Liz Falla was waiting for him with the police Mercedes.

"Congratulations on your promotion, Detective Sergeant Falla. Giorgio Benedetti sends his best."

She was giving him one of her looks again. "Thank you. Good holiday, Guv? How was the weather?"

"The weather was good."

The weather kept them going for a while, a bridge between the personal and the professional.

"The Martello tower on Icart Point is up for sale, Guv."

"So, Giulia Vannoni is leaving the island. How about the marchesa?"

"Well, there was talk she was going to leave when the media were after her, but things have quietened down now. You were right to get away. You're no longer headlines in the *Guernsey Press*, and you don't hear much about the case on BBC Guernsey or Channel Television any more. Are they still on about the Vannoni story in Italy?"

"No. No one is that bothered about two possible, and unproven, murders and a suicide back at a time many people would rather forget. Most of the reporting was of the 'unbalanced American producer kills writer and member of distinguished Italian family' kind. That's the very last thing Monty Lord would have wanted, now that the Vannonis have lost their nemesis, the last real chance of disclosure."

"It was Bella Alfieri who picked up the daggers wasn't it?"

"Wearing a red wig, yes. And Signor Baza was named after the headquarters of the Slovenian resistance at the end of the war. PC Brouard found that on the internet."

They passed the bottom of Fountain Street, where the condemned walked down from Beauregard Tower to a terrible death.

"That business at my place," said Moretti. "It wasn't your imagination, Falla. It was Monty Lord, I'm sure, and if Sydney had stayed there, he'd have got to her. She could have held up the completion of *Rastrellamento*, and that was the last thing he wanted."

"She spooked me." His partner sounded gruff, offhand.

"Okay, she spooked you." Liz Falla could hear the smile in his voice. "But I'd hate to see your grandmother's tall tales cost you the use of your instincts. Remember what you said to me when I was questioning my own?"

"I remember. I met Dwight Ellis in town yesterday — he was asking after you."

Moretti was happy to change the subject. "I'll drop in to the club tonight. You know Dwight?"

"I'm partial to salt beef and red peas, that's how I met him."

Moretti could hear Dwight now in his head, playing. "He's a good musician — you'll have to come and hear him some time," he said. "Sydney Tremaine says you sing like Enya with a touch of Marianne Faithfull. Is that possible, I ask myself."

Liz Falla turned and grinned at him. "And you'll have to come to one of *our* gigs some time," she said. A stray glint of sunlight caught her hair, streaking it with bronze, and Moretti remembered the cat he'd bought from the guy in Grosseto selling fake Etruscan shit. It was up on the windowsill in his kitchen, awaiting a decision.

Too much time has passed, he told himself, and a gift now would look somehow calculated, certainly not spontaneous. So he sat silent, listening to Dwight. He and Garth Machin were now playing a riff on "You're Getting to Be a Habit With Me."

The music was playing once more in his head, thank God. That was all that mattered. Case closed, bury the past.

A thing once done has an end.

More Great Castle Street Mysteries from Dundurn

Samurai Code
Don Easton
978-1554886975
$11.99

This intriguing, suspense-packed novel is the fourth Jack Taggart Mystery in the series commencing with *Loose Ends*, *Above Ground*, and *Angel in the Full Moon*. This time the implacable Mountie Jack Taggart goes undercover to follow the trail of a cheap Saturday-night special found at the scene of a murder.

He traces the gun from the manufacturer to the person it was stolen from and through several criminals until the trail leads him to a suspected heroin importer. Taggart pretends to be an Irish gangster and penetrates the criminal organization, only to discover that the real crime boss is a mysterious figure out of Asia.

Taggart and his partner are unexpectedly taken aboard a private jet where they find themselves alone and without backup in the lair of one of the largest yakuza organized crime families in Japan. East meets west. The clash of culture explodes into violence when their real identities are discovered.

Nightshade
A Sam Montcalm Mystery
Tom Henighan
978-1554887149
$11.99

Deadly nightshade — the poison plant par excellence — and in historic Quebec City at an important scientific conference concerning the genetic manipulation of trees it means *murder*!

Police, RCMP, and a mysterious FBI agent from Washington converge on the scene. But the sharpest eye belongs to Sam Montcalm, a despised "bedroom snooper" from Ottawa whose primary concern is to clear a First Nations activist of the crime. Sam is middle-aged, tough, and sophisticated, yet he's also a lone wolf who feels displaced nearly everywhere, and his relations with his colleagues, the police — and with women — are always complicated. "You're a psychic wound without a health card," a friend comments.

The story moves to its surprising climax as Montcalm follows the trail of murder back to Canada's capital and into the Gatineau Hills, his deep sense of cynicism about human nature confirmed as he closes in on the killer and struggles to come to terms with himself.

Available at your favourite bookseller.

DUNDURN PRESS
www.dundurn.com

What did you think of this book? Visit *www.dundurn. com* for reviews, videos, updates, and more!